The Fortunes of the Farrells

Mrs. George de Horne Vaizey

DODO PRESS

Chapter One.

From Pretence to Reality.

"Berengaria, what do you generally do with your old court trains? How do you use them up?"

The fire had died down to a dull red glow; only one tiny flame remained, which, flickering to and fro, showed a wide expanse of floor, and two easy-chairs drawn up before the fender, on which reclined vague, feminine figures. The voice which had asked the question was slow and languid, and breathed a wearied indifference to the world in general, which was more than equalled in the tone of the reply—

"Really, don't you know, I can't say! I put them away, meaning to use them for cloaks or evening-dresses; but I forget, or they get mislaid, or the maid confiscates them for her own purposes. I expect, as a matter of fact, she makes them up into Sunday blouses."

"You spoil that woman, dear! You are so absurdly easy-going that she robs you right and left. Do take my advice, and give her notice at once!"

"I couldn't, darling, even to please you! It bores me so to deal with strangers, and no one else could do my hair like Elsie. It it pleases her to use up a few of my garments, why shouldn't the poor soul have her pleasure like the rest? That reminds me, Lucille—are you going to the duchess's ball to-night? I suppose it is superfluous to ask, since no entertainment is complete without you nowadays."

"Oh, I suppose so! If I am not too fagged, that is to say. But I have a dinner first, and two At-homes, and people make such a fuss if you don't put in an appearance. One hardly feels up to dancing after struggling through two of the asphyxiating mobs dignified by the name of entertainments; still, I promised Arthur the cotillion, and he will be desolated if I play him false; and I have a new frock for the occasion which is really rather a dream. Silver tissue over satin, and shoulder-straps of diamonds. I had them reset on purpose. I spend quite a fortune on resetting jewels nowadays; but one must be original, or die!"

"My dear, you will be too bewitching! Lord Arthur will be more desperate than ever. My poor little self will be nowhere beside you! I'm going to be sweet and simple in chiffon and pearls. Paquin made the gown. Don't ask what it cost! I tore up the bill and threw it in the fire. Really, don't you know, it made me quite depressed! So perishable, too! I expect I shall be in rags before the evening is over. But it's quite sweet at present—all frilly-willys from top to toe. I do love to be fluffy and feminine, and my pearls really are unique! The princess examined them quite carefully when I met her last winter, and said she had rarely seen finer specimens. I wouldn't wear them at all unless they were good. I cannot endure inferior jewels!"

The speaker lolled still more luxuriously in her chair, then started forward, as the door opened with a bang, and a harsh voice accosted her by name—

"Miss Mollie, your mother wants to know if you have finished darning the socks? She is putting away the clean clothes, and wants to sort them with the rest."

The Lady Lucille—otherwise Mollie Farrell, the penniless daughter of an impoverished house—jumped up from her chair, and clasped her hands in dismay. In blissful contemplation of imagining chiffons and cotillions, the prosaic duties of reality had slipped from her mind, and recollection brought with it a pang of remorse.

"Misery me! I forgot the very existence of the wretched things! Never mind. Tell mother, Annie, that I'll set to work this minute, and put them away myself as soon as they are done. Tell her I'm sorry; tell her I'll be as quick as I possibly can!"

Annie stood for a moment in eloquent silence then shut the door and descended the stairs; while Mollie groped her way across the room, and Berengaria lifted herself from her chair with a sigh, and slipped her hand along the mantelpiece.

"I'll light the gas. How horrid it is, being dragged back to earth by these sordid interruptions! It's always the way—as soon as I begin to forget myself, and enjoy a taste of luxury, back I'm dragged to the same dull old life. I really saw that silver tissue, and felt the coldness of the diamonds against my shoulder; and then—*socks*! Those wretched, thick, ugly socks, with the heels all out, and the toes in rags! I think schoolboys ought to be obliged to darn their own clothes, just to teach them a little care!"

"Well, be aisy; you haven't to darn them, anyway. It's my work, which is the best of reasons why it is left undone. Hurry with the gas, there's a dear. There's no time for conundrums, if I am to finish to-night!"

Another sigh, the striking of a match, and the light sprang up, and showed a tall, girlish figure, clad in a blue serge skirt, and a flannel blouse, faded from repeated washing, and showing signs of a decided shortage of material.

Considered as a costume, it was a painful contrast to the silver and diamonds of the fair Berengaria; but the shabby garments looked their best on Ruth Farrell's slight form, and the face reflected in the strip of mirror above the mantelpiece had a distinct charm of its own. A low brow below masses of brown hair; a flush of carmine on the cheeks; soft lips, drooping pathetically at the corners; and—most striking feature of all—thickly marked eyebrows of almost jetty black, stretching in long, straight lines above the grey eyes. A pretty, almost a beautiful face, full of character, full of thought, full of a restless, unsatisfied yearning.

She threw the burnt-out match on to the fire, and turned to survey the room—surely the most motley and curious apartment that could be imagined! The sloping roof proved at a glance the position under the leads, and a peep at the outside of the door would have shown the word "Attica" painted in bold white letters on the top panel.

Attica—or the land of attic—constituted the boudoirs of the Ladies Berengaria and Lucille, the work-rooms and play-rooms, dens and havens of refuge, of Ruth and Mollie Farrell, and their young stepsisters, Trix and Betty Connor; for it was of generous proportions, measuring a square eight yards or more, and the floor was divided into four equal sections by lines of white paint against the brown of the original staining.

Each sister held an exclusive right to her own domain, and for another to enter therein without special invitation was held as an outrage against decency and good taste.

In the beginning of things, Ruth, as the eldest, had claimed the right of first choice, and, being a young woman who liked her comforts, had instantly and unhesitatingly appropriated the fireside.

Mollie, coming next in order, plumped for the window, it being her sunny habit to look forward to an endless summer; Trix, grumbling vigorously, appropriated the angle made by the blank walls nearest the fire; and poor Betty made her lair in the direct draught of the doorway, and enjoyed a permanent cold in the head from November to March.

A glance at the four corners of the room afforded a very fair idea of the characters of its inhabitants. Ruth's "Fireland" domain had an air of luxury of its own, though the draperies were of simple turkey-red, and the pictures mounted on home-made frames of brown paper. There was a row of shelves against the wall, holding quite a goodly show of volumes, ranged neatly side by side, while a curtained recess at one end contained tea-cups and canister, and a small metal kettle, as scrupulously bright as on the day when it had left the shop.

An old folding-chair had been painted green, and supplied with frilled cushions. There was a sensible little table, holding a hand-machine, and a work-basket—yawning apart, it is true, but neatly strapped to prevent accident; and on the mantelpiece a crowd of photographs, and a few oddments of blue china, all carefully dusted by the owner's hand, and set out with artistic effect.

Last, and crowning luxury of all, a screen stood behind the low chair, manufactured out of a clothes-horse flounced with turkey-red, which was at once the comfort and distraction of Ruth's soul; for while, from her point of view, it was an indispensable comfort, shutting out draughts from window and door, and giving to her little nook the last blessing of privacy, Trix denounced the innovation as the incarnation of selfishness, Betty's teeth chattered with a noise like castanets, and Mollie peered round the corner with her shoulders huddled in a shawl, and her face at once so cheerful, so unreproving, and so bleached with cold, that it was not in human nature to refuse the desired invitation.

Mollie's domain of "Bellevue" comprised the square-shaped window, on the sill of which she cultivated nasturtiums and mignonette in summer, and in the embrasure stood a window-seat covered with blue cloth, that was really the remains of an old winter skirt.

Visitors to "Bellevue" always paused to admire the sprays of flowers which were embroidered here and there on this blue background; and then Mollie "dissembled," as she called it, smiling sweet recognition of the praise, but never once breathing the secret that the whole being and intent of these flowers was to hide the joins beneath.

She also possessed a table and a work-basket; but the former was decidedly ancient and insecure as to legs, while the basket made no pretence of shutting, but looked on unabashed while its contents lay scattered over the rug.

A dressmaker's stand stood in the corner, on which a blouse, more or less complete, was invariably pinned, waiting for the moment when Mollie had time to devote to her favourite occupation. There were no book-shelves, but a litter of magazines behind a cushion on the window-seat, and innumerable photographs were secured to the wall by black-headed pins, to fade slowly but surely into unrecognition in the unbroken glare of light.

Mollie herself pined for curtains to mitigate the draught during the winter months, but the three other inmates of Attica loudly declared that they could not spare a fraction of light, so she gave way smiling, as her custom was. Mollie never grumbled; it was so dull, as she said, and she loved to be gay. An invincible cheeriness of heart carried her gallantly over the quicksands in which Ruth was submerged by reason of her moodiness, and Trix by her quick temper, and made it a physical impossibility to repine over the inevitable.

Fifteen-year-old Trix was in that stage when the Oxford examination seems the end-all and be-all of existence. Her section of Attica was proudly dubbed "The Study," and had its walls covered with maps, class lists, and "memos" of great variety. The desk was strewn with papers and exercise-books, and there lingered in the air that indescribable scent of sponge, slate, indiarubber, and freshly sharpened pencils which seem inseparable from youthful study.

Trix confessed to one weakness,—only one!—an overwhelming greed for pencil-boxes and sharpeners, and the contents of the wooden shelf above the desk testified to her indulgence in this craving. "The girls gave them to me!" she used to say when strangers exclaimed at the number of the piled-up boxes, but she blushed even as she spoke, knowing well that to keep sixpence in her pocket and pass a pencil-box of a new design, was a feat of self-denial beyond imagination.

Dear, chubby, placid Betty was only thirteen, and cared for nothing in the world but her relations, chocolate-creams, and scrambling through the day's classes with as little exertion as possible. She shivered in her corner, poor mite, sucking audibly, to the distraction of her elders, the while she skimmed over her lessons, and looked forward to the time when she would be free to devote herself to the hobby of the hour.

Sometimes it was postcards; sometimes it was stamps; sometimes it was penny toys collected from street vendors. It had once soared as high as autographs, and a promising beginning of three signatures were already pasted into the remaining leaves of an exercise-book. Whatever the collection might be, it lived in heaps on the uncarpeted floor; and when Betty had a tidy fit, was covered with a crochet antimacassar which had known better days, and had grown decidedly mellow in tint.

On this particular afternoon, the two younger sisters were taking tea with school friends, while their elders enjoyed an uninterrupted *tête-à-tête,* when they could indulge in a favourite game. When life was unusually flat and prosaic, when the weather was wet, invitations conspicuous by their absence, and the want of pocket-money particularly poignant, Mollie would cry ardently: "Let's be Berengaria and Lucille!" and, presto! the two girls were transplanted to another world—a world with the magic letter W added to its address, where empty purses and dyed dresses existed not, and all was joy, jewellery, and junketing.

Lucille had lately become the bride of a millionaire and adoring duke; the peerless Berengaria wrought havoc with the peace of Lord Arthur, and had more suitors than she could count on the fingers of both hands. It was a fascinating make-believe; but, as Ruth plaintively remarked, it did come with somewhat of a shock to be dragged back to earth by—socks!

She stood leaning against the mantelpiece, looking on with frowning brows while her sister collected together scattered materials, and carried them and the yawning basket back to the cosy corner in Fireland, where, for the hour, she was an invited guest.

"Quick's the word and sharp's the action!" cried Mollie cheerily. "Now for a grand old cobble; and if there are any heels out to-day, my fine young gentlemen, don't blame *me* if you have to tread on knots for the rest of the week! It's the strangest thing on earth that I can remember nice things year after year without an effort, and yet forget this horrid mending every Saturday as regularly as the day comes round."

"Carelessness!" replied Ruth shortly, and with the candour of near relations. "I couldn't forget if I tried. First thing when I wake in the morning I think of all the bothersome duties I have to do in the day, and the last thing at night I am thinking of them still. But you are so frivolous, Mollie!"

"And you are so morbid, my dear! You don't offer to help me, I observe; and since you are so conscientious as all that, I should think you might lend me a hand in my extremity. There! I'll give you Ransome's for a treat; he breaks out at the toes, but his heels are intact. It's playwork mending for him compared with the other boys."

She tossed a collection of brown woollen stockings into her sister's lap, and Ruth took them up, frowning heavily with her black brows, but never dreaming of refusing the request, though her own share of the household mending had kept her employed during the earlier part of the afternoon, while Mollie was amusing herself elsewhere. She took a darning-egg out of her basket, threaded a needle daintily, and set to work in the painstaking manner which characterised all her efforts; but she sighed as she worked, and Mollie sang, and that was the difference between them.

"Don't make such a noise, Mollie; you make my head ache. Another time, I wish you would do your mending when I do mine, and then we should get a chance of a rest. Just to-day, too, when the girls are out! I hate a large family, where there is never any privacy or repose. I wish the pater could afford to send the boys to a boarding-school. It would be the making of them, and such a blessing to us."

Mollie pursed her lips disapprovingly.

"I'd miss them horribly. They are naughty, of course, and noisy and tiresome, and make no end of work, but that's the nature of boys; on the other hand, they are full of fun and good-humour, if you take them the right way. And they are affectionate little ruffians, too; and so good-looking. I'm proud of them on Sundays, in their Eton suits."

"But there's only one Sunday, and six long days of shabbiness and patches! Bruce ought to have a new school suit; the one he is wearing has descended from the other two, and is disgracefully shabby. I spoke to mother about it to-day, and she said she had intended to buy one this month, but business was bad, and there was the coal bill to pay. The old story! Business always *is* bad, and the coal bill is ever with us!"

Mollie crinkled her brows, and for a fraction of a second her face clouded.

"There's no hope for me, then! I was going to plead for an extra sovereign to carry me to the end of the quarter, for I've spent my last cent, and there are one or two absolute necessities which I shall have to get by hook or by crook, or stay in bed until the next allowance is due. Well; something will turn up, I suppose! It's always the darkest the hour before the dawn, and, financially speaking, it's pitch black at the present moment. Let's pretend Uncle Bernard suddenly appeared upon the scene, and presented us each with a handsome cheque."

"I'm tired of Uncle Bernard! Ever since I was a child I have heard about him and his eccentricities, and his house, and his wealth, and that we were his nearest relatives, and that some day he would surely remember us, and break his silence; but he never has, so now I look upon him as a sort of mythological figure who has no real existence. If he cared anything about us he would have written long ago. I expect he has forgotten our very existence, and left all his money to charities."

"I expect he has, but it's fun to pretend. Suppose he remembered my birthday and sent me a ten-pound note! Fancy me, my dear, with a whole ten pounds to spend as I liked. What fun we'd have! Most of it would have to go in useful things, but we'd take a sovereign or two and have a reckless burst just to see what it was like. A hansom to town, lunch at a real swagger restaurant; and, after that, good seats at a *matinée*, ices between the acts, and another hansom home, instead of shivering at the corner waiting for omnibuses. Oh, bliss!

Oh, rapture! If it could only come true! If uncle would once come to see us, he couldn't help liking us; could he?"

"He'd like me best, because I am pretty," said Ruth calmly.

"He'd like me best, because I am so nice!" contradicted Mollie. And then they looked at each other, and each made a little grimace, supposed to express scorn and contempt, but in reality there was so complete an understanding beneath the pretence that it was almost as expressive as a caress.

After this came a few minutes' silence, while the two needles were woven diligently to and fro; then—

"Mollie!" said Ruth suddenly, "I've come to a decision. I've been thinking it over for ages, so don't imagine it's a whim, or that I don't mean what I say. It's time that one of us turned out and earned some money on our own account, and, as I'm the eldest, I'm the one to go. Business gets worse and worse, and expenses increase, and must go on increasing, as the children grow up. Trix will be sixteen in summer; in less than two years she will leave school, and three grown-up daughters are not needed in any house when the mother is well and strong. I once thought of waiting until then; but I am twenty-two now, and, if I am to do any good, there is no time to waste. You could get along without me even now."

The half-darned sock fell on Mollie's knee, and for once the sunny face looked thoroughly shocked and startled.

"I couldn't—I couldn't! None of us could! What would happen if everything depended on me? You remind me, and keep me up to the mark, and help me out of scrapes. I should be at my wit's end without you. Mother consults you about everything, and the girls obey you, and the boys pay more attention to you than they do to anyone else. Ruth, *everybody* needs you?"

"They love you best," Ruth said quietly. And the dark brows wrinkled in wistful fashion.

It was the truth that she was speaking, no empty striving for compliments; but why was it the truth? She worked hard; Mollie idled. She was conscientious, self-sacrificing, and methodical; Mollie knew not the meaning of method, and was frankly selfish on occasions. She worried herself ill about ways and means, and kept sedulously within the bounds of her small allowance; Mollie took no heed for the morrow, and was in a chronic condition of penury or debt.

Despite these striking contrasts, the fact remained, however, that if any member of the household were ill, or had a secret to confide, or a favour to request, they betook themselves to the heedless Mollie, rather than to herself. Dearly as she loved her sister, Ruth felt a little rankling of soreness mingling with her mystification. She did not yet realise the magic power which cheerfulness wields in this world, or the charm of a sunny face and a ready rippling laugh. Hearts turn to the sun as instinctively as plants, and forgive much for the sake of the warmth and glow.

"They love you best," said Ruth, and honest Mollie did not contradict, but stretched out her hand, and laid it caressingly on her sister's arm.

"But I love you, and I can't do without you, Ruth! I couldn't live alone, for you and I belong to each other. The others are dears in their way; but they are only 'steps,' and we two seem so close together. Imagine Attica without you! Imagine going to bed alone, with no one to talk to about the events of the day! What does the horrid old money matter? We always have been poor, and we always shall be. As long as I can remember mother has been in despair about the bills; but we wriggle through somehow, and we shall go on wriggling. It's horrid of you to talk of going away! Think of me!"

"That's selfish, Mollie. You are the last person I ought to think of just now. Mother comes first, and the poor old pater, and all those children. It comes to this, that I can't stand the present state of affairs any longer. I feel ashamed of taking even the pittance we have; and

I'm tired of the pittance, too, and want to make money for myself, and not have to think a dozen times over before spending a penny!"

Mollie laughed—a pert, derisive little laugh.

"Sounds well, my dear; but, if it comes to that, what *can* you do? You can't teach, for you are not accomplished enough for advanced pupils, nor patient enough for children. Do you remember trying to teach Drummond to read, and rapping his poor little knuckles till they were blue? Besides, talking of pittances, you'd get less than nothing if you did try it. I don't see what you could do to earn a living."

"I could be a hospital nurse!"

"Perhaps you might—a bad one—for you don't like nursing, and would only do it for the sake of the pay. I should have no respect for you if you did that, Ruth. It would be too hard on the unfortunate patients?"

"I could be a companion—"

"People who want companions are old, or gouty, or mad; invariably disagreeable, or why have they to advertise for a friend? I think I see you shut up with a trying old lady, combing the lap-dog's hair, and winding wool! You wouldn't be a very agreeable companion, Ruthans dear. Better make the best of things, and stay where you are."

Ruth made no further protest, but her lips tightened with an expression of determination. Her mind being made up, she was not easily swayed from her purpose. She decided to talk to her mother on the subject on the following morning.

Chapter Two.

An Evening at Home.

The father of Ruth and Mollie Farrell had died when the latter was two years old, leaving his wife but a few hundred pounds with which to support herself and her children. She was a pretty, winsome creature, the sort of woman who attracts sympathy and love, but a most difficult person to help.

Friends came forward with suggestions and offers of assistance, and Mrs Farrell thanked them ardently, and wept, and agreed to all that they said. In words, she was ready to undertake any exertion, however arduous; but when it came to deeds, she was so weak, so incapable, so hopelessly confused, that the school, the boarding-house, and the home for Indian children ended successively in failure.

At the end of three years her scanty capital was almost exhausted; but at this critical moment the Fates—which seem to take special care of the helpless ones of the earth—sent Ernest Connor to play the part of rescuer. He was a round stone in a square hole, that is to say, a student by nature, who, by the exigencies of fortune, found himself doomed to a business life, wherein he was a painstaking but consistent failure.

Nervous and shy, he shrank from the society of women; but it was impossible to be shy with the irresponsible little widow, who confided all her troubles to him on the first day of their acquaintance, and asked his advice with tears in her pretty eyes. To his amazement, he found himself confiding his own troubles in return, and the ready sympathy accorded to them seemed the sweetest thing in the world. A month after their first meeting he asked her to be his wife, explaining honestly his financial position, and the uncertainty of improvement in the future.

"But you will help me!" he said. "The money will go twice as far when you hold the purse!"

And Mrs Farrell agreed with ardour, unabashed by previous failures. She went to her new home full of love and gratitude, and, let it be said at once, never had cause to regret the step in after years.

Ernest Connor was a devoted husband, and a most kindly father to the two little girls; but life was not easy. It was a constant strain to make ends meet, and as Trix, and Betty, and Drummond, and Ransome, and Bruce came in quick succession to fill the nursery, the strain grew even more and more acute.

The elder girls had been educated at a neighbouring high school, but left as soon as they were seventeen, and after that there was no money to spare for music and painting lessons, such as most girls continue as an interest and occupation long after schooldays are over.

Ruth and Mollie were kept busy teaching the babies and making clothes for the family—cutting down Trix's dress to do duty for Betty; laboriously planning little pairs of knickers out of trousers worn at the knees; patching, darning, covering-up, hiding over, turning and twisting; making up something out of nothing, with the lordly sum of fifteen pounds a year each for dress and pocket-money alike. They had never known the luxury, dear to girlish hearts, of choosing a garment simply because it was pretty or becoming. Dark, useful remnants were their lot; sailor-hats in summer, cloth toques in winter; stout, useful boots, and dogskin gloves which stood a year's hard wear.

Many a time over had Mollie stretched forth hands and feet for her sister's inspection, quoting derisively—

"'Her thickly—made country shoes could not conceal the slender contour of her ankles; her rough gloves served only to reveal the patrician beauty of her hands.' Look at that, my love—there's contour for you! There's patrician beauty! What rubbish those books do talk, to be sure!"

Many a time had the girls groaned together over their impecuniosity, and vaguely vowed to "do something" to remedy their condition, until at last Ruth's unrest had reached the point of action, and she determined to seize the first opportunity of a private conference with her mother.

It was not easy to secure a *tête-à-tête* in the house of Connor. On this particular evening, Trix was practising scales on the piano in the drawing-room, while Mollie read a novel, and Betty lolled on the rug; the three boys were busy at lessons, or, as they eloquently described it, "stewing," round the dining-room table. Mr Connor was smoking his pipe and reading the evening papers in his den at the back of the house; and the little, white-faced mother moved incessantly from room to room, no sooner settled in one place than she was seized with an anxious presentiment that she was needed elsewhere.

She was pretty still, in a pathetic, faded manner; and wherever she went she spoke loving, gentle words, and met loving glances in response: but, alas, her efforts seemed rather distracting than helpful! She stroked Drummond's hair, and asked if he was sure his throat was better, just as he was on the point of completing a difficult addition; she told her husband the tragic history of the cook's impertinence, and handed him a heavy bill, when the poor man was enjoying the first quiet rest of the day; she requested Mollie's advice about spare-room curtains at the moment when long-separated lovers were united, and it was agony to lift one's eyes from the page for the fraction of a second.

Husband and children alike answered gently and with courtesy, for, if there was little else, there was plenty of love in this shabby household, and the little mother was the central figure round which everything revolved; nevertheless, her departure was marked by half-involuntary sighs of relief, as if a disturbing element had been withdrawn.

Ruth knew that she would have to bide her time until the younger members of the family had retired to bed; but, too restless to settle down to any definite occupation, she drifted across the drawing-room to where Trix sat, her fingers scrambling up and down the notes of the piano. Trix was tall and lanky; she had grey eyes, set far apart, a *retroussé* nose, dotted over with quite a surprising number of freckles, and an untidy shock of light-brown hair.

In years to come it was possible that she might develop into a pretty girl; at the present moment she despised appearances, and certainly failed to make the best of her good points. Now, as she sat by the piano-stool, with shoulders hunched up and head poked forward, she looked so awkward and ungainly that Ruth's tried nerves suffered afresh at the sight.

"For pity's sake, sit up, Trix!" she cried sharply. "You look a perfect object, bent double like that! You might be deformed, to look at your back! If you go on like this, you will grow so round-shouldered that you won't be able to get straight again, and how will you like that?"

Trix deliberately finished her scale, then faced her sister, and retorted pertly—

"Very much indeed, thank you—if you will only realise that I *can't* help it, and leave me alone! I'd rather be a humpback at once, than be worried morning, noon, and night about deportment, as I am now. My back's my own; I can use it as I like!"

"It's wicked to talk like that, Trix, and very impertinent as well! Who is to tell you of your faults if we don't at home? Other people look on, and say, 'What a fright that girl looks! How shockingly she carries herself!' But they don't trouble to tell you about it, and it is not very pleasant for us when you take it like this. If we did not love you and care for your interests—"

"Oh dear me," sighed naughty Trix, "then I wish you'd love me a little less! I could bear it quite well if you lost your interest, and left me in peace. You and Mollie can do the beauty show for the family; I am content to represent 'intellect and common-sense.' If you want something to do, you might help me with a French exercise instead of nagging. It's simply awful to-day; and if I lose any more marks, it's all up with my chance of getting a prize. Now, then—will you, or won't you?"

Trix's method of asking favours was hardly as ingratiating as might be desired, and for a moment the chances seemed all in favour of a refusal. The colour flamed in Ruth's cheeks, and her black brows drew ominously near together. She was fighting a hard battle against pride and resentment; but, as was usually the case, the better self won. She nodded back at Trix, and said—

"I will! ... Run and bring your books. We won't venture into the dining-room, for the boys make such a noise that one can't hear one's own voice."

There was something very sweet in the absolute surrender of self-will, and Trix, who was the most warm-hearted of mortals, promptly bounded up from her stool and flung her arms round her sister's neck.

"You duck—you angel! You shall nag at me as much as ever you like, and I'll never be cheeky again. It's brickish of you to worry about me at all; but I'll always be a fright, so what's the use? You are pretty enough for the family, Ruth. Ella Bruce's brother watches behind the curtains every Sunday to see you pass, and he says you are the prettiest girl he knows, and are always so nicely dressed!"

"Poor, deluded mortal; may he be forgiven for his blindness! I'm the shabbiest creature in the parish! It's very nice of him to watch; but I wish he would come out from behind the curtains and let me see him. I have not so many admirers that I can afford to have them hidden from view. What is he like, Trix; handsome?"

"Oh, well enough! Ella thinks him a model, but he is too thin and lanky for my taste. He is not half good enough for you, Ruth, anyway. You ought to marry a duke, and retrieve the fortunes of the family!"

"I'm willing, my dear. Produce him, and I promise you I will not stand in the way. I could do quite easily with being a duchess. It would be so soothing to be called 'Your Grace,' and a coronet is peculiarly suited to my style of beauty. I won't have you for a bridesmaid, though, if you stoop like that. Get your book, Trix, and let us set to work. Better take advantage of my good mood while it lasts."

Trix departed obediently, and returned with a pile of books, which she dropped upon the table with a bang, which made the other occupants of the room start in their seats, and for the next hour the two girls wrestled with the difficulties of an advanced Brachet exercise. Truth to tell, Ruth was not much more expert than Trix herself; but she was infinitely more exact, and, by dint of hunting up back rules, and making endless references to the irregular verbs, the result achieved was fairly correct.

It was ten o'clock. Betty and the three boys had departed to bed; Mollie still sat gloating over her novel, with a forefinger thrust into either ear to shut out the sound of the disturbing discussion on moods and tenses. Trix collected her books with a sigh, and prepared to go upstairs in her turn. She looked white and tired, and the freckles on her nose seemed darker and more conspicuous than ever.

"Good-night, old Ruth! Thanks, most awfully! I'll do as much for you some day."

"Good-night, young Trix! Mind you do. I shall remind you when the time comes."

The door opened and closed; Ruth rose wearily, and laid her hand on Mollie's shoulder. Such a charming face was lifted to meet her glance—so fresh, so bright, full of such dazzling youth and vigour! True, Mollie had been lazing all the evening while the others worked; but as Ruth stood looking down at her she wondered for the hundredth time how it was that so little was made of Mollie's beauty in comparison with her own.

The golden hair rippled back in a thick, soft wave; the grey eyes were large, and generously lashed; the laughing lips parted, to show white, even, little teeth; yet a stranger, looking for the first time at Mollie Farrell, rarely remarked upon her good looks.

"What a nice girl! What a dear girl! What a delightful creature!" they cried, according to their different degrees of enthusiasm. They wanted to know her, to have her for a friend, and forgot to think of mere outward appearance.

"What a noise you have been making, Ruth!" said Mollie lazily. "I can't think why you can't be quiet when you get a chance! This book is too exciting for words. I told you how the lovers quarrelled just after they were married, and he went abroad, thinking, of course, that she didn't love him any more; while, of course, she simply adored the ground he trod on, but thought that he had grown tired of her, while he was more madly in—"

Ruth gave an exclamation of impatience.

"Oh, what rubbish! I don't believe such things are possible! If they really loved each other, do you suppose they could keep on pretending while they lived together every day, and when it came to saying good-bye into the bargain? Nonsense! She'd break down and howl, and he would comfort her, and take off his coat. Look here, Mollie—go to bed! I've waited all the evening to have a talk with mother, and you are the only impediment left. Take your book with you if you like,—but go!"

Mollie rose, unwillingly enough.

"I know what you want to talk about," she said, looking into Ruth's face. "I know; and it's not a mite of use. Mother won't let you leave home; she needs you far too much. I shan't go to sleep, for I shall want to hear every single word when you come upstairs. I'll snoodle up to the hot bottle, and read till you come."

The programme sounded very attractive,—to snoodle up to the hot bottle, and lie at ease reading an interesting book,—much more attractive than to linger downstairs by the dying fire, and discuss disagreeable problems with an anxious mother. But Ruth did not waver in her decision, and a few moments later Mrs Connor was caught paying a round of visits to the children's bedrooms—"just in time," as Ruth thought whimsically, "to waken the poor souls from their first sleep!"—and escorted back to the chair which Mollie had vacated.

"Is anything wrong, dear?" she asked nervously. Poor little woman, if a surprise were in store, it seemed so much more likely that it should be disagreeable rather than bright! "You don't feel feverish, or ill, or—"

"No, no, my dear; I just want to talk to you about my own affairs. I'm quite well, and so strong and—and grown-up, don't you know, that it is time I grew independent, and began life on my own account. You have Mollie at home, and Trix and Betty growing up, and I think, mother dear, that I ought not to be dependent on the pater any longer. He has been very good and kind to us all these years; but, still—"

She hesitated, and Mrs Connor looked at her with anxious tenderness. She had honestly considered the welfare of her two little girls as much as her own when she decided to marry a second time, and it had been a constant joy to feel that her expectations had been fulfilled; yet here was Ruth, her firstborn darling, her right hand in household affairs, actually talking of leaving home!

"Aren't you happy, Ruth? Have you not been happy all these years? I thought you were quite content and satisfied."

She sighed; and Ruth gave an echoing sigh, and answered honestly—

"Quite happy, darling, as far as you and the pater are concerned. He could not have been kinder to us if we had been his very own daughters. But satisfied? Oh no, mother; never satisfied for a long time back! How could I be? I don't want to seem ungrateful; but I'm only twenty-one, and it has been all work and no play, and there are so many, many things that I want to do, and see, and feel. I've never been to a proper grown-up dance in my life, for if we have been asked we have not had decent clothes to go in, and we never invite anyone here, so now people have given over asking us even to quiet evenings. I hardly ever speak to a soul outside this house, and I get so tired of it all;—and only fifteen pounds a year for dress and pocket-money! Remember what your allowance was when you were a girl, and all the jolly times you had, and the parties, and the visits, and the trips abroad,—and then think of our lives. It *is* dull for us, isn't it, dear?"

Mrs Connor's pale cheeks flushed with a touch of offence. Not having sufficient insight into girls' natures to understand that there was nothing either undutiful or unnatural in Ruth's lament, she felt herself personally injured thereby.

"Mollie is happy—Mollie is content!" she said briefly.

And Ruth assented with a brief "Yes," and said no more.

If the difference between Mollie's nature and her own was not patent to their own mother, it was useless to enlarge upon it. She waited a moment or two to regain composure, then continued quietly—

"But that was not exactly the point. I did not mean to speak of my own troubles. What I feel is that when business is so bad, it is not right for two grown-up girls to stay at home. You could get on without me, with a little extra help for sewing, and in time I might earn enough, not only to keep myself but to help the others. Honestly, now, don't you think I am right? In my place, would you not feel it your duty to the pater to be independent, and lighten his responsibility, if even by a little?"

Mrs Connor sat silent, torn between two thoughts - dread of parting from Ruth, and a longing to help the overburdened husband, who had come as a rescuer in her own need. No one but herself guessed how it tore her heart to present him with fresh bills, or to ask for money for all the thousand-and-one needs of a growing family. Her very dread and nervousness made her choose inappropriate moments for her requests, and Mr Connor's aloofness from the ordinary workaday world made matters still more difficult. He probably considered fifteen pounds a year a lordly dress allowance for his two step-daughters; certainly he would not have noticed if they had worn the same garments every day for years on end. His own clothes lasted him for an incredible period, and were always neatly brushed and folded. It did not occur to him that girls needed more change than himself.

Mrs Connor sat and pondered. It was terrible to think of parting from Ruth, but the strain of making both ends meet was becoming so acute that some method of retrenchment must inevitably be found. It is easy for rich people to cut down expenses—to give up carriage and horses, dismiss two or three servants, and indulge in fewer pleasures and excitements; but it is a very different matter when there are no superfluities with which to part, but only, as it seems, the barest necessaries of life. Mrs Connor's eyes filled slowly with tears as she stretched out her hand and laid it over her daughter's. It was the signal of capitulation, and Ruth recognised it as such, and felt a sinking of the heart.

"You will let me go, mother?" she asked.

And Mrs Connor answered brokenly—

"If I must, I must! You would come home for the holidays: we should not lose you altogether. But oh, Ruth, not yet! Wait until the beginning of the term. Years ago, when things were at their very worst with me, and I did not know where to turn for help, God sent my dear husband to take care of me and you two babies. Perhaps—perhaps something may happen again. Perhaps, after all, it may not be necessary!"

They kissed each other silently, and parted for the night. Half-way upstairs Ruth remembered that her mother had not once inquired as to the nature of the work she intended to undertake, and smiled whimsically to herself. It was so very characteristic of the irresponsible little mistress of the household!

Chapter Three.

A Proposal and a Refusal.

It was tacitly understood in the household that after Easter Ruth was going to do "something" to retrieve the family fortunes, but what that "something" should be remained vague and undefined. Ruth herself debated the question morning, noon, and night, and, like many another poor girl in the same position, bitterly regretted an education which had given her no one marketable qualification. She could play a little, draw a little, speak French a little, speak German a little less, make her own clothes in amateur fashion, and—what else? Nothing at all that any able-bodied woman could not accomplish equally well. If she had concentrated her energies on one definite thing, and learnt to do it, not pretty well, nor very well, but just as well as it could possibly be done, what a different prospect would have stretched before her now!

If she decided to teach, she must be content to accept juvenile pupils and a poor salary; if she became a companion, she must sacrifice all spirit of independence, and become a dutiful drudge, while she knew in her inmost heart that it would be wrong to take up nursing, since she felt no real vocation for the task.

It was useless to ask advice of anyone at home, so, one afternoon, Ruth betook herself to almost the only intimate friend she possessed,—a middle-aged spinster who kept house for an adored doctor brother. The brother was a friend into the bargain—a tall, thin, clever—looking man of thirty-eight, engrossed in his practice, which was one of the most prosperous in the neighbourhood. Brother and sister were seated at tea together when Ruth was announced, and she looked round the pretty room with admiring eyes. Pink silk lamp-shades, luxurious cushions, bowls of spring flowers, a tea equipage, bright and dainty and complete,—oh, how delightful it all looked after the bare shabbiness of the room at home; and what fascinating clothes Eleanor was wearing!

Despite her affection, one-and-twenty was inclined to think pretty things thrown away upon an antediluvian creature of forty, but if Ruth could have had a glimpse of herself as "others saw her" at that moment, she might have been more content. The subdued lamp-light dealt kindly with the old blue serge coat and skirt, the pink scarf at her neck matched the colour on her cheeks, and the eyes underneath the black brows were unusually bright and animated. She was always a welcome guest at this hospitable house, and it was a pleasant variety to be petted and fussed over, provided with cushions and footstools, and tempted to eat by a fresh supply of hot buttered scones and a delectable chocolate cake studded over with walnuts. Ruth laughed, and dimpled into ever brighter beauty.

"It makes me feel so nice and young," she cried, "as if I were a spoilt only child, instead of the staid eldest daughter of a family! But I ought to be staid; I can't afford to frivol any longer, for I am going to take a most important step, and start life on my own account."

Brother and sister alike looked up with sharp inquiry, and Ruth, understanding, broke into a merry laugh.

"Oh, not that! Nothing half so interesting! Merely going to earn my living, and I came to ask your advice as to how I had best set about it. Nothing is decided so far, except that I am to earn enough money to keep myself, and contribute largely to home expenses. That's the end, but the puzzle is to find out the means."

"Poor lassie!" said Miss Maclure gently. She had a soft, Scotch burr in her voice, and her plain face was full of an almost motherly kindness as she looked at the pretty girl across the hearth. She had private means of her own, and her brother was a prosperous man; but she knew enough of the world to understand the nature of the struggle of which Ruth spoke so lightly.

"It's easier saying than doing, I'm afraid, dearie. There are so many women searching for work nowadays, and for many positions it is necessary to prepare by long and expensive training. We wanted a lady secretary for one of the societies in which I am interested, and we had hundreds of applicants who were expert typists and stenographers, and had all sorts of diplomas to show, but you have nothing of the kind."

"No, nor a penny to spend on training. I must be taken as I am, or not at all. Don't discourage me, Eleanor, please. Mollie runs the cold tap persistently at home, and I really need appreciation. There must be *something* that I can do, if I set my wits to work. I am not going to be a nurse, Dr Maclure, so don't think that I am leading up to a request that you should get me into a hospital. I don't like sick people unless they are my very own, and it would be almost as dull to be shut up in a hospital as to remain at home."

Miss Maclure looked a trifle shocked at this candid confession, but her brother laughed, and said approvingly—

"That's right! I admire your honesty. We have far too many nurses who take up the work without any real fitness, and I should be sorry to see you added to the number. Well, let me see! ... After hospital nursing, the next most popular resort is to turn author and write a novel. Have you any leaning in that direction?"

He looked across at Ruth with a humorous twitching of his clean-shaven lips. Once again she felt conscious that the Maclures looked upon her as a pretty child, to be petted and humoured rather than a serious woman of the world, and once again the knowledge brought with it a feeling of rest and comfort.

She crinkled her brows and smiled back at the doctor, answering frankly—

"Oh yes, plenty of leanings! I should love to write, and Mollie and I are always 'imagining' to make life more lively and exciting; but, when it comes to sitting down with a pen in my hand, my thoughts seem to take wing and fly away, and the words won't come. They are all stiff and formal, and won't express what I want. Mollie gets on better, for she writes as she talks, so it's natural at least. She wrote quite a long story once, and read it aloud to me as she went on, but it was never finished, and I don't think for a moment that any paper would have looked at it. The people were all lords and dukes and millionaires, and we don't know even a knight. I expect it was full of mistakes."

Dr Maclure smiled and rose from his seat.

"Well, I have some letters to write, so I will leave you to have your talk with Eleanor; but I am starting off again on my rounds in half an hour, and shall be driving past your house. It is a disagreeable evening. Will you let me give you a lift?"

Ruth consented eagerly. The blue serge coat felt none too warm in the bleak east wind, and it would be a relief to be spared the chilly walk, and be bowled along instead in the doctor's luxurious brougham. She drew her chair nearer to the fire, and proceeded to confide various whys and wherefores to the sympathetic Eleanor—sympathetic, but hardly responsive this afternoon for some mysterious reason. The while Ruth set forward one idea after another, Miss Maclure sat gazing at her with an intent, questioning gaze, as though too much occupied with her own thoughts to grasp the meaning of the conversation. Ruth felt chilled and disappointed, for during the last few days the constant thought in the background of her mind had been, "Eleanor will advise me! Eleanor will know what to do!"

Miss Maclure was a busy woman, whose name figured in a dozen committees. She knew everyone, went everywhere, and her word had weight in guilds, societies, and associations. What could be more easy than for her to find a pleasant and lucrative berth for a pet girl friend, and settle her in it without delay? Ruth had already imagined a touching scene wherein she had been introduced to her future sphere of work, while those in authority overpowered Miss Maclure with thanks for helping them to find the ideal person to fill the vacant post. But Eleanor said nothing, suggested nothing, only sat staring with those grave, questioning eyes!

It was almost a relief when the half-hour was over, and the doctor gave the summons for departure. Then Eleanor came back to the present once more, and was all that was kind and loving.

"Have you no wraps with you, dear? Is that all you have on?" she asked, as the girl buttoned her thin coat and pulled the scarf higher round her throat; and Ruth answered "Yes," in an irresponsive tone, which effectually put a stop to further remarks. She might speak of her own poverty, but not even Eleanor Maclure herself could be allowed to pity, or offer to supply a want. That was Miss Ruth's idea of proper pride, and she straightened her back, and held her head higher than ever as she crossed the hall and took her seat in the carriage.

Such a luxurious brougham it was, with its well-cushioned seats, its electric reading-lamp attached to the wall, its rack for books and papers, and cosy fur rug! Ruth tucked the rug securely in position, and, looking up, caught the reflection of her face in the strip of mirror opposite. The blue serge toque sat so jauntily on her head that it looked quite smart; the pink tie was undoubtedly becoming. Well, it was a comfort to be pretty, at least! To have been poor and plain would have been quite too depressing. She smiled back in approving fashion, to feel somewhat disconcerted a moment later as the mirror reflected Donald Maclure's face beside her own. He was staring at her with the same intent questioning which she had noticed in Eleanor's eyes, and surely he looked paler, older, more haggard than usual! She turned towards him, warmed into increased friendship by the presentiment that he was in trouble like herself.

"It's so good of you to take me home, Dr Maclure! It may seem curious to you, but it's quite a treat to me to drive about in this comfy carriage. I so seldom travel in anything but shaky omnibuses. I should not object to being a lady doctor, if I could have a brougham like this of my very own. There! We never thought of that when we were discussing my possible fields of labour!"

Dr Maclure bent forward, and glanced out of the window. His horse was travelling quickly to-night; in another ten minutes Mr Connor's house would be reached, and his opportunity over. He turned to face his companion, and said quietly—

"There is another possibility open to you, Ruth, which you have perhaps not considered. Have you ever thought of it, I wonder? Can you guess what I mean?"

The grey eyes stared into his in frankest bewilderment.

"No," cried Ruth—"no! What is it? Something nice? Tell me what it is."

"You have never guessed that I love you; that I have loved you for years, since you were a girl at school? You have never once guessed it all this time?"

He read his answer in the blank face and startled eyes, for Ruth was too utterly taken aback to feel the usual embarrassment. She sat perfectly still, gazing not at him but at the reflection of his face in the mirror opposite. Dr Maclure! Was she dreaming, or was it really his voice which she heard uttering these extraordinary words? Dr Maclure loved her—had loved her for years! It was too inconceivable to be grasped! He asked if she had not guessed his secret, but Ruth had not thought of him at all; he had not entered into her calculations except as "Eleanor's brother"—a nonentity who might be agreeable or the reverse, according as he drove her home on wet evenings, or interrupted a cosy *tête-à-tête.*

She did not reply to the question in words; but he was answered all the same, for she heard him sigh, and saw a quiver pass across the thin face.

"I am too old, Ruth—is that it? You never thought of me as a possible lover?"

"Oh no, never once! You always seemed so busy and occupied, and you have Eleanor to look after you. You have always been very kind to me, but you were kind to Mollie and Trix and Betty as well. I did not feel that you treated me differently from them. You are so clever; and you saw yourself, when we talked this afternoon, I can do nothing.—I don't see how you can possibly like me."

"Don't you?" he asked quietly. "But I do, Ruth; I care more than I can express. I have not spoken before, for you seemed too young. I should not have spoken to-day if you had not told us of this new move. You don't know how hard it is for a girl to go out into the world and earn her living; but I do, and I should like to save you from it, if it can be done. I could give you a comfortable home, and enough money to make life easy and pleasant. It would be my best happiness to see you happy. We could travel; you would be able to help Mollie and the rest. If you married me, your people would be my people, and I should be as anxious as yourself to let them share our good fortune; and I would love you very dearly, Ruth! I seem old to you, perhaps, but my love would be more proved and certain than if I were a boy of your own age. I am a prosperous man, but I want something more from life than I have had so far—something that you alone can give roe. You hold my key to happiness, Ruth!"

Ruth drew back into the corner of the carriage and turned her face into the shadow. She wanted to think. What an extraordinary change in the outlook at life to have happened in a few brief moments! Dr Maclure's wife! Here was an answer indeed to the question which had been occupying her thoughts for the last few weeks!

Suppose—suppose, just for one moment, that she said yes? Suppose that on getting home she walked into the dining-room and announced her engagement to a prosperous and charming man, who was already a family friend and favourite? What fun! What excitement! What pride on the part of the little mother; what transparent relief to the overtaxed pater! Mollie and Trix would begin at once to discuss bridesmaids' dresses, and there would be a trousseau to buy, and all the bustle and excitement of a first marriage in a family. And afterwards? A big, handsomely appointed house, pretty clothes, lots of money, the power to help those whom she loved...

It sounded good—very good indeed! Much more attractive than those nursery governess and companion schemes which she dreaded, despite all her resolutions. It would be delightful to be her own mistress, and do just as she liked...

And then a thought occurred. What of Eleanor? Ruth recalled the intent gaze which had mystified her so much during the afternoon, and felt convinced that Miss Maclure had guessed her brother's secret. What was her feeling in the matter? Was she jealous of a rival in her brother's affections, or loyally anxious for his happiness, regardless of how her own future might be affected? A spasm of curiosity found voice in a sudden question—

"But there is Eleanor. If you married, what would become of her?"

"There would be no difficulty about that. When we took up house together we made a solemn agreement that if either wished to marry in the future the other should not hinder in any possible way. Eleanor has her own income, and many interests in life to keep her happy and occupied. She would live near us, I hope, but you should be entire mistress of your home, Ruth."

He evidently thought she had looked upon his sister's presence in the house as a hindrance to her happiness, but, in truth, Ruth felt a chilly sinking of heart at his reply. The thought of the big house was not half so attractive, shorn of the figure of the sympathetic friend. The library with no Eleanor sitting writing at her desk; the drawing-room with no Eleanor in the deep-cushioned chair; the dining-room with no Eleanor at the head of the table—how blank it all seemed! How dreadfully dull to be alone all day, with only the doctor to break the monotony! Only the doctor! The blood rushed in a flood to Ruth's cheeks as she realised the significance of that one word. She turned impetuously towards her companion, and gripped his arm with nervous pressure.

"Don't tempt me!" she cried earnestly—"don't tempt me! There are so many things that I should like, and I keep thinking of them, when I should think only of you.—I'd love to be rich, and have a nice house, and play Lady Bountiful at home! I'd love to travel about and see the world, instead of jogging along in one little rut; and, really and truly, I dread turning out to work, and am a coward at heart—but,—that's all! I have always liked you very much as a friend, but I can't imagine ever feeling any different. When I was thinking over things just now, I—don't be angry! I don't want to hurt you, only to be quite, quite honest—I thought more of Eleanor than of you! I hardly thought of you at all."

The doctor's thin face looked very drawn and pained, but he smiled in response to her pleading glance.

"I'm not angry, dear. Why should I be? It is not your fault that you do not care, and it is best for us both to know the truth. I feared it might be so. I am too old and staid to attract a bright young girl, but I even now cannot bring myself to regret my love. It has given me the happiest hours of my life, and I hope you will always let me help you in any way that is possible. I think you owe me that privilege, don't you, Ruth?"

"Oh, I do—I do! If it is any pleasure to you, I promise faithfully to come to you whenever I need a friend, and I should like you to help me. That means a great deal, for I am horribly proud. There are very few people from whom I can accept a favour."

He smiled again, but with an evident effort, and Ruth, peeping at his averted profile, felt a pang of real personal suffering at the sight of his pain. It seemed dreadful that she should have such power to affect this strong man; to take the light out of his face and make it old and worn and grey!

The carriage was nearing home; in a few minutes' time the drive would be over, and she would have no chance of continuing the conversation. With a sudden swelling of the heart she realised that she could not part without another expression of regret.

"I am so sorry, so dreadfully sorry to have grieved you! But you would not like me to marry you just for what you could give me;

you would not have been satisfied with that, would you, Dr Maclure?"

His eyes met hers with a flash of determination.

"No," he cried—unhesitatingly—"never! I want a wife who loves me, or no wife at all! One never knows what lies ahead in this world, and if dark days come I should like to feel that she cared for me more, rather than less. It would be hard for us both if she valued only my possessions, and they took to themselves wings and fled. And there is your own future to consider. Love will come to you some day, and you must be free to welcome him. Don't distress yourself about me, Ruth; I have my work for consolation. Before I get home to-night I shall have seen so much suffering that I shall be ashamed to nurse my own trouble."

"Yes," said Ruth faintly.

His words seemed to place her at an immense distance, as if already he had accepted his burden and put it resolutely out of sight. She felt chilled and humiliated, for in the depths of her heart she knew that if Dr Maclure had been persistent in his request, and had condescended to "tempt" her, to use her own expressive phrase, she would very probably have succumbed to the temptation, however much she might have regretted her decision later on. But Donald would have none of her; he wanted a wife who cared for himself, and not for his possessions. Ruth felt almost as if it were she herself who had been refused. It was not an agreeable sensation to experience after a first proposal.

Chapter Four.

A Meeting.

One bright spring afternoon about a week after Ruth's visit to Miss Maclure, Mollie went out to execute some shopping commissions, and on her way home took a short cut through the park, which was the great summer resort of the northern town in which her lot was cast.

She was an ardent lover of Nature, and it was a joy to see the tiny green buds bursting into life on trees and hedges, and to realise that the long winter was at an end.

"Nasty, shivery, chilblainey thing,—I hate it!" said Mollie to herself, with a shiver of disgust. "It might be very nice if one had lots of furs, and skating, and parties, and fires in one's bedroom. People who can enjoy themselves like that may talk of the 'joys of winter,' but, from my point of view, they don't exist. Give me summer, and flowers at a penny a bunch! This dear old park and I have had many good times together. I think I have sampled most of the seats in my time!"

It was, indeed, a favourite summer custom of the Farrell girls to repair to a shady bench under a tree with such portable sewing as happened to be on hand, for when the sun shone in its strength the temperature of Attica was more like that of an oven than a room. The winding paths were, therefore, familiar to Mollie; but they were apt to be puzzling to strangers who, like herself, wished to take a short cut from one side of the park to another.

To-day as she approached the junction of four cross-ways, she saw before her the figure of an old man, glancing irresolutely from side to side, then turning round, as though in search of someone whom he could consult in his perplexity. Besides Mollie herself, there was no one in sight, so she quickened her pace and approached the stranger with the bright, frank smile which came so readily to her lips. Mollie was nothing if not sociable; she never lost a chance of talking if it came in her way; even to direct wandering old gentlemen was more amusing than nothing, and this one had such a curious old-world appearance!

"Can I help you?" she asked brightly; and the old man planted his stick more firmly on the ground, and stared at her with grim disfavour.

"In what way, may I ask, do I appear to be in need of help?"

It was decidedly a snub, but some people are not easily quelled, and Mollie Farrell was one of the number. Instead of being annoyed, she was simply amused, and her grey eyes twinkled with mischief. He was a cross old dear, and proud too! quite amazed that anyone should suppose it possible that he should need assistance of any kind.

"I'm sorry," she replied; "I thought you had lost your way, and that I might be able to direct you. Please forgive me for seeming to interfere."

She took a step forward, but the old man's eyes seemed to hold her back. He was looking at her fixedly beneath his heavy brows; such bushy, black eyebrows they were, and she fancied that the grim expression softened for a moment as he replied—

"You are right. I *have* lost my way! My cabman brought me to the park gates, and as he said there was a direct path across, I thought I should like the walk. As a result, I find myself completely out of my reckoning. It is a stretch of imagination to call this a direct path."

"Oh, it's direct enough when you know it," said Mollie easily, "ever so much nicer than going round by the streets. It is a beautiful park, and we are very proud of it. When the trees are in blossom, it is like fairyland—you can't imagine how beautiful it is."

"Possibly not," returned the stranger curtly. "In the meantime, however, there is nothing particularly alluring in the scene, and you will excuse my reminding you that we are standing in a direct draught. I should be obliged if you could direct me to Langton Terrace without further delay."

Mollie laughed merrily.

"That is just what I have been waiting to do, but you would not tell me where you were bound. I am walking in that direction myself, and if you will allow me I will show you the shortest cut. I know the park so well that I can dodge about from one path to another, and cut off some of the corners. It is cold just here, but the cross-roads are sheltered even now."

The stranger shrugged his shoulders, and said "Humph" in an incredulous manner, and that was his sole reply in words. He turned, however, and walked by Mollie's side, leaning heavily on his stick, and taking such short, laboured steps, that it was evident that the exercise was almost too much for his strength. Mollie longed to offer him the support of her strong arm, but even her audacity failed at the sight of the grim face. She looked inquiringly at his feet, for the symptoms of temper all hinted to the explanation of gout. But no! there were no cloth shoes to be seen, only the trimmest of well-polished boots.

"Perhaps he is just recovering from an attack, or sickening for another," said Mollie to herself. "Anyway, he is ill, poor old fellow, for his face looks quite grey, just like that poor Mr Burgess before he died. I expect he can't help being cross. I should be horrid myself if I were always in pain. I remember that day I had on those new boots that hurt my feet, I quarrelled with Ruth all the way home... The question is, shall I talk, or let him alone? If it were me, I'd like to be amused, to make the time pass. I'll try anyway, and see how he responds."

They had entered one of the smaller paths by this time, and to the right lay the wide, grey surface of a lake dotted over by little islands, the largest of which was connected with the shore by an ornamental bridge. Mollie felt a kind of possessive pride in the scene, and pointed out the beauties thereof as eagerly as though she were the owner of all she surveyed.

"It's the largest lake in any of the parks in the north; some people say it is nearly as big as the Serpentine. I don't know, for I have never been in London. In summer-time hundreds of men come and sail boats—quite great big boats—from side to side. It looks so pretty to see all the white sails floating about in the sunshine."

"Indeed!"

("Doesn't care for boats. I'll try something else.") "Do you see that big island, the biggest of all?" pursued the indefatigable Mollie aloud. "It is full of peacocks. There are dozens and dozens of peacocks! You can see them sometimes strutting about with their tails spread out, and roosting right up in the trees. People say that peacocks are the laziest birds in existence. They go to rest earlier, and get up later than anything else."

"Indeed!"

Still grimmer silence; still slower and more halting footsteps. Presently the stranger stopped short and asked abruptly—

"How far are we still from Langton Terrace? Five minutes' walk—ten minutes? We are more than half-way, I suppose?"

"Not quite, I am afraid. If you are tired, would you not rest on this seat for a few minutes? It is really quite sheltered behind the trees. If you can tell me which end of the terrace you want to reach, it will make a little difference in the way we ought to take. There are three blocks of houses, which are all known by the same name. You wanted to go to—"

"Number 7," said the stranger; and sat down heavily upon the seat. He leant both hands on his stick and rested his chin upon them, as though thankful for the support; and Mollie stood before him staring fixedly at his face.

Aquiline features, sharpened by suffering into yet finer lines, closely-set lips drooping out into lines of fretful impatience, sunken eyes beneath overhanging brows. She studied them one by one, until, struck by her silence, the old man looked up in surprise.

"Number 7, I said. If you live in the neighbourhood, you may know the house, and possibly its inmates?"

"Yes, I know them all; they are nice people and very kind to me. I've known them quite a number of years."

"Mr and Mrs Connor have a large family, I believe—a number of young children."

"Oh, dozens!" replied Mollie easily. She was enjoying herself intensely, but trying to preserve an appearance of innocent calm. "What an adventure," she was saying to herself—"oh, what an adventure. What fun to tell it all to Ruth and the girls! I must remember every word, so as to repeat it in style!" Aloud, she added carelessly, "There are two girls, and lots of little boys. It seems as if there were boys, boys everywhere, wherever you turn all over the house; but they are ubiquitous creatures, so perhaps there are not quite so many as it seems. They are handsome little fellows, and I believe clever too. Mrs Connor is a very pretty woman, and always kind and gentle. Everybody likes her. Mr Connor is nice too. I don't think he is at all strong, and he has to work very hard for that big family."

"Indeed!" The strange old man did not display the slightest sign of sympathy for Mr Connor's anxieties. He relaxed his hold of the stick, and sank wearily against the back of the seat. "There are two step-daughters, I believe—the two Miss Farrells?"

"Ah!" exclaimed Mollie deeply. It was quite a tragic note, as who should say, "Now we are beginning to talk! Now, at last, we reach the real point of the discussion! Just that deep 'Ah,' and no more, until perforce another question must be asked.

"You know the Miss Farrells also?"

"I do!"

"And find them as attractive as the rest of the family?"

"Oh, more—much more! They are darlings!" cried Mollie, with unction, "especially the younger. Her name is Mary, but they call her Mollie, because it suits her better. Don't you always imagine a Mollie very sweet, and charming, and attractive?"

"I can't say that I have devoted any attention to the subject. So Mary is the younger of the two, is she? And the elder?"

"Ruth! she's pretty and serious, and very, very nice; but Mollie is nicer, all the same. When you get to know them, you must promise to like Mollie best, for my sake! I'm so fond of her, that I want everybody to be the same. I like her better than anyone I ever knew!"

The old man smiled grimly.

"You appear to be of an enthusiastic temperament; I fancy I shall prefer to judge for myself when I make the young lady's acquaintance. We had better be getting on now. I am sorry to hinder your progress, but it is not possible for me to move more quickly at present. I should not have attempted the walk if I had known that it was so long; but the cab jolted insufferably, and the sunshine was tempting. Well,—there is nothing for it but to make another effort!"

He pressed his hands on the seat to lighten the effort of rising, but before he had got any further, Mollie stepped forward eagerly, and laid a hand on his shoulder. Her cheeks were flushed with colour, her eyes a-sparkle with excitement.

"Unless you will let me help you! ... I'm very strong; I could support you easily, if you would take my arm and lean on me. I'd love to do it. Do let me? Won't you,—*Uncle Bernard*?"

Chapter Five.

An Invitation.

The old man fell backward on the seat with an exclamation of keenest surprise. His sunken eyes stared into Mollie's face as she bent over him; at the golden hair curling beneath the dark toque, the grey eyes, the curving lips. Each feature in turn was scrutinised as if he were searching for something familiar which had so far escaped notice. Apparently it was not discovered, for the expression of amazement deepened upon his face, and he asked sharply—

"What did you say? *What* did you call me? I don't understand what you can mean!"

Mollie sat down on the bench, and smiled brightly into his face.

"Uncle Bernard! You are Uncle Bernard Farrell! I knew you the moment you said that you were going to Number 7, and asked if I knew the Connors. Of course I know them, because I am—" She hesitated, and Mr Farrell finished the sentence for her.

"You are one of Mr Connor's daughters. The eldest, I presume. I have not the pleasure of knowing your name."

"No-o! I am not Trix. She is a child, only fifteen. I was nineteen on my last birthday. I am,"—for once in her life Mollie had the grace to blush, and looked a trifle discomposed—"I'm Mollie Farrell."

The glance which the old man cast upon her was the reverse of flattering.

"You are Mollie Farrell, are you?" he repeated coldly. "Evidently modesty is not one of your failings, young lady. It might have been wiser if you had allowed me to discover your attractions for myself. Do you consider it quite honest—we will not discuss the question of good taste—to play a double part, and criticise your relations to any stranger whom you may meet in your walks?"

"You asked me; you began it! I should not have mentioned them if you had not asked that question. Then I recognised you, and thought it would be fun. You were not a stranger, you see; you were Uncle Bernard."

"That may be my name, but as I have never seen you before, I can hardly rank as a friend. May I ask how you came to recognise me at all?"

"Oh yes! We have your portraits at home, and mother often talks of you, and the happy times she had when she used to visit you with father when they were engaged. When we were children it was a favourite game for one of us to be Uncle Bernard, and the other guests staying at the Court, and we used to go through all the adventures which father had as a boy,—fall into the mill-stream and be rescued by the dog, and be chased by the bull in the long meadow, and ride on the top of the waggons at the harvest home. We know all about the house, and the tapestry in the hall, and the funny wooden pictures of the Dutch ancestors, and the long gallery where you used to dance at night. Mother loves talking about it. She has not much fun in her life now, poor dear, and that makes her think all the more of her youth. We envy her, Ruth and Trix and I, because we have a very quiet time at home. We are poor, you see. You can't have much fun if you are poor."

"You think that riches are the one thing needful; that if you had enough money your happiness would be assured?"

"Ah!" sighed Mollie rapturously. "*How* happy I should be! I've never had enough money for my wants in all my life, so I can't even imagine the bliss of it. I should not know how to be happy enough."

The old man looked at her silently. She saw that he was about to speak, but the words were long in coming. A cloud had drifted across the sun, and the stretch of park looked suddenly grey and bare. Mollie drew her shoulders together with an involuntary shiver. Something had suddenly damped her ardour of enthusiasm; but it was not so much the bleak wind as the sight of the face gazing into her own, with its set lips, and bleached, joyless expression. For years to come Mollie could recall that moment, and feel again the chill in her veins with which she listened to his reply.

"All my life long," said Bernard Farrell slowly, "all my life everything that I have touched has turned to gold, and everyone I have loved,"—he paused, lingering on the word, and again Mollie shivered in sympathetic understanding—"everyone whom I have loved has *died*!" The wind seemed to take up the word, and repeat it in melancholy echo. "Died! died! died!" wailed the trees, tossing drearily to and fro. "Died!" shivered the ripple over the cold grey lake. The clouds gathered in a pall overhead.

"I'm sorry!" gasped Mollie faintly—"I'm so sorry!" But Mr Farrell stopped her with a hasty gesture.

"Please spare me protestations of sympathy. They were the last thing I wished to evoke. I merely wished to impress upon you that I am in a unique position for judging the worth of riches.—Is it your pleasure that we continue our journey? The afternoon is growing chill."

Mollie rose in confusion, but she did not reply, nor make any further offer of support. There was something in the old man's voice which forbade familiarities. He was no longer merely cross and unamiable; she had caught a glimpse into the secret of a desolate heart, and the sight sobered her youthful spirits.

"First his wife," she said to herself, as she led the way onward—"pretty Aunt Edna, whom mother loved so much. He adored her, and they were never parted for a day till she took typhoid, and died. The little girl died the year after, and he had no one left but Ned. Mother says he was the handsomest boy she ever met, and the cleverest, and the best. Even now, after all these years, she can't speak of the day he was drowned without crying... I always hated to hear that story!

"She says the real Uncle Bernard died with Ned. He seemed to disappear from that day, and an entirely different person appeared in his place. He had been kind and hospitable, fond of having people around him and making them happy; but after that he shut himself up and became a regular hermit. Then he went abroad, and since he came back four years ago and reopened the Court, he has written to nobody, and nobody has seen him. But he has come to see us to-day of his own free will. I wonder why? Something has happened to make him break the silence. What can it have been?"

She dared not ask the question; but, as the feeble steps endeavoured to keep pace with her own, a possible explanation darted into Mollie's mind. The poor old man was ill, very ill; there was an expression on the grey, sunken face which was eloquent even to her inexperience. Death was coming forward to meet him, coming very near; standing upon the very threshold! Strong, happy nineteen shuddered at the thought, and felt an overpowering pity for the waning life.

Mollie longed to comfort the old man with the assurance that there were many still left who could help and minister to his declining days; but her previous overtures had met with so little success that she was afraid of meeting yet another rebuff, and, with unusual prudence, decided to await a better opportunity.

Langton Terrace was reached at last, and Mollie produced a key and opened the door of Number 7. In a household where there are so many children and so few servants, the latchkey was in constant use, and thus it happened that she could bring her guest unnoticed into the house and escort him to her stepfather's sanctum, which was sure to be unoccupied at this hour of the afternoon. She drew forward an armchair, poked the fire into a blaze, and laid Mr Farrell's hat and stick on the table, while he lay wearily against the cushions. He looked woefully exhausted, and Mollie's kind heart had a happy inspiration.

"I shan't tell anyone that you are here until you have had a rest," she said assuringly. "This is the pater's den, and his private property after four o'clock, so you will be quite undisturbed. Just tell me what will refresh you most—tea, coffee, wine? I can bring what you like quite quietly."

"Tea, please—tea, and ten minutes' rest. I shall be better then," Mr Farrell said wearily.

Mollie left the room to prepare a dainty little tray in the pantry, and beg a private pot of tea from the kitchen. The idea of waiting in secret upon Uncle Bernard was delightfully exciting; it was almost as good as running the blockade, to creep past the dining-room door where her mother and sisters were assembled, and listen to the murmur of voices from within.

If they knew—oh, if they knew! She had prepared some crisp slices of toast, skimmed the cream off the milk in defiance of cook's protests, and made sure that the water in the little covered jug was boiling, and not only moderately warm, as the custom was. It was the simplest of meals, but at least everything was as tempting as hands could make it, and Mollie had the satisfaction of pouring out two cups of tea, and seeing the last slice of toast disappear from the rack. She took nothing herself, and preserved a discreet silence until Mr Farrell replaced cup and plate on the table, and condescended to smile approval.

"Thank you, Miss Mollie; I am obliged to you for securing me this rest. Judging from my first impressions of your character, I should not have expected so much common-sense. I feel quite refreshed, and ready to see your mother when it is convenient."

Mollie lifted the tray, and stood for a moment looking down with an air of triumph.

"I'm so glad! I talk a lot of nonsense, but I can be quite sensible if I like, and I *did* want to help you, Uncle Bernard; I'll send mother in here, where you can have your talk in peace. It's the only chance of being uninterrupted."

Mr Farrell made no reply, and Mollie made haste to deposit the tray in the pantry, and rush for the dining-room door. The secret had been kept so long that she felt sore—absolutely sore with the strain. It seemed incredible that her mother and sisters should be sitting munching bread-and-butter as calmly as if it were an ordinary day, when nothing extraordinary had happened to break the monotonous routine. She leant against the lintel of the door and called her mother by name—"Muv! you are wanted at once in the Den. Somebody wants to speak to you!"

Mrs Connor's brow furrowed into the usual anxious lines as she prepared to hear a story of fresh disaster from her husband's lips; but at the doorway two magic words were whispered into her ear which brought the blood into the white cheeks, and sent her trotting down the hall on eager feet. Then came the delicious moment to which Mollie had looked forward ever since the meeting at the cross-roads. She walked back into the room, while Ruth looked up with weary curiosity, and Trix with unconcealed wrath.

"You might have let mother finish her tea in peace! She has been slaving all day, and was just enjoying a rest!"

"What is it, Mollie? Why did the pater come home so early? Is he ill?"

"It isn't pater, my dear. Guess again! A friend of mine, whom I met in the park and brought home to tea. He was rather tired, so I, gave him a private little feed in the study, instead of bringing him straight in here. Considerate of me, wasn't it? He was quite touched."

"He?" repeated Ruth breathlessly. "Mollie, what are you talking about? Don't make a mystery out of nothing! Why can't you say at once who it is?"

"I'm afraid of your nerves, dear. I want to break it to you by degrees. Sudden shocks are dangerous for the young. My own heart is quite palpitating with all I have undergone to-day. I was walking along,—all innocent and unsuspicious,—gazing upon the fair spring scene, when suddenly, glancing ahead, I beheld a figure standing at the junction of the cross-roads. 'Tis ever thus, my love! Fate stands waiting for us where the paths diverge, to point out the way in which we should go. End of volume one ... Do you feel excited?"

Trix grinned broadly, Ruth looked tired and impatient.

"Oh, thrilled, of course! So many interesting people come to see us that it's difficult to choose between them. The piano-tuner, perhaps; or the gasman, to look at the meter."

"I should have walked home with them, shouldn't I, and given them tea in the study? A little higher in the social scale, please!"

"The curate calling for a subscription?"

"Cold; quite cold! Try again! Someone you have often wished to see, but who has never displayed any great anxiety to make your acquaintance in return."

"Uncle Bernard, I presume?" said Ruth sarcastically, not for one moment believing the truth of her words, though her mind instantly reverted to the personage of that mythical uncle who had played so large a part in her mental life. She did not even trouble to look at Mollie as she spoke; but Trix did, and bounded to her feet in excitement.

"Is it—is it? Oh, Mollie, not really! He hasn't really and truly appeared after all these years? You don't seriously mean it? Look at her, Ruth! I believe it *is* true!"

Ruth looked, and flushed the loveliest of pinks. It seemed almost incredible that Trix was right, yet something very much out of the usual course of events must have happened to excite Mollie so keenly. Her cheeks were burning as though with a fever, the hand resting on the table was actually trembling. "Tell me, Mollie!" she pleaded; and Mollie nodded her head in triumph.

"Uncle Bernard himself! The real, genuine article sitting in solid flesh and blood in our very own study, and I'm the one who brought him here. What do you think of *that* for an adventure? I saw an aged, aged man a-leaning on a stick, as the poem says, and I went up and asked him if I could help him in any way. I once read about an old man whose nose suddenly began to bleed in an omnibus. He searched for a pocket-handkerchief, but had evidently forgotten to bring one, and the other passengers began to smile and titter, all except one girl, who opened her bag and presented him with a nice clean one of her own. The old man died soon afterwards, and left her a million pounds as a token of gratitude. I think it's just as kind to escort a stranger through a lonely park when he has lost his way! If Uncle Bernard adopts me and gives me a million, I'll treat you both to a nice new hat.—I asked where he was going, and he said to Number 7 Langton Terrace, and I looked at him. And, Ruth, do you know what I thought of? I thought of *you*! He had black eyebrows like yours, and he scowls, as you do (only when you are cross, dear, not when you're in a good temper), and his lips droop like yours, too. I thought, 'I have seen that face before!' and then I remembered the photographs, and it burst upon me all in a moment. Then he asked me if I knew the Connors, and I said I'd known them for years, and the step-daughters, too, and that they were a charming family, but Mollie was the nicest of all."

"Mollie, you didn't!"

"I did! Why not? It's true, isn't it? When I revealed myself to him, however, he seemed to think that I was rather vain. I must leave it to time to prove the truth of my assertion."

"You are in earnest? You really mean it? Mollie, what has he come for? What has made him remember us after all these years? Has something happened that we know nothing about?"

"I can't tell you. There's only one thing certain,—he is very old and ill, and if he wants to see us at all there isn't much time to spare. He is not at all like the Uncle Bernard mother remembers, but very cross and irritable, and his poor old face looks so miserable that it goes to your heart to see him. I wanted to put my arms round his neck and kiss him, but I would as soon have attempted to embrace a tiger. He snubbed me the whole time. Oh, talk of adventures! *What* an afternoon I have had!"

"If you met him walking across the park he can't have any luggage, and if he hasn't any luggage he can't intend to sleep here to-night," reasoned Ruth thoughtfully. "Perhaps he will just stay to dinner. Pea-soup, cold beef, and apple-pie—that's all there is, and he is accustomed to half a dozen courses, and two men-servants to wait upon him. Poor dear mother will be in despair because she didn't order a fresh joint for to-day. Shall I go to the kitchen and see if there is anything that can be made into a hot dish?"

Mollie pursed up her lips, but, before she had time to reply, the sound of footsteps was heard from without, and Mrs Connor appeared in the doorway, followed by the tall, gaunt figure of Uncle Bernard. The girls rose from their seats as he entered the room, and Ruth and Trix approached him with diffident smiles, while Mrs Connor introduced each by name.

"This is my eldest girl, Ruth; you saw her last when she was a baby in arms. This is Beatrice Connor; she knows you quite well by name, don't you, Trix dear?"

But Mr Farrell betrayed not the faintest interest in Trix or her memories, and barely touched the hand which she extended towards him. All his attention seemed concentrated on Ruth, as she stood before him with her beautiful, flushed face raised to his own.

"This is Ruth!" he repeated slowly. "She is not at all like her sister. I am glad that one of your girls takes after her father's family, Mary. This one is an unmistakable Farrell!"

Mollie turned aside with an expressive grimace.

"I'm cut out already," she told herself. "Ruth's black brows have walked straight into his affections! I might as well resign myself to play second fiddle forthwith."

Mr Farrell accepted an invitation to stay for the family dinner, but it cannot truthfully be said that his presence added to the gaiety of the meal. Mrs Connor was nervous and ill at ease, regretting, as her daughter had foretold, that she had not ordered a hot joint for to-day, and allowed the cold meat to be used on the morrow.

She looked gratefully at Ruth when a small dish of curry made its appearance, in addition to the scanty menu; but Uncle Bernard had spent some years of his life in India, and his ideas of curry evidently differed from those of the plain cook downstairs, for after the first taste he laid down his fork and made no further pretence of eating.

Mr Connor made several attempts to introduce interesting subjects of conversation, but receiving only monosyllabic replies, relapsed in his turn into silence. With every moment that passed, the girls felt less able to imagine the reason for the appearance of a visitor who showed so little interest in the affairs of the family; for Mr Farrell asked no questions, paid no attention to the general conversation, and, for the greater part of the time, appeared lost in his own thoughts.

The three little boys alone were unaffected by the general tension, and chattered about their school adventures in their usual noisy fashion. On another occasion Mrs Connor would have checked them, but anything was better than the dead silence which at one time had threatened the whole table; so she left them unreproved, and Uncle Bernard scowled at them beneath his bushy brows in a manner the reverse of approving.

It happened that Betty occupied the seat immediately opposite the visitor, and it was one of Betty's idiosyncrasies to repeat the grimaces of others with an imitation as faithful as it was unconscious. When, for example, Mollie was speaking, Betty tossed her head, tilted her chin, and arched her brows, to the delight and amusement of the family; and now, there she sat—good, kind, most inoffensive of creatures—drawing her wisps of eyebrows together in a lowering scowl, and twisting her lips into an expression of sour distaste.

The three boys nudged each other and tittered together, and Mr Farrell looked round to discover the reason of their mirth, and beheld Betty's transformed face peering into his own. His glance of indignation made her flush with what appeared to be conscious guilt, though, in truth, the poor child had no idea of the nature of her offence. Mrs Connor beheld the incident with petrified horror, Ruth registered a determination to lecture Betty out of so dangerous a habit, but warm-hearted Mollie rushed headlong into the breach.

"Uncle Bernard, Betty did not mean to be rude! Please do not think she was intentionally disrespectful. She has a habit of imitating people, without knowing what she is about, and I am afraid we laugh at her for it, because it is so funny to watch; but she would be dreadfully sorry to be rude to anyone, wouldn't you, Betty dear?"

Betty's lips opened to emit a hoarse, inarticulate murmur. Uncle Bernard turned his eyes upon Mollie, and said coldly—

"You wish to imply that she was imitating my expressions? Indeed! It is always interesting to know in what light one appears to others. I regret that I failed to catch the likeness."

"Dear Uncle Bernard, shall we go to the drawing-room now? The children use this room to prepare their lessons. We will have coffee in the drawing-room!" cried Mrs Connor eagerly. And the elders filed across the hall, leaving poor Betty reduced to tears of misery, while the boys comforted her by jibes and jeers in true schoolboy fashion.

In the drawing-room a ghastly silence prevailed, broken by fitful efforts of conversation. Mr Farrell had asked that a cab should be ordered by nine o'clock to take him back to his hotel; but, though the time drew nearer and nearer, he still vouchsafed no explanation of the unexpected visit. Surely—surely, before going away he would say something, and not once more disappear into the mist, and let the veil of silence fall around him? The same thought was in every mind, the same wondering anticipation; but it was only when the cab was announced and Mr Farrell rose to say good-bye that he appeased their curiosity.

"I came here to-day to make the acquaintance of my nephew's daughters. I should be glad, Mary, if you would allow them to pay me a visit at the Court. I have arranged to have a lady in residence who will look after them and do what chaperonage is needful. If Monday will suit you, I should like them to arrive on that day."

It sounded more like a command than an invitation, but such as it was it thrilled the listeners with joy. To pay a visit, and above all, to visit the Court, of which they had heard so much, had been the girls' day-dream for so long that it seemed impossible that it had come at last. Ruth's mind flew at once to considerations of ways and means, and she suffered a moment of agonising suspense before Mrs Connor's eager consent put an end to anxiety.

"Oh, I shall be delighted—delighted! The girls will love it, of all things. How kind of you, dear Uncle Bernard! Ruth! Mollie! Are you not delighted to have such a treat in store?"

"Thank you, Uncle Bernard; I should love to come!" cried Ruth warmly. "Mollie and I have often said that there is nothing in the world we should enjoy more than paying a visit to the Court. It is most good of you to ask us!"

"And we will try to behave very nicely, and not bother you at all," added Mollie, her eyes dancing with happiness. "We are to come on Monday week. And will there be other people, too—other visitors, besides ourselves?"

"Probably," said Uncle Bernard curtly. "There are several important matters to be discussed, into which I cannot enter in a short interview. I am inviting you—and others—in order that we may talk them over at leisure. A carriage will meet the train arriving at four-twenty. Good-afternoon, Mary. I shall not see you again, as I leave by an early train to-morrow."

Even as he spoke, Mr Farrell made his way towards the door with an air of finality which forbade further questioning. He had waited until the last possible moment before giving his invitation, and, having obtained an acceptance, was evidently determined to take his departure without further delay. Mrs Connor escorted him to the door, her husband helped him into the cab, offered to accompany him to the hotel, was coldly snubbed for his pains, and came back into the house heaving deep sighs of relief.

"Now for my smoke!" he exclaimed, and hurried off to the study, while Mrs Connor was dragged into the drawing-room and subjected to a breathless cross-questioning.

"Matters of importance to discuss! Mother, what can he mean?"

"Other people besides ourselves! Mother, who can they be?"

"How long does he want us to stay?"

"What are we going to do about clothes?"

"That's just exactly what I'm asking myself!" cried Mrs Connor, referring with equal truthfulness to all four questions at once. "It is most awkward, not knowing how long you are expected to stay, or what sort of a party you are to meet; but, in any case, I am afraid you must have some new clothes. I will have a talk with pater, and see what can be done, and you must divide my things between you. I have a few pieces of good lace still, and one or two trinkets which will come in usefully. I am afraid we cannot manage anything new for evenings; you must make the black dresses do."

Mollie groaned dismally.

"They are so old and shabby! The sleeves look as if they had come out of the Ark. I do so long to be white and fluffy for once. Can't we squeeze out white dresses, mother? I'd do without sugar and jam for a year, if you'll advance the money. Even muslin would be better than nothing, and it would wash, and come in for summer best, and then cut up into curtains, and after that into dusters. Really, if you look at it in the right light, it would be an economy to buy them! I am sure Uncle Bernard would like to see me in white! Now don't you think he would?"

"I'll do what I can, dear—I'll do what I can! I should like you both to look as well as possible. 'Matters of importance!' ... I can't think what matters of importance Uncle Bernard can wish to discuss with children like you. And who are the other guests? And are they also included in the discussion? I don't know of any near relations he has left, except ourselves; but he was even more intimate with his wife's people than his own, and she belonged to a large family. Dear, dear! It is most awkward to be so much in the dark. I do wish he had been a little more explicit while he was about it."

"Never mind, muv; it makes it all the more exciting. We are going to meet someone, and we don't know whom; and to discuss something, and we don't know what; and to stay, we don't know how long. There's this comfort—we can easily take all our belongings, and still not be overburdened with luggage! Ten days—only ten days before we start! It sounds almost too good to be true. But how will you manage without us, dear little mother?"

"Oh, don't trouble about me, dear! I'll manage beautifully. Old Miss Carter can come in to help me if I get too tired; but, indeed, I shall be so happy to think of you two girls staying at the dear old Court that it will do me as much good as a tonic. Now I will go and talk to pater about money matters. We ought to begin preparations at once."

Mr Connor joined in the general satisfaction at the invitation which had been given to his step-daughters, and, though mildly surprised to hear that any fresh equipments would be required, took his wife's word for the need, and produced two five-pound notes from his cash-box, which she was deputed to use as she thought fit.

"If you don't need it all, you can give me back whatever is over," said the innocent male, little reckoning that three feminine heads would lie restless on their pillows that night, striving in vain to solve the problem of making ten pounds do duty for fifty.

Next morning, pencils and paper were in requisition to check mental additions, while Ruth drew up a list of usefuls, and Mollie one of fineries which seemed equally essential. At a most modest estimate it seemed possible to purchase the whole for something under thirty pounds. A painful curtailment brought it down to twenty, but by no persuasion could that sum be halved.

"Unless we play Box and Cox!" cried Mollie, in desperation. "One rain cloak, and an understanding that one of us invariably feels chilly, and stays at home on wet days. One white dress, to be worn in turn on special occasions, while the other languishes in bed with a headache. One evening cloak, ditto. Ditto gloves and sundries. It is the only way I can see out of the difficulty."

"Don't be absurd, Mollie! We shall *both* have to stay in bed if anything special takes place, for we can't afford any extras. I remember once asking Eleanor Drummond's advice about spending my allowance, and she said, 'Wear a shabby dress, if you must; wear a shabby hat, if you have not taste and ingenuity to trim one for yourself out of next to nothing; but never, never, never condescend to a shabby petticoat or shoes down at the heel!' I thought it splendid advice, and have always acted upon it, as far as I could. Let us buy really nice boots and slippers and petticoats before we do anything else!"

"I'll have a silk one, then, and rustle for once, if I die for it!" cried Mollie recklessly. "And the boots shall be thin, not thick, with a nice, curved sole to show off my patrician instep. If I have to content myself with usefuls, they shall be as ornamental as possible. Don't you think we might possibly squeeze out net over-skirts to wear with the black silks, sometimes, so as to make them look like two dresses instead of one?"

"Oh, my dear, I like luxuries as much as you do! It's only grim necessity which makes me prudent. The black net is really an inspiration, and if we make it up ourselves we can manage quite well, and have enough money left for gloves and ribbons, and one fresh blouse a-piece."

For the next week all was bustle and excitement. The girls paid two long shopping expeditions to town, and returned laden with interesting parcels, the contents of which were displayed to an admiring audience in the drawing-room, and then taken upstairs to Attica, which was transformed into a dressmaker's work-room, barriers being for once ignored in consideration of the importance of the occasion.

The five-pound notes became wonderfully elastic, and even after they were expended little offerings came in from friends and members of the family to swell the great sum total. One sent a pretty tie, another a belt, a third a lace handkerchief. Trix supplied a most stylish collection of pens, pencils, and indiarubbers, reposing in her very best box; and Betty, not to be outdone, rummaged among her various collections for a suitable offering. Eventually she discovered a half-emptied bottle of eau-de-Cologne, which had been presented to her the Christmas before, filled it up with water, and presented it to her sisters for mutual use, unperturbed by the fact that the transparent hue of the scent had changed to a milky white.

On the morning of the fifth day Ruth had a conviction that she was sickening with a dire disease; on the sixth, she anticipated a disabling accident; on the seventh, she waited hourly for a telegram from Uncle Bernard, retracting his invitation; on the eighth, she wanted to know what would happen if there was a cab strike in the city; and on the ninth, talked vaguely of blizzards and earthquakes. Something it seemed *must* happen to prevent this long-dreamed-of journey; it did not seem possible that the stars should run placidly in their courses, while Ruth and Mollie Farrell were going a-visiting with a box full of fineries!

Yet the day did break, an ordinary, grey morning, with no sign to distinguish it from another. Looking out of the window, men and women could be seen going calmly about their duties. The postman and newspaper-boy arrived at their accustomed time. No one outside the household seemed to realise that the day was big with fate.

At eleven o'clock a cab drove up to the door; the boxes were piled on the roof; and the heroines of the hour made their appearance in the doorway, immaculately trim and tidy in travelling array. The brothers and sisters were absent at school, so there was only the little mother to say adieu, and stand waving her hand until the cab had disappeared from view.

Once, she too had been young and fair, and life had stretched before her like an empty page, on which the most marvellous happenings might be enrolled. Now, she was old and harassed and poor, and there seemed little ahead but work and worry; yet she could not call life a failure.

"I have had the best thing," she said to herself, as she shut the door and re-entered the empty house—"plenty of dear ones to love, and to love me in return. God bless my two girls, and give them the same sweet gift."

Chapter Six.

At the Court.

The girl whose lot has been cast in narrow places, and whose youth has known few relaxations, should take heart at the thought of the future. There is a good time coming! However long be the lane, the turning must eventually be reached; and then—ah, then, what zest of delight, what whole-hearted, unqualified enjoyment!

If Ruth and Mollie Farrell had been in the habit of paying half a dozen visits a year,—if, indeed, they had even once before started off together on pleasure bent, would they have hailed every incident of the journey with the delight which they experienced to-day? Not a bit of it!

They would have grumbled at the wait on the platform, at the stoppages of the train at country stations, at the draught from the window, the banging of the door, the constant requests for tickets. They would have yawned and lolled back in their corners, and eventually shut their eyes and fallen asleep, regardless of the scenes through which they were passing.

As it was, every fresh stop was a delight. They beamed at the porter who collected their luggage, paid for return tickets with the complacence of millionaires, and thought it lucky that there were ten minutes to spare before the arrival of the train. They tried each other's weight, to the delight of the onlookers; put a penny in every available slot, and made a reckless expenditure in penny magazines. Last, and greatest luxury of all, Ruth actually ordered a tea-basket to be handed into the carriage at a half-way station; one basket to do duty for two, but still a deliberate extravagance, when refreshments had been provided from home; and oh, dear me, how delicious it was to be extravagant for once!

When the train came in, one porter dashed forward to secure window-seats in an empty carriage, another hurried up with rugs and handbags; groups of people standing upon the platform looked after the two girls with kindly glances; everybody seemed kind and interested, as though understanding the nature of their expedition, and wishing them good-speed.

They sat opposite to each other, gazing out of their respective windows, or making an affectation of reading the magazines which lay littered about the seat; but the end was always the same, their eyes met in irrepressible smiles, and they began to talk once more.

Real life was so much more interesting than romance!

"I feel so very Lucille-y!" Mollie declared "Travelling on pleasure, with a tea-basket coming to meet me! It was an inspiration of yours to order it, Ruth! I shall be grateful to you to the end of my life! Let's talk about what we shall do to-night... Let's guess who will be there, and what they will be like. The lady chaperon, now! Should you think that the presence of a chaperon implied that there would be young men in the party? I hope there are."

"So do I," assented Ruth frankly. "But I fancy that they are more likely to be old. Some nieces and nephews of Aunt Edna's, about mother's age, perhaps—middle-aged couples, with caps and spectacles. How will you feel if we are the only young people there?"

"I refuse to imagine anything so ghastly! The couples may have children, mayn't they? I imagine a charming girl who has no sisters, and who will adopt us as her dearest friends, and ask us to stay with her. I rather think she will be dark, and wear eyeglasses, and have a brother who is musical, and has a tenor voice. Then there will be another man—Sir Somebody or other, who has a big estate in the county. He will be very superior at first, and take no notice of us, but in the end he will be conquered by our modest charms and become a devoted admirer. Perhaps there may be some couples, but they will be young and festive, and the chaperon will be a dear old thing with side-ringlets, who will let us do as we like, and take our part with the old man. That sounds about the right thing, doesn't it?"

Ruth smiled happily.

"Ah, well! whoever we meet, I am going to enjoy myself. A change, a change—that's what I wanted. Everything will be different, and there's a world of refreshment in that alone. How thankful I am that Uncle Bernard asked us both, Mollie! It's half the fun to talk things over together."

She lay back in her corner, and gazed out of the window once more, smiling dreamily as a whirl of thoughts flew through her mind. What would have happened before she travelled once more past these flying landmarks? What new friendships would be formed—what experiences undergone—what matters of importance revealed?

Life seemed all to lie ahead; yet from time to time her thoughts drifted back unconsciously to Donald Maclure, and lingered on the memory. She had not seen him since the eventful afternoon, but Eleanor had conveyed his good wishes for a happy visit, and her manner showed she was in ignorance of what had occurred.

Ruth was grateful for a silence which left her friendship untouched, and her thoughts of the doctor were gentle and kindly.

"But I couldn't—I couldn't!" she said to herself excusingly. "I don't want to marry anyone yet. I just want to be young and happy, and have a good time!"

At the half-way station the tea-basket made its appearance, and the girls sat side by side taking turns at the cup, and nibbling at bread-and-butter and plum-cake like two happy children out for a holiday, which in good truth they were.

They made a pretty picture, and more than one of the passengers upon the platform cast admiring glances as they passed by. So far, the carriage had been empty, except for themselves; but, just as the train was preparing to leave the junction, a young man turned the handle of the door, threw a bag on the seat, and leapt in after it. He was on the point of seating himself in the place which Ruth had just vacated, but, seeing the scattered papers, checked himself, and took possession of the further corner, while the sisters studied him furtively from time to time.

He was tall, he was handsome, he was probably about thirty years of age, and he looked thoroughly bored and out of temper. After one casual glance at the pretty sisters, he unfolded a newspaper, and turned from page to page seeking for some item of interest. His eyes were blue, he was clean-shaven, his nose was aquiline, and his nostrils were arched, and had a trick of dilation.

"Like a high-bred horse, who wouldn't like the bridle a single bit," was Mollie's comment, as she turned back to the window; for, after all, the unknown landscape through which the train was now passing was more absorbing than the appearance of a stranger who took so little interest in herself.

She gazed and whispered, and dreamed afresh, until at last the name of a familiar station gave warning that the journey was nearing its end. In another ten minutes the train was due to reach Nosely, and in the interval there was much to be done. Ruth solemnly lifted down the aged dressing-bag, which dated from her mother's youth, and, with a furtive glance at the stranger in the corner, took out a looking-glass and carefully surveyed her hair, pulling it out here, tucking it in there, patting it into position with those deft little touches which come naturally to a girl, but which seem so mysterious to a masculine observer.

The young man in the corner glanced across the carriage with an expression of lordly amusement at the foibles of a member of the weaker sex; and there was even worse to come, for when Mollie, in her turn, had arranged her hair, a cloth brush was produced to remove the dust of travel, and two pairs of well-worn dogskin gloves were thrown into the bag, and replaced by others immaculately new.

Mollie was absolutely without embarrassment in these attentions to her toilet, but it required a little resolution on Ruth's part to ignore the stranger's presence. Only the reflection, "We will never see him again!" supported her through the critical moments during which she trained a fascinating little curl into position on her temple, conscious meantime of a steady scrutiny from behind the newspaper.

It was something of a shock to see the stranger rise from his seat a moment later, and begin making those preparations which showed that he also was approaching his destination; but, although he alighted at Nosely Station, he had disappeared from sight while the girls were still looking after their luggage, and when they took their seats in the carriage which was waiting to convey them to the Court there was no sign of him on platform or road.

"That's a comfort!" remarked Mollie thankfully. "I am glad he did not see where we were going. How superior he looked when we were prinking, Ruth! I don't like him a bit—do you?"

"Oh, I don't know—I can't think! I'm Berengaria, Mollie! I never *was* a poor girl travelling third-class, and changing her gloves at the last moment! I must have been a duchess in my last incarnation, for I feel so thoroughly at home in an atmosphere of luxury!" sighed Ruth, leaning back against the cushions, and glancing languidly from side to side. "Our luggage is following behind in the cart. I hope it will arrive soon, for I want to change my blouse. I suppose we shall have tea in the hall with the rest of the house-party, as they do in books, but I hope they won't be assembled when we enter. I should feel awful walking in, and knowing that they were all staring and criticising our appearance, wouldn't you?"

Mollie laughed gaily.

"Not a bit. I'd criticise, too, and shake hands high up—like this—and be pleasant and condescending. We are Uncle Bernard's nearest relations remember, and the guests of honour... Now, we are beginning to go up the hill! You remember mother said there was a long, winding hill, and at the top to the left stood the lodge gates. Don't talk! I don't want to miss a single thing."

So each girl stared steadily out of her window as the horses slowly mounted the hill path. For the first few hundred yards there were hedges on either side, and beyond them a wide, uneven landscape; then came a little village, grouped round a square "green," with all the picturesque accessories of church, ivy-covered parsonage, thatched roofs, and duck-pond, which travellers look for in a well-conducted English village. This passed, there was another climb upwards, a wider view of the valley beneath, and finally a sharp turn to the left, and a long drive leading to the greystone Court, whose beauties photographs had made familiar.

The butler threw open the door as the carriage stopped, and the travellers thrilled with excitement as they crossed the threshold. First a square vestibule, then the great hall itself, stretching the whole length of the wing, and turning to the right by the foot of the staircase.

The girls' eyes turned in a flash to the tapestry on the walls, and the wooden portraits of ancestors; but besides these historic relics there were many articles belonging to a later and more luxurious age. Carved oak tables, laden with books and magazines; chairs and lounges of every description; a fireplace brilliant with beaten copper and soft green tiles; leather screens shielding cosy corners; cabinets of china and curios.

It was even more imposing than imagination had painted it; but—there was no one there! No Uncle Bernard to speak a word of greeting; no flutter of silken skirts belonging to nice girls who had no sisters, and were dying to adopt other nice girls without delay; no scent of cigarettes smoked by interesting young men, who might have sisters or might not, but who would certainly be pleased to welcome Berengaria and Lucille!

Ruth had knitted her dark brows, and drawn herself stiffly erect; Mollie was prepared to smile in benign patronage on less important guests. It was a trifle disconcerting to see no one at all but a little, black-robed lady, who came hurriedly forward as they approached the staircase and stammered a nervous greeting.

"Miss Farrell! Miss Mary! I hope you have had a pleasant journey. I am Mrs Wolff. Mr Farrell was kind enough to ask me—yes! I hope you are not cold. Your uncle thought you would like to have tea in your own room. It will be brought up to you at once. Mr Farrell desired me to say that he wished to see you both in the library at half-past five. Shall I take you upstairs at once? We have given you one room—a very large one; but if you prefer to have two separate ones, it can easily be arranged—yes!"

The girls protested that they wished to be together, and followed their guide up the broad staircase to a room on the first story, where the curtains were already drawn, and a cosy tea-table spread before the fire. Mrs Wolff had called it large, and she might truthfully have used a more emphatic word, for what had originally been the best bedroom in the house had been, like the drawing-room beneath, enormously enlarged by the addition of a curved, mullioned window, the entire width of the floor.

"One, two, three, four, five, six, seven, eight, *nine*! Nine dear little windows!" counted Mollie rapturously, as the door closed behind the figure of the lady chaperon. "What a view we shall have to-morrow morning, Ruth! Sofas, armchairs, writing-tables, two long mirrors to show the set of our skirts—this is a room after my own heart! I shall have one exactly like it when I marry my duke!"

"But I didn't expect to have tea in it, all the same," Ruth objected, as she took off her hat and jacket. "The house feels very quiet and deserted. If we hadn't uncle's own word for it, I should think there was no one here except ourselves. He might have come to meet us himself! It seems so cold to leave us to strangers!"

"You will be disappointed, my dear, if you expect warmth from Uncle Bernard. My short interview taught me so much, at least. But he wants to see us at half-past five, Ruth. I'll prophesy something—he is going to talk to us about the 'important matters'! It would be just like him to explain his position before we have been an hour in the house, so that there can be no misunderstanding. I'm right—I know I am! We are on the eve of solving the mystery!"

Ruth shivered, and drew closer to the fire.

"Don't make me nervous. It will be bad enough when it comes to the point, without thinking of it beforehand!" she cried.

And it was all the easier to change the conversation, as at that moment a maid entered with a tea-tray and a plate of hot, buttered scones.

Tea after a journey is always a most enjoyable meal, and when it was over the girls made as careful a toilet as could be managed with the materials at hand, the heavier luggage not having yet made its appearance. Shortly before half-past five a tap came to the door, and a maid entered with a double request.

"I have come to show you the way to the library, miss; and if you would kindly give me your keys before you go, I will have your boxes unpacked. What dresses would you like to wear for dinner?"

The horror of that moment was never to be forgotten. Before Ruth's eyes there arose, as in a vision, the patches on the under-sleeves of her morning blouse, the faded dressing-gown, the darns, and make-shifts and pitiful little contrivances of poverty. Her cheeks flamed before the sharp eyes of the abigail, and then flamed again with scorn at her own folly.

"It is all neat and clean and tidy. I *won't* be ashamed of it!" she told herself angrily, as she turned to search for her keys.

But the evening-dresses! The next moment with a mingling of relief and irritation, she heard Mollie's unabashed reply—

"Oh, we have only black dresses! We will wear the net over-skirts, please!"

Just like Mollie, to wear her best clothes on the first possible occasion, instead of prudently storing them up for a special need!

But it was too late to protest; already the maid was leading the way onward. The all-important interview was at hand!

Chapter Seven.

Mr Farrell's Plan.

"Miss Farrell, sir!" said the maid, throwing open the door of the library.

And Ruth walked forward, followed closely by Mollie.

It was a long, narrow room, lined with book-shelves, and the solitary light from a crimson-shaded lamp on the central table gave an air of gloom after the bright illumination of the hall without. On a lounge-chair beside the table sat Bernard Farrell, looking more cadaverous than ever, with a velvet-skull-cap over his whitened locks. He did not rise as his great-nieces approached, but held out his hand in a greeting which was courteous enough, if somewhat cold.

"How do you do? I am pleased to see you. Excuse me for not having met you earlier, but I am not feeling well to-day. I trust you have received every attention since your arrival at the Court. Mrs Wolff had my instructions to look after your comfort."

"Thank you, yes; we had tea in our room—a lovely room. We are looking forward to enjoying the view from that splendid window!"

"Ah, yes; it is very fine in clear weather! Please make yourselves at home, and ask for anything that you need. The servants are good, but they are unused to visitors. Have no hesitation in keeping them up to their duties. Will you be seated? In a few minutes we can, I hope, begin the business of the hour."

He waved them towards some chairs which were ranged before his table. Four chairs! In the twinkling of an eye the girls had grasped both the number and what it implied. Two other guests at least were at present in the house, and equally interested with themselves in the coming discussion. Their advent was evidently momentarily expected, for Mr Farrell turned an impatient glance at the clock, and even as he did so the door opened once more and two young men entered the room. One was tall and dark, with an olive skin, and a curious, veiled look about his eyes, caused by the presence of short but abnormally thick black lashes. Viewed in profile the lashes entirely hid the eye, but the effect of the thick black line was, singularly enough, rather attractive than the reverse. He had a dark moustache, and his chin was square and well-developed.

His companion was—well! the girls felt that they might have guessed it before, as one of the awkward things which was bound to happen. He was the stranger of the railway carriage, the supercilious personage whom they had flattered themselves they would never see again!

Like the two girls, the new-comers had evidently not seen their host before, for they were greeted by him with practically the same phrases; and then came a general introduction.

"I must make you known to your fellow-guests—Mr Jack Melland, Mr Victor Druce—Miss Farrell, Miss Mary Farrell. Mr Melland and Mr Druce are great-nephews of my late wife. Miss Farrell and her sister are my own nephew's only children."

The two young men turned towards the girls with curious glances. Over Mr Jack Melland's face flitted an amused glance of recognition. His companion's dark eyes widened with a curious scrutiny; then the lashes dropped, and hid them from sight. Seen thus, with mouth and eyes alike veiled, the face was a mask devoid of expression; yet Mollie had a conviction that she had surprised something closely approaching disappointment in that fleeting glance. Why the sight of Ruth and herself had affected the stranger in so unpleasant a fashion it was difficult to understand; but the impression remained. Her eyes travelled upward to the face of Jack Melland, and marvelled at the contrast.

"His face betrays him, in spite of himself. His nostrils alone would give him away," she told herself, smiling. "He is cross, the other inscrutable; Ruth is frightened, and I am amused. We look like four school-children seated in a row, with Uncle Bernard as the teacher... When is the lesson to begin?"

At once, apparently; for Mr Farrell lost no time in preliminaries, but began his explanation as soon as the young men were seated.

"I have asked you to meet me here as soon as possible after your arrival, for it is better that we should understand each other from the beginning. You have thought it strange, no doubt, that, after having had no communication with your families for so many years, I should suddenly develop a desire for your company. Circumstances have, however, materially altered for me during the last few weeks by the discovery that it is necessary that my affairs should be settled without delay.

"I have, as you know, no child left to inherit, and as this place is not entailed, it is entirely in my hands to bequeath as I think fit. Until now—for reasons which you may perhaps understand—the idea of making a will has been so painful that I have continually postponed the ordeal; but my doctor, who is also my old friend, has convinced me that I must delay no longer.

"I am suffering from an affection of the heart which makes it impossible that I can live longer than a couple of years, and probably the time may be but a few months. He has urged me, therefore, to settle business affairs, so that I might spend the remainder of my days undisturbed; but to decide on a suitable heir is not an easy matter. I am, as you may have heard, a very rich man, and I hold strong, and perhaps somewhat unusual, ideas as to the qualifications which are necessary for the owner of great wealth. It is not my intention to divide the inheritance in any way, therefore it is the more important to make a right choice."

He paused for a moment, and the four young people looked up sharply. Victor Druce's eyes roved quickly from one to the other of his three companions. Jack Melland's lips closed more tightly than before. Ruth's cheeks glowed with a carmine flush. She was the nearest relation; hers was the first claim! Her heart beat with quick, sickening thuds; only Mollie looked frankly curious and unperturbed.

"As I said before," continued Mr Farrell, "we are, so far, complete strangers to each other; but I judge you all to hold equal rights to anything which I have to leave. Ruth and Mary are my nearest legal relations; but my wife's people always ranked with me as my own, and, other things being equal, I should prefer a male heir. I make no point of the name; the Court is not an estate which has descended to me from many generations of ancestors. My father bought it from the late owner, so there is no real reason why a Farrell should necessarily inherit.

"It is from one of your number, then, that I shall adopt my heir; but, in order to do so, I must have some knowledge of your respective characters and attainments. As I said before, I hold somewhat unusual views. What the world in general would probably consider the best qualification for the owner of a big estate is, in my eyes, an insuperable objection. What I look to find, others might regard as a fault. We all have our own ideas, and must act according to our lights. I wish then, in the first place, to make your acquaintance but do not be afraid that I shall make the task too unpleasant.

"For the furtherance of my plan, I should wish you to lead as full and interesting a life as may be. The Court has been shut up for years, but its doors can now be thrown open for your benefit. You are free to come and go, to invite whom you will, and no doubt the neighbourhood will be eager to meet you half-way. My own health will not permit me to arrange your amusements; but I give you the use of my house, carte blanche as regards expenses, and Mrs Wolff to play propriety—the rest you must arrange for yourselves. If each in turn took the management of affairs for a few weeks at a time, it would meet my views, as helping me to form the necessary ideas of character and tastes."

There was a simultaneous movement of surprise on the part of the listeners, and one and the same word was repeated by four pairs of lips—

"Weeks!"

Mr Farrell smiled grimly.

"You are surprised at the time implied. My invitations were intentionally vague, for I had not at the time made up my mind as to various details. I have now decided that for the proper development of my scheme three months at least will be necessary. I therefore invite you to be my guests at the Court during that period."

Again came the involuntary, simultaneous start of surprise, and Jack Melland cried hastily—

"It is impossible! I am obliged to you, sir; but it is quite impossible, so far as I am concerned. My business—"

"My—my mother!" cried Ruth. "We could not leave her so long; she needs our help—"

Mr Farrell interrupted with upraised hand.

"We will defer objections, if you please! I am prepared to meet and answer them, later on. For the present I ask you to think quietly over the prospect which lies before you, and to consider how far such obstacles as you have mentioned should be allowed to stand in the way. Surely the object is worth some temporary inconvenience or loss. This house, and all that it contains, with various properties bringing in an income of over ten thousand a year, will in due course become the property of one of your number—of the one who best fulfils a certain condition which I consider essential."

"And the condition—the condition?" queried Mollie eagerly.

Mr Farrell looked at her in silence, while a grim smile passed over his features.

"That," he said slowly—"that, my dear Miss Mary,—will be discovered, with other things,—when you hear my will read aloud on the day of my funeral?"

Chapter Eight.

Speculations.

"Well!" exclaimed Ruth, sinking back in armchair number one, at the right of the bedroom fireplace.

"Well!" exclaimed Mollie, sinking back in armchair number two, facing her sister. "Likewise, good sooth! By my halidom! Gadzooks! Of a surety these are great happenings, fair sis!"

"Don't be so tiresome, Mollie! You make a joke out of everything. I want to talk over the position seriously."

"So do I—just dying to. Go on! Where shall we begin?"

"With the time, of course. Three months! I never dreamt of more than a fortnight, at most. Do you think we can possibly be spared?"

"I don't think at all—I know! If it was three years, with such an interest at stake, the poor little mother would jump at it. Three months soon pass, and there will be two people less to feed and wait upon, and a room less to keep in order. Every little tells when people are as hard up as we are, and with the savings mother will be able to pay Miss Carter to help with the mending. It will be good for Trix, too. The more you depend upon Trix the more she rises to the occasion. I have a shrewd suspicion that she is going to cut us out, and be the show daughter of the family. Mother will be blissfully happy building castles in the air; Trix will be blissfully happy playing eldest daughter, and bossing the family. We shall be blissfully happy not pretending, but actually being, Berengaria and Lucille. It's all quite smooth and easy!"

Ruth heaved a sigh, half convinced, half reluctant.

"That's what you always say! I see such crowds of objections. To begin with, I hate the position; it's awkward and humiliating. To stay here on approval, studied like specimens in a case; being on one's good behaviour, and 'acting pretty' to try to get a fortune for oneself, away from other people—bah! It makes me hot even to think of it. I should feel a hypocrite!"

"Don't be high-flown, dear; it's quite unnecessary. You couldn't be a hypocrite if you tried; you are too ridiculously 'proud,' I suppose you would say. I call it quick-tempered! If Uncle Bernard snubs you, you will flare out, fortune or no fortune, and if you feel mopey, mope you will, if he disinherits you the next moment. I shall be honest, too, because I'm too lazy to be anything else; besides, you know, there is always the pleasing reflection that he may *prefer* us to be crotchety! Everything is possible where everything is vague. Imagine how maddening it would be if we kept our tempers, and smiled sweetly from morning till night, and in the end he left everything to that cross Mr Melland, because he considered it necessary for the owner of wealth to have a will of his own!"

Ruth laughed involuntarily.

"You *are* a goose! Not much chance of your being the chosen one, I am afraid. Uncle Bernard is not in the mood for appreciating nonsense; he is too sad and ill, poor old man! That's another hateful thing. I should love to nurse and coddle him, and read aloud, and be good to him generally; but if one does, it will seem— Oh, you know— you understand! It's a loathsome position!"

"If I feel affectionate, I shall act affectionate! He will probably loathe it, so there's just as much chance of injuring one's chance as of bettering it. In fact, if we are to get on at all, we had better try to forget the wretched money, and behave as if it did not exist. If anyone had told us a month ago that we should be staying in a big house with two quite good-looking young men as fellow-guests, and carte blanche to enjoy ourselves as much as we pleased, we would have thought it too impossibly good to be true; but now that it has come true, we shall be idiots if we don't make the most of it. I hope Uncle Bernard keeps to his idea of making us each master of the ceremonies in turn. Won't I make the money fly when it comes to my turn! Picnics and luncheons by day, dances and theatricals by night—one giddy whirl of excitement the whole time long. I'll take the old dear at his word, and give no thought to expense, and entertain the whole countryside until the name of Mollie Farrell is immortalised for ever in grateful hearts. I have always credited myself with a genius for social life; now for the first time you will behold me in the halls of the great, and gaze with surprise at your sister reigning as queen over the assembled throngs?"

"In your one black dress?"

"Certainly not! I've thought of that, too. Suitable equipments must, of course, be part of the carte blanche."

"I am sure nothing was further from Uncle Bernard's thoughts. He looks to me like a man who would never notice clothes, or care what we looked like, so long, of course, as we were respectable. He has more important things on his mind."

"Humph!" Mollie tossed her saucy head. "If he doesn't notice of his own accord, his eyes must be gently, but firmly opened. We stay at his special request; at his special request we entertain and are entertained; it is only reasonable that he should bear the expense of making our appearance do him credit. I'll tell him so, too, if he doesn't see it for himself."

"Mollie, you won't! You shan't! You never could!"

"Couldn't I? You wait and see!"

"And if you did I would never touch a farthing. I warn you, once for all, that it is useless, so far as I am concerned."

Mollie looked at her sister's flushed, defiant face, and laughed her happy, light-hearted laugh.

"Dear old High-falutin'! We won't argue about it. Half a dozen invitations will show you the soundness of my position better than a hundred discussions. Meantime, I'm going to dress. I have a horrible conviction that that maid will return and offer to do 'your hair, madam,' so I mean to be beforehand with her."

Ruth sat still in her chair, enjoying the unwonted luxury of idling, with no disturbing spasm of conscience to remind her that she ought to be mending or patching, or giving Betty a music lesson, or helping Mary to hang clean curtains in the drawing-room. It was delightful to nestle back against the cushions and study one by one the dainty appointments of the room, and revel in the unaccustomed sense of space. Imagine just for a moment—imagine possessing such a home of one's own! The house, with its treasures of beautiful and artistic furnishings, which represented the lifelong gatherings of a man renowned for his taste; the extensive grounds, with gardens and vineries and forests of glass, providing an endless summer of blossom; the income, that in itself was a fortune, and held such inexhaustible possibilities of good. What she could do with it, if it were only hers! With one stroke of the pen she would repay the poor old tired pater for all his goodness in the past, and lift the weight of care for the future from his shoulders. She would heap luxuries upon the dear little mother, who was still a child at heart; so pathetically easy to please that it seemed a sin that she should ever be sad. The girls should be sent to finishing schools, and the boys given a thorough training to equip them for their fight in life. Mollie, of course, should live at the Court, and share equally in all her possessions; and they would travel, and help the poor, and be kind to everyone, and never forget the day of small things! or grow arrogant and purse-proud. Ruth dreamed on in a passion of longing till Mollie, standing before the dressing-table, with her white arms raised to her head, caught sight of her face in the mirror, and uttered a sharp exclamation.

"Ruth! What is it, darling?"

Ruth started nervously and glanced upwards with guilty eyes, but there was nothing alarming in the aspect of the figure which stood over her, white necked, white armed, with the loosened golden hair falling round the anxious face. She caught the outstretched hand, and gripped it tightly between her own.

"Oh, Mollie, I want it! I want it *dreadfully*! When I think of the possibility I feel half wild. If I am disappointed, I believe I shall die! I can't be unselfish, even for you. I want it for myself!"

She was on the verge of tears, but Mollie's matter-of-fact cheeriness had the usual bracing effect. She seemed neither shocked nor surprised, but only anxious to soothe.

"Of course you do; so do we all!" she replied easily. "It's humbug to pretend anything else, only I'm not going to die, in any case, but live and make myself agreeable to the Chosen. If it's you, I shall sponge on you for life, so don't imagine you will have all the fun to yourself. Now get dressed, and don't think about it any more. We must look our best to awe those two superior young men. I am convinced that they look upon us as country bumpkins, and it's most important to put them in their proper position at once, so that we may start fair. If you are going to do your hair in skriggles it will take you an age, so do begin!"

Ruth rose obediently. "Skriggles" was an inelegant but descriptive title for her most becoming coiffure, which she had already decided must be adopted for the first eventful evening at the Court. She set to work at once, and was half-way through her task when the maid appeared, as Mollie had prophesied, paused upon the threshold for one horrified moment, and then hurried forward with an "Allow me, miss!" which could not be gainsaid.

The girls grimaced at one another furtively, but in the end the value of the skilled hands was proved by a dainty finish to hair and toilette which sent them downstairs agreeably conscious of looking their best.

Chapter Nine.

Mr Jack Melland.

In the drawing-room Mr Farrell and his two nephews were standing with their backs to the fire, in the position affected by mankind in that trying wait before dinner. Little Mrs Wolff was stiffly perched upon an uncomfortable chair, twisting her mittened fingers together and looking supremely uncomfortable, and there appeared to be no attempt at conversation. Everyone looked at the two girls as they crossed the wide room, and once again Mollie surprised that curious gleam of disapproval in Victor Druce's veiled eyes. Mr Melland was apparently still on his high horse, a faint flush upon his face, his nostrils curved and dilated. As for Uncle Bernard himself, his set face showed no sign of approval or the reverse; he simply bowed to his nieces, and waved them towards a seat, saying curtly—

"Our party is not complete. I have asked the vicar and his wife to dine with us, and make your acquaintance. They will probably arrive in a few minutes."

"Oh yes!" said Ruth vaguely. Even Mollie suffered a moment's eclipse, during which she sought in vain for an appropriate remark. It was too absurd, she told herself, to sit round the room like mutes at a funeral. What was the use of a lady chaperon if she could not fill up the gaps with harmless inanities? She glanced from one stolid face to another, then made a desperate plunge.

"What time do the posts go, Uncle Bernard? We ought to let mother know of our arrival."

"I have already directed a telegram to that effect to be despatched. May I suggest that you delay any communication on your own part until we have had a future conversation."

Checkmate! Mollie gave a vague murmur of assent, and cast about for remark number two.

"It seems so funny to be here and to see all the things we have heard about so often! I recognise this room quite well from mother's description. There is an alcove behind me, isn't there, with a harp in the corner?"

"The harp was removed years ago. I imagine there are a great many alterations since your mother's last visit. The use of the word 'funny' is somewhat inappropriate, is it not? I see nothing ludicrous in the position."

Check number two! Mollie's wide-eyed perturbation was almost pathetic in its intensity. She was not accustomed to being snubbed in this public fashion, and, after the first shock, a feeling of resentment brought the colour rushing into her cheeks.

"I meant 'curious.' The two words are often used for each other."

"Mistakenly so. Many situations are curious which are not in the least degree amusing."

"They are indeed!" was Mollie's mental comment. "The present, for example; anything much less festive I fail to imagine." Her lips twitched involuntarily as the thought passed through her mind, and, looking up, she met Jack Melland's eyes fixed full on her, with an answering twinkle in their blue depths. For one agonising moment she trembled upon the brink of laughter, when mercifully the door was thrown open to announce the arrival of the vicar and his wife. Mr Thornton was tall and thin, with a much-lined face full of shrewd kindness and sympathy; his wife was a pretty, plump little woman, who looked on exceedingly good terms with herself and the world at large.

"Thank goodness, they will talk! They look alive, not mere graven images," Mollie said to herself thankfully, as the necessary introductions were taking place. Then the squire gave his arm to Mrs Thornton, Mr Thornton offered his in turn to Mrs Wolff, and Victor Druce, evidently obeying a previous instruction, paired off with Ruth, leaving Mollie to his companion.

In silence the little company crossed the hall; in silence they seated themselves round the dinner-table and prepared for the feast. Ruth's grey eyes were brilliant with excitement as she turned from side to side. She did not want to talk; conversation would have been but an interruption at the moment; she wanted but to look and to think.

The walls were covered with portraits of ancestors—Captain Farrell who sailed the seas with Nelson's fleet; General Farrell who fought under Wellington; Lord Edward Farrell, the famous judge; fresh-faced country squires in quaint, old-world costumes. The dim faces looked down from their frames with a curious, haunting likeness running through all; and at the head of the table sat the last of his race, the grim old man to whom death was coming. Ah, it must be hard to look back on so good a race, to realise that no son remained alive to carry on the name, and that one of the strangers now seated round his own table would shortly reign in his place!

Ruth thrilled with pity; her beautiful eyes grew soft and dreamy; and the clergyman, looking at her across the table, could scarcely restrain an exclamation of surprise. He had understood that Mr Farrell possessed only distant relatives, but this girl was a true chip of the old block; allowing for difference of age and sex, here was the same face which was repeated again and again upon the walls—the aquiline features, the melancholy lips, the straight heavy brows.

Mr Thornton knew that the time had come when his host was to choose his successor at the Court, and, looking from one to the other of the four young people, he personally felt no doubt as to the one on whom the choice would fall. Ruth Farrell bore her credentials in her face, and with a thrill, half painful, half amused, he realised how great a factor in his own life this slim young girl might be. As lady of the Court and his own patron, she would have it in her power to ensure his comfort or the reverse. Ah, well, well, it was too early to speculate! The child had a sweet, good face; no doubt all would be well.

While Ruth and the vicar were absorbed in their own thoughts, Mrs Wolff was also silent, overcome with the weight of responsibility which pressed heavily on her unaccustomed shoulders. Little Mrs Thornton prattled of cheery nothings at the other end of the table, and Jack Melland, turning towards his companion, remarked formally—

"I—ah—I think we have met earlier in the day!"

"In the train, you mean; yes! We saw you get out at the station, but you disappeared so quickly that I could not think what had happened to you."

"Nothing mysterious. A dogcart had been sent for me. I jumped into it with my bag, and was out of sight before you had gathered together your possessions."

"Ah, yes; we had boxes in the van." Mollie tilted her head to its characteristic angle and smiled at him with wide grey eyes. "And you watched our toilette across the carriage, little guessing it was for your own benefit. We knew that we were to meet other visitors here, but had no idea who they were or how many there might be. We imagined walking into the midst of a big house-party; hence the preparations. It was only natural we should want to look nice."

"Perfectly! I am glad I was fortunate enough to see the result, since I suppose no one else—"

Mollie shook her head tragically.

"Not a soul! Mrs Wolff met us and sent us straight up to our room. If it had not been for you, the new gloves would have been wasted on the desert air; but now we can console ourselves that our trouble was of some use, after all, since at least half the party had the benefit. Were you also despatched straight upstairs?"

"I was. Afterwards, Druce and I had tea in the billiard-room, and went on to join you in the library. It has been a somewhat trying opportunity; I sympathised with your conversational efforts before dinner."

Mollie's brows went up at this, and she made a sceptical little grimace.

"That is not my idea of sympathy! You stood by and watched me flounder without making a effort to help. It's not at all pleasant to be snubbed before a roomful of strangers. You might easily have remarked that it was a fine day, or that the train was punctual. Anything is better than a ghastly silence."

"But, you see, I had had my innings before you arrived. As a matter of fact I had introduced those very subjects, and added some original remarks on the beauty of the scenery. I fared no better than you, so my fellow-feeling made me sympathise with you, though I had no spirit to try again."

Mollie laughed under her breath, the influence of her surroundings instinctively subduing the usual merry trill. This Mr Melland was an unexpectedly pleasant companion, now that his former gloom and irritability of manner had disappeared. It was as if a dreaded prospect had been removed, and he was luxuriating in recovered freedom. Mollie wondered what the change of circumstances could be; time, no doubt, would show; and, when they had reached a greater degree of intimacy, she would tease him about his sudden change of front, and treat him to a pantomimic imitation of his former gloomy frowns. The prospect pleased her, and she laughed again, showing the pretty dimples in her cheek, while Jack Melland looked at her inquiringly.

"What's the joke? May I hear it?"

"Oh, nothing—I was just imagining! All sorts of things fly through one's head, especially to-day, when we really are in an exciting position. At home my sister and I have a very quiet time, and we get most of our excitement in dreams. We imagine things until they are almost real. Don't you know the feeling?"

"No!" cried Mr Melland bluntly. His brows were arched, his nostrils curved with the old look of scornful superiority. "I have no experience of the kind, and I don't want to have. It's a dangerous habit. We have to live among realities, and very commonplace realities, for the most part; and it unfits one for work to be dreaming of impossibilities."

"No, no, no; it helps one! It is like a tonic which braces one up for the ordinary routine."

"It is like a sleeping draught—agreeable for the time, but mischievous and relaxing in its after effects."

Grey eyes met blue with a flash of defiance, then softened into smiles.

"It depends upon disposition," said Mollie firmly. "We find nothing relaxing about it, but a great deal of innocent amusement. When we are out shopping and want something badly and can't have it, because it costs five shillings and we only possess half a crown, Ruth says to me, 'Let's pretend a letter arrived by the afternoon post to say someone had left us a million pounds! What would you do first of all?' Then we can talk about it for the rest of the walk, and decide what dresses we would have, and where we should live, and the papers we should have in the entertaining room, and the furniture in our bedrooms; and we choose things out of all the shop-windows as we pass, and decide where they shall go. I've furnished my house so often that I really know the rooms, and love them into the bargain."

"And when you go back into the real house you are discontented and amazed at the contrast."

"Oh dear, no! That would be silly. I am so refreshed by my visit to the castle that I can laugh over the shabbiness which annoyed me before. You don't think it wrong to read an interesting book? Very well, then, why is it wrong to indulge in a little fiction on one's own account?"

"Wrong is rather a strong word, perhaps, but there is a great difference between the two. In reading a book you forget yourself in your interest about others; in dreams—excuse me—you think constantly of yourself, and play the part of hero. It is a habit which is inclined to make one consider oneself the most interesting person on earth."

"Well, so you are! To yourself, I mean; you know you are!" cried Mollie, with an innocent *naïveté* which made Mr Melland laugh again. It was seldom, indeed, that anyone was honest enough to confess to self-love, and her candour seemed infectious, for, on the verge of contradicting her assertion with regard to himself, a sudden recollection rushed through him of his own thoughts, doubts, conflicts, and final determination of the past twenty-four hours. Did not every one of these concern himself as a primary, if not an only, motive? Was he not exercised, first of all, by a sense of his own importance, so that the wishes of a dying man availed nothing against the preservation of his own dignity? The laugh gave place to a frown as he replied—

"If it is so it ought certainly to be discouraged. One ought not deliberately to pamper selfishness."

Mollie's eyes dropped to her plate, and her lips pouted in an involuntary grimace.

"Rather inclined to preach," she said to herself naughtily, "and so intensely practical and matter of fact! I must devote myself to the education of his higher faculties. I shall have something to say to you, Mr Jack Melland, the first time that will of yours comes into opposition with my own.—'One ought not deliberately to pamper selfishness.'—Delightful sentence! I must not forget it."

Chapter Ten.

Introductions.

In the drawing-room, after dinner, Mrs Thornton made herself agreeable to the two girls, and was evidently full of interest and curiosity.

"Having the Court open again will make a great deal of difference to the village in general, and to ourselves in particular," she said, smiling. "Mr Farrell has been so invalided of late years that we have seen nothing of him, and it is quite an excitement to dine here again. Dr Braithey told us whom we were to meet, and that, of course, added greatly to the pleasure. I hope you will like the neighbourhood, and enjoy your visit. You must let me help you in any way that is in my power. I hope you will, for I love being with young people and making them happy."

One glance at the kindly face of the speaker proved the truth of her assertion, and both girls assented gladly. A few hours' acquaintance had proved Mrs Wolff to be a mere figurehead of a chaperon, and Ruth shrewdly suspected that her very weakness had been the attraction in Mr Farrell's eyes, since, in consequence, she would be less likely to hinder that display of character and self-will which it was his object to study. Failing Mrs Wolff, then, it was a comfort to meet this brisk, motherly woman, who might be depended on as a helpful confidante.

Mollie glanced at the heaped-up fire, and, with a sudden impulse of friendliness, pulled forward an armchair, saying eagerly—

"Do sit down! Let us all sit down and be cosy till the men come; and will you tell us about the neighbourhood and the people we shall know? We are to be here for three months, and uncle says we can entertain as much as we like. He wants us to entertain, but of course we must know the people first. Do you suppose we shall have many callers?"

Mrs Thornton laughed merrily.

"There's no doubt about that, my dear. Everybody who is anybody within a radius of a dozen miles will think of nothing, and speak of nothing, and dream of nothing else but you and your cousins until they have made your acquaintance. We have not much to excite us in the country, and to have the Court open again, with four young people to act as hosts, is a sensation of the first water. There will be a stream of callers after you have appeared in church on Sunday. You will have a busy time driving over the country returning their calls, and after these formalities are over the invitations will begin. I don't think you will find any lack of hospitality."

The girls looked at each other with tragic glances which said "One black dress!" so plainly to their own understanding that it seemed as if everyone else must interpret the meaning. Ruth flushed, and asked hurriedly—

"Are there many girls like ourselves living pretty near?"

"Oh dear, yes; girls are never at a discount in a country place. Let me see, now, how shall I describe them! In the village itself there is Dora Braithey, the doctor's daughter, a very good, useful worker in the parish; and Lettice Baldwin, who lives with her widowed mother; and the three Robsons, who are what they call good sportsmen, and go in for games; and further afield there is Honor Edgecombe of Mount Edgecombe, a charming girl, and very musical; and Grace and Schilla Trevor; and the Blounts at the Moat have a London niece, Lady Margot Blount, who pays them a long visit every year. She is staying there now, and is sure to call. She is very elegant and distinguished-looking, and we all admire her immensely. My husband thinks her a model of everything that a girl should be."

Ruth and Mollie, staring fixedly into the fire, were naughtily conscious of a dislike towards the immaculate Margot, who had suddenly loomed on their horizon as a formidable rival in the favour of the neighbourhood, while Mrs Thornton unconsciously proceeded cheerily with her recital—

"Of course there are many more, but I am mentioning the most attractive. We have a few young men, too, and most of the big houses have constant visitors for shooting or fishing, so that you can manage to get partners if you want a little hop now and then. And then, as you would suppose, I hope you will find time to take an interest in the parish. I don't ask you to take up any active work, for, of course, as visitors your time will not be your own, but I should like to tell you of our various clubs and enterprises."

"I hope you will not only tell us of them, but show them to us as well. Uncle Bernard wishes us to do exactly as we choose, so our time is our own, and I should like to do some work. I should feel so idle doing nothing but enjoying myself," cried Ruth eagerly.

Mrs Thornton's smile of approval had a somewhat wistful expression.

As her husband had done before her, she looked at these two young girls, and wondered if the time to come would see one of them acting the rôle of the squire and patron, and as such holding almost unlimited power over the parish. They seemed kindly, natural creatures, who would be well disposed towards the vicar and his family; and a woman had more understanding of little things than any mere man.

In the flash of an eye Mrs Thornton's mind reviewed the damp patch on her drawing-room wall, the ill-fitting windows which let in a constant draught; the hopeless ruin of the tiny conservatory, wherein she reared her precious "bedding-outs."

She could not but remember that other squires not only kept their vicar's house in order, but assisted in sending sons to college, daughters to finishing schools, and expressed their interest in the family in a hundred helpful ways; but Mr Farrell had seemed unconscious of the very existence of her precious olive branches, and had never gone beyond the bare duties of his position.

Mrs Thornton was no vulgar schemer for her own benefit, but just a mother of a large family, struggling to make the most of a small income; and a quick repentance for the selfishness of her dreams prompted the desire to help these two young things who were suddenly called upon to fill a difficult position.

"Remember, I am always to be found at home or somewhere about the village. You will soon get to know my haunts, so that you can run me to earth if you need my services. Just come in and out as you like; the oftener you come the better I shall be pleased, for I am so anxious to help you, if you will allow me."

"We will, we will! it is lovely of you to offer; and do please help us now!" cried Mollie eagerly, as the sound of an opening door was heard in the distance, and footsteps crossed the hall towards the drawing-room. "Talk, talk; do talk! I tried before dinner, and got snubbed for my pains; and we are such strangers that it is difficult to know what to say next."

Mrs Thornton laughed.

"I'll do what I can," she promised good-naturedly. "Someone may suggest to Mr Farrell a game of whist. He used to be a crack player, so I don't think he can resist the temptation, and that would leave you young folks free to make each other's acquaintance."

As she spoke the gentlemen entered the room and approached the group by the fireside. Judging from their appearance, the last half-hour had not been particularly lively, for the vicar looked tired and worried, and the young men unmistakably bored. Mr Farrell's set face showed few changes of expression, but a faint gleam of pleasure manifested itself at the mention of his favourite game, and presently the four elders of the party were occupied, while the younger members stood together in a somewhat embarrassed silence.

Left entirely to their own resources, no one knew what to say or what to do; each girl looked first at her partner of the dinner-table, and then shyly across at the other stranger who was to be a daily companion during the next three months. Ruth met no answering glance, for Jack Melland was frowningly regarding the carpet; but for the first time Mollie had a direct view of the eyes which were habitually hidden behind Victor Druce's thick eyelashes, and was surprised to find how bright and friendly was their expression.

"Shall we investigate the conservatory?" he said at once, as if answering an unspoken appeal. "They won't want us to stay here and interrupt the game. I think we had better make a move."

"But may we? Would Uncle Bernard like it?"

"May we! Are we not told to amuse ourselves in any way we choose? Of course we may," he replied laughingly, leading the way forward, while the others followed, nothing loth.

The conservatory opened out of the drawing-room by means of a long glass door, which, being shut, made it into a separate room. A room it was, rather than the ordinary glass passage, for it had a wide, open floor, broken only by spreading palms standing in wooden boxes, and in the midst an old-fashioned pink camellia-tree. Stands of flowers encircled three sides, and a lamp stood out from the walls in a bracket. Given a few rugs and accessories, it would have made an ideal lounge. As it was, there was no provision for visitors, and it was evident that no one but the gardener took the trouble to enter. Mr Druce looked round rapidly, spied a wooden box under one stand, a stool under another, and brought them forward one after another, flicking off the dust with his handkerchief.

"You must have something to sit on. Can you manage with these, or shall I bring chairs from the drawing-room? I don't want to make a noise if I can help it."

"No, no; please don't! These will do perfectly. But what will you do, and Mr Melland? You must not stand all the time."

"Oh, don't trouble about us! We can look after ourselves," responded Jack Melland, pushing the flower-pots nearer together on the staging, and lightly swinging himself into the vacant space. Victor followed his example, and thrust his hands into his pockets.

For the next few minutes silence reigned while the young men took in and quite obviously admired the charming picture made by the two girlish figures against the background of flowering plants.

Ruth's stool had been placed against the camellia-tree, and the pink blooms matched the soft flush in her cheeks, and relieved the sombreness of her black attire. Thus placed she looked charmingly pretty, and held herself with an air of dignity, which was a new accomplishment.

Ruth was an adaptive creature, tremendously influenced by the surroundings of the moment. At home her little head was wont to droop with despondency, and the consciousness that she was poor and unknown and shabbily dressed. At the Court she was intensely, delightfully assured of being Miss Farrell—of possessing the family features, and of being, so far, the recipient of her uncle's greatest favour. And so Ruth now leant back with an air of languid elegance, smiling sweetly at her companions.

Mollie's bright head peeped from beneath the shadow of a palm. She held in her hand a spray of heliotrope, which she had picked in passing, and from time to time bent to smell the fragrance, with little murmurs of delight.

But Mollie was obviously longing to say something, and when the time came that she met Jack Melland's eye she suddenly plucked up courage to put it into words.

"Don't you think we ought to introduce ourselves properly?" she cried eagerly. "We have been told each other's names, and talked politely at dinner, but that's not really being introduced. We ought to know something about each other, if we are to be companions here. I don't know if you two know each other; but we did not know of your existence until to-day. My mother used to stay at the Court when she was a bride, and she loved Aunt Edna, and has often talked to us about her; but she knew very little of her relations, and for the last twenty years or more she has never seen Uncle Bernard until he suddenly descended upon us last week.

"We live in the North—in Liverpool. People in the South seem to think it is a dreadful place; but it isn't at all. The river is splendid, and out in the suburbs, where we live, it's very pretty, near a beautiful big park. The people are nice, too. We are rather conceited about ourselves in comparison with the people in the towns round about. You have heard the saying, 'Manchester man, Liverpool gentleman,' and we are proud of our county, too. 'What Lancashire thinks to-day, England thinks to-morrow.' I really must boast a little bit, because South-country people are so proud and superior, and seem to think that no one but themselves knows how to speak or behave. Someone said to me once, 'You live in Liverpool, then why haven't you a Lancashire accent?' I was so cross. What should she have thought of me if I had said, 'You live in London, why don't you speak like a Cockney?' We are not at all ashamed, but very proud indeed, of coming from the North-countree."

"'Oh, the oak and the ash,
And the bonnie ivy tree,'"

chanted Victor, in a pleasant baritone voice, at the sound of which Mollie flushed with delight, and cried eagerly—

"Ah, you are musical! That's nice. We must have some grand singing matches, but you mustn't sing that ballad. It's Ruth's special property. She sings it with such feeling!

"'And the lad that marries me,
Must carry me home to my North-coun-tree!'"

"Mollie!" Ruth's tone was eloquent of reproof, but Mollie only laughed, and said easily—

"Oh well, of course, if you inherit the Court you will have to change your plans. I wish I could lift it up bodily and put it down among the dear Westmorland mountains; but I'm afraid that's impossible. I think that is all the history we have. No two girls could possibly have led a less eventful life. We have had no money to travel and see the world, and we are not in the least bit accomplished, but we have had a happy time all the same, and we mean to be happy, whatever happens; don't we, Ruth?"

Ruth did not answer, but sat with downcast eyes, staring at the ground. She more than half disapproved of Mollie's candour, despising herself the while for so doing, so she preserved a dead silence, until Jack Melland nobly stepped into the breach.

"Well, if you are North-country, Miss Mollie, I suppose I am Colonial. I was born in India, where my father's regiment was stationed. He died when I was a youngster, and my poor little mother had a hard struggle to keep herself and me. If a fortune had come to us in those days it would have been a godsend, and she would probably be with me now; but she died eight years ago, and I am alone in the world, with no one to think of but myself. I have dingy diggings and a garrulous landlady, but, like you, I manage to have a very good time. I am interested in my work—I'm interested in life generally. I mean to make something out of it before I am done."

He threw back his head with a proud, self-confident gesture. Young, strong, high-spirited, he felt at that moment that the world lay at his feet. All things seemed possible to his unaided powers, and the thought of help was repugnant rather than welcome. The two girls looked at him with the involuntary admiration which women pay to a strong man, while Victor Druce smiled his slow, inscrutable smile.

"A good thing for you that you are not in my profession, Melland! A barrister can't push; he must sit still and wait his turn. I have been waiting a long time, and I can't say that I seem much nearer the Woolsack. Still, one can amuse oneself in London, and I have my home in the country to which I can retire whenever I need a rest. My old parents are alive, and one sister—an invalid. Altogether, I have nothing to complain of in the past, and the future looks pleasant just now. Three months in this charming place—in such society!"

Victor Druce made a graceful little bow, which took in both the girls, and his glance lingered on Mollie bending forward, the spray of heliotrope still raised to her face.

"Stealing already, Miss Mollie! You will get into trouble with the authorities. How do you know that plant was not being specially preserved for exhibition at a show?"

"I hope it wasn't; but it's no use telling me to do as I like, and then to object if I pick a flower. I shall pick them every day—several times a day. I shall always be picking them! I think I shall take the care of this house altogether, and do the watering and snip off the dead leaves. I love snipping! And I shall arrange the flowers on the table, too; they are very badly done—so stiff. Just like a man's taste!"

The two men smiled at each other, while Ruth protested quickly—

"No, you can't, Mollie. I'm the eldest, and I've 'barleyed' it already. You can arrange the vases in the drawing-room, if you like."

"Thank you, ma'am!" said Mollie calmly. "Just as you like."

Judging from the fervour with which she had stated her intentions a moment earlier, the listeners expected that she would dispute her sister's mandate and hardly knew how to account for her unruffled composure. But, in truth, Mollie was already reflecting that flowers took a long time to arrange satisfactorily, and that it would be a bore to saddle herself with a regular duty. Much more fun to let Ruth do it, and criticise the results! She sniffed daintily at the heliotrope, turning her head from side to side to examine the possibilities of the conservatory.

"Well, anyway, I shall take this place in hand! It will make a lovely little snuggery, with rugs on the floor and basket-chairs everywhere about, and an odd table or two to hold books and work, and tea when we like to have it here. I'll have a blind to the door, too, so that we shan't be surprised if visitors are shown into the drawing-room. Is there a door of escape, by the way? I hate to be penned up where I can't run away to a place of safety." She peered inquiringly round the trunk of the palm, whereupon Victor Druce slid down from his perch, and walked to the further end of the floor.

"Yes, there's a door here. If you see anyone coming for whom you have a special aversion you can get out, and hide in the shrubbery. I promise not to tell. Perhaps I may come with you. I am not fond of afternoon calls."

"Don't encourage her, please, Mr Druce," said Ruth quickly. "Mollie talks a lot of nonsense which she doesn't mean; but if people are kind enough to come here to see us, she must not be so rude as to refuse to see them. I am sure Uncle Bernard would be very angry if we did not receive them properly."

But Mollie was obstinate this time, and refused to be put down.

"How do you know?" she asked rebelliously. "He might be very pleased with me for sharing his own retiring tastes! He said himself that he approved of what other people would consider a fault. Perhaps he likes unsociability. There's as much chance of that as anything else!"

Victor Druce came back from his tour of investigation, but instead of taking his former seat, leant up against the stem of a huge palm-tree, whose topmost leaves touched the glass roof, folded his arms and looked down at the two girls with an intent, curious scrutiny.

"It's an odd position," he said slowly, "a very odd position for us all to be plunged in at a moment's notice! None of us have any knowledge of Mr Farrell's tastes, so any attempts to please him must be entirely experimental. If we please him we may thank our good fortune; if we offend, we can, at least, feel innocent of any bad intentions. It's rather a disagreeable position, but I expect the poor old fellow shirks being left to himself any longer, though he would die rather than acknowledge it. It's dull work being left alone when one is ill. Personally, it is extremely inconvenient for me to be away from home for three months, but I shall manage it somehow. One can't refuse a request from a man in his condition, and it would be a pleasure to cheer the poor old fellow a bit, even at the cost of one's own comfort."

There was silence for a moment after he had ceased speaking. Jack Melland stared at the ground, and swung his feet gently to and fro. Ruth knitted her black brows, and Mollie looked puzzled and thoughtful. It was a kind speech. She would have liked to admire it thoroughly, but—did it ring quite true? Was there not something unnatural in the avoidance of any reference by the speaker to his own possible gain?

"I'm afraid I didn't think much of Uncle Bernard; I was too busy thinking of myself. I want to have a good time!" she said bluntly. "It's a lovely, lovely house, and the grounds are lovely, and the spring flowers are coming up, and we can live out of doors, and be as happy as the day is long. I am not going to worry my head about the money, or anything else. I'll be nice to Uncle Bernard in my own way, as nice as he will let me; but he said that we could enjoy ourselves, and I am going to take him at his word, and do every single thing I like. It's an opportunity which may never occur again, as the shop people say in their circulars, and it would be foolish not to make the most of it."

"I want the money!" said Ruth clearly. The pretty flush had faded from her cheeks, and she looked suddenly wan and white. The hands which were resting on her knee trembled visibly. She had evidently strung herself up to what she considered a necessary confession, and her eyes turned to one after another of her companions in wistful apology.

"I want it dreadfully! I have been poor all my life, and have longed to be rich, and I would rather live here, in this house, than anywhere else in the world. If we are going to live together and be friends we ought to be honest with each other from the beginning. It's selfish, but it's true! I want the money, and I mean to do every single thing in my power to get it."

"Bravo!" cried a man's voice suddenly. Mollie was frowning and biting her lips in obvious discomfort; Victor Druce's drooping lids once more hid his eyes from sight as he stood with folded arms leaning against the palm. It was Jack Melland who had spoken—Jack Melland, roused for once to display unqualified approval and enthusiasm. He bent forward on his seat, hands in his pockets, his tall, lithe figure swaying gently to and fro as he faced Ruth with his bright blue eyes.

"Bravo, Miss Farrell! I admire your honesty, and wish you good luck. You are perfectly justified in doing all you can to gain your point, and I sincerely hope you may be successful. It is only right that a Farrell should inherit the Court, and if you were the old man's grand-daughter, you could not possibly be more like him."

Ruth flushed, but did not reply. Victor Druce's measured voice cut like a sword across the silence.

"You are unselfish, Melland! Are you quite sure that you share the honesty which you admire so much in Miss Farrell? Have you forgotten how the question affects yourself?"

Jack Melland jumped lightly to the ground and straightened his long back.

"Unselfish or not, it's the truth. The question does not affect me at all. I am not going to stay!"

Chapter Eleven.

An Early Decision.

"I am not going to stay," said Jack Melland; and whatever his faults might be, he looked and spoke like a man who knew his own mind, and would abide thereby.

His three companions stared at him in silence, and one of the three at least felt a distinct sinking of the heart.

"I was beginning to like him; we got on quite famously at dinner, and I thought we were going to have ever such a good time together. Now we shall be a wretched uncomfortable three, and Mr Druce will like Ruth best, and I shall be out in the cold. How horrid! How perfectly horrid!" grumbled Mollie to herself.

Just because she was so perturbed, however, she would not allow herself to speak, but put on an elaborate display of indifference, while Victor asked curiously—

"You mean that? May one ask your reason?"

"Oh, certainly. I never looked upon myself as having the slightest claim upon Mr Farrell, and I don't care to ruin my business prospects for the sake of an off-chance. Besides, the whole position is unpleasant; I object to being kept 'on approval,' with the consciousness that if I allow myself to be ordinarily agreeable I shall at once be credited with sponging for the old man's favour. I am quite satisfied with my own lot, without any outside assistance."

"Don't you care about money, then?" asked Ruth timidly.

Jack Melland threw back his head with an air of masterful complacency.

"I care about making money. That is to say, I love my work, and wish it to be successful, but I am keen on it more for the sake of the interest and occupation than for what it brings. A few hundreds a year supply all that I want, and I should not care to be burdened with a big fortune. If you come into this place, Miss Farrell, I shall be grateful to you if you will ask me down for a few days' shooting in the autumn, but I shall never envy you your responsibility. To kick my heels here in idleness for three solid months, and know that the business was suffering for want of my presence—nothing would induce me to do it!"

But at this Mollie found her tongue, indignation spurring her to speech.

"You are not very polite to the rest of us! I should not have thought it would be such a great hardship to stay in a lovely big house with three young companions, when summer was coming on, too! I should think there are one or two people in the world who would like it even a little better than poking in a stuffy office from morning until night. But there's no accounting for tastes. When you are grilling with heat in the City you can think of us sitting under the trees eating strawberries, and thank Fate you are so much better off. We promise not to send you any. It might remind you too painfully of the country!"

"Mollie!" cried Ruth in sharp reproof; but Jack laughed with good-natured amusement.

"Oh, I deserve it, Miss Farrell! My remarks sounded horribly discourteous. I assure you if I had the time to spare I should thoroughly enjoy staying on for a time under the present conditions; but as it is quite impossible to remain for three months, I might as well depart at once. I don't suppose Mr Farrell will wish to keep me under the circumstances."

It appeared, however, Jack Melland was wrong in his surmise, for when he announced his decision to his host before bidding him good-night, the old man looked at him coldly and replied—

"I thought I had explained that we would discuss objections at a later date. May I ask what limit you had mentally fixed to your visit when you did me the honour of accepting my invitation?"

"I hardly know—this is Monday. I thought, perhaps until Saturday, or, at the longest, a week."

Mr Farrell waved his hand in dismissal.

"We will leave it for a week, then. On Monday morning next I will discuss the position as fully as you wish. Now, if either of you young gentlemen cares to smoke, the billiard-room is at your service. Please ring for anything you require. Meantime, as it is past my usual hour for retiring, I wish you a very good-night."

"Checkmate, old fellow!" cried Victor Druce, as the door closed behind the stooping figure; but Jack deigned no reply.

The cloud had returned to his forehead, his nostrils were curved with annoyance and thwarted self-will.

The cloud was still there when he came down to breakfast next morning, and did not lighten even at the sight of the well-appointed breakfast-table, and the two pretty girls who were seated thereat. Some meals may be more attractive abroad than at home. A French dinner, for example, has certain points above an English dinner; but we give way to none as regards our breakfast—that most delightful of meals to the strong and healthy, especially in springtime, when the sunshine pours in at the open window, and the scent of flowers mingles with the aroma of freshly made coffee.

The breakfast-table of the Court had all the attractions which one instinctively associates with old country houses. The massive, old-fashioned silver, the revolving stand in the centre, the plentiful display of covered dishes to supplement the cold viands on the sideboard; and, as Mr Farrell invariably remained in his own room until lunch-time, the restraint of his presence was removed.

Little Mrs Wolff busied herself with the duties behind the urn, and Ruth and Mollie in serge skirts and spick and span white blouses looked as fresh as paint, and a great many times as pretty. They were laughing and chatting with Victor Druce, who had donned Norfolk jacket and knickerbockers, and was quite the country gentleman both in appearance and in his manner of leisurely good-humour.

The entrance of Jack in what are technically called "Store clothes," with a gloomy frown upon his forehead, seemed to strike a jarring note in this cheerful scene, and both girls were conscious of a distinct feeling of grievance against the offender. Was it so dreadful a fate to be doomed to spend a whole week in their society? Need a man look as if his last hope in life were extinguished because Fate kept him away from the City for seven days, and placed him instead in the sweet green country, with three companions of his own age who—to put it mildly—were not perfect ogres in appearance!

The necessary greetings were observed. Jack helped himself to a bowl of porridge, and, looking up, asked discontentedly—

"Hasn't the newspaper arrived?"

"Not yet, sir; it will be here by ten o'clock, sir," the butler replied; and Mollie pulled down her lip with an expression of solemn propriety, and added—

"But perhaps I can relieve your anxiety in the meantime. Cotton is down twenty points, very strong and steady, and the Bears are making fortunes. 'Mauds' are fluctuating, but 'Louisa Christinas' are in great demand; everybody is rushing after them. The Bank rate is ten and a half, and Consols have gone up two per cent. General market firm, with a tendency to drop."

"My good child, what nonsense are you talking!" cried Ruth aghast, and the two young men exchanged glances and burst into a laugh; even Jack laughed, though such a feat had seemed impossible a moment before.

"What a thrilling report! You make me more impatient than ever. It is just like my luck to be out of the way when there is a chance of a good thing, though, after all, I don't know if the wisest plan would not be to sell everything one had, and put the money in the bank—eh, Druce? Ten and a half per cent! Where do you get your knowledge, Miss Mary?"

"Oh, I see things in the newspapers, and I hear the pater talking to his friends. Don't call me 'Miss Mary' please, it sounds far too quiet and proper for me. I am never called anything but Mollie, except when I overspend my allowance, and mother feels it her duty to scold me. Are you on the Stock Exchange, Mr Melland? What sort of business is it which you find so attractive?"

"I am afraid you would not be much wiser if I tried to explain. We are what is called 'brokers'; but there are an endless variety of businesses under the same name. I have nothing, however, to do with 'Mauds' and 'Christinas'!"

"Neither have I," volunteered Victor smilingly, "To tell the truth, I have no money to invest, Briefs don't come my way, and I am at present occupied listening to more fortunate fellows, and thinking how much better I could plead myself. It palls at times, but I am fond of the profession, and have no wish to change it."

"No," said Mollie reflectively. "The wigs *are* becoming!" and when the two young men leant back in their chairs and roared with laughter, she blushed and pouted, and looked so pretty that it did one good to see her.

The three earlier comers had finished their meal by this time, but they sat still until Jack had disposed of the toast and marmalade which makes the last breakfast course of every self-respecting Briton; then they rose one after the other, strolled over to the open window, and faced the question of the day—

"What shall we do?"

It was Ruth who spoke, and at the sound of her words the shadow came back to Jack's brow.

"Yes, what shall we do? Think of it—three months—twelve weeks—eighty-four separate days to lounge away with the same question on your lips! I'd rather be sentenced to hard labour at once. Life is not worth living without work. I'd rather be a clerk on sixty pounds a year than stagnate as a country squire."

"You would be a very bad squire if you did stagnate!" cried Mollie spiritedly, throwing back her little head, and looking up at him with a flash of the grey eyes. "You would have your tenants to look after, and your property to keep in order, and the whole village looking to you to lead every scheme of pleasure or improvement, and the vicar looking to you to be his right hand, and all the growing boys looking to you to help them to a start in life, and the old people expecting you to make their last days easy. You would be the hardest-worked man in the country if you did half the work that was waiting for you, and it would be unselfish work, too—thinking of others, and not of yourself."

Jack looked at her, and his face softened.

"That's true," he said frankly. "I'm sorry! You are right, and I am wrong. I'm in a bad temper, and can't see things in their right light to-day. Of course, if one really settled down to it, there would be plenty to do; it's when one is only playing with the position that time drags."

"Well, it ought not to drag to-day, at all events. We must be very dull if we cannot amuse ourselves in surveying the domain, and seeing all there is to be seen. I am going to put on my hat this minute and examine the gardens, and go down to the stables to look at the horses. If anyone likes to come too, they may, but my plans are fixed," cried Mollie, nodding her saucy head; and at the magic word "stables," a ray of interest lit up the two masculine faces.

Ten minutes later the four young people were strolling down the drive, the girls with serge coats over their white blouses, and sailor-hats on their heads, the men wearing their cloth caps with an evident air of enjoyment. They turned the corner of the house, and coming round to the south side uttered simultaneous exclamations of surprise and delight.

Along the entire length of the house ran an enormously wide terrace edged with a balustrade, from the centre of which a flight of marble steps led to an Italian garden, its green sward and stiffly outlined flower-beds flanked by a quantity of curiously cut shrubs.

Beyond this garden the ground dipped sharply, showing first a glade of trees whose fresh spring foliage contrasted with the dark colours of the evergreens; then came a glimpse of a lake, a sweep of park; and beyond all a glorious, wide-stretching view over the countryside. Perched upon one of the highest sites for miles around, this terraced walk afforded such a panorama of beauty as is rarely to be found even in our well-favoured isles, and withal the beauty was of that peaceful, home-like nature which irresistibly endears itself to the heart.

The four young people stood in silence gazing from side to side, and into each mind, even that of the rebellious Jack himself, there crept the same thought. This was indeed a goodly heritage, whose owner would be an enviable person! The possibility of possessing it as a home was worth a far greater sacrifice than anything which had been demanded of themselves.

In those few minutes of silence dreams ran riot, and finally found vent in words.

"When the Court belongs to me I shall have an awning put up on this terrace and sit here all day long," said Mollie; as usual the first to break the silence.

"I shall have a table brought out, and breakfast here every fine morning," said Ruth.

"I'll smoke here after dinner!" said Victor.

"I'll do ditto in every case!" said Jack, then caught himself up sharply—"when I come to visit the Chosen, that is to say! Of course, I'm out of the running. What are you smiling at, Miss Mollie?" For, turning towards her, he had seen the grey eyes light up with a merry twinkle. She shook her head, however, refusing to gratify his curiosity, and sped rapidly down the broad marble steps.

"He is beginning to have qualms! The very first morning, and for a moment his resolution wavered. The spell is working," she told herself triumphantly; for, despite his lack of gallantry, both girls had already candidly admitted that upon Jack's going or staying depended a great part of the pleasure of the next three months. "Don't persuade him; don't mention the subject at all. Let him think we don't care how he decides. Men are contradictious creatures, and the less he is urged the more likely he is to give way," argued Ruth the experienced. And Mollie dutifully agreed.

Chapter Twelve.

A Novel Experience.

Down the winding path, the visitors, as they walked together, came upon masses of daffodils, standing up erect and golden from the carpet of dead leaves which covered the ground. Not the ordinary common or garden daffodil, charming as it is, but named varieties of every description—white trumpeted *Horsefieldi*, stately yellow Emperors, *Bari Conspicui* with its dainty outline of orange; these, and a dozen others were growing in patches, not in dozens or scores, but in literal hundreds, beneath the budding trees. There were violets, too; and white and purple and golden saxifrages peeping out between the stones which bordered the trickling stream—a scene of enchantment, indeed, for City eyes accustomed to gaze only on bricks and mortar. The girls were wild with delight, and flitted about gathering specimens of the different flowers; while the two young men were content to watch them with an air of masculine superiority.

"What is the use of burdening yourselves with all those things at the very beginning of our walk?"

"They aren't a burden, they are a joy. Hold them for me, please, while I get some more," replied Mollie, laying a stack of long-stemmed beauties in Jack's arms, regardless of his look of dismay. "Don't crush them; I want them kept quite fresh."

"What are you going to do with them, if I might ask? There are plenty in the house. It's a pity to cut them just to waste."

"I wouldn't waste them for the world, the beautiful darlings! I'm going to send them home to mother. We will pack them in a box, and take them down to the post-office this afternoon. It will provide honest work for the afternoon," retorted Mollie.

She was too happy, too supremely happy, to be stiff and formal. As she darted from one flower-bed to another she looked like an incarnation of the bright spring morning. There was no room in her mind for doubts and fears. The future simply did not exist; the present was all-sufficient.

From the gardens the quartette strolled onwards past the lake, and across the wide park to the further gates; then, returning, paid a visit to the stables. The groom greeted them with a smile, which showed that he had anticipated their coming; and, like the other servants, hailed with delight a return to livelier days.

"The horses will get some work now, I hope, ma'am," he said, touching his forehead as he addressed himself to Ruth, as the head of the party. ("The Farrell eyebrows again!" said Mollie to herself.)

"They have had it far too easy for a long time back. The master's fond of horses, and we need a good many for driving up these steep hills, as everything has to be brought up from the station; but it's regular gentle exercise as suits 'em best. I've a nice little mare as would carry you, if you'd care to try her. She's in this box. Fanny, we call her. Whoa! Fanny, old girl, come and show yourself! Nice gentle creature, you see, miss: no temper in her."

"But I don't ride," began Ruth, smiling. "I should like to very much; and I don't think I should be nervous, but—"

"Oh, I'd love to ride! Is there a horse for me, too? And would you teach us—would you? Could we come down every day and have a lesson?" interrupted Mollie impetuously.

And the groom wheeled round to face her, and touched his forehead again, his face one smile of delight.

"Ay, would I, miss! Proud to do it. Many's the one I've taught to ride in my time. You settle any hour you like, and I'll have the horses ready for you, and take you a turn across the park. There's some old side-saddles put away in the loft. I'll have 'em down, and put in order for ye. And the gentlemen? You'll not be needing any lessons, I'm thinking."

"Oh no! I think I can manage to sit any horse you have here," replied Victor in a slightly superior tone.

Jack, however, shook his head, and said—

"No use for me. I can't ride, and it's no use beginning. I'm only here for a week."

The groom looked the surprise he was too well trained to express.

"Indeed, sir. Well, I can give you a mount if you change your mind. It wouldn't take long to get your seat; and it's pleasant exercise these spring days. The carriages are round this way, miss. There's a pretty little cart you might like to drive yourself."

He led the way forward; but while the others followed, Mollie hung behind, blocking Jack's way. Something prompted her to speak, an impulse too strong to be resisted.

"Do learn!" she cried entreatingly. "Learn with us. Why won't you? It would be such fun. You said you hated to be idle. It wouldn't be wasted time if you learnt a useful accomplishment."

"Hardly useful to me, I am afraid, Miss Mollie. I have no money for horses. My only acquaintance with them is from the top of a City omnibus."

"But you can't tell what might happen. We might go to war again, and you might want to volunteer. You might grow rich. Besides, you volunteered to come and stay with the 'Chosen,' and then you will certainly find it useful. So you will join us, won't you?"

Jack laughed and hesitated, looking down at the flushed, eager face. It seemed a very trifling matter. He could not tell that with the acceptance or refusal of this light request the whole of his future destiny was involved. He only thought that Mollie was a charmingly pretty girl, and that it would be amusing to practise riding by her side.

"Well! since you put it like that, I can't refuse," he answered laughingly. "We will learn together, Miss Mollie, and good luck to our efforts."

"But what about the riding-habits?" asked Ruth.

"We must get them," said Mollie.

"Where?" asked Ruth.

"At a tailor's," said Mollie. "Bond Street, for choice; only it would be difficult to arrange about fitting. I'm not at all sure that we shan't have to pay a visit to town on this matter of clothes. For the present I mean to consult that maid, and see what can be done until we can get habits well made for us. And—who knows?—there may be some old things stored away somewhere which will come in handy. Anyway, I'm going to begin lessons to-morrow, habit or no habit. You can do as you like."

As there was no time to be lost, the maid was summoned only to proclaim her inability to manufacture riding attire in the space of twenty-four hours, or to produce the same from the household treasures.

"There is the mistress's habit, of course, but that was locked away with her other clothes; and even if I could get at it I wouldn't dare to use it. Mr Farrell keeps everything she wore, and nobody touches them but himself. There's a very good tailor at Bexham, miss—only half an hour's rail from here. Many of the ladies go to him for their things."

"But we want something now—at once! Something to wear to-morrow. Surely you can think of something? Mr Farrell said we were to ask you for everything we wanted, and this is the first thing we have asked for. You must suggest something!" cried Mollie imperiously.

Thus adjured, Emma pursed up her lips, and wrinkled her forehead, leant her head on one side, and stared at the ceiling for inspiration. Presently it came, for the frown disappeared, the lips relaxed into a smile.

"Well, miss," she said, "there's the parson's young ladies; they are nearly as big as you, though they are still at school. They ride with the father in the holiday, for the squire let's them have a mount from the stables whenever they send up. Their habits will be at home, lying idle. They are not much for style, of course, but for a few days, until you have time to get fitted yourself—"

"Emma, you are an angel! It's a splendid idea! Mrs Thornton begged us to let her help in any way she could. We'll call this very afternoon, when we go down to post off the flowers, and I'm sure she will be delighted to lend them. Now we can have our first lesson to-morrow. That's glorious! I do hate to wait when I have planned anything nice."

At luncheon Mr Farrell made his appearance, and listened with polite indifference to the history of the morning's doings as volunteered by his guests. He asked no questions, made no suggestions, and retired into the library the moment the meal was over for his daily perusal of the *Times*. Here for the first time he discovered the inconvenience of the novel interruption to his solitude, for the newspaper was missing from its accustomed place, and, on ringing to make inquiries, he was informed that Mr Melland had carried it off to the billiard-room.

"Tell Mr Melland, with my compliments, I should be obliged if he would allow me to have it for the next hour—and order two copies for the future," he said grimly.

And five minutes later Jack appeared in person the bearer of the newspaper and frank apologies.

"I'm really awfully sorry! I did not know you had not seen it. Would you care for me to read aloud any article? I should be glad to be of use."

"Thank you. My eyes are still quite useful. I prefer to read for myself."

Jack had the good sense to depart without further protest, and Mr Farrell stretched himself on his big chair with a sigh of relief. He took no pleasure in his guests, whose bright young presence depressed him by reviving memories of happier days. If it had not been for the necessity of choosing an heir, he would have cherished his solitude as his dearest possession. He congratulated himself, however, that by reserving one room for his own use he could be still safe from interruption, and, turning to a leading article, read the first few paragraphs with leisurely enjoyment. The writing was excellent, the views irreproachable, in that they exactly coincided with his own. He turned with anticipatory pleasure to the article next in order, when the sound of a light tap-tap came to the door, and Ruth appeared upon the threshold, blushing shyly.

"Uncle Bernard, Mrs Wolff says that you always read the *Times* after luncheon... Would it be any help if I read aloud what you wish to hear? Sometimes, when pater is tired—"

"I am obliged to you. I require no help of the sort. Is there any other subject on which you wished to speak to me?"

The tone was so suggestive of concealed wrath that Ruth quailed before it, and the faltering "No" was hardly audible across the room. Mr Farrell lifted the paper from his knee so that his face was hidden from view.

"Then you will forgive my remarking that I prefer to be undisturbed. We shall meet in the drawing-room for tea."

Ruth shut the door, advanced a few steps into the hall, and stamped her foot violently upon the floor. The thick Turkey carpet reduced the noise to the faintest echo, but an answering laugh sounded from behind a screen, and Jack Melland's eyes looked quizzically into her flushed face.

"Allow me to sympathise. I was sent about my business a few minutes ago. Took back the *Times* by request, and ventured to offer to read aloud—"

"Oh, so did I! His eyes looked so tired, that I long to do something! It's like living in an hotel, to take everything and do nothing in return, but if he is so cross and glares like that I shall never dare to offer again. Do you suppose it will go on like this all the time? Will he avoid us entirely except at meal-times? Shall we never get to know him really? If it is like that, I don't think I can stand it. I shall run away and go home!"

Jack looked down at her with a kindly sympathy.

"Ah, well, it's early days to judge! I don't think it would be consistent with Mr Farrell's plans to remain a stranger. Opportunities are bound to arise as the days pass by. Don't worry about it, but enjoy yourself while you can.—I am going to sit out on the terrace. Will you come, too? It will be quite warm so long as the sun lasts."

They strolled away together, to make acquaintance in a quiet *tête-à-tête,* while once more interruption approached the library in the shape of Mollie, primed for battle. She rapped at the door, received a low growl by way of reply, and had no sooner crossed the threshold than an infuriated voice startled her ears.

"I tell you no! I want no help. I can read without assistance. Am I stone-blind that I cannot be left in peace to read my paper, as I have done these forty years? How many times over have I to answer the same question?"

"But—but—I haven't asked you anything yet!" gasped Mollie blankly. Eyes and lips alike were wide with amazement, but instead of retiring at full speed, as the other two visitors had done before her, she shut the door carefully and advanced towards the fire. "What did you think I was going to say?"

"I have already had two interruptions in the last half-hour; two offers to have my news read aloud—a thing I detest. I conclude you have come on the same mission?"

"No!" Mollie shook her head, half penitent, half amused. "Indeed such a thing never entered my mind. I was selfish enough to be thinking of myself—not you. Something is worrying me. May I sit down and talk to you about it, Uncle Bernard?"

She drew forward a chair even as she spoke, and Mr Farrell made no objection. The *Times* lay on his lap, his thin hands crossed above it, while his sunken eyes were fixed upon the girl's face with a curious scrutiny.

"If it is any argument about going or staying, I have already explained—"

"Ah, but it isn't! I am going to stay. I love staying! I don't know when I have been so happy in my life as I've been to-day, wandering about this sweet old place. It was the most curious feeling this morning before you were down—like living in an enchanted castle where the owner had disappeared! When I gathered the flowers I felt quite like Beau—" She drew herself up sharply—"They were such lovely flowers!"

A short laugh proved that the interruption had come too late.

"As I said before, Miss Mary, you are not overburdened with modesty! I am obliged for my part of the simile!"

But the speaker's eyes were twinkling with quite the most amiable expression Mollie had yet seen, and she laughed unabashed.

"Ah, well, one description is as exaggerated as the other. I didn't mean to say it; it just popped out. You know that I didn't mean to be rude. I wanted to speak to you about something very important—to us, at least. Ruth will be scandalised, but it's bound to come out sooner or later, and I want to understand our position... We told you this morning that we proposed to learn riding."

"You did."

"And you made no objection."

"On the contrary, I quite approved. It is almost essential for your own comfort and convenience it you wish to enjoy a country life."

"Yes! so we thought. But there is one great objection. We have no habits."

"Indeed!"

"No; of course, we have never ridden at home."

"I presume not."

"And we cannot ride without habits. Emma, the maid, suggested that Mrs Thornton might lend us her daughters' just for a few days; but we cannot keep them long."

"Certainly not!"

Mr Farrell made his remarks with an air of polite indifference, which was peculiarly baffling. It was evident that no lead was to be expected from him, and that Mollie would have to put her request in the plainest possible words. Her lips were pressed together in a momentary hesitation between embarrassment and laughter; then she thought of the lecture she would receive from Ruth if her errand ended in failure, and grew strong again. Her eyes met those of Uncle Bernard still fixed intently on her face.

"I wanted to ask you what we were to do about them, and about clothes altogether! You know we are very poor. Ruth and I have fifteen pounds a year to dress on. You have never been a girl, so you don't understand what that means; but though we can get along on that at home and could look respectable for a few days' visit, we can't manage as we are for three whole months, especially when you wish us to go about, and have parties here, and meet your friends on their own terms. We have only those black evening-dresses which you saw last night, and girls can't always wear the same things, as a man does his dress suit."

"I suppose not."

"No they can't. So—"

"So?"

Mollie's cheek flushed with a dawning impatience.

"Uncle Bernard, don't you think you make it very hard for me? After all, it was your wish that we should stay, and we cannot put the pater to more expense. You said we were to have carte blanche. I want to know if that applies to clothes also?"

"I must say I had not anticipated anything of the sort when I made my remark."

"Well then, are you content to have us as we are? It won't be easy or pleasant, but I suppose we *could* rub along if you don't object. People would make remarks, and as they are your friends—"

"It is a great many years since I have troubled my head about what people say. That argument has no weight with me; but, as you say, you remain here and go into society at my invitation, and it is therefore only reasonable that I should make it possible for you to do so in comfort. I am in ignorance as to what is required. What sum, may I ask, would you consider sufficient to make up deficiencies?"

Mollie's smile of rapture was a sight to behold. The victory was won, and won so easily that there had been no fight worthy the name. Her mind flew to Ruth, picturing the scene between them when she retold the conversation; then turned at a tangent to gloat over the thought of fineries to come.

"Ah-ah! That's a difficult question to answer. We shall need riding-habits, and summer things, and evening-dresses, and hosts of etceteras. I could make myself look respectable for twenty pounds; I could look smart for fifty; I could be a vision for a hundred!" cried Mollie, clasping her hands ecstatically, while once again a faint twinkle showed itself in Mr Farrell's eyes. His words were, however, as a rule, decidedly damping in tone.

"That is interesting to know, but something less bewildering than visions might be more in keeping with ordinary life. Very well, then, Miss Mary, order what you please, and tell your sister to do the same, and let the bills come in to me. You can run up to town for the day whenever it is necessary, and no doubt you will enjoy the variety. Is there anything more you wish to say?"

He took up the newspaper in sign of dismissal, but Mollie sat her ground, flushing and knitting her brows.

"Uncle Bernard, you are an angel, and I'm ever so much obliged, but please mightn't we have a fixed sum? It would be so much more comfortable! If it is left like this, we should not know what you would think reasonable or extravagant!"

"And in the other case, I should not know it of you! No; it must be left entirely to your discretion. Get what you please, and as much as you please. I make no restrictions. As I have said before, money is no object to me, but it is my great aim at present to understand your position as to it."

"I understand, but it's very awkward!" sighed Mollie. Her forehead was puckered with thought; she stroked her soft little chin in thoughtful fashion. "I should like to please you, but I am so completely in the dark. A man's ideas are so different from a girl's. If I get all I think necessary, you may think me extravagant!"

"Very possibly I may."

"And if I get less than the best, you might think me mean."

"Very possibly again."

Mollie made an involuntary gesture of impatience, then laughed and tossed her head.

"Uncle Bernard, it is hopeless to try to understand you. There is only one thing to be done; since I don't know how to please you, I must take extra good care to please myself."

"A most sensible conclusion! I congratulate you upon it. I have, however, one request to make. It is my wish that you and your sister should be independent of each other; each acting exactly as she thinks fit, without reference to the other's wishes. Is there anything more that you wish to say? If not, may I suggest that I am generally left free from interruption after lunch?"

"I'll never come again—I promise I won't, but there is a lot I should like to say if you would let me. I'd like to thank you and tell you how much fun and happiness we shall get out of your generosity; but, I suppose, if I did you would hate it, and call it gush. The best thing I can do is to go away at once; but you can't prevent me thanking you in my heart."

She looked at him half smiling, half wistful, longing for some sign of softening which might break down the barrier between them, but Mr Farrell did not even meet her glance. His eyes had already strayed towards his newspaper; he was settling himself in his chair and preparing to resume the interrupted reading. Mollie turned with a sigh and left the room.

Chapter Thirteen.

Learning to Ride.

The riding-lessons duly began the next day, and, continuing each morning of the week, proved a veritable godsend to the four young people, in providing amusement for hours which might otherwise have hung somewhat heavily on their hands. The season was yet too young for outdoor games, and in the early stages of their mutual acquaintanceship it was difficult to keep up a perpetual flow of conversation. Some occupation of general interest was thus badly needed, and this was supplied by the delightful canters over the moors—delightful, despite the drawbacks which were inseparable from inexperience.

On the first morning the girls were kept sternly in hand by the careful groom, each taken in turn for an amble along a quiet road under his own supervision; while the other strolled about, feeling very fine and large as she held up the skirt of her habit, and nonchalantly flicked her whip to and fro.

From the safe vantage of the ground also it was amusing to watch Jack Melland's plungings to and fro, and offer him good advice as to the management of his steed. Jack, needless to say, disdained the groom's good offices, and set forth confident of being able to master any horse by the sheer force of his manhood. His seat was not elegant, certainly, and for once he was at a distinct disadvantage beside Victor, who looked his best on horseback, and was evidently an experienced rider.

On the third day the horses were led to the broad road, crossing the well-treed park, and, after half an hour's patient trotting to and fro, Ruth was started on her first independent canter, which was fated to have an ignominious end; for the horse, impatient of restraint, increased its pace to a gallop, which swiftly left the groom behind and sent its rider's composure to the winds. Her foot slipped from the stirrup, she dropped her whip, clung wildly to the pommel, and, regardless of dignity, screamed for help at the pitch of her voice. It seemed an eternity of time, but in reality it was only a couple of minutes, before Victor overtook her, and leaning forward, seized the reins and brought both horses to a halt.

The groom came running up behind, followed by Jack, jogging painfully up and down on his saddle, while Mollie puffed and panted in the rear. Their faces were all keen with alarm, but fear changed to amusement at the sight of Ruth with hat cocked rakishly at one side and a thick coil of hair hanging snake-like down her back. She looked piteously for comfort, and, meeting only smiles, drew herself up with what was intended to be an air of haughty disdain; but it is difficult to look haughty when with every moment fresh hairpins are falling to the ground, and with the descent of fresh coils your hat is continually assuming a still more impudent angle.

"You *do* look a sight!" cried Mollie with sisterly candour, and Ruth beckoned imperiously to the groom to help her to dismount.

"Take me down! I've had enough of this for one morning. You must give me another horse to-morrow, Bates. I'll never trust myself on this hateful creature again. No, thank you, I prefer to walk on my own feet." She jumped to the ground and stood twisting up her hair, her cheeks aflame with mingled fright and annoyance—a sight, indeed, as Mollie had remarked, though the young men's translation of the term was not perhaps precisely the same as her own.

"I'll put in a thousand hairpins next time," she said angrily, as she fastened the coils to the best of her ability, and straightened the rakish hat. "You had better see that your hair is safe, Mollie, before you have your turn. I am going to sit down on the grass and jeer at you for a change. It's so easy to be superior when you are doing nothing yourself!"

"I shan't hang on to my pommel, anyway, and I won't call, 'Help, murder, thieves!' whatever happens," cried Mollie lightly. "I am going round this curve, so you can all watch and see how well I do it!"

She flicked her horse's side as she spoke with quite a professional air of unconcern, and started off at a brisk canter, holding herself resolutely erect, despite the ever-increasing pain in the small of her back. Echoes of "Bravo! bravo!" followed her down the path and goaded her to increased exertion. A second flip on Prince's back sent him forward at such a surprising increase of speed that, involuntarily, she gripped the pommel; then, remembering her resolve, let go her hold to hang on more and more tightly to the reins.

Prince tossed his head and gave an expostulatory amble. Mollie set her lips and pulled the stronger. She was not conscious that the right hand pulled more strongly than the left, but that it did so was proved by the fact that the horse gradually abandoned the path and directed its course across the grass. The watchers behind gave cries of warning as they saw what was happening, but in her agitation Mollie mistook their meaning for more applause and dashed headlong on her way.

She was so much occupied in keeping her seat that she had no eyes to discover danger ahead, but the groom looked with dismay at the low-spreading trees on right and left, and raced across the grass to intercept her progress. He was too late, however. Maddened by the incessant dragging of the reins Prince galloped ahead, skirting so closely a clump of trees that it was only by crouching low over the saddle that Mollie escaped accident. The watchers drew deep breaths of relief, but renewed their anxiety as once more horse and rider disappeared from sight behind a giant elm, whose branches hung threateningly towards the ground.

Ruth gripped her habit in both hands and sped across the grass after the groom; the two young men galloped ahead; and from one and all came a second cry of alarm, as a moment later Prince sounded his appearance careering wildly along riderless and free.

What were they going to see? A helpless form stretched on the ground; a white unconscious face; a terrible, tell-tale wound? A dozen horrible pictures suggested themselves one after the other in those breathless seconds; but when the fatal spot was reached there was no figure upon the ground, senseless or the reverse; no Mollie was seen to right or left.

It seemed as if the earth had opened and swallowed her up, until a feeble squeak made the rescuers lift their eyes suddenly to the heart of the tree, where a black skirt and two small kicking feet were seen swinging to and fro in the air. Another step forward showed the whole picture, gauntleted hands clutching wildly to a bough, and a pink agonised face turned over one shoulder, while a little pipe of a voice called out gaspingly—

"Catch me! hold me! take me down! oh, my arms! I'm falling, falling, I'm falling! oh, oh, oh—I'm falling down!" And fall she did, so suddenly and violently that the groom, although a stoutly built man, tottered beneath her weight.

The ordinary heroine of fiction is so frail and ethereal in build that when she faints away, under a stress of emotion, the hero gathers her lovely form in his arms and carries her for a couple of miles with delightful ease; but Mollie Farrell was a healthy, well-grown girl; and for one agonising moment it appeared as if the sequel to the adventure was to be an ignominious tumble to the ground of rescuer and rescued.

The moment passed, the groom steadied himself with an involuntary "Whoa!" and Mollie turned to confront her friends, swaying painfully to and fro, with crossed hands pressing against each shoulder.

"Oh, my arms! my arms! They are torn out of their sockets! I know they are! The pain is really hideous!"

"What happened? How did you manage to perform such an acrobatic feat?" cried Jack, now that anxiety was appeased, unable to resist a smile at the remembrance of the pretty, comical picture, and the undignified descent to the ground; but Mollie snapped him up sharply, her sense of humour absolutely eclipsed by the pain she was suffering.

"It wasn't a feat! I saw the bough before me and I thought I should be killed, and I put out my hands to save myself and—I don't know how it happened; but the next moment that horrid, wicked animal slipped from under me, and my arms were jerked nearly out of my body, and I was left dangling in mid-air. It's perfectly hateful of you all to stand there and laugh! I might have been killed outright if it hadn't been for Bates."

"You were only a yard or so from the ground; you could have dropped down yourself without making a fuss. I kept my seat at any rate, and I didn't howl half so loudly!" said Ruth self-righteously. "What made you do anything so mad as to ride in among all those trees?"

"I didn't! It was the horse; he would go, whatever I did," protested Mollie feebly: whereupon Bates shook his head with solemn disapproval.

"We've got to be very thankful as matters is no worse," said the alarmed groom. "I shall have a fine lecturing from the squire when he hears of this, but you will bear me witness as it was against my wishes. If I'd had my way you would never have ventured off by yourselves, for another week at least, but there was no gainsaying you. I'm thinking you'll have had about enough lesson for to-day, and I must look after those horses. To-morrow—"

"To-morrow we'll be good and docile, and do as you tell us. My nerves are too shaken to be disobedient; but don't be afraid; you shan't be scolded for what isn't your fault," said Ruth with her pretty smile. Bates touched his cap and walked off, mollified, while the girls turned sadly homeward. Jack and Victor offered their escort, but, finding it impossible to disguise all traces of amusement, were promptly snubbed and bidden to go and be superior by themselves.

"I do hate men! horrid, patronising creatures!" cried Mollie pettishly, as she limped onwards. "They think themselves so grand because they are stronger than we are, and have no tiresome skirts to hamper them. I don't like riding half as much as I expected. I'm so stiff and sore, I should like to go to bed for a month. I shall lie down this afternoon. I'll get a nice book, and pull the sofa up to the window, and have tea brought up to me; and I just hope it will rain and pour, and they will have nothing to do and be bored to death, and then they will miss me, and be sorry that they were so rude. Laughing, indeed, when I was in danger of my life, before their very eyes!"

"You were safe enough before they laughed, and you did look funny hanging in mid-air! You didn't think it was cruel to laugh at me, and I was just as much frightened as you were!" retorted Ruth; and thereafter a frigid silence was maintained until the Court was reached.

At lunch Mr Farrell appeared with a clouded brow, and vouchsafed only monosyllabic replies when addressed. It was evident that something had displeased him, and, though no reference was made to the adventures of the morning, the young people had discovered by now that he possessed a mysterious power of knowing all about their actions, in sight or out of sight, and felt correspondingly ill at ease. When the meal was over and the servants had left the room, the storm burst suddenly. The sunken eyes gleamed with an angry light, and the tired voice sounded unusually loud and threatening.

"Has neither of you two young men the sense or the prudence to prevent a lady from running a foolish risk? I am informed that Ruth was in danger of having a serious accident this morning. I am not personally able to look after her safety, and she was possibly ignorant of her own folly in attempting more than she could accomplish; but I had imagined that in my absence she had two sufficient protectors—one of whom, at least, I understand to be an accomplished horseman."

Victor flushed deeply, and the lids fell over his tell-tale eyes.

"No one regrets Miss Ruth's fright more than I do, sir. She had been such an apt pupil that I did not imagine that there was any danger in trying a little canter on her own account. Bates disapproved of it, but I am afraid I sided against him. I can only promise to be more careful in future."

"It was no one's fault but my own, Uncle Bernard," interrupted Ruth eagerly. "I was conceited and thought I could do anything I liked, and I have learnt a lesson—that's all! I was frightened, but I hung on so tightly to the pommel that I don't think there was any real danger of falling. I really will be careful not to run any more risks."

"I trust you will. I feel responsible for your safety while you are under my roof, and it will be a severe strain on my nerves if I cannot rely on your discretion. Are you feeling any ill effects from your fright? Can Mrs Wolff help you in any way, or perhaps the doctor—"

Ruth gave an involuntary exclamation of surprise and protest, and the colour rushed into her cheeks. It was so surprising, so extraordinary that Uncle Bernard should betray such concern for her safety and actually suggest sending for a doctor on her behalf. Her heart beat high with the conviction that she was, indeed, his favourite, his Chosen, and that therefore her safety was all-important for the success of his scheme.

She turned her grey eyes upon him with a liquid glance of gratitude, as she faltered out words of acknowledgment.

"Oh no, indeed, it is quite unnecessary! Thank you so much all the same. I am vexed with myself for having upset you by being so headstrong, and didn't hurt myself a bit."

"That is well, then!" Mr Farrell rose from the table and turned slowly towards the door. As he did so he found himself suddenly confronted by another face—a bright-eyed, mutinous girl's face, so transparently charged with speech that he stopped short, uttering an involuntary inquiry—

"Well! what is it? What have *you* got to say?"

Mollie's lips parted, her head tilted to the side.

"*I* was in danger, too! much more than she was. I *did* tumble off! I hung on to the branch of a tree. I might have been injured most dreadfully."

"Ah–ah!" said Mr Farrell slowly. He turned his head aside, and his lips twitched uncertainly. "You! But you, my dear Mary, can take such uncommonly good care of yourself!"

Chapter Fourteen.

Mollie Defends her Uncle.

Mr Farrell walked to the door, and shut it behind him. Everyone stood still, staring at Mollie, and Mollie stared ruefully back.

"Oh!" she cried breathlessly, "oh!" and pressed both palms to her now scorching cheeks. "I've never been snubbed like that in all my life." Then suddenly she laughed a bright, sweet-hearted laugh, utterly free from envy. "I'm nowhere, Ruth, when you are concerned; but there's one comfort, I can do as I like, and no one will interfere! If it is to be a choice between the two, I prefer freedom to riches."

She left the room to make her way upstairs, and Jack crossed the hall by her side. He looked intently at her as he walked, and when their eyes met he said simply—

"You took that well—very well indeed! I congratulate you on your self-control. I could not have kept my temper as you did."

"Oh, I don't know!" returned Mollie easily. "I brought it on my own head. It was stupid to speak of myself at all; but just for the moment I couldn't help feeling aggrieved, because, really and truly, I was in greater danger than she. Uncle Bernard is old, poor thing, and that makes him querulous."

"It ought not to. I call that a very poor excuse. When a man gets to his age he ought surely to have learnt to be patient, even if he imagines himself provoked."

"But he is ill as well. You say nothing about that. Should that make him patient too?"

"Certainly it should. Suffering has often a most ennobling effect."

Mollie stood on the first step of the staircase, her arm on the banister, looking with a challenging smile into the proud self-confident face on a level with her own.

"Have you ever been ill, Mr Melland?"

"I am thankful to say I have not."

"But you have surely had a pain, or an ache, for a few hours at a time? Ear-ache, when you were a child, or toothache later on?"

"Oh, certainly! I've had my share of toothache, and the smaller ailments."

"And when the spasms were on,—were *you* gentle and patient? Did you feel your character being ennobled, or did you rage and champ about like a mad bull?"

Jack laughed. It was impossible to resist it, at the sight of the mischievous face, and the sound of the exaggerated, school-girl simile.

"Well," he conceded magnanimously, "perhaps the champing was the more in evidence. I was not citing myself as a model, Miss Mollie. I know quite well that—that I might be more patient than I am."

"More patient! More! You are not patient at all. You are the most impatient person I ever met. If anyone dares even to have a different opinion from you, you can hardly contain yourself. I wish you could see your face! You look like this."

Mollie drew herself up, making a valiant attempt to draw her eyebrows together, send out lightning sparks from her eyes, inflate her nostrils, and tug the ends of an imaginary moustache at one and the same time; and succeeded in looking at once so pretty and so comical that, instead of being convicted, Jack laughed more heartily than before.

"As bad as that? Really? I must be ferocious! It's rather unkind of you to pitch into me like this, Miss Mollie, when I have just been paying you compliments. It's a good thing I am going away so soon, as I am such a desperate character. There is no saying to what lengths Mr Farrell and I might get if we were long together."

"Oh!" Mollie's face sobered, and a little chill came over her spirits. "You are still determined, then? Nothing has happened to make you change your mind?"

"What should have happened?" replied Jack the ungallant. "There has been nothing behind the scenes, Miss Mollie—nothing that you do not know of. Only I prefer to go back to my work—that's all. I consented to remain for a week to please Mr Farrell, but I don't see that I am called upon to make any further sacrifice. I have my life's work before me, and just now it needs all the attention I can give it. Besides, Mr Farrell and I would never get on; I should be a disturbing element which would not improve matters for any of you. Between ourselves, I think there is little doubt who will be the Chosen, as you express it. Your sister is evidently first in favour. Witness your experience a few minutes ago."

Mollie stared before her, thoughtful and absent-minded. One word in Jack's speech had detached itself from the rest and printed itself on her brain. Sacrifice! He had stayed at the Court for a week as a matter of necessity, and did not feel called upon to sacrifice his inclinations any further. Sacrifice, indeed! The word rankled the more as she realised how differently she herself had described the past five days, and how high Jack Melland's presence had ranked among the pleasures of the new life. When she projected her thoughts into the future, and imagined living through the same scenes without his companionship, it was extraordinary how flat and dull they suddenly became. But he called it a "sacrifice" to stay away from a dingy, dreary office, and preferred the society of his partner to all the Mollie Farrells in the world! He liked her, of course—she could not pretend to doubt that; but just as a grown man might care for an amusing child who served to while away an idle hour, but who was not worth the trouble of a serious thought.

"He thinks I am shallow," thought Mollie sorrowfully, and then suddenly inverted the sentence. "Am I shallow?" she asked herself, with an uneasy doubt creeping over her self-complacency. "I expect I am, for I am content with the surface of things, and like to laugh better than to think. But I'm twenty; I don't want to be treated as a child all my life. It's horrid of him to talk of sacrifices!"

Thoughts fly quickly, but, even so, the pause was long enough to be unusual. Jack looked inquiringly at the thoughtful face, and said smilingly—

"Why, Miss Mollie, you look quite sober! I never saw you so serious before. Is that because I said that your sister was preferred before you?"

That aroused Mollie to a flash of indignation.

"No, indeed; I am not so mean. I'd almost sooner Ruth had things than myself, for I'd have all the fun and none of the trouble. Besides, she wants it more than I do, and would be a hundred times more disappointed to do without. And then you must not blame Uncle Bernard too much. He had a good reason for saying what he did. I deserved it.—You will never guess what I did."

Jack looked amused and curious.

"Nothing very dreadful, I feel sure. You are too hard on yourself, Miss Mollie."

"I asked him for heaps of money to buy heaps of new clothes—"

Jack's whistle of amazement was too involuntary to be controlled. He tried his best to retrieve himself by an expression of unconcern, but the pretence was so apparent that Mollie laughed at the sight, albeit a trifle ruefully.

"Do you mean to tell me seriously that you asked Mr Farrell for money?"

"Yes, I did. I asked him on Wednesday. It seemed the only thing to do, as he wants us to entertain his friends, and go out whenever we are asked, and we hadn't enough clothes to go in. Ruth wouldn't ask, so I had to do it. We have no evening-dresses in the world except those black things that you see every night, and we can't live in them for three months like a man in his dress suit."

"They are very pretty dresses. I am sure you always look charming."

"Oh, don't feel bound to be flattering, I hate obvious compliments!" cried Mollie irritably. She was surprised to realise how irritable she felt. "I only told you because it was mean to let poor Uncle Bernard get the blame." She paused, and over her face flashed one of those sudden radiant changes of expression which were so fascinating to behold. Her eyes shone, her lips curled, a dimple dipped in her cheek. "But he *did* give it to me—he gave me more than I asked—carte blanche, to spend as much as I liked! Next Tuesday morning as ever is, we are going up to town to shop with Mrs Thornton as assistant. Think of it! Think of it! Oxford Street, Regent Street, Bond Street—just to look in at all the windows in turn, and buy what one likes best. Hats,"—two eager hands went up to her head - "dresses"—they waved descriptively in the air—"coats; fripperies of all descriptions, delicious blouses for every occasion, and evening-dresses!—oh, chiffon and lace and sequins, and everything that is fascinating! I've never had anything but the most useful and long-suffering garments, though I have yearned to be fluffy, and now I shall be as fluffy as I can be made! Think of me, all in tulle and silver gauze, with a train yards long, all lined with frills and *frills* of chiffon!" cried Mollie ecstatically, tilting her head over her shoulder, and pushing out her short skirt with a little slippered foot as if it were already the train of which she spoke.

"Indeed, I will think of you! I wish I could do more than think; I should like to see you into the bargain. It is hard lines that I have to leave before the exhibition opens."

"Oh, pray don't pose as an object of pity! Whose fault is it that you are leaving at all?" retorted Mollie quickly. "You have made up your mind to go, and it's a matter of pride with you that nothing or nobody shall prevent you. My poor fineries would be a very weak inducement; but you will have to reckon with Uncle Bernard before you get away, and I don't think he will be easy to oppose."

Jack Melland straightened himself, and his nostrils dilated in characteristic, high-spirited fashion.

"When I make up my mind I never give way," he said slowly.

Mollie tossed her head defiantly.

"So you say; but there is something even stronger than will, Mr Melland."

"And that is—"

"Fate!" cried Mollie dramatically.

The blue eyes and the brown met in a flashing glance; then the girl dropped a demure curtsey, and ran lightly upstairs.

Chapter Fifteen.

In the Village Church.

The shopping expedition was, by common consent, postponed until the middle of the following week, when Jack Melland would have taken his departure.

"Let us make hay while the sun shines. Three is an abominable number, especially when you happen to be the third," said Mollie, sighing. "Mr Druce admires you very much, Ruth. I often see him staring at you when you are not looking; but when I appear upon the scene his eyelids droop, and he does not deign even to glance in my direction. He puzzles me a good deal, as a rule. I rather fancy myself as a judge of character, but I can't decide whether he is really a model of virtue, or a villain in disguise."

Ruth made a movement of impatience.

"How exaggerated you are, Mollie! Why must you rush off to extremes in that foolish fashion? Mr Druce is probably neither one nor the other, but just an ordinary combination of faults and virtues. He is kind and considerate to Uncle Bernard, and very chivalrous to us;—a hundred times more so than Jack Melland, who certainly does not err on the side of politeness. Personally, I don't think any the less highly of people because they are little reserved and uncommunicative at first. It will be time enough to judge Mr Druce's character when we have known him for weeks, instead of days."

"Humph! I believe in first impressions," insisted Mollie obstinately; "and so do you, really, or you would not bristle up when I dare to cast a doubt on his excellence. You are going to like him, Ruth, I can see that quite clearly, and he admires you; so, as I said before, I shall be the poor little pig who stays at home, while you two wander abroad together. It's not exactly the programme which my fancy painted when we came down; but if I devote myself to Uncle Bernard, and cut you both out, I shall have the best of it, after all.

Perhaps, too I may make friends with someone in the neighbourhood,—there is always the chance of that, and I do love meeting new people. I suppose callers will begin to arrive after we have made our first public appearance at church to-morrow. I am quite excited at the prospect of seeing all the people—aren't you?"

"I am not going," said Ruth.

And when Mollie exclaimed and cross-questioned, she flushed uncomfortably, but did not refuse to answer.

"I have made up my mind to go to early service, but not again at eleven o'clock. It's not that I don't want to go; it's because I want to go so much—for the wrong reasons! Ever so many times during the last few days I have caught myself thinking about it, and imagining the scene—everybody staring at us, while we sit in the squire's pew trying to look unconscious, but really enjoying it all the time, and building castles in the air about the future, when we may have a right to be there. We should be thinking most of all of ourselves, and that's not a right spirit in which to go to church; so I'm not going. I'm disappointed, but I've made up my mind."

Mollie leant her head on her hand and gazed thoughtfully before her. The sisters were seated in the great round window of their bedroom, from which such a glorious view of the surrounding country could be obtained; and as Mollie's eyes wandered from the blue of the sky to the fresh green of the trees, and anon to the patches of golden daffodils among the grass, a wonderful sweetness softened her young face.

"But God understands!" she said gently. "He made girls, so He must know how they feel. This is a great occasion for us, and it is natural that we should be excited and a little bit self-engrossed. Mother would think it natural, and make excuses for us, even if we were carried away by our new importance; and God is kinder and more forgiving than mother. Perhaps, when one is quite old and staid, it is easy to sit through a service and never think of self; but it is difficult when one is young. I used to be miserable because every time I had a new hat or dress, or anything that was fresh, I couldn't help remembering it and being pleased that I looked so nice, and hoping that other people liked it too but when I thought it over I came to the conclusion that it was only natural. Look at that lovely view!" She waved her hand expressively from right to left. "When God made the world so beautiful and so full of colour, He must mean us to love pretty things without being ashamed of it; so now I just thank Him for the new things in my prayers, and remember them as some of the things to be thankful for. I'm sure it's the best way. It's cowardice to stay at home because we are afraid of a temptation. Surely it would be far better to go, to thank God for giving us this good time, and to ask Him to send us nice friends, and, if it be His will, to let Uncle Bernard leave us the Court, so that we may help them all at home!"

She broke off, looking round half timidly in Ruth's face, for it was reversing the usual rôles to find herself laying down the law as to right and wrong to the serious-minded elder sister. Would Ruth be annoyed—shocked—disapproving? It appeared that she was not, for the troubled lines had gradually smoothed away from her forehead, and she cried heartily—

"Yes, you are right. I feel you are! Thank you for putting it so plainly, dear. I *did* want to go to church, and now my conscience will be clear, so I can go comfortably, feeling it is the right thing. But oh, Mollie, shall we all four be praying, one against the other, each one wanting to disappoint the others, and keep the Court for himself?"

"Jack Melland won't, for one; and I won't for another. I'm not sure that I want it and all the responsibility that goes in its train. I'd honestly rather it were yours, dear; then I could come and sponge upon you as often as I liked."

"Sponge!" echoed Ruth reproachfully. "As if it would be any pleasure to me if you were not here! What would become of poor Berengaria without her Lucille? We are so grand in real life now that we forget the dear old game; but, when we are back in Attica, we shall be able to play it better than ever, now that we really know what it feels like to be rich and have everything one wants!"

Mollie did not answer, and both girls sat silently gazing before them, while their thoughts wandered northwards to a shabby, crowded house, and to a sloping-roofed attic under the leads, in which so many hours had been spent. Mollie smiled, remembering the little make-shifts and contrivances, seeing the humour of them, and feeling again the glow of triumph with which each difficulty had been surmounted.

Ruth shuddered with a mingling of fear and repulsion.

Oh, how bare it was—how poor, and small, and unlovely! the few small rooms, the shabby furniture, the little plot of grass in front of the door which did duty as a garden. Could it be possible that in a few short months she might have to return and take up life once more under the old conditions? The thought of Dr Maclure's handsome house had been a distinct temptation to her when he had asked her to be his wife; then how much more the beautiful old Court?

"I would do anything to get it!" thought poor Ruth desperately. "Oh, if I could only find out what Uncle Bernard wants! It is terrible to be in the dark like this!"

The next day was Sunday, and the ordeal of church-going proved to be much less trying than had been expected, for the congregation was mainly composed of villagers, who looked too stolid and sleepy to trouble themselves about the appearance of strangers, even when seated in the squire's pew. The pew, moreover, was situated in the front of the chancel, so that it was all the easier to pay whole-hearted attention to the service. Coming out through the churchyard, the girls were conscious of glances of interest directed towards themselves by various little parties who plainly composed the gentlefolk of the neighbourhood.

At the gate one or two carriages were waiting in readiness to convey their owners home, the best appointed of which was presently occupied by an old lady and gentleman, whom Ruth recognised from Mrs Thornton's description as being the couple whom the renowned Lady Margot Blount was about to visit. She said as much to Mollie, when the carriage had passed by, and the four young people were strolling together in easy country fashion along the road.

"Did you notice, Mollie? Those must be Mr and Mrs Blount, who live at the Moat. I should know them anywhere from Mrs Thornton's description. I wonder whether they will call, and if Lady Margot Blount will come with them? She was expected this week, I think."

She was interrupted by a sharp exclamation, and turned with her two companions to stare in amazement into Victor Druce's transformed face. For once amazement had broken down the veil which gave a tinge of mystery to his personality; his sallow cheeks showed a streak of colour, and his eyes were wide open and eager.

"Lady—Margot—Blount!" he repeated incredulously. "Here, in this village! You say she is expected to meet those people who have just driven past? Is it possible? Who told you about her?"

Ruth stared at him, amazed in her turn by his energy of manner.

"Mrs Thornton told us so, the night she dined at the Court. We asked her what girls were in the neighbourhood, and among the number she spoke of Lady Margot as a constant visitor to her uncle and aunt. Why are you so surprised? Do you know her in town? Is she a friend of yours?"

Victor hesitated, biting the ends of his moustache.

"I can hardly call her a friend. We are not in the same set; but I saw a good deal of her last autumn. Some people I know were getting up tableaux for a charity bazaar, and asked us both to take part. There were a good many rehearsals, so that we grew for the time pretty intimate; but she went off to Egypt for the winter, and I have heard nothing of her since the night of the performance."

"But have thought a good deal all the same!" said Mollie shrewdly to herself, looking at the dark face, which looked so handsome in its unaccustomed animation.

If Victor Druce often looked like that, he would be a fascinating companion. To have the power so to influence him and excite his interest would be perilously attractive. A few hours before, Mollie had been almost prepared to declare that she distrusted and disliked this new acquaintance; now she was conscious of a distinct feeling of envy towards the unknown Margot.

"How interesting that you have met already! Mrs Thornton was so enthusiastic in her praise, that she roused our curiosity to fever-pitch. Do tell us what she is like! We are longing to know."

But Victor did not appear inclined to be communicative. The heavy lids fell over his eyes, and he murmured a few non-committal sentences. It was difficult to describe a girl so as to give any real idea of her appearance. He was not skilled at word-painting. If Lady Margot was so soon expected, would it not be better to wait and judge for themselves? Mollie shrugged her shoulders impatiently, and forthwith began her catechism.

"Tailor short?"

"Er—medium; not small, not too tall."

"The perfect mean? I understand! Dark or fair?"

"Dark eyes, chestnut hair."

"Oh, that's not right. She has no right to monopolise the beauties of both complexions. And chestnut hair, too, the prettiest shade of all! Is she a real, true beauty, or only just pretty, like ordinary folk?"

"That must be a matter of personal opinion, mustn't it, Miss Mollie? Ideas vary so much on these subjects."

"Checkmate!" sighed Mollie to herself. "He won't say what he thinks, and I can't be so rude as to ask directly, though it's just what I'm dying to know." Aloud, she said carelessly, "Oh, I've no doubt I shall think her lovely, and adore her as I do all lovely people; that is, if she doesn't scare me too much. Is she formidable and *grande dame*, or lively and easy-going?"

"That again must surely depend upon circumstances," replied Victor sententiously, whereat Mollie tossed her head, declaring that he was as aggravating as Uncle Bernard himself, and almost as enigmatical.

As for Ruth, she walked along with compressed lips and frowning brows. It was not possible for a girl to find herself thrown into close companionship with two young men, and not wonder in the recesses of her heart if perchance friendship might not eventually develop into something warmer. Ruth and Mollie had both thought and dreamed, and to each it had occurred that possibly some such ending of the great problem might have occurred to Mr Farrell himself. There was no barrier of near relationship to prevent two of the young people making a match, if they were so disposed; and while Uncle Bernard, so far, seemed to favour his elder niece, he had expressly stated that he would prefer a male heir. Ruth's favour was not easily won, but as both young men appeared agreeable, gentlemanly, and good-looking, it had been a distinctly pleasant experience to look forward and wonder if he,—if I,—if perhaps some day, long ahead, when we know each other well... All girls have such dreams, and understand how their existence adds savour to a situation. It was not a little trying, then, when Jack Melland insisted on returning to town, and Victor Druce, in his turn, must needs betray an undoubted interest in another girl.

"Tiresome thing!" murmured Ruth to herself; referring, needless to say, not to Victor, but to the innocent Margot herself. "I knew I should dislike her from the moment when Mrs Thornton mentioned her name. Why couldn't she be happy in town, with all her grand friends, instead of rushing down here to interfere with us the moment we arrive? She is sure to hear the reason why we are here—everyone knows it; and if she is mercenary she will like Victor better now that he has a chance of inheriting the Court, and, when he knows her connection with the neighbourhood, she will seem to him more desirable than ever. Uncle Bernard would be pleased, and think her a suitable mistress for the Court, and they will get everything, and we'll get nothing, and go home as failures... Mother will be disappointed, and everything will be duller and pokier than ever..."

So on and so on, conjuring up one gloomy vision after another, as was her unhappy custom, until at length she saw herself stricken in years, broken in health, lonely and unloved, with nothing in prospect but a pauper's grave. A strange ending, indeed, to that first public appearance from which so much had been expected!

Chapter Sixteen.

Kismet.

When Sunday evening arrived Jack Melland was surprised to feel a distinct strain of regret in realising that it was the last evening he should spend at the Court. He was still not only determined but eager to return to his work at the beginning of the week, and had counted the hours until his release should arrive; but, as the days passed by, he had become increasingly alive, not only to the beauty of his surroundings but to the unusual charm of feminine society. After a lonely life in London lodgings, it was an agreeable experience to come downstairs to a perfectly appointed meal, set against a background of tapestry and oak, to be greeted by bright girlish faces, and kept amused and interested from morning till night.

Mollie was a fascinating little creature—witty, audacious, and sweet—hearted, though, as yet, too much of a school-girl to be taken seriously. As for Ruth, she was a beauty, and might become dangerous to a man's peace of mind on a longer acquaintance. That was an additional reason why Jack was set on leaving the Court, for, as she was obviously first favourite, it would be a distinct stroke of diplomacy for a man to link his chances with hers. Jack's nostrils inflated in characteristic manner as he told himself, that this would not be his fashion of going a-wooing, but he was less scrupulous in prophesying for his neighbour. "Druce will make love to her! she'll marry Druce!" he told himself confidently; and his thoughts flew ahead to the time when the young couple would reign over the Court, and dispense the favours which were now in Bernard Farrell's hands.

Well, it was a goodly heritage! Even in seven short days several scenes had printed themselves upon his memory. The drive across the park, with the great north front of the house lying grey and chill in the distance; the south terrace flooded with sunshine; the gardens sloping to the level of the lake; and beyond them the open stretch of country. And in all probability Druce was to be the master of it all.

He seemed a good enough fellow, but was he worthy of the position, and of the wife who would go with it? Would he make her happy?—the sweet, beautiful thing! Happiness did not come easily to her as it did to her sister. If her husband neglected her, or fell short of her ideal, the wistful expression, which was one of her charms, would soon develop into a settled melancholy. Jack conjured up a vision of Ruth's face—emaciated and woebegone—and felt a pang of regret, allied with something curiously like remorse. It seemed as if by going away he were deliberately leaving her to Druce's tender mercies, so certain did he feel as to the result of the three months' companionship. For the first time a rankling doubt of the wisdom of his decision disturbed his complacency. When he was back in his dingy lodgings would he think longingly of the Court, and reproach himself for having thrown aside the chance of a lifetime; and if the business failed, despite all his efforts, and he found himself thrown adrift on the world, how should he feel then, remembering what might have been?

These reflections brought a frown to Jack's brow, but he was too proud to show any sign of wavering to his companions; and in the old man's presence was careful to make no allusion to the coming departure. On Monday morning the subject was to be officially discussed; but, until the prescribed hour arrived, it would have been a brave man or woman who dared open it in Mr Farrell's presence.

As for Mr Farrell himself, so far from looking forward to the interview with foreboding, he seemed in an unusually amiable frame of mind as he took the head of the table on Sunday evening, actually deigning to question his guests as to the day's doings, and the impressions which they had received. In their replies the young men were, as usual, brief and practical, Ruth tactfully reserved, and Mollie unflatteringly honest. But to-night Mr Farrell seemed determined to take no offence, and even vouchsafed a grim smile at the sound of the quaintly vigorous language.

"You will have to curb that rebellious tongue of yours, my dear Mary, if you are to get through the next few weeks without trouble. The good people about here are not accustomed to such picturesque exaggerations, and will take everything you say as literal fact, so you had better beware. You will probably have a number of visitors this week, so it would be as well to arrange to be at home as much as possible in the afternoons. Calling is a more serious business in the country than in town; and when people have taken the trouble to drive eight or nine miles, it is a disappointment to find nobody at home." He turned towards Jack, and continued: "Of course, this restriction does not apply to you, or to Druce. Your presence will not be expected; and if you agree with me, the further afield you can be, the better you will be pleased. There are some charming excursions which you could manage in an afternoon's ride, and, from what I hear, your horsemanship has improved so rapidly that you could easily manage them. Bates will be happy to give you any directions you may require; or, still better, to accompany you as guide."

These remarks were so markedly addressed to Jack, that no one but himself could venture to reply, and his self-will was so much ruffled by the deliberate ignoring of his expressed determination that he was instantly aflame with wrath. His nostrils curved, his brows arched, his lips opened to pronounce a sharp disclaimer, when suddenly he caught sight of Mollie's face gazing at him across the table; and if ever a face cried "Don't!" with all the eloquence of pleading eyes and parted lips, Mollie's said it at that moment. The message was so unmistakable and ardent that it demanded obedience, and to his own surprise Jack found himself murmuring conventional words of thanks, instead of the heated disclaimer which he had intended.

Later on in the evening he followed Mollie into a corner of the drawing-room to demand a reason for her unspoken interference.

"It was not honest to seem to agree when I have no intention of being here for a single afternoon. Why wouldn't you let me speak?" he demanded; whereupon Mollie pursed her lips, and said thoughtfully—

"I hardly know. You were going to be cross, and it is Sunday—our first Sunday here. I didn't want it to be spoilt by angry words. If you must disappoint the old man, do it gently. Don't answer back, even if he is annoying. You will be glad afterwards—when he is dead, and you have nothing to regret."

Jack looked down at her in silence. Was this the pert school-girl, whom he had just deemed unworthy of serious consideration? The face into which he looked seemed of a sudden that of a woman rather than that of a child—soft and sweet, grave-eyed, with lovely, serious lips. The very voice was altered, and had an added richness of tone. It was like catching a glimpse into the future, and beholding the woman that was to be, when girlhood's bright span was over. Instinctively Jack's manner altered to meet the change. The supercilious curve left his lip, his keen eyes softened.

"Thank you, Miss Mollie," he said gravely. "You are quite right. I'll remember!"

She thanked him with a luminous glance, and turned away; but he wanted to see her again, to hear her speak once more in that beautiful new voice. Before she had taken three steps he called to her eagerly—

"Miss Mollie! One moment! I expect I shall be packed off, bag and baggage, as soon as I have announced my decision; but Mr Farrell does not make his appearance until lunch-time, so we have a whole morning left still. Will you come for a last ride with me after breakfast?"

"Yes," said Mollie simply.

Her heart beat high with pleasure, because Jack had assented so readily to her request, because he had wished to spend his last hours in her society. For the moment she forgot the blank which would follow his departure, and was wholly, unreservedly happy. It was the old, sparkling, girlish face which was turned upon him—the vision had disappeared.

The next day neither Ruth nor Victor offered to join the riding-party, though they had not any settled plans for the forenoon. Mollie had told her sister of Jack's invitation of the evening before, and Ruth was too proud to make a third unless she were specially asked to do so. She strolled into the grounds to interview the gardener about sending in an extra supply of plants and flowers to beautify the house for the expected callers, while Victor shut himself in the library to write letters.

Jack looked well on horseback, as tall, upright men always do, and Mollie glanced at him admiringly, and thought regretfully of her new habit, which was even now in the tailor's hands. It did seem hard that she should have to wear a shabby, ill-fitting coat while he was here, and that the new one should come home almost as soon as he had departed. Her sigh of self-commiseration brought his eyes upon her, and he sighed in echo as he cried—

"Last times are melancholy occasions! I hate them, even when the experience has not been altogether pleasant. There is a sadness about turning over the leaf and ending another chapter of life. This chapter has been a very short one, but uncommonly jolly. Don't think that I haven't appreciated it, because I am going away. I have enjoyed every hour of this week, and when I am back on the treadmill I shall think longingly of you all many times over. I hope we may often meet again."

"It is not very likely, is it? You will go your way, and we will go ours. Ruth and I have never been in London, nor you in Liverpool. We may all live until we are old and bald, and never meet again," said Mollie dismally; whereupon Jack looked at the shining plaits which were coiled at the back of her head, and laughed reassuringly.

"I can't imagine you bald, nor old either, and I expect to see you many times over before you have the chance of changing. The Chosen, whoever he or she may be, must surely have the good manners to invite the rest of us to visit a house which might have been our own; and I have a special claim, for by retiring from the lists I increase your chances. Personally, I have made up my mind to spend many holidays here—shooting and riding, and enjoying myself generally. I hope you won't object, if you happen to be the chatelaine?"

"Ah, but I shan't! I have no chance against the other two; but I also intend to spend my holidays here, and I tell Ruth she must send home hampers every week. It has always been my ambition to get hampers, and she could send such splendid ones from the Court—game and poultry and eggs, and nice out-of-season fruits and vegetables, which would be such a help in the housekeeping! I am afraid sometimes that we count too much on Uncle Bernard's fancy for Ruth's eyebrows, for if he changed his mind and left everything to Mr Druce, it would be a terrible disappointment. And there are three months before us still. He may change a dozen times yet."

"I think most probably he will. Better stick to your resolution, to have a good time, and not bother your head about the future. I shall be most anxious to know how things go. Druce has promised to send me a line now and then. Will you jog his memory in case he forgets?"

Mollie promised, all the more readily that Victor's letter would naturally bring a return, which would serve to bridge over the separation. It seems curious to remember that little over a week ago she had not known of Jack Melland's existence. He had made but a brief appearance upon the scene, but it would not be easy to forget him, or to fill the vacant place.

Both riders relapsed into silence as they neared home; but, as they clattered into the stable-yard, Jack turned towards Mollie with rather a forced air of triumph, and cried—

"Do you remember your warning, Miss Mollie, that Fate was stronger than will? Ever since we set out this morning the words have been ringing in my ears, and I have been expecting some accident to happen which would keep me here in spite of myself. I have looked for it at every turn of the road as if it were bound to come."

Mollie shivered nervously.

"Oh, how horrid! I am glad you did not tell me. I should have been nervous, too, for I am superstitious about presentiments. They so often come true."

"Well, this one at least has not. Here we are safe and sound, and all risk is over!" cried Jack, dropping his reins, and jumping lightly from the saddle without waiting for the groom to come to the horse's head.

He was anxious to assist Mollie to dismount before Bates came up; but even as his feet touched the ground he slipped, staggered uncertainly for a moment, and sank to the ground with a groan of pain. The groom rushed forward; Mollie leapt inelegantly but safely to the ground, and bent over him with anxious questioning. His face was drawn with pain, and he bent forward to grip his foot with both hands.

"My—ankle! I slipped on something, or came down on the side of my foot. I don't know how it was done; but I've given it a bad wrench, if nothing worse. You'll have to cart me up to the house, Bates. I'm afraid it's hopeless to try to walk."

"No, indeed, sir! Don't you trouble. I've got an old bath-chair stored away in the stables. We'll lift you into that in no time, and take you up as easy as possible."

He turned off as he spoke, and Jack and Mollie were left alone. For a moment she stood silently by his side; then their eyes met, and he said wearily—

"Kismet! Fate is too much for me. For better or worse, Miss Mollie, it is evidently ordained that I must stay on at the Court!"

Chapter Seventeen.

New Experiences.

The village doctor came to doctor Jack Melland's damaged ankle, and the patient fumed and fretted beneath his old-fashioned treatment.

"Bandaging me and laying me up by the heels for weeks at a time; it's folly!" he declared angrily. "The man is twenty years behind the times. If I were in town I should have had one of those Swedish fellows to massage it, and be about in half the time. Just my luck to go in for an accident in a place where one can't get proper attention!"

"But you groan if anyone comes near your foot; wouldn't it hurt dreadfully much to have it massaged?" Mollie asked.

Whereupon the invalid growled impatiently—

"Hurt? Of course it would hurt! What has that to do with it, pray?"

"Lots," returned Mollie, unabashed. "I should think so, at least, if it were my ankle. I can't endure pain."

"I'm not a girl," growled Jack the ungracious, between his teeth.

There was no denying the fact that he did not make an agreeable invalid. In the first realisation of his accident he had meekly bowed his head to Fate; but ever since he had, figuratively speaking, kicked against the pricks, and repaid the kindness of his companions by incessant grumblings and complaints. He hated having to give up his own way; he hated being tied to a sofa and a bath-chair; he resented offers of help as if they had been actual insults, and hindered his recovery by foolhardy attempts at independence.

"How would you like to be an invalid for life?" Mollie asked him severely after one of these outbursts. "There was a young man in mother's district, every bit as strong and big as you, and a sack of something fell on his back while they were trying to haul it up into a warehouse. He was taken to the hospital, and they told him that he would never walk again, never even sit up again. As long as he lived he would be a helpless cripple. And he was just going to be married, too!"

"Well, I'm not, thank goodness!" cried Jack bluntly. "Why do you tell me such gruesome stories? My own troubles are quite enough just now. I don't want to hear any more horrors."

"It was just to distract your mind from yourself that I did tell you. Once upon a time I met a man who read me a beautiful lecture upon the dangers of being selfish and self-engrossed. I'll tell you his very words, if you like. They made a deep impression upon me at the time," said Mollie naughtily. But instead of being amused, Jack was only irritated afresh.

In these first days of invalidism Mollie's influence was the reverse of soothing, for Jack was not in the mood to be teased, and if his inner determination could have been put into words it would have been that he objected to be cheered up, refused to be cheered up, and insisted upon posing as a martyr; therefore, it followed that Ruth's gentle ministrations were more acceptable than her sister's vigorous sallies. If he could have seen again the Mollie of whom he had caught a glimpse on Sunday evening, Jack would have chosen her before any other companion; but, as she had made place for a mischievous tease, he preferred to look into Ruth's lovely anxious eyes, and to dilate at length upon his symptoms to her sympathetic ear.

Mr Farrell's behaviour at this critical juncture did not throw oil upon the troubled waters. He took care that Jack should have every attention, and inquired as to his progress with punctilious regularity; but he plainly considered a sprained ankle a very trivial affair, which, needless to say, did not coincide with the invalid's views of the case; moreover, he absolutely refused to believe that the accident was responsible for keeping Jack at the Court.

"It is only right to tell you, sir, that I had finally made up my mind that I must return home to-day, as I could not agree with your conditions," Jack informed him on their first interview after the doctor had paid his visit; whereupon the old man elevated his eyebrows with that air of ineffable superiority which was so exasperating, and said—

"And I, on the contrary, had made up my mind that you should stay. It is satisfactory to me that the question is decided in my favour."

"By an accident, sir. By an accident only. If I'd been able to move—"

Mr Farrell held up his hand with a deprecatory gesture.

"In that case I should have called your attention to certain arguments which would have brought about the same result. Believe me, my dear Jack, it would have made no difference."

Jack's face flushed angrily. He forgot Mollie's entreaty, forgot his own promise, and answered hotly—

"I cannot imagine any arguments that could keep me here against my will. As soon as I can get about again I must return to my work. This accident is only delaying my departure for a few weeks longer."

"So!" Could anything be more aggravating than that little bow and smile which accompanied the word. "In a few weeks, my dear Jack, many things may happen; therefore, it is superfluous to discuss the subject at present. When the time arrives I shall be ready to meet it."

He turned and left the room, while Jack raged in helpless fury upon the sofa. It was insufferable to be treated as if he were a boy who could be ordered about against his will. When John Allen Ferguson Melland said a thing, he *meant* it, and not all the old men in the world should move him from it, as Bernard Farrell would find out to his cost before many weeks were past.

For three whole days Jack's ill-temper continued, and, like most angry people, he punished himself even more than his companions, refusing to sit in the drawing-room to see callers, and insisting on remaining all day long in a dull little room at the back of the house. He grew tired of reading. His head ached with the unusual confinement; just because he was unable to move he felt an overpowering desire for half a dozen things just out of reach, and the day stretched to an interminable length. On the fourth morning depression had taken the place of ill-temper, and he was prepared to allow himself to be petted and waited upon, when, to his dismay, Victor came to his bedroom with the news that the girls had gone up to town, accompanied by Mrs Thornton.

"They said, as you preferred to be alone it would be best to keep to their plans," said Victor cruelly. "I am off for a ride, and shall probably make a day of it, and lunch *en route*. I was thinking of going to Barnsley. It is quite a decent-sized place. Would you like me to try if I could find a masseuse for your foot?"

Jack looked up sharply; but Victor looked as he usually did. His face was set and expressionless, as it always was when his eyes were hidden. It was natural enough that he should make such a suggestion, seeing that he had heard many lamentations on the subject, natural and kindly into the bargain, yet Jack felt an instinctive unwillingness to accept the offer.

"He wants me out of the way," came the leaping thought, while he bit his lip, and appeared to ponder the question.

A few days before he himself had heartily echoed the sentiment; but now that Fate—or was it something else?—had interfered to keep him at the Court, Jack's views had slowly altered. It might be that there was a duty waiting for him here, some duty which was even more important than his work in town; and, if he shirked it, the consequences might fall upon others besides himself. The two girls' faces rose before him,—Ruth's shy and anxious, Mollie audaciously reckless,—children both of them in the ways of the world, though innocently confident of their own wisdom. If by staying on at the

Court he could safeguard their interests, it would be well-spent time which he should never regret.

To Victor's astonishment his offer was quietly but firmly refused, and he set out on his ride marvelling what had happened to bring about such a sudden change of front.

Meantime, Ruth and Mollie were enjoying their first experience of that most delightful feminine amusement—shopping in London. They drove to the doors of world-famed establishments, entered with smiling self-confidence, and gave their orders, unperturbed even by the immaculate visions in black satin who hastened forward to receive them; so marvellous and inspiring are the effects of a purse and a cheque-book behind it!

Mrs Thornton was purse-bearer, and, to do her justice, enjoyed the occasion as much as the girls themselves. She had been personally interviewed by Mr Farrell and coached for her part, which was to chaperon the girls, take them to the best places in which to procure their various requirements, but on no account whatever to direct the purchases, or limit their extent.

"It is a good test; I wish to study it," said the old man, which speech being repeated, Ruth looked grave, and Mollie laughed, and cried—

"There is only one question I shall ask you, 'Do I look nice?' and one piece of advice, 'Which suits me best?' and you are free to answer them both. In the present instance these hats are all so fascinating that it would be a sin to choose between them. I shall take them all!"

"Mollie, don't be absurd. You shall do nothing of the kind. Four hats, and you have two already! It would be wicked extravagance!" protested Ruth vigorously.

But Mollie persisted, and the attendant volubly declared that indeed "madam" was wrong. Six hats was a very moderate allowance. Madam would need different hats for different occasions,—for morning and afternoon, for fine and wet weather, for ordinary and dress occasions. Would she herself not be persuaded to try on this charming model, the latest French fashion, "ridiculously cheap at three guineas?"

"Thank you, I'll take the white hat, and the black chiffon. They will answer all my purposes," declared Ruth frigidly.

She was shocked at Mollie's wanton extravagance, and all the more disapproving that she herself badly wanted to be extravagant too, and wear dainty colours for a change, instead of the useful black and white, if only her sensitive conscience could have submitted to the outlay.

If hats had been a pitfall, dresses were even worse, for here the prices were largely increased. It was a new experience to be ushered into what looked more like a luxurious house than a shop, and to find oneself confronted by a row of tall, willowy young women dressed in tightly fitting black satin garments, so marvellously representing dress-stands that they might have been mistaken for them had it not been for the elaborately dressed heads.

"This is a very expensive place—just for your very best dresses," Mrs Thornton ventured to explain; and the order, "Summer gowns for these young ladies," having been given, presto! the animated dress-stands disappeared through a doorway, to return a few minutes later to promenade slowly up and down the floor before the dazzled eyes of the beholders, each one attired in a different costume. Blue, green, white, lavender, and yellow—perfect of cut, distracting of make—it was, indeed, a problem to choose between them! And while they hesitated, lo! another disappearance, and another triumphal entrance even more gorgeous than the first.

"If I thought I should look as nice as they do, I'd have four at least, but I shan't; my waist is twice as big, and I never learnt to glide," sighed Mollie humbly. "How much is the blue, please? I think that would suit me best."

The price of that simple—looking frock gave Ruth an electric shock. It was actually more than the whole of her yearly allowance. She looked it over, making a rapid estimate of the cost of material and trimming, and felt convinced she could have bought them all out of a five-pound note. And then it could be made at home. Ah, no, that was just the difficulty! The material was a detail, in the making-up thereof lay all the charm and effect. She came out of her calculations to hear Mollie say calmly—

"And I shall want them both home by the end of a week! Now my sister will choose, and after that we will see some evening gowns."

Ruth took her courage in both hands, ordered one dress, and took advantage of the first moment of solitude to rebuke Mollie in irritable undertones.

"Do think what you are about! I'm the eldest, and it's most unsuitable for you to be better dressed. You ought to let me decide, and follow my example."

"But I promised Uncle Bernard that that was just what I would not do."

"Even if you did, he never intended you to order a whole trousseau. How will he feel when he sees the bills?"

"I don't know; I think he will feel nice when he sees my clothes. Oh, Ruth, do enjoy yourself when you have the chance! He gave you carte blanche—why on earth can't you take it?"

But that was just exactly what Ruth could not do. The fear of the bill—the fear of Uncle Bernard's displeasure, loomed so largely before her eyes, that she dared not indulge her longing for needless fineries. In every shop the same story was repeated, Mollie giving a lavish order with beams of satisfaction, Ruth reducing hers by half, and feeling sore and aggrieved. Each appealed in turn to Mrs Thornton for support and approval, until that good lady became quite dazed and bewildered, and was thankful to find herself once more in her quiet home.

Arrived at the Court, Mollie danced up to Mr Farrell, who sat reading by the library fire.

"I'm back again, Uncle Bernard," she cried; "I've had a beautiful time! I don't think I ever enjoyed myself so much! I'm bubbling over with gratitude. I've spent heaps of money! You said I might, and I've taken you at your word; and oh, I have got such lovely things in exchange!"

Mr Farrell looked at her grimly, but made no reply. His eyes turned towards his other niece, who stood silently in the background.

"And you," he queried, "have you been equally fortunate?"

Ruth's face clouded.

"I got what I needed," she said; "I have a headache. I'm going upstairs to rest."

Chapter Eighteen.

Mollie's Revenge.

Three weeks had passed by. May had begun—an old-fashioned, well-conducted May—which was really like a foretaste of summer, instead of the shivery disappointment which so often condemns us to fire and furs. Jack's ankle was still troublesome, and though he could limp a few steps with the aid of a stick, his outdoor exercises were for the most part restricted to peregrinations in the old bath-chair. According to his account the period had been one of much tribulation, when patience and forbearance had been tried to their limits by the unnatural conduct of Miss Mollie Farrell. Instead of behaving like the proverbial ministering angel, Mollie proved uncertain, coy, and hard to please, and so full of mischievous pranks that Jack declared that his hair was turning white, though, if the truth be told, he looked remarkably bright and happy.

One morning it happened that a chance remark of Jack's offended Miss Mollie's dignity, and she vowed that she would be revenged. It seemed, however, that she had forgotten her displeasure for when Ruth and Victor went off to the village after lunch, she offered herself for the post of chairman, and wheeled the invalid to his favourite position beneath a flowering chestnut in front of the house.

The ankle was comfortable, and Jack, having lunched well, felt at peace with mankind and womankind into the bargain, and quite inclined to enjoy a pleasant talk. No sooner was he settled, however, than Miss Mollie drew a book from her pocket, and sitting down on the grass at a few yards' distance, deliberately turned her back upon him and began to read.

Jack watched these proceedings in silence, recognising both that he was being punished for having annoyed his companion in the morning, and also that he could not better frustrate her intentions than by preserving an appearance of undisturbed complacency. Accordingly, he sat quietly, studying the pretty figure in the blue linen dress, and noticing with satisfaction that the pages were flicked over more rapidly than was consistent with careful reading.

The book was evidently dull—so much the better! Miss Mollie might find her own punishment even heavier than his. He himself had nothing to read, but that did not distress him. A man is not to be pitied if he cannot make himself happy for an hour or so, even with a sprained ankle, when there is a charming landscape to gaze upon, of which a pretty girl makes the foreground.

Jack smiled lazily to himself as he thrust his hand into the tail-pocket of his coat, but his expression changed tragically as his fingers groped in vain for the bulky pouch which he had refilled just before leaving the house. Now, what in the world had happened to that pouch? Could it have fallen out of his pocket? Impossible! It was too securely weighted down by its own size. It could not have fallen, but it could easily have been stolen by the hands of his mischievous charioteer as she wheeled him across the grass. Jack had no doubt that that was exactly what had happened, and he congratulated himself on having smothered an exclamation of dismay, as he saw Mollie's head lifted cautiously from the pages as if to listen for the expected explosion.

Jack smiled to himself, knowing full well that her patience would soon be exhausted, and with it the limit of his punishment. It would be a joke to pretend to be asleep when, at last, it pleased her ladyship to turn round! The little witch no doubt was fully aware how pretty she looked, and fondly imagined that he was wrapt in admiration. It would be a useful snub to find that he had forgotten all about her. So Jack rested his head against the cushions of his chair, folded his arms, and kept his eyes rigorously shut for the next few minutes. He felt delightfully at ease, and the rays of the sun shining through the branches were at once so subdued, and so comforting, that it came to pass that what he had plotted in fun came about in earnest, and at the end of a few minutes his lids were tightly closed, and his breath came through his lips in long, regular respirations.

Mollie heard the sound, and smiled derisively.

"As if I should believe for one moment that he had gone to sleep!" said she to herself, with a tilt of the saucy head; but as the moments passed by, the perfection of the imitation began to disturb her equanimity; the last breath, for example, approaching perilously near a snore! She turned cautiously, inch by inch, until a glimpse of the bath-chair could be obtained, with a fair head drooping upon the cushions. Jack was asleep! Actually, and in very truth he had calmly slumbered off in defiance of her displeasure.

Mollie arose in her wrath, and stood over the unconscious figure, meditating upon the next step. If Jack Melland imagined for one moment that she was going to mount guard over his slumbers, he would find himself vastly mistaken; yet she dared not leave him unprotected, for the ground sloped away from the tree, and a violent movement on the part of its occupant would be enough to send the chair racing down the incline. She stood and pondered, then, drawing a handkerchief from her pocket, crept on tip-toe to the back of the chair and tied the handle to a convenient bough. It would be almost impossible for Jack, crippled as he was, to raise himself and turn round sufficiently to undo the knots; so, after testing their firmness a second time, Mollie took a circuitous path to the house, there to amuse herself for an hour or more, until Mr Jack had time to awake and repent himself of his audacity.

The awaking came unexpectedly quickly. Perhaps Jack's slumbers had been disturbed by Mollie's movements, quiet though they had been; certain it is that she was hardly out of sight before he stirred uneasily, blinked once or twice, and finally sat erect in a spasm of remembrance. He had fallen asleep, not in pretence but in actual fact; for how long he had slept he had no idea, but meantime the bird had flown, no doubt with feathers much ruffled by wounded pride.

Jack did not believe that Mollie had gone out of sight; he pictured her standing a few feet away, squeezed up against the branches of a tree, with blue skirts held tightly together lest a fold should betray her presence. Anxiety for his safety would soon bring her rushing to his side; so he threw himself back in the chair to set it a-going; failed to make it move, jolted forward, and again found it immovable.

Then he grew suspicious, and craning over his shoulder beheld the tell-tale handkerchief with the tight little knots twisted purposely well out of reach.

So this was Mollie's revenge, to leave him stranded in the middle of the park until such time as it might please her to set him at liberty! Jack hardly knew whether to be more amused or indignant at the sense of his helplessness. It seemed so preposterous that a chit of a girl should be able to keep him prisoner, that for a moment he seriously contemplated getting out of the chair and limping back to the house. How contrite she would be when she returned to find the chair empty; how full of contrition, and anxiety about his welfare!

The prospect was not unpleasant; but after nearly a fortnight's invalidism, he dreaded doing anything to retard convalescence, and the more he measured with his eye the distance to the house the more convinced he became that it was beyond his power to accomplish. It would be ignominious, indeed, to have to give in half-way, and be discovered by his tormentor sitting prone upon the ground waiting her arrival.

Jack determined to be wise in his generation and remain where he was; but it was dull work sitting alone, without paper or book to while away the time, and as his chair was turned away from the drive he had not even the distraction of watching for the return of Ruth and Victor. He took out his pocket-book, searched through its contents for anything of interest, made a few calculations on an empty page, and thrust it impatiently into his pocket. Then he studied his strong white hands, trying to imagine that they looked thin and delicate, carried out a systematic search through every one of his pockets, lest, perchance, anything at all interesting might have wandered into one of them by mistake; looked at his watch and groaned to find that it was still a full half-hour to tea-time. At last when patience was well-nigh exhausted, the crunch of footsteps on the path delighted his ears, and he called out a vociferous greeting—

"Hallo! are you back? Thank goodness for that. I was just looking out for you."

No answer. The footsteps came to a momentary pause, then crunched on again quicker than before. Jack cleared his throat and roared still louder—

"I say, I'm here! Don't go without me; I'm alone; I want to go up to the house."

Silence still; another pause and then a deliberate walk onwards, which roused Jack to veritable anger. This was evidently not Ruth but Mollie, and Mollie must be taught that there was a point when a joke ceased to be a joke, and that, bound or free, Jack Melland must be obeyed. When he spoke again his voice was not loud any longer, but cuttingly cold and severe.

"Will you kindly come here and unloose my chair; I refuse to be kept a prisoner any longer."

The footsteps paused abruptly; the swish of a silken skirt came across the grass, and a woman's clear, high-bred voice cried abruptly—

"A prisoner! Oh, what is the matter? Please tell me what I can do. I would have stopped at once, but I did not think you could possibly be talking to me."

Jack looked up in amaze, and beheld a tall girl clad in grey, a little head beautifully poised on an unusually long neck, and a pale, oval face, out of which looked a pair of deep, violet eyes. The stranger was not beautiful, not even pretty, but in the way she spoke, in the way she moved, in the way she stood looking at him, with the folds of her dress held together in one slender hand, there was an air of distinction which marked her out from the ordinary run of womankind.

Jack felt overcome with embarrassment as he remembered his imperious summons, and so much at a loss to explain his predicament that for a few moments he could not find words, but just lay back in his chair staring at her with horrified eyes.

The stranger evidently perceived his embarrassment, for she came a step forwards and said tactfully—

"I think you must be Mr Melland. May I introduce myself? My name is Margot Blount I have been lunching at the vicarage, and took the opportunity of calling upon Miss Farrell before the carriage comes back for me at five o'clock. I shall be so glad if I can be of any service to you *en route*."

"Thank you; you are very kind. I am awfully sorry that I should have shouted at you in that threatening way," said Jack, smiling in his most fascinating manner, and he could be remarkably fascinating upon occasion. "The truth is I am a cripple at present with a sprained ankle, and my—er—attendant has chosen to run away, and leave me tied up to this tree. I was getting tired and impatient, hence the summons."

"Ah," exclaimed Lady Margot, smiling, "I can guess who the attendant was! Miss Mollie Farrell, was it not? I have heard so much of her from Mrs Thornton that I am quite longing to see her. Is she at home this afternoon—and her sister?"

"I am not sure about Miss Farrell; she went out for a walk after lunch; but in any case she is sure to return very soon. Miss Mollie is—somewhere! It is impossible to be more explicit. Probably some of the servants will be able to find her for you."

"I hope so, but first what can I do for you? Shall I untie this noose and set you free?"

"Thank you; I should be much obliged. Then, perhaps, you would kindly ask the butler to send someone to bring me in. I shall hope to see you later on."

Lady Margot rustled to the back of the chair, and bent over the knotted handkerchief. It was tied as if the knots were never intended to be undone, and presently she paused to take off her gloves before attacking it again, while Jack expostulated and apologised for the trouble he was giving. Finally, regardless of her light draperies, Lady Margot knelt down on the ground so as to work more conveniently, and in the midst of her efforts a saucy face peered suddenly round the corner of a tree a few yards distant, and Mollie hove into sight, with head thrown back and arms a-kimbo in would-be threatening attitude. From her position Jack's broad shoulders hid from view the grey figure behind the chair, and he guessed as much, and took a wicked delight in the thought.

"Well, Mr Melland, I hope you feel refreshed by your slumbers, and have awakened in a better frame of mind," cried Mollie loftily. "Will you say you are sorry, and be taken to have tea on the terrace, or be obstinate and stay here by your lonesome little self?"

"Neither, thank you; I have been fortunate enough to find a friend in need, so am no longer dependent on your good offices. Allow me to introduce you—Miss Mary Farrell—Lady Margot Blount!" said Jack dramatically.

Tableau!

Mollie's arms dropped to her sides and her face grew scarlet under the garden-hat. So far from rising to her position as hostess, it was the visitor who came forward to shake hands and speak the conventional words of greeting. It was, indeed, a cruel Fate which sent just this visitor at just this very time! Half a dozen times over during the last fortnight had Mollie donned one of her grand London dresses and sat primly in the drawing-room, with intent to receive Lady Margot in style, and impress her with a sense of her own dignity and importance! And then to be discovered behaving like a mischievous school-girl, and be taken at such a disadvantage that she could not even find her voice! It was too annoying!

"Good-afternoon, Miss Farrell! I was coming up to the house to call upon you and your sister. I am so happy to have found you at home; and, do you know, I believe Mr Melland will have to fall back upon your help, after all. My efforts have not been at all successful. You tie such good knots!" cried Lady Margot, in a tone of enthusiasm which seemed to imply that the tying of knots was one of the rarest and most valuable of accomplishments. Looking into her face, Mollie's embarrassment died a sudden death, and she found herself smiling back with a delicious sense of comradeship and understanding.

"Oh, I know the trick. I can undo them in a moment, and then won't you come and have tea with us on the terrace? It is all ready, and it seems a sin to be indoors on this lovely day. My sister will be there waiting for us; she was just coming up the path by the lake as I turned the corner."

"Oh, that is nice!" said Lady Margot. She looked as if she were about to ask another question, but checked herself, and strolled along beside the bath-chair, chatting alternately to Jack and Mollie with an ease and grace which might have come from long years' acquaintanceship. As they turned the corner of the terrace she was a step in advance, and Mollie saw her stop short for the fraction of a moment while the colour rushed into her pale cheeks. She had surprised a pretty little tableau—a tableau to which the inhabitants of the Court had grown accustomed during the last few days—Ruth seated on her chair, her lovely head drooped shyly forward, Victor leaning impressively towards her, his dark eyes bent on her face. They were too much engrossed to hear the approaching footsteps, but the sound of the chair crunching over the gravel at last aroused their attention, when Victor turned round, and leapt to his feet, white and breathless.

Chapter Nineteen.

"The Ogre."

It was not a successful tea-party; for the fact of Victor's previous acquaintance with Lady Margot, so far from acting as a bond of union, seemed to cast a constraint over all. The meeting between the two had been cool and unnatural. They persistently avoided speaking to or looking at each other, and it seemed to Mollie's critical ear as if even Lady Margot's voice had altered in tone since she had turned the corner of the terrace. She chatted away as easily as before, but the friendly manner was replaced by something colder and more formal. As she sat with veil turned back, the full rays of the sun shining upon her face, it became more obvious than ever that, in spite of chestnut hair and violet eyes, Lady Margot fell far short of beauty; but, none the less, the eye dwelt upon her in fascinated attention, so graceful was the pose of the small, stag-like head, so finely cut the curve of chin and cheek; while the smallest action, as of lifting a cup to her lips, became a veritable joy to behold.

She was the incarnation of grace, and, looking at her, Mollie became uncomfortably aware of roughened hair, sunburnt hands, and a dozen little deficiencies of toilette. Even Ruth suffered from the comparison, and, despite an obvious effort to sustain her rôle as hostess, there was a strained, unhappy expression upon her face which went to Mollie's heart.

It was a relief to all when Lady Margot rose to take leave; but when she offered her hand to Victor in his turn, he said eagerly—

"Mayn't I walk down with you to the vicarage? It is so long since we met! Please let me take you so far!"

"Oh, certainly, if you can spare the time!" replied Lady Margot with a careless indifference of manner which made her consent almost more blighting than a refusal.

Victor winced beneath it, but made no comment, and the two tall figures walked slowly down the terrace. Immediately they had disappeared, Jack summoned a servant to wheel him into the house, and the girls were left alone.

They sat silently for a long time, as true friends can do without offence, Ruth gazing ahead with grey eyes which saw nothing of the beauty of the scene; Mollie glancing from time to time at her troubled face, then turning quickly aside, lest her scrutiny might be observed and resented.

At length Ruth spoke, letting her figure drop back in her chair with a gesture of weariness—

"I wonder how it is that nothing is ever as nice as one expects? If we could have looked forward two months ago, and seen ourselves as we are now, we should have imagined ourselves the happiest creatures on earth; but I am not. Sometimes it seems quite perfect for a few moments, but something always happens to rub off the bloom. Uncle Bernard is cross, or Mrs Wolff stupid, or—or something else! I believe we are not meant to be happy in this world!"

Mollie looked up with a quick flush of dissent.

"Oh, I think that is such a grudging idea! I hate to hear people say it, and I can't think how they can, when they look round, and see how bright and beautiful everything has been made! If God had meant us to be dull and sad, would He have made all the flowers different colours, and every season different from the last, and the sunsets and the dawn, and the wonderful changing clouds? It is just a gorgeous feast to delight our eyes of colour; and all the animals are so cheerful, while they are young, at least—they skip and dance by instinct, so surely we must be meant to be happy too!"

"I don't know," Ruth objected slowly. "Animals have not souls and responsibilities, but we have, and that keeps us serious. The average man and woman is not happy, if you can judge by appearances. I remember reading about a man who walked about the streets of

London all day long to see how many people he should meet with a smile on their faces. I forget how many there were—half a dozen, perhaps—terribly few!"

"Well, there would have been thousands, if people were half as grateful as they should be. Do you know, I sometimes think that what must grieve God more than almost anything else is that so many people refuse to be happy, in spite of all He can do, and go on forgetting their blessings, and making themselves miserable about little bits of silly worries and bothers day after day. Imagine if you had a child who was always grizzling, in spite of all your love and care! How would you feel?"

"But a child is a child. We may be meant to be serious."

"You can be serious without being glum. You can be happy without being thoughtless."

"Ah, Mollie dear," cried Ruth, turning to her sister and holding out her hand with a rush of tenderness—"ah, Mollie dear, happiness is a gift, which you possess and I do not! I am sad even on this lovely day, in this lovely place. It may be wrong, but I can't help it, yet I don't think I am ungrateful."

"You are happy enough as a rule; but you do 'sup sorrow with a spoon' when you get the chance, old dear! An hour ago, for instance, the sky seemed remarkably bright, and I could make a shrewd guess at the reason of this cloud; but, if I did, I expect you would snap off my head for my pains!"

"Yes, I should—I certainly should; so be careful what you say!" cried Ruth hastily. Then, as if eager to change the subject—"Here is James coming out with the afternoon letters. I hope there is one from home. It seems ages since we heard!"

"Trix! For me. How lovely! I'll read it aloud!" cried Mollie, tearing open the envelope, and unfolding several odd sheets torn out of an exercise-book and covered with large, untidy handwriting. Trix's characteristic epistles were always welcome, and this afternoon's specimen had arrived in the very nick of time to stop an embarrassing discussion, and cheer Ruth's drooping spirits.

Mollie lay back in her chair, and began reading in her clear fresh tones—

> "Darling Moll,—While you are basking in the lap of luxury, this poor critter is snatching a few precious moments from 'prep' to answer your last epistle, and give what news there is. First and foremost, mother is as well as possible, and goes about with an 'open your mouth and shut your eyes, and in your mouth you'll find a prize' expression, which puzzles her friends into fits. Poor mum simply dies to tell them that one of her daughters will shortly become a millionaire! But she shuts her lips up tight, and looks more mysterious than ever, because, of course, there is a chance that it may not come off. Don't let me ever see your faces again if it doesn't, that's all!
>
> "Fancy you having all those fine clothes! I can't imagine how you would look respectably attired. Kindly remember Beatrice Olivia for any cast-off fineries. Hair-ribbons especially desired. I've nothing left but an old Navy-blue, twisted up like a tape.
>
> "We had a general intelligence examination at school this week. Stupid old things! One question was, 'What is the complementary colour to red?' I had never heard of a complementary colour in my life, and I was just racking my brains to think what to say, when my eyes happened to light on Miss Smith's carrots. 'Ah, ha,' thinks I, 'I have it!' So I put down 'auburn,' and was jolly well pleased with myself until lunch-time came, when I was telling Gladys my answers, and Miss Bateson heard me, and went into perfect fits! It seems complementary means something idiotic about two colours making a white light—as if they ever could!

Anyway, I think my answer was very pretty and tactful—don't you? and I hope it will soften Smithy's hard heart.

"Another silly question was, 'Order a dinner for a class of twelve Board-school children, and state what quantities of each article are required.' One girl ordered a pound of roast beef and a pound of potatoes for each child, and ten and a half yards of Swiss-roll for the whole class! I ordered the 'scrag-end of the neck.' Haven't the least idea what it means, but I thought it sounded cheap. I likewise gave them suet dumplings for pudding. Hope they liked them!

"Is Mr Melland's ankle getting better? Have you had any more callers, invitations, rides, excursions, or excitements generally? Please answer my questions next time, and don't ignore them, as you generally do. Drummond had a fine adventure yesterday. Another small boy dared him to stick his head between our railings, and he did, but it wouldn't come out! He pushed, and the small boy pulled, and a crowd collected right across the pavement, making kind suggestions, and commenting on the size of his ears. Whenever he tried to get back, the railings caught them, and they stuck out like sails. Finally his pride gave way, and he howled, and a friendly policeman coming along, poked the rails apart with a stick, or did something or other, and out he came with a rush. He looked very crushed in every sense all the evening, so we hope it may be a lesson to him.

"The next-door girls have new hats—mustard straw, draped with green, and roses under the brim. It seems so sad to reflect that the poor dears probably imagine they look quite nice!

"How is the Ogre? Does he still live in his den, and growl when you appear? I should be very glad he did shut himself up, when he is so cross and disagreeable!

> "Well, ta-ta, my darlings! I miss you at home, but I can't say I pine for your return, for it's quite pleasant to be Number One for a change, and boss Attica and the Muz. Take care of yourselves, behave prettily, and don't forget the hair-ribbons.—Your loving Trix."

"Wild child!" said Ruth, smiling. "She does write the most absurd letters! Better tear that up at once, Mollie, or burn it when you get into the house. You have such a trick of leaving things about, and it isn't safe. Uncle Bernard might—"

She started violently, and Mollie jumped to her feet as a harsh voice interrupted the sentence—

"Uncle Bernard has already had the pleasure of hearing the way in which a member of your family writes of him to a visitor in his own house. Ideas of loyalty seem to have altered since my young days, when it was considered a breach of decent feeling to eat a man's salt and speak slightingly of him behind his back!"

Ruth sat silent, crimson to the roots of her hair; Mollie shuffled miserably from one foot to another, but did not shrink from the old man's angry gaze.

"But how did you hear, Uncle Bernard? Have you been sitting behind this open window, listening to us all the while we have been talking? I don't think it is quite fair to do that."

"Don't you, indeed! I happened to be reading in my armchair, when you came and planted your chairs immediately outside. I was the first-comer, you observe, not yourselves, and I cannot say I was interested enough to listen to your conversation until my attention was attracted by the description of myself. I presume the very descriptive title was originally your invention?"

He planted his stick on the ground, and stared fixedly in Mollie's face. The grey eyes fell before his, and she answered hesitatingly—

"I'm—I'm afraid it was."

"And do you think it was good manners to write in such a way of your host?"

"No, I don't; I think it was hateful. But—"

"But?"

Mollie took a step forward, and laid a timid hand on his arm.

"But, in a sort of way, it is true. You shut yourself up, and you do growl, and even when you are kind, you pretend to be cross. We have tried and tried to be friends with you, but you won't let us. We have said over and over again that we felt as if we were living in an hotel, and it has been a trouble to us all. I don't wonder you feel angry; but don't you think you are a wee bit in the wrong yourself?"

Mr Farrell stared down at the eager face, the wide grey eyes, the little hand upon his arm, then deliberately drew himself away, saying coldly—

"You would make a good lawyer, my dear. You have a clever trick of evading an awkward question, and shifting the blame from your own shoulders. You will excuse me if I say that I can scarcely consent to discuss my own conduct with a girl of your years. The point I mentioned was your own conduct in writing disrespectfully of your host."

"I know, and I've said already that it was horrid; but it was not so horrid as you think. Trix is my sister, and we all have a habit of exaggerating and using stronger terms than we really mean. We have a habit of giving nicknames, too. They are not complimentary as a rule, but we don't mean to be unkind. If you read some of Trix's other letters, you would see that we have not been altogether ungrateful. Will you read them? I have them all upstairs, and could bring them down in a moment."

"You are very good. Judging from the specimen I have heard, I think I would rather decline the honour."

"Yes; but you ought not to decline! It isn't a question of enjoyment; it's a question of justice to Ruth and to me. You accuse us of being disloyal and ungrateful, so it's only fair you should hear our defence. I will bring down the letters, and you can read them at your leisure. They may bore you a little, but you will see that we are not so bad as you think, and that we have not always been uncomplimentary."

She walked hastily towards the house, leaving Ruth and the old man alone. He stood leaning on his stick, staring fixedly at her with his sunken eyes; but her head remained persistently drooped, the dark lashes lying on the flushed cheeks.

In the tension of that silence she could hear the beating of her own heart, and her ears strained nervously for the sound of returning footsteps. She had not long to wait. With a clatter, Mollie came scrambling out of the library window, the letters in her hand.

"There's our defence! Please read them before you scold us any more."

Mr Farrell took the letters, thrust them into his pocket, then stood silently, as if waiting for something more.

Mollie stared at him curiously, but he paid no attention to her; his gaze was fixed on Ruth's bent figure and downcast face. At length, surprised at the prolonged silence, she lifted her eyes with a frightened glance, and immediately Uncle Bernard broke into speech.

"Yes, I was waiting for you! Have you nothing to say on your own account?" he demanded sternly. "You seem content to sit silently and let your sister fight your battles. Is it because you are innocent of having offended in the same way yourself?"

Ruth's cheeks flushed to an even deeper rose.

"I," she stammered—"I—I'm sorry! I didn't mean—"

Mr Farrell turned to re-enter the house.

"Ah," he said coldly," so it was cowardice, after all! I understand. It is an interesting discovery!"

Chapter Twenty.

Receiving and Paying Calls.

Two days later Mr Farrell returned Trix's letters with a brief "Thank you!" which Mollie had enough tact to receive without remark. She was not conscious of having gained in the old man's graces, though Ruth was sadly conscious of having fallen from favour. Victor was evidently for the time being the *persona grata,* his remarks being received with attention, and his wishes carefully carried out.

Mollie confessed to herself that Victor's manners were perfect where his host was concerned, and wondered why it was that she found herself constantly suspecting his motives. What if he were playing a part to win the old man's favour? Was it not the unhappy feature of the situation that they were all, more or less, doing the same thing?

Meantime, callers arrived daily. Stout, middle-aged matrons, with pompous manners; thin matrons, precise and formal of speech; tall elegants, with flowing robes and Parisian millinery; sporting-looking women, with short skirts and motor-caps. One after another they drove up to the door and sat for a few moments in the drawing-room, going through the same stereotyped conversation: "How pleasant to have the Court opened once more! How do you like Raby? How delightful to have such delightful summer-like weather!" Then they drank a cup of tea, nibbled a piece of cake, and said: "*Good*-afternoon! *So* pleased to have met you! We shall hope to see you again *very* soon!"

Occasionally the matron brought a daughter in her train, and still more occasionally a shy, depressed-looking husband; but at the best of times the calls were not cheerful occasions, and Ruth and Mollie looked forward with little pleasure to paying their return visits.

"Though it must at least be more interesting than receiving at home, for we shall see other people's houses, and the way they arrange their drawing-rooms. I do love studying strange drawing-rooms!"

said Ruth meditatively. "In country houses they ought to be charming—all chintzy and smelling of pot-pourri! All the same, Mollie, I'm disappointed in the neighbours. They aren't a bit thrilling, as we expected."

"People generally seem uninteresting at first. They may turn out to be perfect darlings, when we know them better. I dare say they drove away saying the same thing of us, for we behaved like a couple of marionettes, sitting dressed up in our best, saying, 'Yes, indeed!' 'No, indeed!' 'Very much, indeed!' 'Thank you so much!' as if we were wound up by machinery. We must really launch out, and say something a trifle more original!"

It was quite an exciting occasion when the girls set out on their first calling expedition. It was an ideal May afternoon, and the prospect of driving over the countryside in an open carriage, behind two prancing horses, was in itself a delight.

Victor was to make one of the party, but Jack refused contemptuously to accompany them if only for the drive, declaring that even a sprained ankle had its silver lining if it let him off so boring a function. He was sitting in the hall, waiting to cheer—or more strictly speaking, to jeer—the departure, when Ruth came downstairs buttoning her gloves, and, to her surprise, Mr Farrell was also present.

Both men looked up critically as she appeared, but neither glance was altogether approving. Her new dress looked too old and staid for so young a girl; moreover, her expression was fretful and worried. As she reached the spot where the two men were seated, Victor came into the hall from the doorway and looked round impatiently.

"Are you ready, Miss Ruth? The carriage has been waiting for some time now."

"Oh, I have been ready for ages! It's Mollie who is the laggard. She has been dressing ever since lunch, and is dressing still. I don't know when she will be finished."

Mr Farrell turned imperiously to the butler.

"Be kind enough to send a message to Miss Mary that I object to having the horses kept waiting. Three o'clock was the hour arranged, and it is already a quarter past. Ask how soon she will be ready!"

The man departed, and there was an uncomfortable silence for several minutes, broken at last by the banging of a door and the sound of racing footsteps. A white-and-blue vision came flying down the staircase, with filmy skirts floating behind, white feathers drooping over the golden hair, a cobweb parasol unfurled, and held triumphantly aloft.

"I'm sorry! It took such ages to fasten, and I had to take my hair down and do it up again to get the hat at the right angle. I wanted to fasten my gloves, to give you the whole effect, parasol and all. There!" Mollie strutted to and fro, turning her head from side to side like a sleek, self-satisfied pigeon. "How do you like it? Don't you think I look rather—nice?"

The two young men laughed aloud, and Mr Farrell said drily—

"Fine feathers make fine birds! I am glad to see that you have honoured my friends by wearing your fineries for their benefit. Ruth, I presume, prefers to keep hers for another occasion?"

Ruth dropped her eyelids and vouchsafed no reply. There was a little lump in her throat at that moment which would have made it difficult to speak in her usual voice. It was hard to have denied herself for naught, and less than naught, for Mollie's extravagance seemed more to the old man's taste than her own prudence. It was not the first time that the difference in their attire had been the subject of little edged remarks, which had made her bitterly regret the lost opportunity.

Seated in the carriage opposite Victor, she was still further depressed by the fear that he was also comparing her with Mollie, to her own disadvantage; but there was no hint of such a thought in his look or manner. The dark eyes met hers with sympathetic understanding. At every point he deferred to her opinion with a subtle flattery which was inexpressibly soothing to her wounded feelings.

The occupants of the first house on the list were not at home, so a sheaf of cards were left, and the carriage sped on another mile to Number 2, where the family were discovered superintending the arrangements of bedding-out plants round the front lawn. They greeted the visitors with easy cordiality, consulted them on the knotty question of geraniums *versus* begonias, escorted them round the gardens, and were vociferously reproachful when they refused to stay another half-hour to partake of tea.

As the carriage drove up the drive leading to the third house, a masculine figure was seen rushing to conceal itself behind the bushes, and the visitors had hard work to conceal their smiles when their hostess sent an urgent message to summon her husband from the grounds, and, on hearing that he could not be found, expressed her conviction that he would be woefully disappointed to have missed the pleasure of making their acquaintance.

"A fellow-feeling makes us wondrous kind! I don't feel a bit of a grudge against that fellow," Victor said laughingly, as they drove off once more. "With your permission, I am going to follow his example and make a bolt of it when we get back to the high-road. I shall enjoy the walk home, after being cramped up all afternoon. You will excuse me, won't you?"

"But we are going to the Moat. That's the next house on the list. Don't you want to see Lady Margot?" cried Mollie, outspoken as usual.

Both girls stared at him in amazement, but there was no sign of embarrassment on the handsome, smiling face.

"Very much, of course, but not enough to face another drawing-room catechism, accompanied by draughts of strong tea. There will be no escape this time, so you must be generous, and let me run for it, like poor Mr Granger! I have been very good and docile, but if you only knew how I am longing for freedom!"

There was no gainsaying such a request, nor, indeed, did either of the girls particularly wish to do so.

They made no objections, therefore, but, putting Victor down at the cross-roads, drove on their way in great good-humour.

The Moat was a picturesque old house, though by no means so imposing as the Court. The man-servant reported that Mrs Blount was not well enough to receive visitors, but that Lady Margot was at home and disengaged; and the visitors were shown into a pleasant, sunny apartment, where Margot herself was seated reading. She looked up apprehensively at the sound of the opening door; but at the sight of the two girls her expression changed, and she came forward to greet them with an eagerness which could not be mistaken.

"This is good of you to come so soon! And I am alone, so we can have a delightful chat all to ourselves. Bring tea, Wilson, please. Do come and sit down, and let me make you comfortable! My aunt is not downstairs to-day, and I was getting so bored with my own society that I am doubly pleased to see you! There are so few girls of my own age in this neighbourhood that I find it rather dull after the rush and bustle of town. It is so good of you to be here at the same time as me!"

"It is very nice for us," responded Mollie brightly; while truthful Ruth hesitated to find some reply which would be at once polite and non-committal. "But isn't it a strange time for you to come to this quiet place, when London is at its brightest and gayest?"

"Ah, thereby hang many tales!" cried Lady Margot, laughing. "The most important is, perhaps, that I am not strong enough to go through a season just now; but I have no intention of being dull even in Raby. We must amuse each other and do all kinds of nice things together. The great lack on my visits, so far, has been to find any other girls with whom I could be intimate; but now that you are here it will be quite different."

"But we are only country-cousins, Lady Margot. You will find that we are very ignorant of the things that have made up your life. We are very poor at home, and have had to do most of our gaieties in imagination," said Ruth; while Mollie gave a little gurgle of laughter, and cried—

"Let's tell her about Berengaria and Lucille!"

Lady Margot looked her curiosity, and, when the nature of the game was explained in detail in Mollie's breezy language, went into peals of delighted laughter, and rocked to and fro in her chair.

"How lovely—oh, how lovely! I do think it is too funny! I must call you Berengaria and Lucille. Do you mind? Such wonderful names! How did you manage to hit on them? I used to imagine, too; and what do you think was my dream? Instead of being a lonely only girl, I was a large family of grown-up sisters, and schoolboys coming home for the holidays, and little dots in the nursery—all in my own little self. You can't imagine how dull it is to be an only girl!"

"No," asserted Ruth doubtfully. "But rather nice to get all the petting and consideration! When you are the eldest of seven children, you are always expected to set an example, and it is very wearing at times. How delightful that you amused yourself 'pretending,' just as we did! That makes quite a bond of union between us!"

"Yes, indeed! But lucky creatures, your dream seems about to come true, while I am as lonely as ever. Your position at the Court is so romantic! You don't mind my speaking about it, do you, because everyone knows, and is so interested in the result? Of course, one of you must be the lucky heir; and then we shall be neighbours, and see each other constantly. Which is it to be—Berengaria, or Lucille?"

"Mollie!" said Ruth.

"Ruth!" said Mollie. "Don't believe her, Lady Margot. She is a wee bit out of favour the last few days, but I haven't a chance beside her. She has the Farrell eyebrows, you see, and the Farrell frown, and poise of the head. When she is sitting in the dining-room, you could tell at once that she was a descendant of the oil-paintings. I often see Uncle Bernard looking from her to them, and he is far more amiable to her than to any of us, as a rule. We all agree that she is far and away the chief favourite."

"Really! You discuss it among yourselves, and come to the same conclusions. How interesting!" said Lady Margot. "And the two men—your cousins—do they have no chance at all, poor things?" she asked lightly.

"They are not our cousins. They belong to different sides of the house, and we had never met till we came down here. Mr Melland refuses to be considered as a 'candidate,' and is staying only till his ankle is better. Mr Druce,"—Ruth hesitated uncertainly—"he is very nice to Uncle Bernard. They talk together a good deal. Sometimes I think his chance is very good."

"He is certainly second favourite, so far; but we have more than two months still before us. I intend to cut them both out long before then. May I have one of those dear little scones? I am quite hungry after my drive!" Mollie said, as she in turn was presented with a dainty Worcester cup.

She watched Lady Margot with intent eyes, as she flitted about the room, placing little tables beside her guests for their greater convenience.

"Such a plain dress, and almost no jewellery, and her hair so simply done; but she looks a Lucille through and through, as I should never do, however fine I might be!" she said admiringly to herself.

"We must think what we shall do to amuse ourselves, mustn't we? You have begun your round of dinners already, I hear; but in Raby they are apt to be a trifle too agricultural. All the men talk about their crops at this time of the year, and, as the prospects are generally bad, they get gloomier and gloomier as each course comes on. Mr Druce told me that Mr Early has paid you a visitation, so, if you take his conversation as a sample, you can judge of the combined effect. I don't ask what he talked about, because I know!"

"Yes," murmured Ruth vaguely, while her eye met Mollie's in an involuntary appeal. "Mr Druce told me!"—But Mr Early's call had taken place only three days before, nearly a week after Lady Margot's visit to the Court. "Mr Druce told me!" That meant that Margot had met Victor yesterday or the day before, and had talked with him some time, for the prosy Mr Early would not be an early subject of conversation. Victor often went out riding alone, and there was no reason in the world why he should not call on an old acquaintance. But why make a mystery of it, and avoid the call to-day by an obvious subterfuge? Ruth was very quiet for the rest of the visit, and Lady Margot glanced at her more than once as she chatted with Mollie. When tea was over she came out to the porch to watch their departure.

"*Au revoir,* Berengaria—*au revoir,* Lucille!" she cried gaily, as the carriage drove away; but as she turned from the door, the smile faded from her face, and was replaced by a very thoughtful expression.

"I see—I see it all! Poor pretty thing!" she said tenderly to herself. "I am sorry for her and for poor Margot, too! Which of us, I wonder, is the more to be pitied?"

Chapter Twenty One.

Preparing for the Garden-Party.

Mrs Thornton took counsel with her husband as to the best form of hospitality she could show to the squire's visitors.

"I want to be one of the first to entertain them formally. It is a duty in our position," she explained. "The girls have been to tea several times, and that dear Mollie runs up to the nursery as naturally as if she were at home; but I think we ought to do more. The squire will expect it; and then the question is, dear—what can we do?"

"Just so." The vicar smiled, half amused, half quizzical. "The means at our disposal are distinctly limited. We can't ask them to dinner, because the staff is incapable of cooking and serving an extensive meal."

"And there are only three sherry-glasses left, and Mary broke the round glass dish last week—the one I always used for the trifle. And the dinner-service... We really must buy a new dinner-service, Stanford!"

"We really must, Agnes—some time! I think all the objections taken together put the dinner-party out of the question. Would not a somewhat more formal tea—"

"No." Mrs Thornton shook her head decidedly. "A formal tea is the most depressing function imaginable. If it was a little later on, I would suggest a hay-party. As it is, I am afraid it must be a garden-party, pure and simple."

The vicar laughed.

"Simple, it certainly would be. Our poor little lawn, one tennis-court, and the flower-garden a mass of weeds! We can't afford a band of minstrels, or even the ordinary ices and hothouse fruits. I am afraid it might be rather a failure, Agnes."

But Mrs Thornton refused to be discouraged.

"Nonsense, dear! People don't expect extravagant entertainments at a vicarage! The children and I can undertake the weeding, and when that is done the dear old herbaceous borders will look charming! The lawn is not big, but there is delightful shade beneath the beech-trees, and we can draw the piano up to the drawing-room window, and get a few people to sing for us—Maud Bailey and Mrs Reed; and I believe Mr Druce has a fine voice. I'll ask him to be very kind, and give us a song. As for refreshments, I can give good tea and coffee, and the best cream for miles around, and people can exist without ices for once in a way. Given a bright, fine day, I could manage beautifully!"

"I have no doubt you could. But why go through the ceremony of asking my advice, Mistress Thornton, when your mind has been made up from the beginning? Go your ways—go your ways! I wash my hands of all responsibility!" cried the vicar, laughing, as he walked back to his study, leaving his wife to sit down to her desk and make out a lengthy list of guests, which included everyone of note for miles round.

During the days to come Mr Thornton often sympathised with his wife on the amount of work she had undertaken in order to entertain the squire's guests; but, even to his unobservant eyes, it was apparent that, so far from being exhausted, she throve beneath it, and appeared brighter and younger than for years past. All work and no play has an even more depressing effect upon Jill than on Jack, and Mrs Thornton was by instinct a hospitable creature, who would have loved nothing better than a houseful of guests and a constant succession of entertainments. With small means, a large family, and a straggling parish, her time and energy were for the most part engrossed in sheer hard work, so that the prospect of a little "jollification," as she laughingly expressed it, came as a welcome variety.

The invitations to the Court were sent out first, to make sure of the most important guests, and down came the girls with notes of acceptance, and a hundred curious questions.

"Who is coming? What are you going to do? What dresses shall we wear? Can we help?" they asked eagerly; whereupon Mrs Thornton laughed, and replied hesitatingly—

"It is most incorrect; you ought to know nothing of the make-shifts, but just drive down to enjoy the completed effect; but, yes,—I cannot resist the pleasure of your company. Come, if you like, and I'll promise you some real hard work."

"That's right; and you'll find us so useful! We have been born and brought up on make-shifts, and can make anything out of nothing, and a box of tacks—can't we, Ruth?" cried Mollie, in the brutally outspoken manner which always brought a flush into her sister's face.

It was not so much foolish shame at the fact of poverty, but the stab of painful repugnance which came with the remembrance of the bareness and lack of beauty which characterised the old life. After a month's sojourn at the Court the day of small things seemed far away, and she shrank at the possibility of returning to it as a permanency.

When Mrs Thornton began to enumerate her difficulties, and escorted the girls from one room to another to ask their advice upon various knotty points, it was like the probing of a wound to Ruth's sensitive nerves. The house itself was roomy and well built, but in a hopeless state of disrepair. The paint was worn and dingy; the wallpapers so old-fashioned and discoloured that all Mrs Thornton's painstaking efforts after cheerfulness and beauty were foiled by the inartistic background.

"I shed tears over the drawing-room paper when I was first married," said Mrs Thornton, with a laugh and a shrug. "But, as one gets older, there are so many more serious things to cry over that one learns to be philosophical. I thought I might put some big, spreading branches in these old pots to cover the walls as much as possible, for we must have some rooms available in case of a shower. A wet day is too terrible a catastrophe to contemplate, so we won't even imagine it. Given sunshine and unlimited borrowing, we can struggle through. Think of it, my dears—I have invited over a hundred people, and we possess twelve teaspoons!"

Mollie gurgled with laughter in her hearty, infectious manner.

"I'd give up sugar for the day, and do without. That's one off the list. Shall we ask the butler to send down a supply? I'm sure he has hundreds stowed away in those great plate-chests."

"My dear, no! I should not think of it!" cried Mrs Thornton, aghast. "I can manage quite well without troubling the squire. Pray don't repeat any of my thoughtless remarks to him. My husband says that my tongue runs away with me far too often."

Ruth protested politely, but Mollie preserved an unusual silence for the rest of the visit. She was evidently thinking hard, and the result of her cogitations was, that when she returned to the Court she paid a surprise visit to Mr Farrell in his sanctum.

The old man was sitting reading in his favourite chair, and as he looked up it struck Mollie that he looked more alert than she had seen him since her arrival. The voice in which he answered her greeting was certainly less wearied and fretful than usual. He looked, if such a miracle could be believed, almost pleased to see her.

"Well,—so you have returned from your wanderings!"

"Yes, here I am, come to bother you again. There's a whole half-hour before you need begin to dress, and I've something very important to talk to you about."

"What does that mean, pray? More new dresses? I should have thought you could hardly have come to the end of the last supply by this time."

"Goodness, no! They will last for years. It is something far more important."

Mollie seated herself on a low chair directly opposite the old man, leant her elbows on her knees, her chin on her hands, and said hesitatingly—

"Uncle Bernard!"

"Mary!"

"Do you remember the first evening we were here, when you spoke to us about our visit? You said that you might possibly allow each of us in turn to act as master or mistress of the ceremonies for a short time?"

"I believe I did say something of the kind. It occurred to me that it might be an interesting experiment."

"And did you mean that we could really do what we liked, about money and everything else, just as if we were really and truly the real owner in your place?"

Mr Farrell smiled somewhat grimly.

"If your sister asked me that question, I should say 'Yes.' Knowing as I do your capacity for extravagance, I am a little more cautious. Within reasonable limits that is, however, what I meant to imply."

"Ah!" sighed Mollie deeply. "But it all depends on what you call reasonable. At any rate, you can only refuse, and things can be no worse than they are at present. Please, Uncle Bernard, may I begin my reign from to-day?"

"Your reign! You put it forcibly, my dear—more so than is perhaps quite pleasant in my ears. And you are the youngest of the four; your turn should come last, not first. When the others have had their trial—"

"But they have never asked for it; they don't want it, and I do; and you said nothing about taking turns when you made the suggestion. If you let me begin, they could take warning from my mistakes. I don't think you would find they disliked the arrangement. Do, please, be kind and say 'Yes.'"

Mr Farrell reflected for a moment, bringing the tips of his fingers together.

"As you say, you are the first to express any desire to take me at my word. If it pleases you to assume the reins of government for a short time, I have no objection."

"You mean it really? I can begin at once, and give what orders I like?"

"Subject, as I have said, to some possible restrictions if your enthusiasm carries you too far. There is evidently some big scheme looming behind this request. You had better let me know the worst at once. What is to be your first extravagance?"

Mollie's head still rested in the cup of her hands. She looked at him steadily, with a little flame of determination in her grey eyes.

"I am going to have the vicarage painted and papered from top to bottom. It's disgracefully shabby! The paper is hanging off the walls in some places, and where it isn't, it would be almost better if it were, it is so ugly and worn. It is too bad to expect Mr and Mrs Thornton to do all the hard, depressing work of the parish and keep bright and cheerful themselves, when their home is enough to give the blues to a clown! It looks as if it hadn't been touched for a century!"

Mr Farrell lowered his eyelids and sat in a grim silence, while the clock ticked a full two minutes. Mollie, watching his face, saw the thin lips grow thinner and thinner, as they were pressed the more firmly together; the horizontal lines in his forehead deepened into furrows. There was no mistaking the fact that he was displeased, and deeply displeased, even before the cold eyes met hers once more.

"I had no intention now, or at any other time, of allowing you to assume control over the whole parish! My proposition referred simply to this house and your own entertainment. I am still capable of looking after my own property."

"But—" began Mollie, and stopped short.

Even her courage failed before the obvious retort that the property was not looked after, but allowed to fall into dilapidation; but Mr Farrell understood without the need of words, and his eyes flashed with anger.

"You must permit me to judge for myself! When my day is over, whoever comes into possession can squander my money as he or she sees fit, but I cannot hurry the time forward, however much you may desire it. You must be patient and wait. It may come sooner than you think."

Mollie sprang to her feet with an exclamation of mingled pain and anger.

"Oh, Uncle Bernard, how cruel! How can you say anything so horrid and unjust! It isn't true, and you know it isn't true, and I don't deserve it! I only asked for what you yourself suggested."

"I never suggested that you should interfere with my property, and criticise what I had chosen to do or left undone. As for not deserving reproach, you must have made very sure of stepping into my shoes since you wish to wear them while I am still here. No doubt I appear to you a mere cumberer of the ground; but it is my ground, I would have you remember. You cannot take liberties with it yet awhile."

"I don't want it! I never want it! I'll go home to-morrow! You have no right to taunt me like this!" cried Mollie, trembling with such a storm of indignation and wounded feeling as she had rarely known in her bright, easy-going existence.

A rush of ugly words came to her lips, and struggled for utterance, while Mr Farrell sank back in his chair, and lay crouched against the cushions, one thin hand pressed heavily over his heart. The look, the action, brought Mollie to herself with a stab of recollection.

Whatever he had said to wound her pride, she had no right to forget his weakness, his danger, his lonely, piteous age. Anger died a rapid death, and gave place to an even keener sympathy. When Mr Farrell looked up again, it was to find the grey eyes wet with tears, and the lips trembling with emotion.

"Oh, you poor old man—you poor old man! Why will you make it so difficult? Why won't you let us love you and be a comfort, instead of a trouble? We would, if you would allow us. We want to, but you keep us at arm's length, and scold and sneer. I am not thinking of myself. I am young and strong, and I have my home and my dear little mother. I shall be happy, whatever happens. It's *you* I am sorry for! I hate to see you ill and lonely. You have given a great deal to me; can't you be generous enough to take something in return? There are only two months left. The time is nearly half over. Can't we be friends—real friends—until the end?"

She drew nearer as she spoke, and saw no rebuff in the watching face, until at last she sank on her knees before him, and timidly touched his hand.

"Uncle Bernard, speak! Say something to me!"

Still the old man hesitated; but his hand lay quietly in hers, and did not try to escape.

"What can I say?" he asked slowly at last. "I believe you are a good child; I believe you are honest; but my days are past for making friendships. I have felt deeply in my time, but the power of loving died away with everything else which made life worth living. I cannot promise what is impossible."

"But you can at least give me a chance of loving you. I won't ask any more favours if you will just talk to me a little sometimes, without sneering at me, and let me walk with you about the grounds and be a little bit of a companion. Will you? You might get to like me a little bit in time, and it would not be quite so lonely."

"I can imagine things less impossible. You are a good child; but remember, Mollie, my liking or not liking has nothing to do with my choice of an heir. The condition to which I referred might easily apply to one who appealed to me in no other way. It is only right to warn you."

But the listener took no heed of the warning. Her face was one radiant beam of delight.

"You called me 'Mollie'!" she cried. "It was the very first time! That really does sound as if we were going to be friends?"

Chapter Twenty Two.

Mr Farrell Makes his Will.

It was not in human nature—not in Mollie's nature, at least—to resist "showing off" a little after that momentous interview, and her sudden familiarity with their host filled her companions with amazed curiosity. Ruth had naturally heard all that had passed, and loyally stifled the dawning of envy, but the young men were at a loss to account for what seemed to them a mysterious change of favourites.

"Miss Mollie is outstripping us all! She has stepped into the position of first favourite this last fortnight," Victor Druce said, as the four young people sat on the terrace steps waiting for tea, a few days after the visit to the vicarage.

He laughed as he spoke, but in a half-hearted manner, and tugged heavily at the ends of his moustache, while he scrutinised Mollie's face through half-closed lids. She beamed at him gaily in response, scorning mock-modest protestations.

"Oh yes; we understand each other ever so much better! I have been impressing upon him ever since our first meeting that I am really very nice, and at last he is beginning to realise it for himself. He likes me very much. He told me so with his very own lips; but he told me something else, too."

"Yes! May we inquire—"

"Oh, certainly! It is quite as interesting to you as to me. Liking has nothing whatever to do with the mysterious condition; he may quite probably choose the one of us he cares for least, as his heir. 'Curiouser and curiouser,' as Alice said; isn't it?"

"Humph! There may be a chance for me, after all," said Jack lightly.

Victor knitted his brows, and tugged once more at his moustache.

"He said so definitely—you are sure you are not mistaken? Then how can one possibly judge? That upsets all our theories at a blow."

"That's what I thought myself. I felt sure that it would be Ruth, but now I am all at sea; but, for my own part, I'm glad. It is easier to be good friends when there is nothing mercenary involved."

Mollie smiled her sunny, candid smile, and lay back in her deck-chair, her hands clasped easily behind her head. It was delightful to laze in the sunshine, to feel at peace with all the world. The present was so all-absorbing that she had no time to worry her head about the future; but Ruth sat by her side, with unseeing eyes bent upon her book, while the swift thoughts surged through her brain.

She also had felt inwardly convinced that Uncle Bernard's choice would fall upon herself, who was so truly a daughter of his race, and it had been a shock to learn that there was nothing to be deduced from his signs of preference; but of late days there was another problem which was becoming of even more vital interest than the heirship of the Court.

Even as she sat there, with averted head, she was acutely conscious of Victor's presence. She seemed to know, without looking in his direction, the absorbed, contented expression of the dark face. She knew it so well by this time—knew it in an aspect which no one saw but herself; for when they were alone together, it was as if a mask fell away, and revealed the true man. Then he looked at her with open admiration, spoke unreservedly of himself, and drew her out to tell of her own life, and hopes, and ambitions. And there were even more thrilling moments, when the talk ceased, and they sat side by side, silent, yet absorbed, acutely conscious of each other's presence; delightfully, inexplicably confused.

At such moments Ruth confessed to herself that this man, whose very existence she had been unaware of a few weeks before, was fast becoming to her the most important person in the world, and it seemed as certain that he reciprocated her feelings. At such moments, yes! but certainty died away into uneasy doubt, as upon the approach of a third person—even the insignificant Mrs Wolff herself—Victor fell back into his carefully conventional manner.

It was not that she expected or desired any demonstration in public. Ruth was by nature far too reserved to welcome such an exhibition; but the two attitudes were so widely divided, Victor's care in keeping them apart so sedulous, that she could not but be perturbed. Ruth's heart had never before been touched; but love needs no apprenticeship, and she felt by instinct that such self-control was unnatural. Surely, surely, if he really "cared," there would be moments when his eyes would involuntarily meet hers, when his voice would soften in tone.

Then there was Lady Margot Blount! What was the real history of that acquaintanceship? Why did Victor affect to avoid her, while really meeting her in secret?

While Ruth sat dreaming, tea was brought out, and Mr Farrell came limping down the terrace to join the party. It was not often that he favoured them with his presence at the afternoon meal, but the day was so fine and sunny that it was really warmer out of doors than in the house, and as he sat he spread out his wrinkled hands, evidently enjoying the newly-found heat.

Ruth waited upon him with a pretty deference, while Mollie chattered on in her usual unabashed fashion. The old man appeared to pay no attention, but he evidently listened more closely than he cared to admit, for a casual mention of Margot Blount's name evoked a quick glance and question—

"You all seem to speak of Lady Margot in a very familiar fashion; I have not the pleasure of her acquaintance, but from all I have heard I should not imagine she was inclined to make friendships lightly. You have met her—how often? Once or twice?"

He looked at Mollie as he spoke, but Mollie deliberately avoided his eyes, turning towards Victor in a marked manner, which left him no choice but to reply. It was a mischievous impulse to avenge herself and Ruth for his desertion of a few days before, and to discover the truth about that secret meeting of which Margot herself had spoken. Her face seemed solemnity itself to the casual observer, but as he looked at her Jack choked suddenly over his tea, and hitched his chair in an opposite direction. He would have laughed outright if he had looked one moment longer. As for Victor, his dark eyes shot out a spark of annoyance, just one; then he answered with smiling unconcern—

"Lady Margot and I are not quite strangers, sir; I met her in town a good deal last year. We have some friends in common. It was only renewing an acquaintance when we met again the other day."

"Indeed—indeed!" Mr Farrell looked unusually interested and alert. "I am glad to hear that. The Blounts are some of the most important people in the neighbourhood. In the old days there was a strong friendship between the two families, which I should be pleased to see renewed. You were introduced to the old people when you called at the Moat, I presume?"

Here was a direct question which could not be avoided. Jack and Mollie turned towards Victor with glances of elaborately veiled curiosity. Ruth clattered the tea-cups together, carefully averting her eyes. Anxious as she was to hear the reply, she hated the knowledge that Victor was being placed in an awkward position,—hated the consciousness that the others were enjoying the embarrassment.

The pause lasted but a moment; then Victor spoke in his most casual tones—

"No; I have not seen them yet. I have run across Lady Margot once or twice in my morning rides, and had the opportunity of a talk with her, so I thought it better to defer a more formal call. Miss Farrell was kind enough to leave my card, but I did not wish to put myself too much *en evidence*!"

Mr Farrell frowned.

"You had better go soon, then—the sooner the better. As you know the niece, there is all the more reason for paying due respect to the uncle and aunt. You will no doubt receive an invitation after this exchange of visits, and it must be returned as soon as possible. I knew the girl's father in his youth. He was a fine fellow. If she is like him, she must be worth knowing. She cannot be very young,—nearer thirty than twenty, I should say. It is a wonder that she is not married, or engaged. Is she engaged, do you happen to know?"

Again the others waited, leaving Victor to reply, and for the first time a faint flush showed itself on his cheek.

"I believe not. There was no talk of it last autumn. I have heard no rumours—"

"I am surprised at that. It is a poor family, and she will have little or no money; but the name and position ought to count for something. They would be almost more valuable than money to a young man beginning life."

"I am thankful that I have no name or position! I should like my husband to value me for myself, not for what I possessed!" cried Mollie quickly.

It gave her an uncomfortable feeling, amounting almost to an augury of ill, to hear Uncle Bernard talking of Margot Blount with such unusual interest. The first definite wish which he had expressed was in connection with her name; his last remarks virtually sanctioned with his approval any aspirations which Victor might secretly treasure. Lady Margot Blount could hardly be expected to marry a struggling barrister; but if that barrister were the possible heir of the Court, his importance became at once largely increased.

Victor was unfailing in his efforts to please his host, and the result of this conversation would inevitably be a closer intimacy with the Blount family, which, even if it led to nothing more serious, would of a certainty cloud Ruth's happiness. Mollie was by no means sure that she approved of Victor as a suitor for her beloved sister, but, with delightful inconsistency, she hated the idea of his daring to care for anyone else, and the thought lent an unwonted edge to her voice—

"It's horrid to talk about marriage in that mercenary fashion, as if it were a pure business arrangement. When I hear such remarks, I'm thankful that I haven't a penny piece in the world!"

"If that is your feeling, you would be in a most unfortunate position as the owner of the Court. It would be a pity to disturb your equanimity, my dear."

Mr Farrell stretched out his thin hands on his knees, looking at her with quizzical eyes, whereupon Mollie forgot her anger, and gave one of her gay, infectious laughs, nodding her head towards him in mischievous, new-found familiarity.

"Ah, you had me there! But I might be like Queen Bess, you know, and prize my kingdom above any man; or, if one came along whom I really wanted to marry, I'd send him to slay dragons and carry off golden apples, to prove his devotion and disinterestedness. Don't cut me off through any mistaken scruples, Uncle Bernard. I'd really make a delightful chatelaine, and I should enjoy it so! No one appreciates the real object of money more than I do!"

"And what is your idea of the 'real value,' if one may ask?"

"To spend, of course!" she answered audaciously. "It is the only thing to do, for if you keep it, it's just a dull collection of coins. I love spending! Now, if I became a big heiress to-morrow, would you like to know what I should do?"

"Extremely; it would be most interesting!" said Mr Farrell.

"Yes, Miss Mollie, do tell us!" urged Victor.

Jack looked up with a puckered brow, half amused, half anxious, and Ruth murmured a gentle "Mollie dear!" Mollie was not to be deterred by encouragement or warning. She lay back in her chair, tapping off each item on her fingers as she spoke, her face one beam of mischievous enjoyment.

"I'd settle annuities on all my relations and friends. I'd buy the most exquisite presents, and send them round to everyone who had been kind to me in my poor estate. I'd give huge donations to governess's Homes, and funds for poor gentlewomen, and send them flowers, and fruit, and game. I'd go to Liberty's, and buy artistic furniture, and hire experts to superintend decorations, and, while the house was being put in order, I'd go a voyage round the world, and buy stacks of lovely things at every port, and see all the sights, and come home laden with spoils! Then I'd settle down, and,"—she chuckled complacently—"I *would* have a good time! I'd have every single thing I wanted, and never think of what it cost!"

"Until the bailiffs arrived; which would be surprisingly soon, I should imagine!" said Uncle Bernard drily. "You have not much idea of the responsibility of wealth, my dear. I prefer not to discuss the point, however. My own views, which are peculiar, are set forth in the Will which is lying in the desk in my room."

The four young people looked up sharply. The same question was on the lips of each; but it was Victor's eagerness which first found words—

"The Will?—Now! But surely—?"

Mr Farrell's lips twisted into a grim smile, as if he had of deliberate purpose provoked their curiosity.

"You are surprised that I have already come to a conclusion. It is by no means unchangeable; but, in the extremely precarious condition of my health, I do not think it safe to delay matters indefinitely. This Will was drawn up last week, and is based upon my impressions up to the present time. If I live it is extremely likely that I may alter my mind once and again; but it should be a comfort to you all to feel that, at the worst, I am not unprepared."

He looked from one to the other with the same faint, mocking smile, his gaze lingering on Ruth's troubled face. Her eyes expressed a questioning so intense as to be almost wild; then slowly they fell before his, and a crimson tide rushed over her cheeks.

Chapter Twenty Three.

Hard at Work.

Preparations for Mrs Thornton's garden-party went on uninterruptedly during the next week, and grew in fervour as the great day approached. Everybody had accepted, as the hostess announced with a groan and a laugh; and the vicar threatened to be called abroad on urgent business, so alarmed was he at the prospect of the fashionable throng which was to invade his shabby precincts. When, however, Mrs Thornton made up her mind to carry out a plan, she was not easily damped; and aided by Mollie and the younger members of her brood, she weeded, and forked, and clipped at the over-grown garden, until it really began to assume quite a presentable appearance.

"I daren't weed," Mollie explained, "for I'm a poor town thing, who would probably pull up your most cherished seedlings; but my arms are so strong that I can mow with the best, so I'll take the grass in hand, if someone else will trim the borders."

"But your face, my dear—your face!" cried Mrs Thornton, staring with dismay at the crimsoned countenance beneath the straw hat. "I'm ashamed to let you work so hard! What would your uncle say if he saw you now?"

"Something uncomplimentary, no doubt. I know I am magenta, but fortunately it isn't lasting. I asked Mr Druce if he would help me this morning, and do a little rolling into the bargain, but he would not give up his ride."

Mrs Thornton pursed up her lips, stared first at the ground, then at the sky, then across into Mollie's face.

"He is very fond of riding!" she said mysteriously. "I see him pass every morning, going in the same direction, and always alone. How is it that none of you ever go with him?"

"Jack Melland is still lame, and Ruth and I are only beginners. We have little canters together in the afternoons sometimes, but in the mornings he prefers to be free to go longer distances. He goes ever so far—miles and miles. One morning last week he met Lady Margot Blount somewhere near the Moat."

"And one morning this week also, for my husband saw them together, and if I were inclined to gossip, I should say it was oftener than once. My dear Mollie, how charming! Are we going to have a love-story to enliven the summer? Nobody ever gets engaged or married in this sleepy place, and this would be truly exciting! But I thought at one time—excuse my saying so, won't you, dear?—I quite thought he admired your sister, and that there might be a match there!"

"Of course, he admired her—no one could help it; but please never hint at anything of the sort to Ruth. She is very reserved, and would hate to be talked about!" cried Mollie hastily.

Across the lawn Ruth's graceful figure could be seen kneeling in front of a bed of flowers which she was fastening to supporting sticks in her usual neat, methodical fashion. No one could have recognised that bed as the same confused broken-down mass of blossom which it had been an hour earlier.

"There! now they do look as if someone loved them," said Ruth to herself, straightening her weary back, and brushing the soil off her fingers.

After the Thorntons' more casual work was over, she had made a careful round of the beds, giving those dainty finishing touches which add so largely to the effect. Now her work was finished, and, seeing Mrs Thornton and Mollie standing together, she rose stiffly, and walked across the lawn to meet them.

"Have you finished? I think I have really come to the end of the beds, and everything looks delightfully 'cared for'! I shall bring my camera down on Thursday, Mrs Thornton, and take some snapshots of your guests in pretty corners of the garden. Did you know I had taken the photographic fever? I bought myself a really, really nice camera, and I want to take mother a collection of views of the Court when we go home. She will value it more than anything else, for I shall snap all her favourite bits in the grounds, and take the interiors with time-exposures. They will be nice to look at when we are away, and someone else reigns in our stead!"

She shrugged her shoulders as she spoke, and Mrs Thornton patted her arm with kindly encouragement.

"Nonsense—nonsense! You are tired, dear, and that makes you look at things through blue spectacles. Come into the house, and we will have tea, and discuss the great question of where my guests are to sit, if anything so dreadful as a shower should happen! Two armchairs, you see, half a dozen small ones, more or less unstable (if anyone over seven stone attempts the green plush there'll be a catastrophe!), and one sofa. Now, put your inventive brains together, and tell me what I can do. There is plenty of room for more furniture, but no money to buy it, alas!"

"Let them sit on the floor in rows; it would be ever so sociable!" said naughty Mollie.

Ruth knitted her brows thoughtfully.

"Have you any chair-beds? We could make quite elegant lounges of them, pushed up against the wall, covered with rugs and banked up with cushions; or even out of two boards propped up at the sides, if the worst came to the worst!"

"Oh–oh! Chair-beds! What an inspiration! I have two stored away in the attic. They are old and decrepit, but that doesn't matter a bit. They will look quite luxurious when the mattresses are covered with sofa-blankets; but I don't know where the cushions are to come from. I only possess these three, and they must stay where they are to hide the patches in the chintz. I might perhaps borrow—"

"No, don't do anything of the kind. Use your pillows, and Ruth and I will make frilled covers out of art-muslin, at threepence a yard. They will look charming, and lighten up the dark corners. We are used to that sort of work at home. We made a cosy corner for the drawing-room out of old packing-cases and a Liberty curtain, and it is easier and more comfortable than any professional one I ever saw. The silly upholsterers always make the seats too high and narrow. We made a music ottoman of the inside, and broke our backs lining it, and our nails hammering in the tacks; but, dear me, how we did enjoy it, and how proud we were when it was accomplished for seventeen-and-six!

"I'm beginning to doubt," repeated Mollie solemnly, "whether it is half so amusing to be rich as it is to be poor. When you can get everything you want the moment you want it, you don't appreciate it half so much as when you have pined for it, and saved up your pennies for it, for months beforehand. When we get a new thing at home, the whole family pay visits to it like a shrine, and we open the door and go into the room where it is, one after the other, to study the effect, and gloat over it. It *is* fun; isn't it, now? Confess that it is!"

"Ye–es," agreed Mrs Thornton doubtfully. "But where you have to wait too long, the sense of humour gets a little bit blunted, especially as one grows older, Mollie dear!"

She sighed as she spoke, and her eyes roved pensively round the discoloured walls, those same walls whose condition had fired Mollie to make her unsuccessful appeal. The girl's thoughts went back to that embarrassing interview, not altogether regretfully, since it had ended in bringing about a better understanding between her uncle and herself. Perhaps, though he had refused her request, it would linger in his mind, and lead to good results. Nothing but the unexpected was certain about Uncle Bernard.

The next afternoon the vicarage drawing-room presented a rather chaotic appearance, as Mrs Thornton and her assistants prepared the important couches. Ruth sat in the middle of the floor running up lengths of brightly coloured muslins on a sewing-machine, while the other two wrestled with the difficulties which attend all make-shifts. With the greatest regard for ease and luxury, the beds were pronounced decidedly too low to look genuine, and the rickety legs had to be propped up with foundations manufactured out of old bound volumes of magazines, bricks from the garden, and an odd weight or two from the kitchen scales. The sofa-blankets also turned out to be too narrow, and persisted in disclosing the iron legs, until, in desperation, one end was sewn to the mattress, allowing the full width to hang down in front.

At last the work was finished, and the hot and dishevelled workers retired to the hall, and, re-entering the room to study the effect, in true Farrell manner, pronounced the "divans" to look professional beyond all fear of detection.

The next achievement was to place a tapering bank of plants against a discoloured patch of wallpaper, and many and varied were the struggles before the necessary stand was arranged. Eventually an old desk formed the bottom tier, a stool the second, and the baby's high chair the third and last. Draped with an old piece of green baize, with small pots of trailing *Tradescantia* fitted into the crossbars of the chair, and the good old family *Aspidistras* ("as old as Mabel!" explained Mrs Thornton, stroking one of the long green leaves affectionately) taking the place of honour, the effect was so superior and luxurious that the vicar had to be dragged from his study to exclaim and admire.

"There, just look at our divans! Did you ever see anything look more luxurious? Who could ever suspect they were only a make-up? Sit down and see how comfortable this is!" cried Mrs Thornton volubly; whereupon the vicar sat down heavily in the centre of the seat, and promptly descended to the floor amidst a heaped-up pile of bedding, pillows, *Sunday at Homes*, and broken bricks.

He gasped and groped wildly with his hands, and the sight of him sitting prone among the ruins was so comical that both girls went off into peals of laughter. The humorous side of the accident was not, however, quite so apparent to the mistress of the ceremonies.

"That tiresome, tiresome bed! I might have known as much! It used to collapse with me regularly when I was nursing Mabel with scarlet-fever!" she cried impatiently. "Now we shall have to begin from the beginning, and make it up again. How tiresome of you, Arthur, to be so heavy!"

"I will spare you the obvious retort, dear. Let us be thankful that I was the victim, and not Lady Elstree, whom you would certainly have escorted to the seat of honour to-morrow. If you will allow me to help, I think I could manage to make things fast."

At this critical moment a loud rat-tat sounded at the door, and Mrs Thornton rushed to peep out of the window.

"Horrors, a visitor! Mary will show her into the room, I know she will! That girl has no more sense than a doll! Ruth—Mollie—Wallace! pick up the things on the floor; throw them behind the sofa! Pull the sewing-machine to the wall! There's no room for anyone to tread! Of all the tiresome, aggravating—"

"Nonsense, dear—nonsense!" cried the vicar, laughing. "Leave things as they are. You have quite sufficient excuse in the fact of expecting a hundred people to-morrow. There will be no room to tread then, if you like!"

He turned towards the door as he spoke, and Mrs Thornton hastily smoothed her hair as it opened wide, and Mary's eager voice announced—

"If you please, mum, a 'amper!"

"A *what*?"

The vicar and his wife pressed forward eagerly, and, lo! on the well-worn oilcloth of the passage lay a large wicker hamper, addressed to "Mrs Thornton, The Vicarage, Raby," and bearing on the label the name of a well-known London fruiterer. To cut the string and tear it open was the work of a moment, when inside was revealed such treasures of hothouse fruits as left the beholders dumb and gasping with admiration.

There in profusion were grapes, peaches, giant strawberries of the deepest red, pineapples,—each one more perfect and tempting than the last, in their dainty, padded cases.

The vicar stood looking on, stroking his chin, and smiling with enjoyment at his wife's delight, as she bent over her treasures, exclaiming and rapturising like a girl in her teens.

"How lovely! How charming! How delightful! My fruit-table will be a triumph! This is exactly what I needed to give the finishing touch to my preparations! I've never seen finer fruit—never! Wallace, Wallace, won't we be grand?"

"So grand that I am afraid the churchwardens will have serious doubts as to the school funds," said the vicar, laughing. "I have twenty pounds in hand at the present moment, and really—"

"Oh, don't be a goose! Of course, everyone will guess that it is a present. I shall say so myself on every opportunity. But who from? Who can have thought of such a thing?" Her eyes turned with sudden questioning to the two girls. "Ruth, Mollie—did you?"

"Indeed, no! I didn't think of it, I am sorry to say!" said Ruth; and added honestly, "I am too hard up to pay for all those lovely things!"

"And you know nothing about it, really?"

"Really and truly, not a thing!"

"You don't think that perhaps the squire—"

Mollie recalled the snubbing which she had received on suggesting the improvements to the vicarage, coupled with the various cynical remarks to which Mr Farrell had given utterance on the subject of this very garden-party, and felt convinced that he was not the anonymous donor; but these things were not to be repeated, so she remained silent, while Ruth and Mrs Thornton wondered and speculated.

No one could be thought of more likely than the squire, for the parishioners, as a rule, were not overburdened with money, nor the few who were, with generosity.

"I have never had such a thing done for me all the years I have been here—never once!" cried Mrs Thornton, waxing almost tearful in her excess of gratitude. "And to send it anonymously, too—so modest and unassuming! The dear, kind, thoughtful creature. I shall never rest until I know who it is?"

Chapter Twenty Four.

The Day of the Party.

The morning of the garden-party was bright, almost perilously bright even for June; but there was exhilaration in the sight of the blue sky, dappled with fleecy white clouds, which formed such an exquisite contrast to the velvety green of the landscape, and a delicious sense of luxury in strolling about in the sun, and feeling rid at last of the treacherous wind.

The squire's guests breakfasted upon the terrace, to the mild disapproval of Mrs Wolff, who could not understand why people could not be content to remain comfortably indoors, instead of picknicking in gipsy-like fashion on every possible occasion. Her small, pinched face expressed the annoyance which she had not the courage to put into words, and as soon as her duties were over she hurried back to the shelter of the house. Immediately she had disappeared Jack boldly demanded another cup of coffee, and set to work on toast and marmalade with a fresh access of appetite.

The opportunity was too good to be resisted. Ruth flew indoors for her camera, and stood a few yards off focusing the table and its occupants, and waiting for a picturesque moment in which to snap. It came at last, just as Jack was forgetfully indulging in an enormous bite, a bachelor habit which had become a standing joke among his companions. Mollie had stolen a half-eaten piece of toast from his plate one morning, and measured the gap with an inch tape, to his everlasting embarrassment, so that the pictured memorial was hailed with delight.

Needless to say, Jack wished to have his revenge, and immortalise Mollie scraping the sugar out of the bottom of the cup in school-girl fashion, and finally Bates was pressed into the service and instructed how to snap, so that a complete group might be taken.

By this time it was ten o'clock, and Mollie announced her intention of going down to the vicarage to help in the final preparations for the afternoon's entertainment. She took for granted that Ruth would accompany her; but Miss Ruth had her own ideas as to the employment of the next few hours, and they had nothing to do with Mrs Thornton's garden-party.

On her way downstairs to breakfast she had overheard Victor telling a servant that he had no orders for the stables this morning. The inference was, therefore, that he intended to stop at home, and the thought had instantly darted into her mind that if Mollie went off to the vicarage there would be an hour or two before lunch, when—when—

Ruth blushed guiltily to herself when she got so far in her calculations; but it was such a delight to enjoy a quiet *tête-à-tête* talk sometimes, instead of the general impersonal conversation. So it came to pass that when Mollie announced her intention of going down to the vicarage to help in the final preparations, Ruth absolutely refused to accompany her.

"I've done my share," she said. "To-day I am going to be a visitor pure and simple, and drive down when everything is ready for my reception."

Mollie shrugged her shoulders resignedly.

"Well, somebody has got to do it, and, thank goodness, I'm not poor-spirited enough to leave a friend in the lurch at the last moment! I shan't be satisfied until I see the last chair in order; but I don't see any reason why I should walk. There is a pony-carriage in the stables, and if anyone had any nice feeling they would drive me there and back!"

Jack laughed, and limped across the terrace.

"Anyone, singular; they, plural! Your grammar is deficient, Miss Mollie; but I suppose your modesty forbade you to be more explicit.

I have lots of good-feeling, and nothing to do, so I shall be charmed to escort you, if you will give the order. It would take me too long to get down to the stables."

It was evident that Jack's offer was pleasing to Mollie, for she thanked him with a smile as bright as her words, and a quarter of an hour later on they were driving together across the park behind the sleek little pony, Mollie chatting gaily as usual, Jack listening with an air half amused, half bored. Despite his accident, he was looking strong and well, his skin bronzed by the outdoor life of the last few weeks; but the old haughty, intolerant expression, which had seemed his chief characteristic at first meeting, was still noticeable in curving lip and nostril. Not an easy man to convince against his will, nor one to be easily affected by the presence of a pretty girl.

"How cross Uncle Bernard was when I told him about the mysterious hamper! One would think he grudged poor Mrs Thornton having anything nice!" said Mollie severely. "He nearly snapped my head off when I asked if he had sent it. I should not have thought much of that, if he had not denied it in so many words, for he might have been trying to put me off; but after what he said there can be no more doubt on the subject. I wonder who could have sent it? Mrs Thornton says she will never rest till she finds out."

Jack flicked the pony impatiently.

"Why can't she be content to take it quietly, and not worry any more? That's the worst of women—they must make a fuss! If the man who sent it wanted to be thanked, he would have put in a card. If he didn't, it shows that he prefers to be anonymous, and it's bad taste to go ferreting round trying to find out what she is not intended to know. I should tell her so straight, if I were you."

"No, you wouldn't, because, being a woman, you would be consumed with curiosity, as I am. Now, I wonder why you said the 'man'?" queried Mollie, tilting her head on one side, and staring at him with mischievous eyes. "What makes you think it was a man? Couldn't it as easily have been a woman?"

"Oh, quite; but I prefer to use one pronoun and stick to it, instead of muddling them up as you do. Why are you always in such a hurry to snap a fellow up?" cried Jack irritably.

Mollie made a naughty little *moue*.

"I thought it was the other way about! I was most mild and lamb-like, when you snubbed me for my grammar, abused my sex, and accused me of bad temper. It shows how little you know of my beautiful disposition!"

Jack flicked the pony again, his face darkened by a frown.

"No, I don't know you—how should I? You never give me a chance. You show me only the frivolous side of your character. You are always laughing, joking, frivolling. In all these weeks I have only once had a glimpse of your real self. You evidently do not wish me to know you in any real or intimate sense; but that is your own fault, not mine."

"If you have seen it only once, it cannot be my real self," said Mollie quietly. She had grown, not red but white, as she listened to Jack's words, and her heart had begun to beat in an agitating fashion hitherto unknown. She felt as if somebody had suddenly dealt her an unexpected blow, for until this moment she had fondly imagined herself to be good friends with Jack Melland. "You do not know me, because, perhaps, there is nothing to know, beyond the frivolous, silly creature you dislike so much!"

"There you go again, exaggerating and catching up my words! Who said I disliked you? We were not talking of likes or dislikes. We were talking of knowing each other properly. I wouldn't trouble my head if you were an ordinary, empty-headed girl, but I know you are not. There is another side to your character, and I want to see and know you in it, but you evade me, and refuse to show yourself. I suppose I am not worth the trouble of talking to seriously?"

Mollie shook her head dejectedly.

"I am not evading, I am not hiding anything. I'm nineteen, and out for a holiday. It's the first taste of luxury I've ever known. I enjoyed it so much,"—unconsciously to herself she used the past, not the present, tense—"that surely it was natural for me to be light-hearted. I am not highly educated, and I've lived a very quiet life. It's only natural that I seem stupid in comparison with other girls you have met. I suppose they are very clever and well read?"

Jack kept his eyes on the road, mentally classifying the girls with whom he had been most closely brought in contact in his town life. Yes! they were for the most part accomplished and clever; but were they not also apt to be discontented with their lot, given to grumbling at the restrictions of home life, and to imagine themselves ill-used and unappreciated? Mollie's radiant good-humour and unconsciousness of self were qualities unknown among them. What poor, anaemic images they appeared beside her! Yet he was continually provoked by the very cheerfulness which he mentally approved. Jack frowned, puzzled and disquieted. As a rule, he was at no loss to account for his prejudices, but for once he found himself completely mystified. What exactly was it that he wanted of Mollie Farrell, the lack of which rankled in his veins? He could not tell, and annoyance with self gave an added touch of irritation to his tone.

"Oh, if you cannot distinguish between becoming a bookworm and talking seriously once in a way, there is no more to be said! I'm sorry I spoke. Now I suppose you will be offended with me, and the day will be spoiled?"

It was not a gracious speech, but Jack did not feel gracious, and he had not much control over his temper. An inner voice informed him that he was behaving like a cad, and he acknowledged the truth of the indictment, while in the same moment he was prepared to reply more irritably than before.

He had not the chance, however, for Mollie's eyes met his without the faintest shadow of reproach. There was a subtle change in her expression, but it spoke neither of offence nor anger.

"No, I am not vexed; that would be stupid, for it would only make things worse. It is my nature to look on the bright side of things. I know I am thoughtless, but it won't last. I shall be serious enough some day—perhaps sooner than we think. Don't grudge me my little hour!"

The face raised to his looked so young and wistful that Jack felt a pang of the same remorse which one feels who has wounded a little child. He averted his eyes and drove on in silence, thinking, thinking.—The clever town girl would have been mortally insulted if he had dared to criticise her manners or attainments, and would have justified herself by a dozen plausible arguments. Mollie was ready to admit everything against herself, and only anxious to save him from any feeling of embarrassment.

She talked on impersonal topics all the rest of the way to the vicarage, and her smile when she bade him good-bye was resolutely cheerful, but he hated himself as he realised that for the first time there was an effort involved. As he turned the pony round the corner of the little lane which bordered the lawn he heard Mrs Thornton's surprised exclamation, "Why, Mollie!" and the half-laughing exclamation, "It's nothing! The sun is so strong, it made my eyes—smart!"

Jack Melland set his teeth and drove on in a tumult of feeling such as he had never known before in the course of his self-satisfied existence. Blundering, presumptuous wretch that he was! If any trouble came to Mollie Farrell, he would feel as guilty as if he himself had deliberately brought it to pass!

Chapter Twenty Five.

Confidences.

While Mollie was busy at the vicarage, Ruth took her book to her favourite seat, and prepared to spend a quiet morning; but to her delight, Victor joined her, and took his place by her side, before she had been seated more than a few minutes.

"He will see Lady Margot this afternoon. He need not ride ahead in the hope of meeting her," came the involuntary bitter thought; but it was impossible to harbour jealousy for more than a minute when alone in Victor's company. Every word, every look, every tone, was filled with a subtle flattery which was not only soothing but inspiring into the bargain, for we are always at our best in the society of those who appreciate us.

Ruth gazed, with the old delightful sense of well-being, across the beautiful grounds, in which the long slopes of green and wide-spreading trees had already grown dear and familiar as old friends. Surely every day it became more certain that this would be her home of the future, since Jack was still determined to return to town the moment he was sufficiently recovered from his accident, and Mollie's extravagance was plainly distasteful to Uncle Bernard. As for Victor, if he really—really meant... Ruth did not finish the sentence even to herself, but at the bottom of her mind lurked the inevitable reflection that she stood a double chance.

Evidently Victor's thoughts had, to a certain extent, followed her own, for he broke the silence by saying suddenly—

"That was an extraordinary statement of Mr Farrell's the other day,—that he had already made a will. I suppose it is a wise precaution under the circumstances, but it gave one rather a shock to know that things were already settled."

"Yes, poor old man! one hates to realise how ill he must be. He does not seem to have grown any worse since we came, so far as an outsider can judge, but he must feel his weakness increasing."

Ruth puckered her brows in a distressed fashion, too much occupied with her own thoughts to notice Victor's quick glance of inquiry.

His concern had not been for Mr Farrell or his sufferings, but he was quick to change his tone in response to hers.

"I expect he does," said Victor, "though he is too well-plucked to complain. The doctor told me the other day that these fluctuations are part of the disease, and mean no real improvement. He does not give him long, though he thinks it will probably be six months or more. It must be more or less of an effort to him having us here, and if his mind is already made up, I wonder he does not prefer to go back to his solitude."

"He said he might still change, you remember. The will is only made in case of accidents. It does seem strange to think of it lying there all the time, and that one peep at it would end all our wonderings. I *should* like to see it!" cried Ruth with an outspoken honesty which apparently shocked her companion.

"Be careful what you say, Miss Ruth! Farrell is just the sort of cross-grained old fellow to take all sorts of ideas into his head if he heard you. And, besides, you can surely guess for yourself what name you would find!"

Ruth lifted her face to his in quick inquiry. The brown eyes were for once fully open and looking down at her with an expression half smiling, half melancholy. "You know it would be your own!" he said softly, and she flushed in quick denial.

"No, no; it's impossible to be certain. I hope, of course, but— At first I thought Uncle Bernard liked me best, but lately Mollie seems to have cut me out."

"But we are told that liking has nothing to do with the great decision."

"I know, and that does away at once with so many qualities with one fell swoop, that one can hardly tell what is left. It puts amiability out of the question, and unselfishness and cheerfulness, and—and tact, and everything which makes us care for a person or not. When they are gone, what is left?"

"A great many things, just as Mr Farrell's knowledge of our characters and actions is far more extensive than you suspect. We meet at meals, and in the evening, and for the rest of the day one would imagine that we are beyond his ken, but I have discovered that to be a mistake. In some mysterious fashion he knows all that we do, and guesses fairly accurately what we think! ... Would you imagine, for instance, that he knew that this seat was our favourite resort, and that we have enjoyed some very pleasant *tête-à-têtes* here during the last few weeks? Would you imagine that he knew who gave me that white rosebud which I wore as a button-hole last night?"

Ruth's face was a rose itself at that moment, a red, red rose, as the colour flew from her cheeks up to the roots of her hair. Her eyes wavered, and fell.

"How can he know? How do you know he knows?" she queried confusedly; and Victor shrugged his shoulders.

"How, I can't tell you, but I suspect his man James is a useful source of information. I know that he knows, because of several caustic remarks which he has let fall from time to time, to which my legal experience easily gives me the clue. I have come to the conclusion that he knows pretty well what we are about every hour of the day!"

"Even when you go out riding by yourself, and meet Lady Margot in the lanes?" questioned Ruth, stung by a sudden rising of jealousy, which she was unable to control. The words were no sooner spoken than regretted, and regret deepened into shame as Victor turned his calmly surprised eyes upon her.

"Certainly! as I told him myself in the first instance. Since then I have been fortunate enough to meet her again once or twice. The good vicar saw us together on one occasion; I presume he hurried home forthwith to spread the news over the parish. In these dead-alive places the most casual acquaintance is magnified into a scandal, but fortunately Lady Margot is a woman of the world who is unaffected by silly chatter. She has a dull time at the Moat, and is glad to meet a fellow-creature with whom she can have a few minutes' conversation. Personally, I don't care what the whole parish pleases to say. There is only one person whose opinion matters. ... Ruth! what are you trying to imply?" He moved nearer to her as he spoke, until the arm which rested on the back of the seat almost touched her shoulder. "Lady Margot is pleased to be friendly and gracious, but she does not belong to my world. She is a star far above the head of a poor struggling barrister, even if he were fool enough to aspire to her, which he certainly would not do so long as there are inhabitants of his own sphere a hundred times more beautiful and more attractive."

Ruth shook her head, her eyes fixed shyly on the ground.

"If the barrister were the heir to the Court, it would make all the difference in the world. Uncle Bernard spoke very warmly of the Blount family. It might increase your chance," she urged, compelled by some impulse which she could not understand to argue against her own wishes. "Perhaps the condition has something to do with ambition, and pride of race."

"In that case, again you score the advantage, for you are his direct descendant. I think myself, however, that it refers entirely to money. He has warned us that he has peculiar ideas on the subject. Probably he is on the look-out for a similar peculiarity. He has consulted me, and Melland also, I believe, on several matters in connection with the estate; but my ideas are purely businesslike, and Melland is hopelessly happy-go-lucky, so there was nothing original in either his advice or mine. No! from whichever point of view I consider the question, I always come to the same conclusion. You are the nearest heir; you are a Farrell in name as well as appearance. You are not extravagant nor thoughtless like your sister. To Melland, as well as to myself, the result is a foregone conclusion. I would congratulate you on the spot if I could do so honestly.—I wonder if you will in the least understand what I mean, when I say that I wish it had been any one of the four rather than yourself?"

The face that was raised to his was for a moment simply shocked and surprised, but under his steady gaze comprehension dawned, and Ruth turned hastily aside, saying, in a tremulous voice which vainly struggled to be defiant—

"I shall remind you of that unkind speech when you are living in state, and I am toiling for my daily bread. I could not have believed you would be so unkind."

"I am not afraid, for that day will never dawn. Remember it, rather, when you are reigning here, and a poor fellow stifling up in town refuses the invitations because he longs to accept, and dare not, remembering the difference between us!"

It was pretty plain speaking, and Ruth did not pretend to misunderstand its meaning. At that moment all doubts died away. She believed herself to be loved, and as her lover considered himself in an inferior position to her own, she was generous enough to show him her own feelings in return. The dark lashes rested upon her cheeks, her lips quivered like a child's, as she said softly—

"If I did own the Court, if Uncle Bernard left me everything he possessed, it would be worthless to me if—if I were separated from the friends I cared for most."

Chapter Twenty Six.

A Shattered Ideal.

By four o'clock that afternoon the vicarage grounds presented a festive appearance, as the hundred guests strolled to and fro, arrayed in light, summer-like garments. The tennis-lawn was occupied by a succession of players, a ping-pong table stood in a quiet corner and attracted a certain number of devotees, and the grass-plot in front of the study window had been marked out for golf croquet. For those less actively disposed there were seats in the prettiest corners, and an endless supply of refreshments served on little tables under the trees.

Ruth was looking lovely and radiant, blissfully conscious of Victor's presence, even if he were at the further end of the garden; of a dress and hat which suited her to perfection, and of her own importance in the eyes of the assembly—Miss Farrell, the squire's nearest living relation, his image in appearance, and reputed to be his favourite. Surely this must be the future mistress of the Court! The intoxicating whisper followed her wherever she went, and heightened the flush in her cheek.

"Berengaria!" cried a laughing voice; and she turned to see Lady Margot Blount standing by her side, holding out a slim, gloved hand. While most of the girls present were arrayed in chiffons and laces, she wore a perfectly simple lawn dress, with a coarse straw hat shading her face; but the accessories of shoes, gloves, belt, parasol, and dainty jewelled fastenings were all of an immaculate perfection, and with her tall, graceful carriage she was by far the most striking figure present.

The two girls had met several times at different houses in the neighbourhood since the formal exchange of calls, and it was not Margot's fault that the friendship had not progressed still further. She was always cordial, almost demonstrative in manner, eager to plan fresh meetings and mutual occupations. It was Ruth who persistently put obstacles in the way. In spite of Victor's protestations, she instinctively recognised in Lady Margot a formidable rival, and the knowledge gave her courage to disregard her uncle's expressed wishes, and neither give nor accept informal invitations.

To-day, however, in the flush of her success she was full of good-will to the whole world, and the former jealousy was replaced by commiseration. Poor Lady Margot, poor everybody whom Victor did not love as he loved herself!

"Oh, Lady Margot, I am so glad to see you," she cried frankly. "Do come for a stroll with me! I am so tired of being asked how I like Raby, and talking commonplaces to curious strangers. Doesn't it all look bright and pretty? If only it will keep fine to the end."

"Oh, we may have a shower, but I don't think it will be anything more serious Yes; Mrs Thornton has done wonders. Shall we take this path? It is the narrowest and quietest, so there is the less fear of interruption."

Ruth turned in the direction indicated with a somewhat doubtful look. A narrow path, bordered on one side by prickly gooseberry-bushes, was hardly the promenade for her perishable fineries; but while she hesitated Margot led the way forward, and she followed, drawing her skirts tightly together. Even so, disaster awaited her, for in the interest of an animated discussion some of the filmy folds slipped from the hand which held the parasol, dragged along the ground, and finally caught with a rip and a jerk, leaving a long jagged tear at the hem.

Of the two exclamations, Margot's was far the most distressed.

"Oh, my poor Berengaria! How thoughtless of me to bring you here! It's all my fault. I am such a plain-hemmed creature myself that I forgot your frills. You must fasten it up at once or you may trip. I can give you some pins, and there is a little summer-house at the end of the path, where you can sit down and fasten it properly. I'll stand before the door and screen you from the public gaze."

RUTH SAT MOTIONLESS; IT COULD NOT BE VICTOR'S VOICE?

[*See page 295*

"Oh, thanks, it will be all right; I am thankful it was not further up. The hem can always be shortened," said Ruth practically. She sat down in a corner of the summer-house, the windows of which were screened by thickly growing tendrils of hop, and, spreading out the tear, began to pin it daintily together, while Lady Margot mounted guard outside.

A minute passed—two minutes—then came the sound of a man's quick tread, and a voice spoke, a voice broken by a quiver of emotion which could tell only one tale.

"Lady Margot! You here? I have been looking for you all afternoon. Why did you hide yourself in this out-of-the-way place? You knew I should be waiting."

The pin fell from Ruth's hand, she sat motionless as a statue behind the leafy screen. It could not, could not be Victor's voice!

"I have not been here many minutes," Lady Margot replied quietly. "I knew we should meet sooner or later; but you are a public character to-day, and I must not monopolise your attention."

"Monopolise!" cried the voice again, the familiar voice with the strange, unfamiliar thrill. Ruth's head dropped forward and her hands clasped the seat on either side. "You talk of monopolising, while I starve all week with just a chance five minutes now and then to keep me alive! I rode for about three hours yesterday morning without even a glimpse of you in the distance. I have been counting the hours until this afternoon."

"Count them just a little bit longer, then; I have not spoken to half my friends, and we would certainly be interrupted. Do me a favour and go back to the lawn now, and later on—say in half an hour—come to me again, and you shall have your reward."

"I'd wait a hundred years if I could have what I wanted at the end!" said the voice passionately.

Footsteps crunched down the path, then came silence, and the falling of a shadow across the doorway. Ruth lifted an ashen face, and saw Lady Margot looking down upon her with tender, liquid eyes.

"Dear," she said gently, "you heard! I *meant* you to hear. Don't think me cruel; it was the truest kindness. You and I have something to say to each other. I know a quiet nook where we can be alone. Come, Ruth—come with me!"

Ruth rose mechanically and followed her guide through a door in the wall, which led to a square piece of ground, bare and ugly,—a cabbage-patch in name and in deed. There against the unromantic background the two girls stood looking at each other, face to face with the great question of their lives.

"Ruth," said Margot gently, "let us be honest with each other. It is the only way. This man—Victor Druce—has come into both our lives; let us find out where we stand! Shall I tell you my story first? I met him last summer, when we were thrown constantly together for six weeks, and he attracted me. I came nearer loving him than any man whom I had met. Why, I don't know. I saw he admired me; but others had done that, and when I was alone and could think about him quietly there were many things about him I did not like. Still, he fascinated me. I thought of him a great deal during the winter. I looked forward to seeing him again. He was not of my world, and it seemed impossible that anything serious could come of it; but I dreamt dreams... Then I came here, and found, to my amazement, that he was staying at the Court. He met me one morning going out for my ride, and since then it has often happened. From the first his manner was different; more assured. He told me of Mr Farrell's proposition, and insisted that the chances were in his favour. He wished me to look upon him as the future owner of the Court; a man who would be in my own position. He has been making love to me all these weeks, Ruth, but he has not definitely asked me to marry him. That's my story! Will you tell me yours in exchange?"

Ruth looked drearily round the bare, ugly patch. A moment before she had been living mentally and physically in a land of roses; now, in an instant, the scene had changed and the beauty had disappeared.

"I think," she said slowly, "that he has been making love to me too... He has insisted from the first that I am Uncle Bernard's favourite, the others think so too, and he has made me believe—only this morning he made me believe—that he was afraid to speak plainly because of the difference in our position. He said I should be a great lady, and he would be working for his bread far away, and thinking of me." Ruth's voice broke pitifully, but the red flamed in Margot's cheek, and she reared her proud head with a disdainful gesture.

"So! It is as I thought; he has been playing a waiting game, making love to us both, but keeping himself free until he saw how the land lay. If he inherited, Lady Margot Blount would be useful in society; if he were cut off, he would reserve the chance of marrying the heiress. And we have both been deceived, and have imagined that he was in earnest! I have seen him on the stage, and congratulated him on his success, but I was not prepared for such finished acting in real life."

"No!" said Ruth drearily, "you have not been deceived; he was not acting with you. I heard him speak just now, and I felt the difference. Oh, Margot, he is playing with me, but he is in earnest with you; he does really love you!"

Margot's lip curled scornfully.

"It is hardly my idea of love. If I am ever married, it shall be to a man who will risk something for my sake, not to a mercenary who thinks first of himself. I suspected something of this from the first afternoon I called at the Court. You were sitting together on the terrace, and something in his attitude... Oh, well, why dwell on it any more?—it is none too pleasant. Ruth dear, you have avoided me, and I have seemed to force myself upon you, but I was determined to find out the truth, for both our sakes. It is better so, is it not?"

Ruth's dull glance of misery was pathetic to behold.

"I suppose it is," she said slowly, "but just now I cannot feel glad. Everything seems over. I was so happy, and it will be so difficult to go on living in the same house, meeting at every hour of the day. It is easier for you, for you need not see him unless you wish, and you do not care as I did."

"Don't I?" queried Margot gently. "He has been first in my thoughts for nearly a year, Ruth, and you have known him for a few weeks. It is not easy for me, either; but we must both realise that the Victor Druce of our imagination never existed, but was a creation of our own brains. This man—this adventurer—who has used us as his tool, must never suspect that he has caused us pain; we must play our parts without flinching, and let him see more and more clearly that we desire nothing from him. It will be difficult, but there is nothing else for it, if we are to keep our dignity. Ruth, you have plenty of will-power;—one can see it in your face; you will not let this man deceive you again with his plausible words?"

Ruth shook her head. The grey eyes shone hard and bright, then suddenly brimmed with tears.

"Perhaps, after all, he is not worse than I am myself. Perhaps I deserve this lesson. Another man asked me to marry him before we left home. I did not love him, but he was well-off and had a nice house, and for a few minutes I was tempted. I told him so, and he said he did not want me if I could not care for himself alone... Perhaps if he had begged very hard I might have said 'yes.'"

Margot smiled—a very kindly smile.

"The cases are not precisely similar, are they? Instead of playing a double game you were absolutely honest; much more honest than is usual on such occasions. And he was a wise man. I think I should have liked that man! Compare him with Victor Druce sometimes, Ruth; it may help you to be brave... Now I am going back to the garden to act my part. We will meet and talk again, but we can't stay away any longer just now without attracting attention... Just tell me one thing before I go—Can you forgive me for shattering your dream?" She held out her hand, and Ruth took it in both hers.

"I have nothing to forgive. It is only wakening a little sooner; that's all!" she said tremulously.

Margot bent down lightly, and touched her forehead with her lips, then turned swiftly away, and Ruth was left alone. Poor, disenchanted Ruth, wideawake at last, in the midst of the deserted cabbage-patch!

Chapter Twenty Seven.

Jack Melland's Secret.

When Mr Farrell's guests assembled for dinner, on their return from the garden-party, it was at once evident that the old gentleman was in one of his difficult moods. From the beginning he had affected to disapprove of Mrs Thornton's extravagance in attempting to entertain on so large a scale, while sedulously keeping himself informed as to every detail of the preparations. The anonymous present of fruit had furnished him with a subject for much satirical comment, as had also the girls' endeavours to beautify the house and grounds.

Now he found a fresh grievance in the fact that dinner was delayed a few minutes past its usual hour, and that the young people appeared depressed, rather than elated by their experiences. Ruth's plea of a headache was justified by her wan looks; Jack was moody, and even Victor was for once silent and distrait. It was left to Mollie to stem the tide, and she raised herself nobly to the effort, albeit her own heart was none too light.

"It went off beautifully, Uncle Bernard! Shall I tell you all about it from the beginning?" she cried, smiling at his grim visage across the dinner-table; and when he declared his lack of interest in the whole concern, she smiled again, and refused to be convinced. "Oh, but you must hear, because in a kind of way it was your party, as you are the patron, and give them all that they have... There were such crowds of people, and they looked so gay. Old Lady Everett wore a magenta satin, quite the most awful garment I ever beheld, and she got hot, poor dear, and it matched her face. And such an awkward thing happened; she brought a little basket with a few under-sized grapes, about a pound, perhaps, and presented them to Mrs Thornton with such an air of munificence, and then turned round and saw the table spread with all that exquisite fruit! She was quite angry even when Mrs Thornton explained that it also was a gift."

"Why need she have explained at all? No other woman would have thought of doing so. Why should a clergyman's wife be expected to explain her private affairs to any inquisitive stranger? Surely it is her own business what she puts on her own table?" This from Jack, in a burst of querulous impatience which brought his host's eyes upon him with an answering flash.

"If a woman in a public position provides what is obviously unsuited to her means, the least she can do is to offer an explanation. A clergyman's means do not run to expensive entertainments."

"Exactly; yet he is expected to entertain, and to humble his pride to do it in an inferior style to his neighbours. And his wife is expected to accept paltry gifts from her neighbours which another woman in her position would look upon as an insult, and to be thankful for the chance. I suppose she often is thankful, poor creature, as she has not the means of providing properly for herself."

Mr Farrell put down his knife and fork, and, leaning back in his seat, stared fixedly in Jack's face. His thin lips worked, and his eyes gleamed ominously.

"May I ask if you are speaking in general terms, or individually of the clergyman's wife in my own parish?"

Jack shrugged his shoulders.

"Oh, I suppose she would be included, since her husband's income is insufficient for her needs."

"You are aware, of course, that I am responsible for that income?"

"I suppose so—in a way, since the living is in your gift."

"And what grounds may you have for considering it insufficient?"

Jack burst into a short laugh, undeterred by the appealing glances cast upon him by three frightened feminine listeners.

"What grounds? Why, the house is an advertisement of shabbiness; the vicar's coat is green with age, and the poor little kiddies look as if they had come out of the ark! Mrs Thornton has pluck enough for a dozen, or she would never keep things going as she does; but she looks an old woman before her time."

"Then it is your deliberate conclusion that I ought to increase the Vicar's stipend?"

Under cover of the tablecloth a little hand stole along and laid a gentle pressure on Jack's arm. He turned and met Mollie's eyes, grave and appealing, with no trace of the frivolity of which he had complained earlier in the day, and, at the sight, his irritation died a sudden death. Mollie must indeed have forgiven him when she condescended to so sweet an intimacy. The rush of joy which accompanied the thought put him at once at peace with all men.

"The labourer is worthy of his hire, sir," he answered quietly. "I call Thornton a rattling good fellow, and I should like to see him relieved of monetary troubles. It's hard lines to expect a man to be an example of all the virtues when he is constantly wondering how to make both ends meet. I don't set much store on money, as you know, but I should enjoy being in the position to do a good turn to a man like that."

Mr Farrell's sunken eyes gave forth a malicious gleam.

"You speak with feeling. Perhaps you have been enjoying a foretaste of the experience. Surely you must be the generous Unknown who contributed the hamper of fruit of which we have heard so much during the last few days!"

There was a simultaneous gasp of surprise round the table, and everyone turned to stare with curious eyes at Jack's scarlet face. Scarlet, with an embarrassment which plainly proved the truth of the accusation; with anger, too, and thwarted self-will. His nostrils inflated in the old haughty manner, as he replied coldly—

"I thought we were discussing Mr Thornton's income! I fail to see what the hamper has to do with the case."

Mr Farrell gave the short, staccato sound which did service for a laugh.

"Your pardon! It is to me a very interesting sidelight. I am indebted to you for stepping in to make up for my deficiencies."

"It was very kind of you, Mr Melland—very, very kind! You don't know how much pleasure it gave. I envy you for having had such a nice thought," said Ruth earnestly. For a wonder Mollie was silent, while Victor shrugged his shoulders, and cried, between a sneer and a laugh—

"You are a sly dog, Melland. I had no idea that you were such a devoted admirer of the redoubtable Mrs Thornton."

The sneer brought Jack to his bearings in a moment. Every trace of embarrassment disappeared as he faced Victor across the table, wide-eyed and defiant.

"It is the truth, none the less. I admire Mrs Thornton immensely. She is a capital little woman, and fights the odds like a Spartan. This garden-party business was a great event in her life, and she prepared for it by a series of make-shifts. I got sick of hearing about them. Poor little soul, why shouldn't she be able to do the thing decently once in a while? She's been very kind to us; it was little enough to do in return."

"Oh, well, everything is comparative. You must be pretty flush to send about hampers of that description. I have never tasted finer fruit. I am sorry that such generosity is beyond my means," said Victor, whereat Jack scowled all the more.

"You would have spent as much on your lunches and teas if you had been in town these last weeks. What is the use of money if you can't be reckless once in a way? I am sorry that this subject has come up;

but, as it has, I must ask you all to be good enough not to speak of it to Mrs Thornton. She would gush, and I loathe gush. The secret is my own, not yours, so you must please respect my wishes."

Once more Ruth came to the rescue.

"Of course, we will keep your secret. We have no right to tell without your consent," she said decisively.

Her grey eyes smiled at him across the table with a wistful sweetness. This man, at least, was true and honest. Quick-tempered he might be, self-willed and impatient, but one could never imagine Jack Melland playing a double part, nor selling his soul for greed. And yet—and yet, one glance from Victor's eyes had power to affect her as Jack Melland's most earnest effort could never do; and Uncle Bernard, sharp-sighted as he was, treated Jack with far less confidence and favour.

"But I was never sure of him all the time, except for those few hours yesterday," she thought. "I *felt* there was something behind. When Dr Maclure spoke to me that afternoon I knew that he meant all, and more than all, that he said; but it is not easy to make the imitation like the real thing. The moment I heard him speak to Margot I knew the difference—oh, such a difference! I shall never be deceived again."

She sat trifling with her fruit, unheeding the conversation around her, yet dimly conscious that a passage-at-arms was still being carried on between Mr Farrell and Jack; the former indulging in caustic remarks at the young man's expense, Jack replying with more or less irritation.

A sudden gleam of excitement on Victor's face recalled her wandering thoughts, in time to hear Jack reply quickly—

"You are quite right, I am an invalid no longer. I walked about most of the afternoon and feel none the worse. I can manage even the stairs with a little help. In another few days I shall be ready for work. There will then be no need for me any longer to trespass—"

Suddenly he stopped; and though Mr Farrell sat waiting in silence for several moments, he did not attempt to finish the sentence; for another gentle pressure on the elbow had reminded him of the wisdom of self-control. He sat with downcast eyes and firmly shut lips until Mr Farrell's mocking voice broke the silence.

"Since Mr Melland has nothing more to say, it would perhaps be as well if we made a move. I will ask you to excuse me for the rest of the evening, as I am feeling fatigued."

He rose as he spoke and turned towards the door, but even as he did so he staggered, and uttered an exclamation of pain. Mrs Wolff echoed the cry and sank back in her chair helpless and unnerved; but in an instant Victor was at his side, supporting him with a strong, steady arm.

"Send for James," he said, addressing the butler in the quiet tones of one who knows how to keep his head in an emergency. "Let me help you into the hall, sir; you will have more air there. Lean upon me!"

They moved slowly forward together, the bowed figure seeming momentarily to shrink in stature, while the glimpse of cheek, as he turned towards the door, was so ashen in colour that the girls clasped each other's hands in dismay. Then James appeared, alert, composed, capable, a carrying-chair was brought forward from some secret hiding-place, and the invalid was borne upstairs to his room.

"It's one of his 'turns,' miss," the butler explained to Ruth. "He used to have them constantly, but it's the first since you came. We'll send down for the doctor, and he'll probably stay all night. You can never tell how things may go!"

Jack Melland limped off towards the deserted smoking-room. Five minutes before, as he sat resolutely silent, he had determined to go to Mr Farrell as he sat in the library that evening, and, in the quiet of a *tête-à-tête*, announce his determination to leave the Court before the week was out; but now, once again, circumstances conspired against him. There was a greater question at stake than his own miserable comings or goings, for the shadow of death hovered over the Court, and none could tell what the morning might bring forth.

Chapter Twenty Eight.

Mrs Wolff.

The next morning Mr Farrell was reported better, though unable to leave his bed. His old friend, the doctor, had stayed with him for the greater part of the night, and had now taken his departure, pronouncing all immediate danger to be over. A few days' rest would no doubt make the patient much as he had been before, to outward seeming, though to the professional eye, a little weaker, a little nearer the end.

At breakfast Mrs Wolff fussed in a feeble, self-injured manner because she was not admitted to the sick-room.

"It is so dreadful for him to be left without a woman! I can't think how he will be nursed without a woman!" she repeated monotonously, while her hearers breathed an earnest wish that, when their turn came to be nursed, it might not be by a woman of her calibre. Mr Farrell was a hundred times better off with his quiet, capable James.

A shadow of depression rested upon all the young people, though Ruth could not help feeling thankful for a reasonable excuse for a sadness which had nothing to do with Uncle Bernard or his health. Now, no one would wonder if she were sad or silent, and she would escape the questioning she had so much dreaded. Immediately breakfast was over she announced her intention of devoting the morning to photography, and disappeared indoors, while Victor took his accustomed path to the stables.

Mollie would have followed her sister, but Jack detained her with an appeal which could not be denied.

"Stay and talk to me a little while; do! or I shall think you are offended by my stupidity yesterday. I have to thank you for your reminder last night. If you had not stopped me I should have spoken even more strongly than I did, and have been filled with remorse. As it is, I don't think anything I said could have been responsible for this attack. Considering all things I kept pretty cool, didn't I now?"

"I think you did," conceded Mollie, smiling. "No; I expect it has been coming on for some days, and that was why he was so cross. You generally find people are ill if they are more than usually snappy. Poor Uncle Bernard! I wish one could help; but I am glad he has not Mrs Wolff to fidget him. Do you know," said Mollie, fixing her candid eyes upon Jack's face, and inwardly rejoicing at having hit on an impersonal topic of conversation,—"do you know Mrs Wolff is an unending problem to one! I think about her for hours at a time, and try to puzzle her out, but I never get one step further."

"Really!" Jack searched in his pockets for materials, and began rolling up one of the everlasting cigarettes. "I'm surprised to hear that. I should not have thought she could have occupied more than two minutes. For my own part I find it impossible to think of her at all. She was born; she exists; she will probably die! Having said so much, you have exhausted the subject."

"Not at all," contradicted Mollie frankly. "There's lots more to consider. What is she really, and what is the real life that she lives inside that funny little shell? And was she ever a child who laughed and danced, and raced about, and was good and naughty, and played with toys, and lived among giants and fairies? We *lived* fairy tales, Ruth and I, and had giants to tea in a nursery four yards square. And we hunted ferocious lions and tigers, who either turned out kind and harmless, or were slain by imaginary swords. Did Mrs Wolff always know exactly that two and two make four, and never by any chance made a delicious pretence that it was five? And when she went to school had she a chum whom she adored, and wrote letters to every other day filled with 'dears' and 'darlings,' and did she ever shirk 'prep,' or play tricks on the teachers, or sit up to a dormitory supper?"

"Certainly not! She was a good little girl who never soiled her pinafore, nor dreamt of anything she could not see, and she worked hard at school and remained persistently in the middle of the class, and gained high marks for neatness and decorum. She never had a chum because she is incapable of caring for one person more than another."

"But what about 'poor Mr Wolff'? Surely she must have had, at least, a preference for him! That's another problem—how did anyone come to fall in love with her, and what did he fall in love with, and why, and when, and where? I long to know all about it, for it seems so incomprehensible."

Jack laughed with masculine amusement at her curiosity.

"Not incomprehensible at all. I can give a very good guess how it happened. She was a timid, shrinking, little thing, rather pretty—her features are not at all bad—and 'poor Mr Wolff' was a big burly fellow who took a fancy to her because she was a contrast to himself. She didn't say much, so he credited her with thinking the more. She agreed with everything he said, so he considered her the cleverest woman he knew. He discovered his error, no doubt, in sackcloth and ashes, poor fellow; but mercifully he had not to endure many years of disenchantment. I can't imagine a worse fate than being tied for life to an automaton!"

"Humph!" Mollie pondered, pinching her soft chin between thumb and finger. "He might not be so particular as you... Did you ever... Have you ever,—I mean, did you ever meet..."

Jack blew a cloud of smoke from between his lips with a half-embarrassed smile.

"Did I ever meet a girl whom I imagined might be my Mrs Wolff! Is that what you want to ask? Yes - once!—for a passing moment. We met, and I caught a glimpse of her face, and recognised it as the fulfilment of a dream. Then she disappeared. Romantic, isn't it, and disappointing into the bargain? I am not a sentimental fellow, I suppose, for I have never even imagined myself in love, though I have known scores of charming girls; but at that moment I realised possibilities!"

"But, oh, how disappointing! Did she really disappear? Couldn't you find her? Is there no chance that you may meet again?"

"Sometimes I think there is; at other times it seems impossible. In any case, I am powerless to help, or to hinder."

"I should not say that if I were a man! I would search the world over till I found her!" Mollie sat silently, with bent head and thoughtful air, then suddenly lifted her eyes to his with a sweet, grave glance. "I hope you *will* meet! I hope you will be very happy together some day,—you, and your Lady of Dreams!"

Jack looked at her, and his face changed strangely. He said nothing, not even a word of thanks for her good wishes, and presently got up from his seat, and limped into the house, leaving Mollie depressed and self-reproachful.

"I suppose I should not have said it. He thinks it 'gush,' and won't condescend to answer. I wonder what she was like? Dark, I suppose, and stately, and serious; the very opposite from me. She will appear again some day, and they will be married and look so handsome together. I'm awfully, awfully glad; at least, I should be if Uncle Bernard were not ill. That makes one feel so dull and wretched that one can't be glad about anything," said poor Mollie to herself.

Jack did not appear again; and she was not in the mood to take any interest in Ruth's photographic efforts, so she strolled through the grounds and gathered an armful of flowers to send home to the little mother. This was always a pleasant undertaking, and just now there was a special reason for choosing the freshest and most fragrant blossoms, for the last few letters had hinted at a recurrence of the old money troubles.

"Something is up!" wrote Trix, in school-girl parlance. "Father and mother are talking in his den all the evening, and she comes down to breakfast with her eyes swollen with crying, and he looks like a sheet, and doesn't eat a bite. Horrid old business again, of course. How I hate it! We shall have to scrape a little more, I suppose; and where we are to scrape from, I'm blest if I know! My blue serge is green, and the boys' Etons shine like the rising sun. It was a fine day on Sunday, and they fairly glittered going to church. I don't want to give you the blues, but thought I'd better tell you, so that you could write to cheer them up, and also be more assiduous in your attentions to the old man. You must and shall get that fortune between you, or we shall be bivouacking in the workhouse before you can say Jack Robinson! My heart too truly knows the signs full well!"

Mollie recalled these expressive sentences, and sighed in sympathy.

"Poor old Trix! too bad that she should be left at home to bear the brunt, while we are living in the lap of luxury. I expect it is just one of the old crises, and we shall worry through as usual, but it is depressing while it lasts. I can't endure to see mother with red eyes. She will smile when she sees these roses, bless her! I defy anyone not to enjoy opening a box of flowers; and when we go home we will cheer them up again,—fortune or no fortune. Dear old Trix shall have some of my fineries made down, as a change from the green serge."

Mollie's spirits lightened perceptibly as she loitered about the garden, for to a town-bred girl it was luxury indeed, not only to look upon a wealth of roses, but to be able to gather them lavishly as she pleased. When the basket was full of half-opened beauties, ranging in every shade, from white to the bloomy crimson of "Prince Camille," she turned to more shady corners for the sprays of ferns and foliage, which are even more prized than flowers themselves by the unhappy dwellers in cities, then returned to the house to find a box and pack it for the post. The terrace was empty, but Mrs Wolff was sitting knitting just inside the drawing-room window.

"Your uncle is better," she announced, as Mollie approached. "He has had a quiet sleep since breakfast, and James thinks he will be able to sit up for an hour or two to-morrow. I haven't seen anything of Ruth or Mr Melland. Mr Druce came back from the stables to say that he was not going to ride to-day, but take a long walk, and he would be sure to be home in time for lunch. He is always so kind and considerate!"

The poor little woman looked wan and dispirited, and Mollie reflected with a pang of remorse that she herself had shown little consideration for her feelings. Even a nonentity, it appeared, could feel dull when left by herself in a big, empty house, and also could appreciate a little act of thoughtfulness. Victor disappeared so regularly for the morning hours, that it seemed strange that he should have especially explained his intentions this morning of all others; but perhaps he had done so, just because to-day was distinguished by a special load of anxiety which he was anxious not to increase. Mrs Wolff lived in a constant state of fidget, and even so little a thing as the uncertainty whether the household would assemble punctually to partake of the luncheon which she had ordered, might easily add to her distress.

"He is awfully considerate at times; much more than the rest of us," Mollie admitted to herself. "He never forgets the least little thing that Uncle Bernard says or does, or likes or dislikes, while I—silly, blundering thing!—always try to help him out of his chair at the wrong side, or stumble over his sticks."

She stood looking down at Mrs Wolff with a new impulse of sympathy. Hitherto, they had seemed divided by an impassable gulf, but this morning the girl's usual radiant sense of well-being had died away, and left a little rankling ache in its place. "Uncle Bernard's illness, and this new bother at home," was Mollie's explanation even to her own heart, but the result thereof was to fill her with pity for the life of a woman whom nobody loved, and who was homeless in a land of homes.

She sat down beside Mrs Wolff, determined to make the hour before luncheon pass more cheerfully than its predecessor, and a few judicious questions soon set the good lady's tongue prattling over past and future. She said that as a girl she had always had a partiality for blue merino, and had owned a Dunstable bonnet, trimmed with roses, which was said to be particularly becoming. It was a pity that roses faded so in the sun; ribbons were more economical wear. Did Mrs Connor buy her fish wholesale from Whitby, or retail from a fishmonger? They did say there was a great saving in the former way, only you got tired of cod, if it were a very big fish...

The worst of a large house was having to keep so many servants! A friend of hers, who was "reduced," said she had never known what comfort meant till she came down to two. That James really took too much upon himself! Talking of black-currant jelly—how beautiful the peaches were on the south wall! Her cousin's little boy—Eddie, not Tom—fell over a garden barrow the other day, and it might have been most serious, for the shears were only a few yards away. Children were more trouble than pleasure. Poor Mr Wolff always regretted having none, and she used to remind him of the school bills, and the breakages, and the dirt in the house...

Had Mollie ever knitted comforters for deep-sea fishermen? They said their ears did get so cold. There was nothing like an onion boiled really soft, and made into a poultice for ear-ache. Her cousin's little boy—Tom, not Eddie—had it very badly. Dear, dear, to hear his shrieks! They found onion much better than camphorated oil. When Mr Farrell died, she supposed whoever came into possession would re-cover the drawing-room furniture. It needed it, and you got lovely patterns from London...

On and on the stream flowed, until Mollie felt dazed and bewildered. Mrs Wolff evidently felt it such a treat to have a listener that she was capable of continuing for hours at a time, and it was only the sounding of the gong for lunch which brought an end to the monologue.

In its passing it had seemed a quiet, uneventful morning; no one guessed what importance its coming and going would assume in the near future.

Chapter Twenty Nine.

An Unpleasant Interview.

Mr Farrell kept to his determination to see none of his visitors until he was able to come downstairs, but he sent a message by James, to the effect that he would be annoyed if his indisposition were allowed to interfere in any way with social engagements. Therefore, dinner-parties being the order of the day, the four young people feasted abroad every evening, and spent the afternoons at various tennis and croquet parties instituted in their honour.

The rush of gaiety was in full swing, and the list of invitations which ought to be accepted stretched so far ahead that it seemed as if there would be little time left in which to entertain in return. In earlier days the girls had delighted to discuss gorgeous and bizarre ideas, smacking more of the Arabian Nights than of an English country house, by the execution of which they hoped to electrify the county and prove their own skill as hostesses; but of late these schemes had been unmentioned. Ruth was too much crushed by her disappointment to have spirit for frivolities, and the shadow of the universal depression at home, as well as at the Court, cast its shadow over Mollie also.

In a half-hearted way both girls were glad of the engagements which prevented *tête-à-têtes*, which had grown difficult and embarrassing, yet with the unreasonableness of her sex Ruth felt doubly hurt to realise that Victor shared in her relief. She had expected to have difficulty in avoiding him, and to hear reproaches for her coldness, but neither expectation was fulfilled.

"I suppose he thinks that he has made things safe with me by that last conversation, and can afford to take a little holiday and enjoy himself. He does not want to compromise himself too far!" Ruth told herself, with a touch of bitterness which had developed during the last few days.

She knew that Victor's long absences in the morning were spent in trying to waylay Lady Margot in her walks and drives, and had the best authority for knowing him to have been successful more than once, for Margot had been present at one of the dinner-parties and had seized an opportunity to have a quiet word.

"I have met Mr Druce twice this week. I could have avoided him by staying in the grounds, but I do not wish to rouse his suspicions. He won't risk anything definite until matters are decided between you and Mr Farrell, and then he shall learn his lesson. From which of us he learns it, it does not matter. In the meantime, I shall make no change, and he can come and go as he sees fit."

"You must be very—very sure of yourself!" said Ruth wistfully; at which Margot reared her little head with a haughty gesture.

"Absolutely sure! If he had dared to ask me six months ago, I might have given up everything to be the wife of the imaginary Victor, but now I will not alter the slightest plan out of consideration for the real Mr Druce. I can trust myself; but,"—she turned a grave, direct gaze on the other's face—"can *you* trust me, Ruth? I don't concern myself about appearances, so it is possible you may hear rumours which may not seem in keeping with our agreement. Can you trust me enough to believe that, however strange things may seem, I am really considering your interests even more than my own?"

"I think I can—oh yes, I am sure I can!" replied Ruth hesitatingly.

But even as she spoke a doubt crept up in her mind. If Victor did, indeed, become the owner of the Court, and remained persistent in his wooing, could Margot withstand him? She had loved him once. Would not the old feeling revive, and prove too strong for argument? It was Ruth's nature to distract herself with doubts and fears, and the little conversation did not help to raise her spirits.

On the fifth morning after Mr Farrell's seizure he came downstairs to his study, and was reported by the doctor to be in fairly good health. He did not appear at luncheon, however, and there was something darkly mysterious about James's manner when he came into the dining-room when the meal was nearly over to announce that his master wished to see the young ladies, with Mr Druce and Mr Melland, in the library at five o'clock.

"And me—surely he wishes to see me also!" Mrs Wolff cried, in an injured tone.

But James only bowed, and repeated inflexibly—

"Only the young ladies and gentlemen, ma'am. I understand that he wishes to see them on business."

Business! That word was enough to keep five minds working busily during the hours between luncheon and the time appointed for the interview. Had Uncle Bernard come to some definite conclusion during those quiet days upstairs? Was the period of probation over, or did the summons simply imply some new and eccentric phase of the old routine?

Conjecture ran riot; but at the first sight of the old man's face all pleasant expectations died a sudden death, for it was fixed in a stern, unbending anger, such as his guests had never seen before. Hardly replying to their congratulations and inquiries, he motioned them impatiently to the seats ranged in readiness facing his chair, exactly as they had been on that first important interview five weeks before. Only five weeks, thirty-five short days, yet each of the squire's guests felt as if a lifetime of experience yawned between that day and this!

"I have sent for you, as it is necessary to speak on an unpleasant topic, which, however, cannot be avoided," Mr Farrell began. "It is painful for me to open it, especially as I am urged to avoid excitement; but I have no alternative. You may remember that shortly before I was taken ill, I referred to the draft of my will which was lying in this desk." He stretched out his hand, and laid it on the polished surface. "It was kept here with other important papers, arranged in a special manner, which I have adopted for years, partly for the sake of neatness, partly to ensure them against interference, for it is impossible that they should be touched without my knowledge. This morning, on coming downstairs, my first task was to add some memoranda to one of these papers. I opened the desk, and discovered at once that my will had been opened and read—"

He stared grimly across the room, and four flushed, bewildered faces stared back at him. The silence lasted for several moments; then Jack spoke in his haughtiest and most intolerant tone—

"You do not, of course, wish to imply, sir, that you suspect us of having any hand in the matter? I presume you want our help in unravelling the mystery? My own detective powers are not of a high order; but if you will explain your system—"

Mr Farrell interrupted him with a raised hand.

"Thank you, I prefer to make my own inquiries. As I said before, it is a disagreeable duty; but when a duty is forced upon one, the best course is to perform it in the most strict and business—like manner possible. You are the people most concerned in my will, the people who would naturally feel most interest and curiosity in seeing it; therefore, apart from sentimental considerations, on you the first suspicion must fall, and it is right that I should question you before outsiders."

Jack's eyes flashed. He rose from his chair and limped across the floor, as if unable to keep still.

"I am afraid it will be of little use. If a fellow is sweep enough to pry into another man's secrets, he is equal to lying about it into the bargain, and in that case you have no chance in finding out the truth. You have been upstairs for five days. It is impossible to account for all that may have happened during that time."

"I have been upstairs five days, as you say, but it happens that I can reduce the time to a much narrower limit. On the evening after I was taken ill, it occurred to me that I had not locked my desk the night before, as I expected to return to the library as usual after dinner. I sent James downstairs to make sure. He found it open, locked it, and brought me back the key. The lock is a patent one, and has not been tampered with, therefore whoever examined the will must have done so on Wednesday morning or afternoon."

Victor looked up quickly.

"You allowed your man to lock it, you trusted him with the key?"

"Certainly. He has been twenty years in my service, and knows exactly what provision I have made for his future. He will not need to work after my death, and has no personal interest in my will. Moreover, I trust him as I would myself."

Mr Farrell spoke sharply, evidently annoyed that any doubt should be cast upon his favourite. As he finished his eyes met Mollie's fixed upon him with an angry challenge, to which he was not slow to respond—

"Well, what have you to say, young lady? Can you throw any light on this mystery?"

"I have not opened your desk and pried among your papers, if you really mean to ask me such a question. I have lots of faults, but I've never been suspected of anything so mean as that, and I don't care to stay in a house where anyone can believe it possible! I don't want to see the horrid old will! We should all have been content and happy if it had not been for the thought of it; and I never want to hear it mentioned again. I don't know how you dare insult us so, Uncle Bernard!"

"That will do, Mollie; you have given me your answer. There is no need to get excited. You had better go back to the drawing-room while I speak to your companions."

The squire leant back in his chair, waiting for her to go; and, willing or unwilling, there was no defying that grim silence. Mollie marched across the floor with defiant tread, opened the door, and closed it behind her with a bang, so expressive of temper that Jack could not resist a smile. It vanished quickly enough, however, as he listened to Mr Farrell's next words—

"I must ask you to tell me in so many words whether you know anything of this matter. If a sudden access of curiosity should have proved too strong for resistance, a candid confession would be the best means of obtaining forgiveness. I could overlook anything better than deceit." He looked at the three young faces before him with a scrutiny that had something pathetic in its earnestness; but, as it met with no response, his expression hardened. "Perhaps you would be good enough to tell me, in the first place, whether any of you were in the library on Wednesday?"

He looked at Victor as he spoke, and the dark eyes met his without a moment's hesitation.

"I went out for a long walk immediately after breakfast, and returned when luncheon was on the table. Afterwards Melland and I smoked on the terrace until it was time to drive over to a tennis-tea. I forget which house it was held at, but I remember we heard that the carriage was at the door, and had to rush for it. That was so, wasn't it, Melland? I think I should have little difficulty in proving an alibi for the whole day."

Mr Farrell hesitated for a minute, then turned towards Jack.

"And you, Melland?"

"Oh, I was about the house! I don't remember going into the library, but I might have done so half a dozen times, and forgotten all about it. You gave me permission to borrow books as I chose, and I have been constantly in and out. I could not undertake to say positively what I did on any particular day."

"Ruth?"

Ruth lifted a miserable face, and shot a glance across the room. There was none of Mollie's righteous indignation in that glance, only a nervous shrinking which amounted almost to fear.

"I—I was in the library, Uncle Bernard! I photographed it several times that morning. It seemed a good opportunity, as you were upstairs, and I wanted the room for my collection."

"You were photographing. That means that you would be some little time alone in the room?"

"Yes—no; I came and went. Not so very long," stammered Ruth hesitatingly. It was terrible to be cross-examined like this, with the eyes of the three men fixed upon her, grave and questioning. She looked wistfully at the door, and half rose from her seat. "I know nothing—I did nothing! I can tell you nothing more! May I go now? There is no use staying any longer."

"One moment, please! You all deny having touched the will, and I shall, of course, accept your word; but you must help to find the real culprit by giving me every clue in your power. Was any reference made to the will in your presence? Has anyone, for instance, expressed curiosity respecting it and its contents?"

Victor's eyes turned to Ruth with a glance which brought the colour rushing into her cheek. He did not speak, but his expression was too eloquent to be misread. The old man looked keenly from one to the other, and his voice took an added sharpness as he spoke—

"Well, Druce, out with it—out with it! What is it that you have to say?"

"Nothing, sir—nothing worth repeating. Your question reminded me of a chance remark; but I would rather say no more about it."

"You have said too much already. Pray go on, since you have begun!" cried Ruth, with a sudden blaze of anger. Her small head was thrown back with a defiant gesture, and the Farrell eyebrows met in a straight black line across her brow. "*I* spoke of your will, Uncle Bernard—I said I wished that I could see it. I *did* want to see it! It was impossible to know that it was lying there, and not feel curious."

"Of course it was. We were all curious, but some of us had not the honesty to confess it," Jack cried quickly. "Surely it is not necessary to keep Miss Ruth any longer, sir? She has told you that she can give you no more information. It is cruel to the girl—" He broke off as if afraid of speaking too strongly; and Mr Farrell lay back in his chair with a sudden weary slackening of muscle.

"Yes, yes, she may go; you may all go! We can prove nothing at present; but time will show—time will show!" And he raised his hand with a gesture of dismissal.

Ruth and Victor rose and hurriedly left the room only Jack stood his ground, nervously tugging at his moustache. He had something to say, and was determined to say it, but the sight of the old man's figure in its physical and mental depression turned his anger into commiseration. It was in almost an apologetic voice that he broke the silence.

"I stayed because I wanted to have five minutes' quiet talk with you, sir. My ankle is now practically well, and I am anxious to return to town. Please don't think I am unappreciative of your kindness in wishing me to stay, but as I said before I have no wish to be considered as a candidate for your fortune. It is owing to my accident that I have remained so long, and not to any change of mind. I hear from my partner that the business is suffering from my absence, and we have had such a struggle to work it up to its present condition, that you can understand I am in a fever to get back."

Contrary to his expectation Mr Farrell showed no sign either of surprise or anger. Perhaps he had been expecting the announcement as a result of convalescence, perhaps he was simply too weary to feel any strong interest in passing events. In any case, his face scarcely changed in expression, as he replied—

"After five weeks' visit to the Court you still keep to your original opinion, that the chance of possessing it is not worth a little inconvenience, or even monetary loss?"

Jack pursed his lips with an impatient dissent.

"Oh, the Court is beautiful—an ideal place in every respect. I would go through a good deal to earn it—in a straightforward fashion. What I object to is the mystery, and the idleness, and the feeling of competition. You have every right to manage your own affairs in your own way, sir, but you must allow me the same privilege. You must have found out by this time that I have a large amount of obstinacy in my composition. I have made up my mind that for every reason it is my duty to return to town."

"You have calculated, of course, that even if your business succeeds to an extraordinary extent, you are never likely to make anything like as much money as will come to my heir?"

"I have always heard that you are enormously wealthy. You are probably quite right; but,"—Jack paused in front of the lounge-chair and looked down at the shrunken figure from the height of six-foot-one,—"looking back on your own life, sir, has your greatest happiness come from the amount of your possessions? Has it increased as they increased? Can you honestly advise me as a young man to sacrifice everything for money?"

There was silence for several minutes, while Mr Farrell winced and shrank within himself, as if the words had touched a hidden sore. He never referred to his own domestic life; but it was well-known that for years it had been one of ideal happiness, and that with the loss of wife and son, his real life had closed for ever. He avoided a direct reply to Jack's question by asking another in return.

"There are other things which many men consider more important. I have sometimes imagined that you would agree with them. Have you reflected that in returning to town you may be leaving behind even more than land or fortune, and thereby losing a dearer chance of happiness!"

The blood rushed into Jack's face. He could not affect to misunderstand the drift of the old man's words, but to acknowledge their truth was impossible, and the orthodox protests seemed to come of their own accord.

"What do you mean? What am I leaving? I hardly understand..."

Mr Farrell laughed shortly.

"Young people seem to imagine that their elders cannot see what is happening under their eyes. I have watched you and Mollie, and thought that there might possibly be an interesting *dénouement* to your friendship. She has faults, but she has a kind heart and would make a good wife."

Jack's face stiffened.

"Hadn't we better keep her name out of the discussion, sir? I have the greatest respect and admiration for both your nieces, but, as far as anything further is concerned, I am not in a position to think of marriage. It may be years before I can keep a house, and I would never tie down a girl indefinitely."

"In this instance it might happen that the girl had a house of her own! Did it never strike you that you would be doubling your chances if you linked them together?"

"I am not a fool, sir! Of course I realised as much from the first, and have wondered if it was part of your scheme. My idea of marriage, however, is to be able to keep my wife, not to accept support. It may be a weakness in my nature, which makes me wish to be head of my own household; but weakness or not, there it is, and I can't get rid of it. It would be detestable to me to marry an heiress, and if I were a girl I should despise a man who was content to live on his wife's money."

"Just so—just so! Very praiseworthy sentiments, no doubt; but I should have been glad to know that the child had a protector. The stepfather is a broken reed, and the mother is a child herself; however, you place your pride and your prejudice first, and that's the end of the business. You will go back to town, she to the North—a very effectual separation!"

He shrugged his shoulders expressively; but Jack's eyes gave out a sudden flash, he straightened himself, and cried eagerly—

"There are trains, there are boats—if it comes to that, it is only two hundred miles. If she were in trouble, one could *walk*! It would make no difference if the woman one wanted were at the end of the world—one would get to her *somehow* when the hour arrived! Difficulty is an inspiration, sir, when one is young!"

"Yes, yes; when one is young—when one is young!" The smile which had lightened the old man's face died away at the sound of those last words. He raised his hand and pushed the thin locks from his brow. "Well, it is your own life—you must live it in your own way! I cannot benefit you against your will. If your mind is made up I have no strength to argue the point. You had better arrange to leave to-morrow afternoon, and give instructions to that effect to the servants."

Jack's start of surprise was entirely disagreeable. He had not expected to be dismissed in this summary fashion, and the thought of so speedy a break with the new life came upon him with a positive shock. To-morrow! To-morrow, then, at this very hour he would be back in the dingy lodgings which did duty for home, preparing to sit down to a solitary meal, to spend a solitary evening, to sleep and wake up to a day's work in the stifling City, where the thought of green fields and rose-gardens, and wide, stretching lawns would seem as unreal as a dream. A weight of depression settled on him, as he exclaimed—

"To-morrow! But—unless you wish it, there is no hurry—I could wait until the end of the week. If I left on Saturday, I could still begin work on Monday."

"For what object? Since you have decided not to remain, it is better for all reasons that you should return at once. You have put your work before everything else—then why delay in getting back to it? For my own part, since you refuse to consent to my conditions, it would simplify matters if you returned at once. The position is difficult, and my strength is rapidly failing. I should have been glad if you had consented to grant me these few weeks out of your life, but, since it is not to be, I prefer to finish the matter once for all." He held out his hand as he spoke. "Good-bye, Melland—my best wishes! I shall not see you in the morning!"

Jack took the proffered hand, and held it in silence, his face a study of perplexity and remorse. An Englishman hates to express his emotions, but to a generous nature the sting of ungratefulness is even more abhorrent. At that moment it seemed a little thing to spare a few months of strong, young life to gratify the whim of a dying man. Jack's heart reproached him, and he spoke in eager accents.

"If I could be a help to you, sir—if I felt that my presence gave you pleasure or comfort, I would stay willingly as long as you wished; but you have kept so much apart, that there has been no opportunity—"

Mr Farrell disengaged his hand, and turned aside with a wearied air.

"Good-bye, Melland!" he repeated. "I wish you a pleasant journey!"

So far as any change of voice or manner was concerned, he might not have heard the young man's protest. Jack turned away, miserable and abashed. It was the last time he ever saw Bernard Farrell alive.

Chapter Thirty.

Fresh Trials for Ruth and Mollie.

Meanwhile, Ruth and Mollie were crying in each other's arms in the privacy of their bedroom—that is to say, Ruth was crying and Mollie was storming and shedding an occasional tear more of anger than distress.

"I've never been so insulted in my life, and I won't stand it from fifty thousand Uncle Bernards! I'll tell him so, and make him beg my pardon and yours too, darling! Don't cry! It makes your nose so red, and you hate to look a fright!"

"Oh, Mollie, we were far happier at home when we thought we were so badly off! What was the use of coming here to have our hearts broken? I loved that man, I thought he loved me, and now I can only despise him. He deliberately tried to fasten suspicion upon me this afternoon, and I can never prove my innocence, for I *was* in the library, and alone for quite a long time, on and off. What can I do, or say, if they won't take my word?"

"Everybody will, whose opinion is worth having Victor Druce thinks of nothing but his own advantage; and I won't allow you to say you cared for him."

"It's easier said than done! Can you practise what you preach? You don't say anything, but I know,—I can see! When Jack goes away, will you find it easy to forget all about him?"

Mollie's face changed. Excitement disappeared, to be replaced by a sweet and serious dignity.

"I shall never forget him," she said quietly; "but he is in love with another girl—he told me about her the other day—so our lives must be spent apart. I shall never be as happy as I might have been, but I'm going to be as happy as I can. I *won't* mope! We were happy enough just to be together a few weeks ago; let's go back to where we were, and forget all about the tiresome men!"

"It's easier said than done," sighed Ruth once more. She sank down in a chair by the window, and, leaning her head on her hand, gazed drearily across the park, beautiful in the changing light of late afternoon. With what joy and confidence had she regarded the same scene a few weeks ago, her heart expanding in the happy certainty that some day it would be her own, and with it unlimited powers of helping those she loved. Now, between Victor's faithlessness and her own fall from favour, hope had gradually died away, and the future seemed to hold nothing but bitterness and regret.

Ruth's heart turned homewards with yearning affection. The love of the little mother was a certainty which could be depended upon through good report and ill; nothing that could be said against her child would shake her trust and faith, she would be even more tender in failure than success.

The dear old pater, too—how good he had been all these years, making no distinction between his step-daughters and his own children, except perhaps to show a more anxious care for their needs! He worked so hard, and was so absolutely self-denying and uncomplaining; it was not his fault if he did not possess the power of money-making. When she was at home again she would be more thoughtful of his comfort, more affectionate and sympathetic. She recalled all the step-brothers and sisters whose very existence she had grudged at times, each name bringing with it some kindly, humorous recollection. How truly lovable they were, despite their faults!

Then Ruth's thoughts roamed a little further afield to the few intimate friends of the family, foremost among whom came Eleanor Maclure and her brother. What would Eleanor say if the grand expedition ended in ignominious failure? A good many words of sympathy, of cheer, and a few simple heart-to-heart truths, pointing out the spiritual side of the puzzle, spoken in that soft Scotch voice which was so good to hear. Ah yes, it would be a help to meet Eleanor again. And the—the doctor!

During the first weeks of her stay at the Court, Ruth had been so much absorbed in the present that she had had no leisure to think of old friends; but during the last few days the vision of Dr Maclure's face had risen before her not once but many times—strong, earnest, resolute, with steady glance and square-built chin, such a contrast from that other face with the veiled eyes, which seemed to hide rather than reveal the soul within.

In the midst of soreness and humiliation it had been a comfort to remember that such a man had loved her enough to wish to make her his wife. She recalled the conversation in the brougham with new sympathy and understanding. Had he suffered as she was suffering now? Did his life also stretch ahead blank and grey because of that little word from her lips? Her heart yearned over him, yet felt mysteriously lightened at the thought.

"There's the postman's collie!" cried Mollie's voice, interrupting her reverie. "That means that the evening post is in. I'll run down and see what there is for us."

She disappeared for a few minutes, then reappeared carrying one letter in her hand.

"From mother, to you. Open it quickly, dear! It is an age since she has written. I only hope and pray it is good news!" But, alas! that aspiration was shattered at the sight of the first few sentences.

"My darling girls,—I have delayed writing as I could not bear to cloud your pleasure, but I can keep back the truth no longer. You must be brave, dears, and help me to be brave, for it is no half and half trouble this time. We are quite, quite ruined, and Heaven only knows what is to become of us!

"It is not the pater's fault in any one way. For the last two years he has been doing a good deal of business for a man who appeared to be in very good circumstances. At first he paid up his accounts most regularly, but lately they have sometimes been allowed to run on from month to month. I don't understand business, but it seems that this is often allowed, and as he had been such a good client, and had met his payments regularly before, the pater felt safe in trusting him, and paid out all his own little capital to finance the business of the last few months, which was unusually large.

"He expected to make such a handsome commission as would set us on our feet again; but it was all a deliberate fraud. Other poor men have been taken in in the same way, and that scoundrel has disappeared, leaving us to bear the brunt. I hope I may be able to forgive him some day; just now, when I see the pater's broken heart and think of you, and all those children, it's too difficult.

"Everything that we have or can raise in any way will not pay what we owe, and the pater cannot carry on his business without some capital. The future is very dark; but God has helped me through many dark days, and He will help us still. Trix is splendid! She went of her own accord to the headmistress and offered to teach one of the junior classes in exchange for Betty's education, and a few finishing classes for herself. Miss Bean came to see me, and it is all arranged, for she says Trix has a genius for managing children, and will be a valuable help. She is a good woman, and is glad of the opportunity of helping us, so that difficulty is overcome; but there are oh, so many others to be faced!

"What is to be done about the house—the boys—yourselves? Pater and I have talked until we are too tired and puzzled to talk any more, but, so far, no light has dawned.

"Write to the pater as well as to me, for he has been good to you, and will value your sympathy. Oh, my darlings, it is hard that this should have happened just now to spoil your happy visit! My heart aches for your trouble, for these things are so hard when one is young. I hope, I trust, I pray that the future may be so bright for you as to make up for all the anxieties you have had to bear. Tell Uncle

Bernard our trouble; you and he must decide what you had better do.

"I long for your help and comfort, but leave the decision entirely in your hands. Every one is good and sympathetic, and the pater has had most kind letters from his friends in town. We have this great comfort that his good name is untarnished, and that there is no shadow of disgrace in our misfortune. God bless you, my darlings! If we are rich in nothing else, we are rich in our love for one another.—Your devoted Mother."

The girls looked at each other in a long, breathless silence. Ruth laid her hand across her heart with a little gasp of pain.

"Oh, mother! Poor little mother! And we are away, we who should be her best comforters! There is only one thing to do,—we must go home at once!"

"Yes," assented Mollie firmly, "we must go home to-morrow."

Chapter Thirty One.

A Fateful Decision.

It was all decided. The interview with Uncle Bernard was over, the last farewells spoken, and the boxes packed in readiness to go to the station. In less than an hour the Court and its inhabitants would be a thing of the past.

Out of consideration for Mr Farrell's health, the girls had decided not to tell him of their bad news until the morning.

"He has had enough excitement for one day," Mollie said; "let him be quiet to-night. To-morrow morning we will send up mother's letter for him to read, and ask to see him as soon as possible after breakfast. That will give him time to think over the situation and decide what to do. He must guess that we will want to return home, but if he wishes to keep us he can easily do so. Oh, to think that with a few strokes of the pen he could make us all happy again! I don't know how much money the pater needs, but it would probably be the tiniest sum out of Uncle Bernard's great fortune. Suppose he offered to send a cheque—suppose he gave us a cheque to send, and all was peace and joy again! He could—he might—oh, surely he *will*! What is the use of being rich if one can't help people in trouble?"

But Ruth sighed and shook her head.

"Rich people have not much patience with failures, and the poor old pater has not the gift of success. I am afraid Uncle Bernard will be more inclined to blame than to help." And as events proved she was right.

Mr Farrell sent word that he would be at liberty at ten o'clock in the sitting-room adjoining his bedroom, and the first few minutes of the interview proved that his attitude towards the family trouble was one of scornful impatience rather than sympathy. He was apparently quite unprepared for the girls, determination, and would not at first believe in its sincerity.

"You are surely joking," he said scathingly. "If your parents are in such straits as you describe, how do you propose to help them by giving them two more people to keep and feed? It appears to me that your room would be more valuable than your company."

Ruth flushed painfully.

"We hope to be able to help, not to hinder. When a child like Trix has already found work, we ought not to lag behind. It would be impossible to go on living in the lap of luxury, wearing fine clothes, eating fine meals, being waited upon hand and foot, while our own people are in actual need."

"Unless—" interrupted Mollie, and then stopped short, while Mr Farrell turned sharply towards her.

"Unless what? Finish your sentence, if you please."

"Unless you will help them for us!" gasped Mollie, crimson, but daring. "It would be so easy for you to lend the pater what he needs, and he would promise to pay you back—we would all promise! We would work night and day until it was made up."

Mr Farrell smiled sardonically.

"At last! I knew it must come. It would not be Mollie if she had any scruples about asking for what she wanted. No, my dear, I never lend. It is against my principles to throw good money after bad. At the risk of appearing a monster of cruelty, I must refuse to interfere in your stepfather's affairs. There are still six weeks of your visit here to run, and I shall be pleased to relieve him of your support for that time; otherwise—"

"We are much obliged, but we have decided to go home. You wished to be able to judge our characters, and you have had enough time to do so, with very unsatisfactory results, if we are to judge from yesterday's conversation!" cried Ruth, with a sudden burst of indignation. "If you can believe us capable of prying into your desk, you will surely not be sorry to get rid of us altogether!"

The old man looked at her long and thoughtfully.

"Yes," he said quietly, "it's a pity—a very great pity—that the two things should have happened together. It is as unsatisfactory to me as to you that you should leave before the culprit has been discovered. But it is useless now to argue the point if your minds are already made up. Taking everything into consideration—the peculiar circumstances with regard to my will, your original acceptance of my invitation—do I still understand that you wish to leave me to-day?"

"It is our duty to go home. Yes, we have quite decided," said Ruth.

The old man's eyes turned towards the younger girl.

"And you, Mollie?"

"Yes, uncle; I'm sorry, but we can't leave mother alone just now."

Mr Farrell sat silent, his eyebrows lowered, his head hanging forward on his chest, so that it was difficult to see the expression of his face; but the pose of the figure suggested weariness and disappointment. Suddenly he stretched out his hand and touched an electric bell. A servant appeared almost immediately, and was asked a hasty question—

"Is Mr Druce still in the house?"

"I believe so, sir. He was in the morning-room a few minutes ago."

"Go down and tell him that I should be obliged if he would come up here at once."

The girls exchanged puzzled glances as the servant departed on his errand; but they did not dare to speak, and, as Mr Farrell relapsed into his former downcast attitude, the silence was broken only by the sound of Victor's approaching footsteps. He entered the room confident and smiling, but drew up with a start of surprise at seeing the two girls. He was evidently disappointed at their presence, and vaguely uneasy; but after the first involuntary movement his features quickly resumed their mask-like calm.

"You sent for me, sir. Is there anything I can do?"

Mr Farrell raised his head and looked at him thoughtfully. It was seldom indeed that he allowed himself to show any sign of interest in his young companions, so that this steady scrutiny was the more remarkable. Even Victor's composure suffered beneath it, for a tinge of colour crept into his pale cheeks, and he moved uneasily to and fro.

"What is it, sir?" he repeated. "I hope nothing fresh has happened to distress you."

"Thank you, Druce. My plans have been still further upset this morning, as, owing to news received from home, my nieces have decided to leave the Court at once. That means that three out of the four whom I selected for my experiment have, of their own accord, refused to carry out the conditions. Under these circumstances, I think it is only right to offer to release you from your promise, if you prefer to return home at the same time. Everything will be changed, and you may not care to stay on with only myself as a companion."

Victor's eyelids dropped, and a quiver of emotion passed over his face. Ruth saw it, and, with a sinking heart, realised that it resembled exultation rather than grief. He was silent for a moment, but when he spoke nothing could well have been more dignified and natural than words and manner—

"If it will inconvenience you in any way to entertain me alone, I am, of course, perfectly ready to leave; but if you give me the choice—if it is left to me to decide, sir—I should prefer to keep my promise, and stay for the remainder of the time. I might perhaps be of some help to you when you are alone."

The strained expression on Mr Farrell's face gave place to one of unmistakable satisfaction.

"That is good!" he replied heartily. "I am glad to find that you at least have some appreciation of the nature of a bargain. It will be lonely for you, but I am the more obliged for your decision. I won't keep you any longer just now, as we shall have other opportunities of conversation, and I have my adieux to make."

The door closed behind Victor, and Mr Farrell turned immediately towards his eldest grand-niece, as if anxious to get through an ordeal.

"Well, Ruth, I must bid you good-bye. I trust you will have a pleasant journey, and find matters at home less serious than you anticipate."

"Thank you, Uncle Bernard." Ruth extended a cold little hand, and stood hesitating by his side, while his sunken eyes dwelt upon the face which in feature was so like his own. "I've enjoyed the time—part of the time—more than anything else in my life! I'm sorry if I have done wrong in any way; I wanted only to please you!"

"For my own sake, or for what I could give?"

The question came sharp and abrupt, and Ruth's cheeks flamed beneath it. She hesitated painfully, gathering courage to speak the truth.

"Oh, I know I have been mercenary! I'm sick of being poor, and I love the Court and the easy, luxurious life. I wanted the money more than anything in the world; but it's all over now, and it's partly your own fault, for you *did* tempt me! Please forgive me before I go!"

"I forgive you, Ruth. It is quite true that I tempted you, and you are not fitted to bear temptation. But there is no need to bear enmity. Good-bye!"

He held out his hand again—held it at a distance, and with a formality which forbade a warmer farewell; and Ruth turned away, downcast and miserable. Those words, "You are not fitted to bear temptation," seemed to denote that in his mind there still dwelt a lingering suspicion lest she might have yielded to her anxiety to look at the will, and had then lacked the courage for confession. Well, it was all over, and it was useless to protest. So perish earthly hopes!

Mr Farrell turned towards his remaining niece.

"Well, Mollie, and so you also are resolved to leave me?"

"There was only one alternative, Uncle Bernard, and you refused it. If you won't help mother, we must lose no time in getting to work. We are breaking no promise, remember. We said we would stay if she could spare us, and now the time has come when she needs to have us back."

"You believe you can find work—work which will pay—a child like you, with the plainest of educations?"

"I am sure of it. I am not going to teach, but I shall be able to do something. I should be ashamed of myself if I couldn't—a big, strong creature like me! I am sorry to go—much more sorry than you will believe! I've been very happy these few weeks."

"I know you have. I have known more than you are aware of, perhaps. But you will not regret your departure so much, as Jack Melland is leaving at the same time. He has been your special companion, I think."

The blood flew to Mollie's cheeks under the scrutiny of the sunken eyes, and, to her consternation, spread even higher and higher, until she was crimson to the roots of her hair. She tried in vain to answer with composure, but could only stammer confusedly—

"He has been very nice. I like him the best—better than Mr Druce. But he decided—we decided,—our reasons for leaving are absolutely independent of each other, Uncle Bernard."

"I know—I know!"

He turned aside, and remained silent for a few minutes, as if to allow her time to recover composure, then once more held out his hand in farewell.

"Well, good-bye, Mollie. We also must agree to forgive and forget!"

Mollie bent over his chair, one hand resting on each arm, the embarrassment of a moment before dying a sudden death in the face of a parting which, in the nature of things, must be for ever.

"Uncle Bernard," she said softly, "if your Ned were alive, and you were in trouble, you would like him to hurry home to you, whatever it might cost! And if She were alive, and poor and distraught, you would rather he worked for her, than left her that he might fill the greatest post on earth. Judge us by that thought when you feel inclined to be hard! I know you don't like kissing people, so I am going to kiss you instead. There! Good-bye; and God bless you!"

She turned away with tears in her eyes, but half-way to the door the sound of her own name made her pause.

"Mollie!" he cried, in a sharp, resolute voice, which sent her heart beating with sudden hope.

But, even as her eyes met his, his expression changed once more.

"No, no; it is better as it is! I have nothing to say!"

Mollie turned away sadly and walked out of the room.

Chapter Thirty Two.

Leaving the Court.

The news of the girls' sudden flight spread to the vicarage, and brought Mrs Thornton rushing up to the Court, hot and panting, and almost incoherent with curiosity and dismay. When she heard of the trouble which was the cause of their departure, her best side came out, and she helped the girls in both word and deed through the last difficult hours. It was a comfort to find someone who agreed with their decision, and was convinced that they were acting aright in returning home, even in defiance of Uncle Bernard's wishes.

"The maid cries, and Bates looks as if he would like to murder us, Mr Druce keeps out of the way and says nothing, and Jack Melland, who is so keen on taking his own way, has half a dozen compromises to suggest. Actually he offered to go to Liverpool himself and find out if we could be of any use if we returned! It was sweet of him, but we must be of use. There is no option in the matter, and it is not reasonable to expect mother to discuss private affairs with a stranger."

"Of course not; but I love him for having suggested it. Of course, no one wants you to go, dear Ruth. It is a terrible collapse to all our bright schemes, but with such trouble at home you have no choice, and there is nothing gained by staying on for a few odd days. Better hurry back and bend all your energies to see what can be done to retrieve matters, and look forward to the day when you will return for good."

Ruth shook her head hopelessly, and for once Mollie followed her example.

"Ah, that will never be! There is no more hope. We are leaving against Uncle Bernard's wishes, and at the very worst possible time, for he is angry and upset because there is no way of finding out who opened the desk and read the draft of the will. We are all indignant at being suspected; yet it seems strange that an outsider should be so interested. It is terribly unfortunate, especially for Uncle Bernard, for he can't help feeling his confidence shaken; and yet, so far as we can see, nothing will ever be found out."

"Yes, it will all be explained some day," said Mrs Thornton solemnly. "Don't ask me how, for I can't tell. I only know that evil deeds are the most difficult things in the world to hide, and that in the most wonderful and unexpected ways they are discovered long after hope of detection has been abandoned. It will be so in this case also. Whoever is mean and wicked enough to allow you, dear children, to bear an unjust suspicion in addition to your own trouble, will be put to the shame he deserves. As for your coming back again, I will not give up hope if you do. I can't afford to lose all my castles in the air. It is decided that one of you is to be Lady of the Manor, and put our societies out of debt, and pay for a parish nurse, and take my dear girls about when they come home, and make life a fairy tale for us all. You have raised my expectations, and I intend to go on expecting! Seriously, dears, whatever Mr Farrell may say to you just now, in the first heat of disappointment, I cannot believe he will really think less of you for giving up your own pleasure to hurry back to your mother. Mr Melland has only himself to thank if his name is struck off the list; but you were willing and anxious to stay, and are the victims of circumstances. If I were in the squire's place I should think all the more highly of you for your unselfish devotion, and I believe he will, though he will never confess as much in words. But time will show! Meantime, my poor dears, we will think of you every day, and pray for you that you may be shown what to do, and have strength to do it. I have had my own share of money troubles, and would never try to belittle them in my own case or in the case of others. They are very hard and sordid, and far-reaching. There was a time in my life when money seemed in the background of every thought, and I could not get away from it; but I have learnt to trust instead of worrying, and that's the great lesson of life. It isn't mastered in a day; it took me years to learn, and many bitter experiences, which I hope you may be spared; but try, dears, to do your best, and leave the rest with God! Then comes the 'quiet mind' which will keep you calm and restful through all outward troubles."

The two young, wistful faces gazed into hers, and her eyes filled with tears of pity.

"Now tell me honestly—shall I help you best by staying, or by going away at once? I have arranged to do whichever suits you best. If you need any help."

"Oh, thank you! The best help of all would be to stay and drive down to the station with us. The packing is all done—in a way! But I expect that in our haste we have left lots of things behind, for we worked together, and in such a hurry and confusion that we hardly knew what we were about. Poor Elsie has packed our new garments in the new trunks, and watered them with tears. I expect it will be months before they are opened. We shall have no use for such fineries now."

"You can never tell what may happen, but if you don't, there is no cause to grieve. They have served their day, and have given you pleasure. Never mind if you have left some oddments behind; Elsie can send them on. I never have a visitor at the vicarage that I have not to expend my substance posting toothbrushes or sponge-bags or stray garments after their departure."

Truth to tell, Mrs Thornton was much relieved at being allowed to accompany the girls to the station.

The Vicar's wife possessed even more than her share of feminine curiosity, and was longing to discover in what fashion Victor Druce said good-bye to Ruth.

He was already waiting in the dining-room when she went down with the girls a few minutes later to partake of some light refreshment before starting on their long journey, and nothing could have been more unobtrusively sympathetic or attentive than the manner in which he waited upon them, anticipating every want, and ministering to it with eager hands. The room itself was so spacious that unconsciously the little party split into groups; and Mrs

Thornton found herself *tête-à-tête* with Jack Melland, obviously in the worst of humours.

"Can you do nothing? Is there nothing you can say to knock a little common-sense into those girls' heads? It's the maddest trick, rushing off like this in defiance of the old man's wishes. What can they do at home—a couple of children like that? They are better out of the way. At any rate, one of them might have stayed—Mollie, for instance—and kept things going here till she saw how things worked out. They have no right to rush off together at a moment's notice!" he cried irritably; whereat Mrs Thornton smiled involuntarily.

"Isn't it rather a case of people in glass houses, Mr Melland? You have set a bad example without half the excuse of these dear girls. It seems to me their plain duty to return to their parents when they are in trouble, so I have not attempted to dissuade them in any way."

"But—" Jack made a slight but eloquent gesture of the head in Victor's direction. "It's such a walk over for somebody else! I can't bear the thought of it. This place ought to belong to one of those girls—it is theirs by rights. It maddens me to see them throwing away their chance, for I'm afraid Mr Farrell will never forgive them for going against his wishes."

"Don't be too sure!" returned Mrs Thornton, nodding her head sagely. "Mr Farrell is not half so obstinate as he pretends, and however annoyed he may be to-day he can't help softening when he remembers that they have put all their own pleasures and self-interests on one side to return to work and worry for their mother's sake. If he wanted a test of character, surely nothing could be better than this! I don't think it will be by any means a 'walk over' for Mr Druce. My firm belief is, that Ruth and Mollie have as good or even a better chance than they had before."

"I say," cried Jack cordially, "you *are* a brick!" He turned towards her with a bright, boyish smile, which took years off his age. "You don't know how you have cheered me by saying that! I hated to think of them as being out of the running; but you will rub it in, won't you? Don't let Druce have it all his own way! Impress upon the old fellow what you said just now—unselfishness and hard work, and all that sort of thing. You will know how to do it, so as to make him see that he ought to admire the girls more for going than staying."

Mrs Thornton smiled indulgently.

"I can try, at least. I'm only sorry that I can't do the same for you. You have not the excuse of home troubles, and I'm afraid Mr Farrell—"

"Oh, never mind me; I don't count! I have been out of the running from the first, and it is only through an accident that I have stayed so long. I don't want anything from Mr Farrell but good-feeling and a fair judgment. It cut me up to say good-bye when I saw how feeble he looked. I don't want you to plead my cause, because I relinquished my claim long ago; but if you get a chance, you might just let him know that I was genuinely sorry to leave him for his own sake."

Jack's manly, straightforward speech was just what Mrs Thornton expected from him, and she gladly consented to convey his message to Mr Farrell.

"I will, with pleasure," she said, "and I shall have the chance before many days are over. Wonders will never cease! When I said just now that the squire was not so hard as he pretended, I spoke out of a full heart. What do you think of his suggesting—actually suggesting to my husband that the vicarage might need renovations, and asking him to send me up to give him my ideas! I nearly fainted when my husband told me. Now, do you think he thought of it himself, or did one of you kind creatures suggest it to him?"

"I didn't, I know. It would have been as much as my life was worth; but I suspect Miss Mollie may have had something to do with it. She spoke pretty strongly on the subject to me, and she has the courage of her convictions."

"Oh, that Mollie!" murmured Mrs Thornton under her breath. "I have never met her equal. The dearest, the simplest, the most affectionate of girls!" Her eyes moistened suddenly, and Jack's face softened in sympathy as he looked across the room to where Mollie stood by her sister's side. She met the two glances bent upon her, and walked forward in response, leaving Ruth and Victor by themselves.

Poor Ruth! Her heart beat fast with agitation and a last desperate hope born of Victor's soft tones and regretful eyes. For the moment it seemed that the last few days must have been a nightmare, and that he really did "care"; in which case she was prepared to forgive everything—nay, more, to believe that there was nothing to forgive.

If, in this moment of trouble and humiliation, he would place himself by her side, nothing that she could do in the future would be enough to prove her gratitude and devotion. But, alas! even as Mollie turned away, Victor's manner altered, and he became nervous and ill at ease. The long, eloquent glances which had been safe enough in the presence of a third person could not be risked in a *tête-à-tête*, and Ruth's hopes died a final death. She sat trying to eat her sandwiches, and feeling as if every bite would choke her, while Victor feebly struggled with commonplaces.

The sound of carriage-wheels could be heard drawing near to the door; the last, the very last moment had arrived! Ruth raised her beautiful, sad face and gazed steadily at Victor, and he stopped short in the middle of a sentence, and turned guiltily aside. He could not meet her eyes.

After that all was bustle and confusion—servants crowding to say good-bye, villagers bobbing farewell curtseys at their doors, elaborate regrets and hopes for a speedy return from acquaintances at the little station, tears from Mrs Thornton, and a last glimpse of Victor's tall figure standing motionless on the platform; then they were off, and Jack tactfully busied himself behind his newspaper until the first painful moments were past.

When he ventured to lower the screen, both girls were perfectly composed and dry-eyed, gazing out of their respective windows. His eyes turned from Ruth to dwell upon Mollie at the further end of the carriage. The fashionable young woman had disappeared, and he saw again the simple girl in shabby serge coat and close-fitting hat with whom he had travelled weeks before, yet there was a difference which his fastidious eyes were quick to note, a dainty precision in the way the clothes were worn, a perfection of detail, a neatness of coiffure.

Mollie was too clever and adaptive to have missed the lessons of the last few weeks, and the change of expression was even more marked. The audacious school-girl had disappeared, and in her place sat a woman, with a grave, set face, and eyes that stared into space, seeing things that were far away.

Jack's heart contracted with a stab of pain. He dropped his paper, and with one long step crossed the carriage and seated himself by her side. Ruth turned in her seat to stare more persistently out of her window, and the clattering of the train made it impossible to overhear a conversation.

"Mollie!" said Jack softly.

She turned her head and looked at him, neither startled nor smiling, but with a patient sadness, the sight of which brought with it yet another stab.

"For Heaven's sake, Mollie, don't look like that! Things will right themselves again, or you may find that they are not so bad as you expect. In any case, there's a pleasure in helping to pull them straight. It may be a tug just at first, but that only means more satisfaction in the end. Don't look so sad! I can't bear to leave you looking like that."

Mollie gave a flickering smile. She had not been thinking of business troubles, but naturally Jack could not guess that.

"Once on a time—do you remember?—you wished that I could be serious. You should not complain because your wish is fulfilled," she said slowly; and Jack put up a protesting hand.

"Don't! don't! I was a fool! I didn't know what I was saying. You were made to be happy; you should always be happy if I could arrange it for you."

Mollie smiled again, but with the same obvious effort.

"I hope you will be happy," she said; "I hope some day we may hear good news from you. I don't mean about money; you can guess what I mean."

"Yes," said Jack gravely; and there was silence for another five minutes, while the train approached nearer and nearer to the junction at which he was to alight, to catch the express for town.

"I hope I shall hear good news of you, too," he said at last. "You will be busy at first, and there may not be much to tell, but later on—in a few weeks' time, when you see how things are going—will you let me know? I shall be so interested to hear; and at any time if I can do anything, if you need anything done in town, or if I could help by coming North, you would be doing me a good turn by letting me know. I mean it, Mollie; it is not a polite form of speech."

"I know; thank you; I will promise," said Mollie, with, for the first time, a little break in her composure. Her lip trembled in a pathetic, childlike fashion, and, as if afraid of herself, she bent forward and addressed a pointed question to Ruth.

Ten minutes later the junction was reached, and Jack stood outside the carriage saying his last farewells. Ruth talked persistently in a high, cheerful voice, and Jack bit his moustache and cast furtive glances at Mollie's white face. She smiled at him bravely as the train steamed away, and waved her hand, calling out, "Good luck! good luck!" Then they turned, the two poor girls, and clasped each other tightly.

"Oh, Lucille, my poor Lucille!"

"Berengaria, Berengaria, how horribly it hurts!"

Chapter Thirty Three.

Back to Poverty.

Trix was at the station to meet them—a greatly developed Trix, as became a young woman who not only provided for her own education but also that of her sister. The door-knocker had disappeared, and her lanky locks were screwed into a knot about as big as a good-sized walnut; she wore a discarded black skirt of Ruth's, which reached down to her ankles, a blue blouse, white sailor-hat, and brown shoes. Ruth's heart contracted with pain when she saw her, and even Mollie felt a pang of dismay. So shabby, so unkempt, so obviously poverty-stricken! Was it really possible that Trix had looked like this six weeks before, and that the sight had caused no consternation?

Plainly Miss Trix was rather pleased than otherwise with her appearance, and was decidedly patronising to her half-sisters, ordering them about, and treating them with the lenient forbearance which a busy worker might be expected to show to two elderly, incapable drones. She interviewed the porter as to sending home the luggage, and only consented to the hire of a cab when it was proved to her own satisfaction that the cost would be about equal. She took Ruth's purse from her hand to tip the porter, looking at him the while with such a severe and determined air that his grumbles died upon his lips; finally, she gave the cabman instructions to stop at a certain shop, where—as she informed her sisters triumphantly—potatoes could be bought three-halfpence a peck cheaper than in more fashionable neighbourhoods.

"Good gracious, Trix, you don't mean to take home potatoes in the cab!" gasped Ruth, fresh from the delightful luxury of the Court, where no one thought what anything cost, and every luxury of the season appeared of its own accord upon the table; but Trix smiled at her benignly, and replied—

"Certainly; two pecks! And any other vegetables I can pick up cheap. It will help to pay for the cab-fare. Not that you will get any of them to-night, for we have knocked off late dinner and afternoon-tea, and have one late tea instead. Cold tongue for you to-night, as you have had a journey. Mother wanted to have a chicken. The idea! 'No, indeed,' I said; 'let them begin as they must go on. Our chicken days are over!'"

"I think yours are, any way. You seem to have grown into a very old hen," cried Mollie disconsolately. She looked across the cab at the businesslike young woman, and wondered if a few weeks of home under the new conditions would work a similar transformation in herself and Ruth. It was a comfort to remember that Trix's vocation kept her out of the house for the greater part of the day, for it would be distinctly trying to be "bossed" as a permanent thing.

Perhaps Trix's thoughts had wandered to the same subject, for her welcome was the reverse of encouraging.

"Can't think what you've come back for!" she declared candidly. "Mother thought of sending for you last week, but I told her it was absurd. It will make more work, and both the servants are going. We gave Mary notice, and Kate said she couldn't abase herself to be a 'general' after her bringings up. Goodness knows who we shall get! I sat for two hours in a registry-office yesterday afternoon, when we had a half-holiday, and didn't see a single creature who could be bribed to come. 'Nine in family; one servant, cellar kitchens; washing done at home.' Sounds so attractive, doesn't it? And yet I suppose we ought not to afford even one. If we lived in the country we could do the work alone, but cockroaches! No really refined mind can cope with cockroaches, and they simply swarm in the back kitchen... Mother's terribly cut up that you have left the Court. If I had been in your place I'd have stayed on, and persuaded the old man to help father out of his difficulties."

"Oh, Trix, as if we hadn't tried! You talk as if no one had any sense but yourself! You are very clever and important, no doubt, but even your earnings will not keep the family. There is a little work left for Mollie and myself!" cried Ruth hotly.

Whereupon Trix elevated the red marks which should have been her eyebrows, and exclaimed coolly—

"Hallo, still snapping! I thought you would be quite good-tempered after such a holiday!"

It was indeed like being at home again to hear a squabble between Ruth and Trix within the first ten minutes.

When the house was reached, there was the little mother standing in the doorway, smiling and waving her hands in welcome; but at the first sight of her both girls felt a sudden choking sensation in the throat, so wan did she appear, so bleached in colour, such a tiny, frail little creature to be burdened with the care of an impecunious household! She clung to her girls, and her girls clung to her, and presently they were seated together round the dining-room table, on which, in spite of Trix's dismal prophecy, appeared a tray of the ever-welcome afternoon-tea.

"After their journey, Trix dear! I thought just this once," murmured Mrs Connor apologetically. "Dear Ruth, how sweet you look! Is that a new coat? No, I see it is not; but it looks new, with that charming collar and vest. And your hair, dear; and Mollie's, too! So beautifully done! I suppose the maid taught you? Oh, darlings, I'm thankful to have you back, but I should never have sent for you! You were on the spot, and could judge best what to do. Did you—did you let Uncle Bernard know of our trouble?"

The strained eagerness of the small face, the involuntary tremor in the voice, smote the girls to the heart. Ruth turned her head aside, herself on the verge of tears, while Mollie said brokenly—

"We sent him your letter to read, and when he said nothing I asked him point-blank if he would lend father enough money to put things right just now, and promised that we would all work to pay him back."

"Yes, dear—yes! And then?"

"He wouldn't. He jeered at me, and said he made it a rule never to throw good money after bad. He would keep us for the remaining six weeks, if we agreed to stay, but more than that he must refuse to do. So there seemed no alternative, mother dear, but to come straight away and try to help you ourselves."

"Yes, dear—yes. Bless you! You were quite right!"

Mrs Connor tried to speak bravely; but it was as if the last gleam of hope had died out of her tired eyes, and her hands trembled as she clasped them in her lap. She herself had not realised until this moment how much she had counted upon Uncle Bernard's intervention, and now the last hope seemed gone. She shivered, and put her hand to her head; then forced herself to smile, as she met the girls' anxious gaze.

"It's always the darkest the hour before the dawn. You must talk things over with pater, dears; my head is so confused. I shall be thankful for your help in the house, and no doubt something will turn up for you, as it has done for Trix."

"Mother," cried Ruth, with an outburst of irritation, which was the result of tired-out nerves and body, "Trix is insupportable! She behaves as if she were the head of the house! How can you let her give herself such airs and domineer over you so? I shan't stand it for one, and the sooner she understands it the better. I am not going to be ordered about by a bit of a chit of seventeen, and apologise to her if I dare to have as much as a cup of tea!"

"Hu–ush, dear!" Mrs Connor cast an apprehensive glance towards the half-opened door, through which Trix's voice could be heard superintending the carrying of the luggage. "She is such a child! Young things are always inclined to go to extremes; and she has been so good! I don't know what I should have done without her! We must not let her feel slighted because you have returned!"

That was true enough; Trix had borne the heat and burden of the day, while her stepsisters were amusing themselves, in blissful ignorance of the gathering troubles. Ruth's irritation was silenced by the reminder, and she listened quietly while Mollie pressed her mother for details of the present situation. Alas, it was even worse than had been expected! It was so bad that it could not well be worse, and it seemed ridiculous to talk of what they could afford, since, as a matter of fact, they could afford nothing at all. It was a matter of speculation whence the next twenty pounds was to come.

"'Man's extremity is God's opportunity!' Some friend will be raised up to help us through this strait. It is not often that we are brought to a point when we realise our own helplessness so plainly. Let us look upon it as an opportunity, and watch to see what He will do. 'Be not dismayed, neither be afraid, for the Lord thy God is with thee whithersoever thou goest.'"

Mrs Connor's voice sank to a rapt whisper, her face shone with that wonderful grace and exaltation which the Christian knows in the midst of his trial; but her daughters looked at her pinched cheeks and haggard eyes, and felt their hearts sink within them.

It was a dreary evening—how different from the triumphant home-coming which fancy had painted so often during the weeks of absence! The house felt unbearably cramped and airless. It was dreadful to have no garden, after having practically lived out of doors; and oh, what a contrast the evening meal presented from the repast served nightly in the old oak dining-hall!

When people are in the extremity of anxiety and poverty, they have no heart to attend to the little superfluities which add so much to the beauty of daily life; there was not a single flower on the table, nor in the half-lit drawing-room, where Trix sternly forbade the lighting of a second lamp. Mr Connor sat silent and haggard, and his wife poured out tea and smiled a pathetic, patient little smile, as the children catechised the travellers.

Was the Court a jolly big house? Were there strawberries in the garden? Did the footmen wear white stockings, like the Lord Mayor's Show? What was the name of the horse that bolted? What did they have for dinner every night? On and on went the endless catechism, which the sisters tolerated only as an improvement on silence. They had no wish to visit Attica, but retired upstairs to their bedroom at the earliest possible moment to mingle tears of misery.

"I—I feel as if I should burst!" cried Ruth expressively. "My heart is so full that I can't bear another thing! Everything seems to have happened at once, and I feel crushed!"

"It's so bad that it must get better! it can't possibly get worse!" said Mollie, persistently hopeful in the midst of her misery.

But alas, her prophecy was not justified by events! Mrs Connor crawled about the house for another week, looking every day smaller and more fragile; and then a morning came when she could not rise from bed, and all other anxieties seemed to dwindle in significance when the illness took a serious turn, and her precious life itself seemed in danger.

Chapter Thirty Four.

The Silver Lining.

Ruth and Mollie constituted themselves nurses, Mollie, as the more robust of the two, insisting upon taking as her share the arduous night duties. Trix found time to attend to the housekeeping between school hours, the younger children were housed by sympathetic friends, and on the once noisy house settled down that painful silence which prevails when a fight is being waged between life and death.

At the beginning of the illness Ruth was dismayed to see a stranger in Dr Maclure's place, but on the third day he appeared, bringing with him an atmosphere of comfort and security. One felt now that all that was possible from human skill and care would be done for the dear invalid, and, busy man as he was, Dr Maclure found time for several visits a day, until the first acute anxiety was passed. Until then his intercourse with Ruth had been solely that of physician and nurse, but one morning, when the invalid's temperature and pulse both showed a satisfactory decline, he walked into the dining-room on the way to the door, and motioned Ruth to a seat.

"Sit down for a moment. I want to have a little talk with you. It is a doctor's duty to see that a nurse does not overtax her strength, and you are looking very ill these last few days. I am going to prescribe a tonic which I want you to take regularly, and you must contrive to have a walk each day, and, if possible, a rest in the afternoon. You might lie down on the sofa while your mother is dozing."

Ruth flushed, and shook her head in pretty disclaimer.

"Oh, I am all right! Don't trouble about me. I have not half such a hard time of it as Mollie. The nursing doesn't tire me a bit; it is other things which make one feel rather ill at times."

"Just so. And it is about those other things that I want to speak. Eleanor and I have been abroad for a month, and have heard little or no home news. I was ill—that is to say, feeling rather worn out," corrected the doctor, with a sudden flush of colour to his thin cheeks, "so we decided to treat ourselves to a holiday. I found on my return that Mrs Connor was ill, and heard rumours which strengthened my own conviction that her trouble was more mental than physical. It is not giving a doctor a fair chance to keep back anything from him in a case of this sort. I want you to tell me honestly, as a friend and physician, if anything can be done to set her mind at rest."

"We are ruined, that's the trouble! The pater has lost every penny—not by his own fault, but through some wretched man who has deliberately cheated him for months back. He can't even go on with what business is left, for want of capital, so we have arrived at the point when we don't know what to do next. We look pretty much as usual, I suppose, but we are just as much paupers as if we lived in the big workhouse over in Smithdown Lane!"

Dr Maclure paced slowly up and down the room, stopping immediately in front of Ruth's chair.

"But, excuse me—your uncle? Surely he will help at a crisis of this sort. Before I went abroad I heard great stories of your life at the Court, and of the very marked preference which he showed to yourself. It seemed a foregone conclusion that his choice had fallen upon you, and, if so—"

"Ah, that was a month ago! Many things have happened since then. Uncle Bernard doesn't like me as much as he did. He discovered my weaknesses, and accused me of being a coward. I am not a coward, as a rule, but I wanted so badly to please him that I was afraid to be natural, as Mollie was. Before we came away someone went to his desk and read the draft of a will which he had mentioned a few days before. It was not altered or tampered with in any way, but, of course, it was a mean thing to pry into his private papers, when he had put us on our honour by speaking of it. We all denied it, but just because I had been afraid before, I know he suspects that I did it, and dare not confess.—Then we came away against his wishes. Jack Melland left, too, so only one out of the four remains, and he is certain to be the heir."

"You mean Mr Victor Druce?"

Ruth started, raising a flushed, bewildered face.

"Yes; but how,—what do you know about him?"

"Trix brought some of your letters to show us. His name was mentioned very often, Ruth. I had a presentiment that you two would be more than friends. You must forgive me, but one's perceptions grow keen when one's interests are strong. I thought that very probably Mr Farrell had some such hope in inviting you and Mollie to meet these two men."

"Perhaps he had. I have thought so, too, but, in any case, it has come to nothing. Jack Melland cares for nothing but his work, and Mr Druce—"

Ruth hesitated, possessed by a sudden impulse to confide her own troubles to this man, who loved her, and would understand. Her lids dropped till the dark lashes lay on her flushed cheek; she clasped her hands nervously together. "He made love to me as long as I was in favour, but it was only pretence. He really cares for another girl, but he thought I should be a better bargain if I were Uncle Bernard's heiress. He has taken no notice of me lately, but we found him out before that,—I and the other girl. She is good and charming, and in every way better than I am, and she had cared for him, too. I expect he will try to marry her now that I am in disgrace, but she will never accept him."

"And you, Ruth? Has it gone very hardly with you, poor child?"

There was silence for several moments before Ruth lifted a thoughtful face.

"I—don't—know!" she said slowly. "It was a shock to me at first, and I felt as if I could never believe in a man again, but since I came home I have hardly thought about him, and if I had cared as much as I imagined that would have been the worst trouble of all. I think it was just part of the experience. Can you understand? Summer-time, and the lovely country, and the holiday feeling, and nothing to do but laze about, and amuse ourselves together. It seemed—don't laugh!—so natural to fall in love."

Dr Maclure did not laugh, but a smile flashed over his face, full of immeasurable relief and pleasure.

"I do understand," he said heartily. "You have had so few chances of enjoying yourself with young people of your own age. It was, as you say, quite natural, but I hope you will have no more to do with the fellow. He is a pretty contemptible specimen, by all accounts."

"Oh no!" Ruth reared her little head with a haughty gesture. "I could forgive a great deal to a man who really loved me, but nothing to an adventurer who cares only for his own gains; I am sorry the dear old Court will fall into such hands, for he cannot make a good master, and, as far as we are concerned, it will cease to exist. That dream has come to an end, Dr Maclure!"

"Well, one must hope it will be replaced by something more lasting. Don't trouble too much about Mr Connor's difficulties. I feel quite convinced that some arrangement can be made to tide him over the present crisis. You may not live at the Court, but it is equally certain that you are not going to the workhouse."

He held out his hand, and Ruth said good-bye with a little tremor of relief and thankfulness in her voice. Dr Maclure was a man of few words, but what he said he meant, and his quiet, assured manner made him seem a veritable rock of refuge in the midst of the storm.

Ruth felt happier and more hopeful than she had done for many a long day, despite the uneasiness caused by the doctor's appearance. His skin was bronzed by his tour abroad, otherwise he must have looked shockingly ill, for he was thin and worn to a marked extent. Remembering the date of his illness, it was impossible not to connect it with her own refusal, and Ruth's heart softened at the thought. "He has suffered for me, as I have suffered for Victor! He is a real man; true and strong and honest. Everywhere people run after him and admire him, but he cares only for me. How much he cares! His poor, thin face! All this time while I have been forgetting, he has been thinking of me, and grieving himself ill."

Sad though the reflection might be, there was comfort mingled with it. The sore, slighted feeling of the last few weeks could not survive while a man of Donald Maclure's calibre placed her first among women.

That very evening, after his second visit to the invalid, the doctor was closeted with Mr Connor for an hour, and after his departure the latter joined his step-daughters in the dining-room, where Mollie was eating her deferred dinner in preparation for the night's watch, and the first glance at his face proved that a light had arisen in the darkness.

"The worst is over!" he said tremblingly. "Maclure has come to the rescue. He is a good fellow—a noble fellow! God will reward him; I am to draw upon him for necessary expenses for the next few months; and I have no doubt the business will go well—so many men have come forward and offered to support me if I could keep going. This will be the best possible medicine for your mother, and for us all. It will give us heart to work, and we shall have to work hard to pay off the loan."

Ruth set her lips in a determined fashion, which gave a new expression to her face. She was thankful beyond words for help in this time of need, but the fact that it had come from Donald Maclure, of all people, made the debt difficult to bear. He had already offered much, and had been rejected. She felt oppressed by his very generosity.

That night when she went to bed, Ruth unfolded the little bundle of letters which she had received from Raby since her return home, and read them over with lingering attention. No word from Uncle Bernard, though both girls had written to him more than once, telling him of their mother's illness and progress towards recovery. Not a line from Victor, though he must have known of the added trouble. A short, manly letter of sympathy from Jack Melland, who had heard of the bad news through Mrs Thornton—a letter addressed to Ruth, with "kindest regards to her sister"; three long, underlined epistles from that lady herself, and one sheet covered with a beautiful, distinctive handwriting, and signed "Margot Blount." Ruth opened this last letter first of all, and passed hurriedly over expressions of condolence to the more practical part of the message.

"And now, Ruth, you must not think because Fate has separated us in this hurried manner that you have seen the last of me. I want to be your friend now and always, and hope to see a great deal of you in the future. Mrs Thornton says that you wish to find some work. I am neither rich nor clever, but I know a great many people, and I have some little influence, so I can certainly help you there. Write, dear, and tell me if you have any special vocation in view, or if you are willing to take the best chance that offers. I have a rich and gouty relation whose companion is shortly to be married. I could recommend you for the post, when you would be well paid, and live in luxury; but I know you would feel prisoned, and long to throw cushions at her occasionally. I should! There are numerous societies and guilds also to which I belong, and to one of which you might be appointed as secretary or treasurer. Then you would be your own mistress, and free; but is freedom worth much in London lodgings? I can't fancy you roughing it by yourself, and I keep hoping against hope for some sudden turn of the tide which may still make it unnecessary. Don't settle to anything before telling me first. I know I can find something really good if you give me time.

"Mr Druce is very much in evidence, acting host at the Court, and visiting far and near. He tells me that Mr Farrell consults him on every point, and gives him carte blanche to do as he likes; and I hear as much from other sources, more reliable. As his position becomes more assured, his attentions increase; but he will not make the fatal mistake of burdening himself with a poor wife until there is no possibility of mistake. Therefore, it may some day be my painful duty to refuse to become mistress of the Court; but the refusing itself I shall enjoy. You would not, for you have a gentle nature; but Mr Druce shall find that he cannot play with Margot Blount for naught!"

Ruth could see in imagination the haughty tilt of Margot's graceful head, and the flash in her eyes, as she wrote those words, and did not envy Victor his hour of awakening. Evidently the whole countryside now looked upon him as the accepted heir, and even hopeful Mrs Thornton ceased to prophesy for the future.

"I have seen Mr Farrell twice this last week, but have not succeeded in making him mention your names," she wrote in her last letter. "I talk continuously of you—in what vein you can imagine!—and read extracts from your letters; and he listens intently, but makes no remarks. I can see him mentally pounce on anything which gives him fresh insight into your life here, as if he were still interested in the study of your characters; but the moment I stop speaking he turns the conversation to impersonal topics. Only one thing he has done which I thought really thoughtful. Ruth's camera was found lying about, and he gave instructions that it was to be taken down to the photographers the same day, and copies printed from all the films, so that your mother might receive them as soon as possible. I believe they were sent up yesterday, so that you may expect them soon, and perhaps a letter at the same time. Mr Druce is kind and amiable, and very much the man in possession. I don't take to him, but my husband believes he will make a good squire."

"Will," not "would"! This from Mrs Thornton was conclusive indeed! Ruth dropped a salt tear on the back of the sheet as she folded it up. It was good news to hear of the trouble Uncle Bernard had taken on her behalf. Surely, surely he would not forward the photographs without enclosing some sort of an answer to her many notes!

For the next few days Ruth's heart leapt every time the postman's knock sounded at the door; but, when the longed-for packet arrived, the words, "Photographs only," written on the back, killed her hopes at a glance. The pictures themselves were fairly successful, and gave a happy half-hour to the invalid, who bent lovingly over each familiar scene.

"It takes me back to my youth to see the dear old rooms again! How successful you are with interiors, Ruth; but you have no photograph of the library, one of my favourite haunts. How did you come to leave that out?"

"I didn't. I took it twice over. I'm sorry, dear, but I expect they were failures," said Ruth wearily.

She could not guess that on these missing pictures hung the fate of many lives.

Chapter Thirty Five.

Love's Conquest.

Six months had passed by, taking with them the keen edge of anxiety, but leaving behind the dull, monotonous routine which is almost as hard to bear. It is not enlivening, to be obliged to work instead of play, to look ten times at a sixpence before you dare spend it, to consider what you can do without, rather than what you can have, and to see no prospect ahead but continual cheese-paring and self-denial; and when you happen to be young and full of life, it is harder than ever.

With Dr Maclure's help, Mr Connor was able to continue his business, and his City friends rallied round him, doing their best to put work in his way; but, even so, there were pressing debts to be settled besides the loan which one and all were anxious to repay, so that housekeeping expenses had to be reduced to a minimum. It was decided that one of the elder girls must stay at home, while the other tried for work abroad, and it was at once a relief and a blow for Ruth when Mollie was chosen as mother's help. She had dreaded the irksome duties of mending, cooking, dusting, and everlasting putting to rights, which would have fallen to her share, but it would have been a comfort to have been chosen!

"Don't feel hurt, darling; it's a pure question of suitability," Mrs Connor had explained anxiously. "Mollie is stronger than you are, and has a more adaptable temperament. She won't feel the little jars as you would, and will get on better with the maid. It is the art of a good general to place his forces in the best position."

"Yes, of course, dear. It's quite—quite right! Arrange everything as you think best," replied Ruth sweetly, kissing the little, wistful face as she spoke; for Mrs Connor was still very fragile, and by Dr Maclure's orders had to be spared all possible worry.

The same orders were extended to forbid Ruth from taking advantage of Lady Margot's offer to procure work at a distance.

"Unless it proves absolutely impossible to find a suitable post here, I don't think it would be wise to subject your mother to any further anxiety. She would be constantly worrying about your welfare, and that is the very thing we wish to avoid. Would it be a great disappointment to you to give up going to London?" he inquired, with a quick, grave look at Ruth's face.

"It would be a blessed relief. I'd a million times rather be at home; but what can I find to do? I am ashamed to think how incompetent I am! Here we are back again where we were three months ago, Dr Maclure, when I worried you and Eleanor about a vocation!"

Ruth smiled, then flushed crimson at a sudden remembrance of how that conversation had ended. She was immeasurably thankful to the doctor for looking in an opposite direction and continuing to talk in the most matter-of-fact manner.

"It occurred to me last night that I knew of a post which might suit you for the next few months. The secretary of our Home for Nurses is on the point of breaking down, and needs a good rest. The work needs no special knowledge; it consists mainly in answering endless notes of inquiries, and in keeping some very simple accounts. I could soon coach you up in what is necessary. You would have to be there from ten to six—not heavy hours, as things go. I think I could secure the post for you for, say, the next three months, if you cared to accept it."

"And how much should I get?"

"Miss Edgar's salary is forty pounds; you would get a fourth of that—"

"Ten pounds!" Ruth stared at him with dilated eyes. "Ten pounds! Every day from ten to six for three whole months, and only ten pounds! Dr Maclure, do you know it is a real, true, honest fact that I paid twenty pounds for a ball-dress only a few weeks ago? I've got it now in a box upstairs!"

The doctor smiled.

"I should like to see you in it! I hope I may some day. It certainly seems a good deal of money, but I suppose it is very fine, and will last a long time."

"But it won't! It's a mere wisp of gauze, that will only be fit to burn after being worn two or three times. And I should have to work for six months to earn enough to pay for it! How shocking! What a terrible difference there is between the lives of the rich and the poor!"

"Ah, there you have touched on a great problem! After you have had some experience of being a working woman, you may not care to buy any more twenty-pound dresses, even if the opportunity offers. I know that the payment is small, but I am afraid you would find it difficult to get more without any special knowledge or training. It is hard for you, especially coming so soon after your taste of luxury; but if you can face it—"

"Oh yes, indeed! I'll take it, and be thankful; and perhaps, if I do very well and keep the books nicely, I may be worth fifty pounds next time!" said Ruth, with a charming courage, which might well have aroused any man's admiration.

Dr Maclure made no remark, and turned his head aside. He had a habit nowadays of looking at other things when he was speaking to Ruth. So it happened that while Mollie worked at home, Ruth went forth every day to her monotonous task, trudging along the same well-known path, in sun and rain, heat and cold—for the secretary's leave of absence had to be prolonged—until Christmas was close at hand, and the ten pounds' salary had doubled in value.

"I shall be able to buy myself a new mackintosh and a pair of good stout boots," Ruth said to herself, as she trudged home one dismal

December evening, and felt a suspicious dampness in the soles of her tired little feet.

She had no idea what a charming figure she made in her long, dark coat, with her hair curling in wet rings about her face; for she carried no umbrella, as her cloth toque defied the weather, and she preferred to keep her hands free to hold her skirts from contact with the muddy roads. The pink-and-white face, with its delicately cut features, and straight black brows, shone out like a flower among the tired, colourless-looking throng of workers who wended their way homeward; and her expression was bright and alert, despite the dismal surroundings.

Ruth was surprised at her own happiness of late. Her work was dull and monotonous, and she had few pleasures to relieve it; yet, for some mysterious reason, she was more truly content at heart than in those days of ease and luxury, which seemed like a dream of the past. Six months had passed since that memorable day when she and Mollie had bidden adieu to the Court; and Uncle Bernard still lived, and was apparently in the same condition.

Mrs Thornton kept her friends well informed of the news of the neighbourhood, so that they knew that, though Victor Druce had ostensibly returned to town at the expiration of his three months' visit, he was constantly running down and bringing friends with him for a few days' shooting, with the privilege of a son of the house. For the rest, Margot Blount had returned to town, and Jack Melland's communications were limited to an occasional picture-postcard bearing half a dozen words of greeting. Mollie made no comment on the briefness of these missives, and was always cheery and busy, but sometimes on her return from her day's work Ruth would look at her anxiously, and wonder if it were only imagination that Mollie looked different, thinner and older—a woman rather than a girl. Perhaps after all she had the harder path—shut up in the house, without the daily variety of seeing fresh rooms and fresh faces. The regular constitutional, too, was in itself health-giving, and though Ruth received much pity at home on the score of her long, wet walks, it was astonishing what pleasant surprises loomed out of the fog at times. She smiled to herself, and a dimple dipped in her cheek.

The good old fairy days were not yet over, when a tired Cinderella, trudging through the mire, was suddenly provided with a comfortable carriage, springing as it were out of the earth to carry her to her destination. It was extraordinary how often Dr Maclure's brougham "happened" to be travelling in the same direction as herself on wet evenings; and although the doctor himself was conspicuous by his absence, the coachman was wonderfully quick to recognise one figure out of many, and to draw up with a "Just driving past your house, miss. Can I give you a lift?"

Ruth had no doubt that it was the master, not the man, who was responsible for these meetings, and the conviction brought with it a glow of content, of which as yet she failed to realise the meaning. Nevertheless, her heart beat with a pleasurable excitement as she threaded her way through the crowded streets, wondering if once again the fairy equipage would be sent to the rescue, if it would appear at this corner or the next. At last, through the driving sleet, she recognised the familiar outline of the brougham drawn up beside the pavement, but for once the coachman sat stiffly on his box, while the master stepped forward to meet her.

"Miss Ruth, it is a shocking evening! I have a call to pay in this neighbourhood. Do let George drive you home before you are wet through."

Ruth stood still and looked at him. The drops of moisture were thick upon hat and coat, her soft cheeks were damp with rain, but her eyes danced with a spice of mischief which was more like Mollie than the grave, elder sister of the family.

"I'll drive with pleasure on one condition—that you will first allow yourself to be taken to your patient's house," she replied demurely, adding when the doctor hesitated in embarrassment: "It is such a very odd neighbourhood for a patient to live in, in the midst of these great blocks of offices! I think we may perhaps have to drive you a long, long way."

For a moment Dr Maclure did not reply; he merely held open the door of the carriage, waiting until Ruth should have taken her seat; then he leant towards her, the light from the lamps showing the nervous tremor of his lips.

"I will come in too, on one condition—that you are willing to drive beside me all the way, Ruth!"

What did he mean? Ruth started and flushed, for the tone of voice was even more eloquent than the words themselves. The moment which she had vaguely expected, dreaded, and hoped for, had come suddenly upon her, provoked by her own jesting words. She did not know what to say, or how to say it, only one definite thought stood out distinctly in the confusion of her mind, namely, that Dr Maclure was standing unprotected in the damp and cold. She held out her hand towards him, and cried tremulously—

"Don't stand out in the rain! Oh, please come in! We will go where you like?"

Dr Maclure leapt lightly to his seat, and the coachman whipped up his horses without waiting for instructions. A coachman is only an ordinary man after all, and George had seen how the wind blew for many a long day. He took care not to drive too quickly, nor to choose the shortest routes, satisfied that for once his master was not in a hurry.

Inside the brougham Dr Maclure held Ruth's shabbily gloved little hand in his, and asked earnestly—

"Can you give me a different answer this time, Ruth? It has been a weary waiting, and I seem to have grown worse instead of better. I fear it is an incurable complaint! Can you give me a glimmer of hope, dear, or is it still quite impossible?"

Ruth shook her head and nodded and smiled, and sighed, and shed a few bright tears, in a whirl of delightful confusion.

"It's—it's not impossible at all! I think I am quite sure. I have been growing surer and surer all this time. But am I good enough? You remember that six months ago I fancied myself in love with someone else?"

"I can afford to forget that episode, and even to be thankful for it, if it has shown you your own mind, so that now you are 'quite sure'! Oh, Ruth, it is too good to be true! Can you really be happy with a dull, old fellow like me? No country seat, you know; no life of ease and luxury, just a comfortable, commonplace house, with a husband who is too hard-worked to have much time for play. I have no fortune to offer you, dear, except love—there's no end to that wealth!"

Ruth turned her beautiful eyes upon him with a smile of perfect content.

"But that's everything!" she cried. "I shall be the richest woman in the world!"

Chapter Thirty Six.

Margot's Answer.

A week later Victor Druce was sitting *tête-à-tête* with Margot Blount in the drawing-room of her aunt's London house, a cramped little house in a fashionable neighbourhood. The house was generally let furnished during the season, and inhabited by the impecunious owner at those odd seasons of the year when she had no invitations which made it possible to saddle other people with the cost of food and maintenance. Just now there was a gap of a few weeks between the last shooting-party and a Christmas gathering in the country, so the house had been reopened, and friends flocked to call and leave cards, foremost among them Mr Victor Druce, a young man of importance, nowadays, as the accredited heir to one of the finest properties in the kingdom.

"I am not at home to anyone else this afternoon," Margot announced to the servant, as Victor took his seat beside her. She smiled to herself as she spoke, an odd little smile, whose meaning her visitor was puzzled to decipher. It was a great compliment to be allowed a private interview, but there was a mysterious something in Margot's manner which detracted from his satisfaction. He watched her as she poured out tea at the inlaid Turkish table, with eyes in which admiration and anxiety were equally mingled. He had known many women more beautiful, but never one with such an air of grace and distinction; every movement of the slim body and white tapering fingers was a poem in itself, and the coils of chestnut hair shone like burnished gold. Even in the poorest of surroundings Margot would look an aristocrat, and reflect credit on her husband's good taste.

While he was drinking his tea and listening to the pretty flow of conversation about everything in general and nothing in particular, which seems to come so naturally to women of the world, Victor was busy painting a mental picture of a wonderful, rose-coloured future where he would reign as master of Raby Court, with Margot acting chatelaine by his side. The exclusive county families might have hesitated to welcome a stranger, who was moreover a "City man," but, with Margot Blount as his wife, he would have the entrée into any society.

Victor congratulated himself on his usual good luck, inasmuch as this desirable partner was the girl of all others whom he would have selected for her own sake. A year ago he had looked upon her as a star entirely out of his own sphere, for he had the poorest of prospects for the future, but now, as by the stroke of a magician's wand, a fine position was almost assured, and he could approach Margot if not as an equal, still as a match whom nobody need disdain. Almost, but not quite! There lay the rub.

The old squire still lingered on, dying by inches as it were, and preserving to the last his grim enigmatical silence. Victor had not heard one word from his lips to substantiate his hopes; but actions—which, as the proverb says, speak louder than words—all seemed to range themselves in his favour. His three rivals had retired in disfavour, and, receiving no replies to their first letters, had gradually ceased writing, so that there was at present no correspondence between them and the squire, while he himself was a constant visitor, and was even allowed carte blanche in inviting and entertaining his friends. The very servants about the place spoke of him as "the young master," and the local tradesfolk lost no opportunity of begging his patronage in the future. Surely, surely he might be done with doubts, and allow himself the joy of speaking out all that was in his heart!

"A penny for your thoughts, Mr Druce," cried Margot gaily. "You have not been listening to me for the last ten minutes. It must have been a very pleasant day-dream to engross you so completely."

"It was," said Victor simply. For once he was thoroughly sincere, and voice and manner both testified to the change. "I was thinking of you," he added, looking at her with the dark eyes which could be so eloquent upon occasions. "My daydreams have always been of you for the last year!"

"Always?" echoed Margot sceptically. She selected a little cake from the basket by her side, and nibbled it daintily with her small white teeth. "Really? I am surprised to hear that. I fancied that you were more catholic in your tastes. It is very flattering of you to include me in your dreams, but I am not presumptuous enough to expect to occupy the entire stage!"

"Presumptuous!" echoed Victor reproachfully. The vague uneasiness which had possessed him since the beginning of the interview was deepened by the unconcealed irony of her tone; and he realised suddenly that he must speak plainly, since it was dangerous to play fast and loose any longer. "What a word for you to use of yourself! It is I who am presumptuous to dream of you as I do; but a man is not always master of his thoughts. I think you must know what my feelings have been ever since we met. I fell hopelessly in love with you at first sight—hopelessly in every way, as it seemed at that time; but, all the same, my fate was sealed, and the world held no other woman."

"Really?" queried Margot again, in the same voice of scepticism. "But, then, how wonderfully you act, Mr Druce! I have seen you only occasionally during the year, but I cannot say that you impressed me as a man who had lost his interest in my sex! At one time I made sure—a good many people made sure—that you had a very definite preference. That was at the beginning of your stay at the Court, when Mr Farrell seemed so devoted to his charming grand-niece. Do you remember the afternoon when I came to call, and found you two sitting together upon the terrace? What a charming picture you made! The old house makes an ideal background for a *tête-à-tête*!"

Victor's eyes lit up with a flash of relief and triumph. Margot was jealous—that was the reason of the change of manner which had puzzled him all the afternoon. She was jealous of his attention to Ruth Farrell, which she evidently looked upon as disloyal to herself. As he could not deny the evidence of her own eyesight, the wisest plan was to throw himself upon her generosity and forgiveness.

"Ah, you must not be hard on me! You were out of reach, and the time and the opportunity were there. She was a pretty girl, and not disinclined for an innocent flirtation. You would not confound so trivial an incident with my feeling for you? Ruth Farrell is a charming girl in her own way; but—"

"But not so charming as she was! She has fallen from favour all round, poor little Ruth, since Mr Farrell transferred his favour to another!"

Victor leapt from his seat, and strode across the room to her side.

"Margot, what is the matter? Why do you speak to me in that voice? Leave Ruth Farrell alone—she is nothing to you or to me. I have been waiting to ask you a question, but I can wait no longer. If the Court is mine, if Mr Farrell makes me his heir, as we all expect, will you share my good fortune? Will you be my wife, and make me the happiest man on earth? I could give you a home which would be worthy even of you!"

He bent over her as he spoke; but Margot pushed back her chair, and rose to confront him, her head almost on a level with his own.

"Really, Mr Druce, you are too original in your methods! A conditional proposal is quite a novelty in my experience. *If* you inherit? And what if by chance you are disappointed? It is still possible, you know! There are some people who believe that the squire is deliberately misleading us all, and that the property will go to Ruth Farrell, despite all appearances. I should like to know exactly how I stand before I commit myself to a reply. Does your offer still hold good if Ruth inherits in your place?"

Victor's eyelids sank, and a dull red flush showed on his cheeks.

"It is impossible!" he protested. "Why will you conjure up such a position? Mr Farrell has never mentioned his niece's name since she left the Court. He treats me like a son; I come and go as I choose. It is preposterous to believe there can be any doubt on the subject!"

"But suppose there were? Suppose the impossible happened, if you like to put it in that way?"

"If I were back in my old position—worse than my old position, for these months of idleness have not helped me on—I—I should be no match for you, Margot. You would not care to marry a pauper!"

"Nor you an equally impecunious bride! My title would be of service to you as master of the Court, but a commoner with a substantial fortune to her back would be a better bargain for a budding barrister. Such a commoner as—shall we say Ruth Farrell, for example? Mr Druce, you ought to succeed in your profession, for you have shown wonderful forethought in the management of your own affairs. It was an admirable idea to provide for both emergencies, while leaving yourself free. The only drawback to success is that Ruth and myself happened to be friends, and were mutually anxious that the other should not be deceived. Under the circumstances, you will not be surprised that I must decline to consider the problematical offer of the Court and its master. I will live unmarried all my days, or I will marry an honest man and a gentleman!"

Victor stood gazing at her, a figure cut in stone. For a few moments stupefaction held him dumb; then his face worked convulsively in the effort of speech.

"You have known all along—you have deliberately waited, intending to deal me this blow?"

Margot bent her head gravely.

"Yes, I have waited! I am able to take care of myself, but I wished to make quite sure that Ruth was safe. To-day I was glad to feel that it was unnecessary to wait any longer. You will be interested to hear that Miss Farrell is happily engaged to an old friend of the family. It sometimes happens that the cleverest of schemers falls between two stools. The position is undignified, but you have only yourself to thank. I think we have nothing more to say to each other, Mr Druce. I have the pleasure to wish you—Good-bye!"

She had touched the electric bell a moment before, and now the door opened and a servant stood awaiting her bidding. In his presence it was impossible for Victor to reply. For one moment he stood glaring at her, a picture of impotent fury, then slowly turned and left the room. As the house door closed behind him, the electric bell pealed once more, and the servant turned back to the drawing-room.

"I am not at home in future to Mr Druce! Please remember!" said Lady Margot.

Then her eye fell on the envelope of a telegram which the man was carrying towards her. She tore it open, saw at a glance that it came from Mrs Thornton at Raby, and read the following message:—

"Squire died suddenly last night. Husband, Druce, Melland, summoned to funeral on Thursday. Will write details."

It was a duplicate of a message which was even then speeding on its way to the two grand-nieces in Liverpool.

Chapter Thirty Seven.

Bernard Farrell's Heir.

"I'm not sorry; I'm *glad*!" cried Mollie, while a rain of tears rolled down her cheeks. "He was old and was tired, and everyone he loved had gone before him. It will be like going home to meet them again. He was grim and cross and suspicious, but I loved him all the same, and in his queer way I am sure that he liked me too. I'm thankful he is at rest! ... 'Will write details.' Thursday!—that means that she will write on Thursday evening. Mrs Thornton is nothing if not businesslike. We shall hear from her by the second post on Friday. By Friday at ten o'clock we shall know our fate. To be, or not to be—that is the question. Oh, I hope—I hope he has remembered us a little! There is no chance of inheriting the Court, as we once dreamt of doing; but still, there is a hope, and it will be a shock to bury it for ever. I used to feel comparatively indifferent; but the strain of these last six months has made me greedy; while you, you dear goose, who used to be all ambition, are in such a ludicrous condition of bliss that you can hardly rouse yourself to take any interest in the question! What it is to be engaged!"

Ruth tried to look contrite, but succeeded only in smiling seraphically.

"When you are perfectly happy it is impossible to be happier, and I honestly don't care very much. I should like Uncle Bernard to leave me a nice message, and I shouldn't at all object to a legacy, which would provide my trousseau; but the Court itself would be a white elephant to me now. Donald adores his work, and would not give it up for any consideration, so we could never live there ourselves."

"You might lend it to a poor but deserving family! Astonishing as it may appear, there are a few other people in the world beside yourself and Donald, and they are not all going to be married and live happily ever after!"

This time Ruth did, indeed, look contrite, and that without an effort.

"Oh, Mollie, I am horribly selfish! Forgive me, darling! I honestly do forget everybody but ourselves sometimes; and it is hateful of me, for when I am so happy I ought to be more sympathetic, instead of less. I am, when I remember! I am so bubbling over with happiness and good-will that I feel inclined to kiss everyone I meet. But there is so much to be thought about, and every time we meet there seems to be more, and I get lost in dreams."

"Bless your heart, don't apologise to me. I like it!" cried Mollie heartily. "I know your heart is right; and it's a poor thing if lovers can't live in a world of their own for a few weeks of their life. I'm thankful beyond words that your future is settled. But oh, what a help a few hundreds would be to the rest of us just now! I feel as if I could hardly live until Friday morning, I am so anxious to hear the news! And the mysterious condition, Ruth! Do you realise that we shall know all about it in three more days?"

"I wonder!" sighed Ruth dreamily. Then, with sudden animation, "If it is good news,—if either of us came in for something really big, Mrs Thornton would wire! She simply could not wait. She is far too impulsive!"

It was an unfortunate suggestion, as it added tenfold to the strain of waiting. The minutes seemed to drag on Thursday afternoon and evening; but no telegram appeared, and Mollie's heart sank heavily. She knew better than her sister how difficult it was to make both ends meet, and what a long and arduous task it would be to pay off the loans which had tided the family through their time of need, and she was tired—as any natural, high-spirited young thing would be—of all work and no play, and eagerly longing for a respite. Mr Farrell had expressly stated that he would not divide his property; but that did not prohibit small legacies, and when he knew that his nearest relations were in straits, surely—surely...

Mollie was up and dressed even before her usual early hour the next morning, for sleep was impossible in such a whirl of nervous anxiety. Ruth kissed her before departing to her work, and said—

"Rush down to me, dear, if there is anything good to tell. I shall look out for you about eleven."

Mollie set about her household duties with great fervour, so as to make the long hour pass by more quickly. At last ten o'clock struck, and almost at the same time came the sound of the postman's rat-tat. She flew to the door, arriving at the very moment that three letters fell into the box.

One was of that long, narrow shape, which inevitably foretells a bill; a second was unmistakably a circular; the third— Mollie stared at it, turned it over, looked at the postmark, stared at the writing again, in a whirl of bewildered dismay. It could not be an ordinary, unimportant letter from the children's aunt at Brighton! It could not! The thing was impossible! Yet why, then, the address to Trix, the well-known writing—most of all, the horrible postmark?

She put her hand to her head, wondering if it were true, or only a horrible nightmare that Mrs Thornton had not written, after all!

The little mother came creeping out of the dining-room, and, seeing her child's blanched face, was persistently optimistic. Absurd to give up hope because a letter did not come by the first possible post! A hundred things might have happened to cause a delay; and, even if it had been posted in time, the post-office was not always infallible.

Mrs Farrell recalled stories of belated letters from her own experience, and related them at length, while Mollie went numbly about her work. The disappointment was severe, and seemed like a foretaste of worse to come. Nevertheless, as time went on, her naturally buoyant nature asserted itself, and, as each delivery drew near, excitement grew to fever-pitch.

One o'clock, and a letter for the maid; three o'clock, and the postman walked past the door. Poor Mollie! The sound of his departing footsteps rang like a knell in her ears, and two hot rebellious tears rose to her eyes. It did not seem possible that anything would have prevented the kindly Mrs Thornton from keeping her promise except sheer inability to communicate bad news; and bad news meant that her own name and Ruth's were not mentioned in the will, and that everything went to Victor Druce. Oh, it was hard to give up so much to so unworthy a supplanter!

The children came home from school and settled down to their "prep." Mrs Connor retired to her room for a rest, and Mollie took her way to her stepfather's little den to set a match to the fire, and hold a newspaper before it to make it blaze cheerily in preparation for his return. It was one of the pleasures of the day to make the sanctum look cheery and home-like for the tired man, and to-day there was an additional impetus in the knowledge that he would share in her own disappointment.

Mollie knelt by the grate, holding the newspaper in place—a tired, disheartened little Cinderella, who would have liked to lay her head on the table and indulge in a good cry. But such luxuries are not for the brave-hearted; so she resolutely blinked away the rising tears, and, rising to her feet, lighted the crimson-shaded lamp on the writing-table. Its rosy light had a wonderfully beautifying effect on the little room, giving an air of luxury to the commonplace furnishings; and when the curtains were drawn, and the easy-chair drawn up to the fire, it was as bright and cheerful a little interior as one need wish to see.

Mollie looked round with a glance of satisfaction, then suddenly rushed into the hall at the sound of a loud knock at the door. So soon! She had not expected the next delivery for another half-hour at least. No letter appeared in the box; so, with wild visions of a legal missive, registered for greater safety, she threw open the door and peered out into the night.

A man's tall figure stood on the step; but it was not the figure of a postman. Mollie leant forward—the light from above shining on cheeks flushed from contact with the fire, and ruffled golden head—leant forward, and stared into his face with incredulous eyes.

"Mollie!" cried a well-remembered voice, which broke into an eloquent tremor over the name.

"You!" cried Mollie! "Mr Melland! It can't be! What does it mean? You can't really be here!"

He laughed at that, and took a step forward, like the masterful Jack of old.

"I am here; it is myself, and nobody else! I'll tell you all about it if you will let me in. It's rather cold to-night, you know."

She held the door wide open at that, and hurried him across the hall into the little, pink-lighted room, which she had just prepared for another's reception. There they stood face to face, staring at each other for a breathless moment.

"I thought you were in Raby—"

"So I was yesterday. I left this morning, and came down by the first train."

"Mrs Thornton promised to write. I thought you were the postman just now; and, of course, one cannot help being curious.—Have you come to tell us anything nice? Did Uncle Bernard remember us at all?"

"He has left your sister his wife's rubies. They are very beautiful, I am told, and of considerable value."

"Oh, I am glad! Ruth will be pleased; and she will be able to wear them when she is married. How beautiful she will look! And—and me?"

Jack shook his head.

"Nothing? Not even a word to say he forgave me for coming away?"

"There is a letter. You will see it later on. What I meant was that your name was not mentioned in the will. He left you no legacy."

Mollie sat down in the easy-chair, and leant her head against the cushions. In spite of all that had passed, in spite of every determination to be prepared for the worst, the blow fell with crushing weight. She was conscious of a feeling of physical weakness, as if the body shared with the mind in grieving over the vanished dream; but she tried bravely to smile and look unconcerned.

"Then I suppose he—Victor Druce—inherits all?"

Jack looked at her with anxious eyes.

"You expected it, didn't you? You are not surprised? It seems to have been generally taken for granted for the last six months."

"Yes; so Mrs Thornton said. If it had been anyone else I should not grudge it so much. And you are left out too! I wish—oh, I wish it had been different!"

Jack Melland took a step forward, and bent over her chair.

"Mollie," he said softly, "shall we console each other? I have been waiting until this question was settled before coming to see you. It seemed an endless time to wait, but I couldn't come till I knew the truth. How could a poor fellow, with a few beggarly hundreds a year, approach a girl who might be one of the biggest heiresses in the kingdom? But I didn't forget you—I couldn't forget. I have been thinking of you night and day. It was all the harder to be silent when you were in trouble; but it was the straight thing to do. You can't tell what it means to me to see you again! When you opened the door just now, and the lamp-light showed me your little golden head—"

He broke off, with the same strange quiver in his voice which had marked his first utterance of her name; but Mollie shrank back still further in her chair, staring at him with troubled eyes.

"What do you mean? I don't understand!"

"It's simple enough—only that I love you, and want you to love me in return!"

"But—don't you remember?—you told me about her—the girl you met, and loved at first sight. Suppose you met her again, and felt the same; then you would be sorry if I—"

"Oh, Mollie, do you mean to say you have remembered all this time, and never guessed! It was yourself, darling; there never was anyone else! I think I must have cared for you from the first, though I did not realise it, for I was irritated that I could never get you to be serious. You were like a child out for a holiday—full of fun and mischief—and I wanted to talk of deeper things. Then one day for a moment you showed me a glimpse of your real self—the sweet, womanly heart that lay beneath the gaiety; and as I looked at your face I recognised it, Mollie. It was something I had dreamed of when I did not know I was dreaming, and wanted, without knowing what I wanted! I saw that look again five minutes after I had told you of my lost love, as you looked at me and wished me happiness. Why did you look sad, Mollie? Were you—were you sorry at all?"

Mollie put her hand to her side with a gesture as natural as it was charming.

"It hurt," she said simply. "I never, never dreamt that you meant me, and I have tried hard not to think of you ever since; but I didn't succeed very well... Why did you always write to Ruth instead of to me?"

Jack laughed happily, and with a lover's privilege seated himself on the arm of the easy-chair, and took Mollie's hands in his.

"Because, as I told you before, you darling, I was waiting. And do you really think you could make up your mind to marry me on next to nothing, and live in a tiny house, and wrestle with the household bills? Do you think I am worth the sacrifice?"

Mollie smiled at him, shyly confident.

"I'm so improvident that I'm afraid I'd marry you on nothing. I haven't a copper of my own, remember. You will have a penniless bride. Oh, I wish more than ever that Uncle Bernard had left me something, so that I might help you! It does seem hard, doesn't it, that Victor Druce should get it all?"

Jack hesitated a moment, tugging at his moustache with his unoccupied hand.

"I didn't say that, you know. I never told you that he did."

"Jack!"

The name slipped out so naturally on the surprise of the moment that there was a prolonged interval in the conversation, while Jack acknowledged the compliment. Then Mollie returned to the attack, laughing and rosy.

"You asked if I were surprised. You said everyone had taken it for granted!"

"Exactly; so I did. But for once everyone was mistaken. Druce has not come in for the property."

"Then, who—who—"

"Someone equally unworthy—an ungracious rascal of a fellow called Melland. It is all mine, Mollie—all that there is to leave!"

And then Jack did a pretty thing—a thing that he would have sneered at as high-flown and sentimental a few months before; but no man really knows himself or his capabilities till he loves and is beloved. He slipped off his seat, and knelt on the floor at Mollie's feet.

"And I have come to you," he said gravely, "to ask you to share it with me, for it's worth nothing, and worse than nothing, if I have not you by my side!"

He held out his hand as he spoke, and Mollie laid hers in it, while her face confronted him, white and tense with excitement.

"I can't—I can't believe it!" she gasped. "It is too wonderful! You and me! That lovely, lovely place; and we the masters of it, able to do as we like—just as we like, all the summer days, and the winter days, and the beautiful spring, and no more anxiety and trouble! Jack—Jack!"

Her head went down on his shoulder, and he held her fast while she shed a few natural tears of joy and thankfulness.

"My poor girl—my dear girl! Yes, it is all over, and the money is as much yours as mine. I feel sure Mr Farrell meant it to be so, and that you will find something to that effect in this letter he has left you. He discovered my secret before I left Raby, and said plainly how much he wished it success. There, darling, read your letter! I hope you may find some kind words to comfort your heart."

Mollie broke open the envelope, which he handed to her. It was a solemn business, reading a message from the dead, and her big eyes looked quite awestruck as they scanned the page. There were only a few words, written in a small, tremulous hand:—

> "My dear Mollie,—I leave you nothing, hoping that you may share all. That is my strong wish, and I believe I am helping on your happiness by an apparent neglect. Try to forgive me for refusing your last request. It would have been easier to consent, but I considered that a short period of anxiety would be a blessing in disguise, if it showed you who were

> your true friends. If a man comes forward and offers you his love in the days of obscurity and poverty, that man's love is worth having. I hope and believe it will come to you. I thank you for your kindness to an old man. Forgive him for all his offences, foremost among them an unfounded suspicion.—Your friend and kinsman, Bernard Farrell."

"There! You see how right I was?" cried Jack in triumph. "In effect, we are joint heirs, and have equally free hands in the disposal of the money. You must settle an income on your mother which will ensure her against anxiety, and then you can come away with an easy mind, and help me to turn into a country squire and learn my duties to the tenants. You told me once that he would be hard-worked if he were conscientious, and I want to do the thing well while I am about it. This is December. I mean to be married in January, at latest!"

Mollie laughed, but with a somewhat tremulous sound. The change of scene which had taken place within the last quarter of an hour was so complete, so extraordinary, that she felt dazed by the shock. Not only had undreamed-of happiness come to herself, but with it such relief and ease for all belonging to her, that they would rejoice equally with herself. It did indeed seem more like a dream than a reality, as, with Jack's arm round her waist and her head resting contentedly upon Jack's shoulder, they drifted off into one of those delightful conversations which follow all happy betrothals.

"Do you remember?" queried Jack. "Do you remember?" echoed Mollie. "What did you mean when you said?"

"How did you feel when you heard?"

"When did you first begin?"

"And are you quite sure you will never, never—" It is all as old as the hills, and as new as to-morrow morning, though each separate pair of lovers imagine in their innocence that they own the exclusive monopoly.

"Jack!" cried Mollie at last, sitting suddenly upright and clasping her hands in amaze. "Jack, imagine it! All this time I have forgotten the most thrilling part of all. The condition—the mysterious condition! What was it? What did you do, or leave undone, which made you different from the rest of us?"

Chapter Thirty Eight.

Conclusion.

"Aha!" cried Jack. "I wondered when you were coming to that! It was indeed something of which we could never have thought! Mr Farrell had learnt by sad experience that real happiness cannot be purchased by money, so had determined to leave his fortune to the one who cared for it least—that is to say, to the one who put other things first—love—whole-hearted, disinterested love, such as he himself had felt for his beautiful wife; and honest work, enjoyed for its own sake more than for what it will bring! Ruth was out of the running from the start, for she showed so plainly that, to her, money meant happiness. There must have been a time when he wavered in favour of Druce, who played his part remarkably well; but on the whole, it was my obstinate, ungracious self which approached nearest to his ideal. He knew that I loved you, but that I should never venture to ask you to be my wife if you were a great heiress; so as he himself writes, he left you nothing, hoping that you would share all. I want you literally to realise that, darling—and to feel that the money belongs as much to you as to me!"

Mollie smiled at him in her sunny, candid fashion.

"Oh, I shall!" she said simply. "I mean to. There are so many things that I want to do for the dear people here, and they would like them better if they came from me. Uncle Bernard was a dear, sweet old thing to scheme for our happiness, and I adore him for it. I certainly put love before money, for I would marry you if we had to play an organ in the streets or sing sentimental ditties out of tune, but it will be like a fairy tale to live in the Court—with you!"

"It will, indeed! I don't feel indifferent to fortune any longer now that it has brought us together. When the Will was read aloud yesterday, I did not know whether I was standing on my head or my heels. I rushed down to the vicarage, and good little Mrs Thornton cried upon my neck, literally she did, Mollie!"

Mollie smiled at him with love-lit eyes.

"But oh, Jack, there's something else—Victor? What about him? Was he terribly disappointed? Did he get nothing?"

"No! not a cent!"

"Did Uncle Bernard leave no word of explanation or good-bye?"

"There was no note, but there was an envelope and an—an enclosure," said Jack gravely.

He put his hand in his waistcoat-pocket and drew from his pocket-book an unmounted photograph.

"Druce opened this in the library after the Will was read, stared at it for a moment, then threw it in the fire, and dashed out of the room. It fell on the grate and the lawyer picked it up and gave it to me."

He held out the photograph as he spoke, and Mollie bent eagerly over it. It was Ruth's missing picture of the library at the Court—one of the longtime exposures which she had taken on the eventful morning when the desk had been opened in the squire's absence. The nearer part of the interior was clear and distinct, but the further half was blurred as if something had moved while the plate was still exposed, while leaning over the open desk was a man's figure, dim and blurred indeed, but recognisable in a flash as that of Victor Druce!

Mollie's face was white to the lips as she raised it to meet Jack's glance, and he put his arm round her protectingly.

"Yes; I knew you would be shocked! It is easy to see what happened. After Druce went out, ostensibly for the day, he slunk back unseen, and entered the library by the window. The blur across the picture shows in which direction he crossed to the desk. Meantime, Ruth had put her camera in position, and as the exposure would be a long one in such a dark room, she had gone away and left it there. Druce would never notice the little camera perched on a side-table, and when he heard Ruth returning he, no doubt, hid himself hastily behind the curtains; but he had remained sufficiently long at the desk to give a definite impression of his figure. The camera was discovered after you left, and the squire had the plates developed in the village. He must have had the curiosity to examine them before sending them on, and one can imagine his feelings upon finding the solution of the mystery which had troubled him so much. I have no sympathy for Mr Victor Druce; I am only profoundly thankful that Ruth escaped his clutches. Don't let us talk of him any more. We want only pleasant subjects on this great night, sweetheart!"

"And there are so many pleasant subjects to think of. It will be such a lovely experience to play fairy godmother to people who have had a bad time; the first of all comes the dear pater. There's his key in the latch! Be nice to him, Jack; he has been so good to us!"

"Come, then!" said Jack, rising, and holding out his hand towards her. "Let us go to meet him together, and you shall tell him that he has a new son, and that all his troubles are at an end?"

The End.

Lightning Source UK Ltd.
Milton Keynes UK
UKOW04f0653100118
315876UK00001B/49/P

9 781406 546903